F

TYRUS

ALSO BY PATRICK CREEVY
FROM TOM DOHERTY ASSOCIATES

Lake Shore Drive

TYRUS

AN AMERICAN LEGEND

PATRICK CREEVY

A TOM DOHERTY ASSOCIATES BOOK
NEW YORK

TYRUS: AN AMERICAN LEGEND

Copyright © 2002 by Patrick Joseph Creevy

This book is printed on acid-free paper.

A Forge Book
Published by Tom Doherty Associates, LLC
175 Fifth Avenue
New York, NY 10010

www.tor.com

Forge® is a registered trademark of Tom Doherty Associates, LLC.

Library of Congress Cataloging-in-Publication Data

Creevy, Patrick.
    Tyrus : an American legend / Patrick Creevy.
        p. cm.
    "A Tom Doherty Associates book."
    ISBN 0-765-30014-1
        1. Cobb, Ty, 1886–1961—Fiction. 2. Detroit Tigers (Baseball team)—Fiction. 3. Children of murder victims—Fiction. 4. Baseball players—Fiction. 5. Detroit (Mich.)—Fiction. I. Title.

PS3553.R353 T97 2002
813'.54—dc21

2002022801

First Edition: July 2002

Printed in the United States of America

0 9 8 7 6 5 4 3 2 1

For Robert Creevy,
in loving memory

TYRUS

Book One

THE CAUSE

Chapter One

THE FAMILY GUN

Nobody felt harder pain. The boy was dead certain. Who else, not nineteen days gone, lost a father the way he did? Taking two blasts from a shotgun, dead on, at just paces? Do people know what a shotgun can *do* at that distance? Do they have a clear picture of the nightmare? And who had to watch his own mother being taken in, then, and charged with this kind of killing? Or had to read in his hometown paper words that spun rumors like those spun by the *Royston Record* about the Cobbs? Unstoppable little whispers, racing off like lightning all across the state of Georgia, about a wife and a lover. About a husband who'd been warned in secret to "watch his house." For when the husband wasn't there, what? Why didn't the paper just go ahead and say it! That his wife's lover would be right there for him, taking his place in his own bed. Why didn't the *Record* say that right out loud! It went ahead and floated off third-hand things about a pistol that was supposed to have been seen in his dead father's coat pocket but that was now, supposedly, missing. Pure rumor. When you don't stop at that, why not just make yourself happy. And damn *say* that Senator Cobb had set up his wife so he could catch her in the act of adultery and then *murder* her, or her lover, or both of them in his bed—but that instead it was his wife who surprised him, two times, with the family shotgun, as he stood on the roof outside their bedroom window. His wife with her lover by her side.

The boy knew every word from the *Record* exactly. And these—that "Mrs. Cobb's claim that she thought it was a burglar in her window is doubted by many"—these he'd repeated to himself in raging anger more times than he could count in the two weeks now since her arrest. "By many." He wished it were by *all*, Joe Cunningham, his best friend, included, so he could write off every last one of 'em until the end of time. Friends. Call them former friends. What do they all want, anyhow? They want a tragedy—their little bit of small-town Shakespeare. You can't get a good story out of a mere accident.

But where in hell did he find himself now? Ironies he'd had enough of in the preceding two days to last him for the next thousand years. For, hour after hour, Augusta to Atlanta, Atlanta to Cincinnati, Cincinnati to Toledo, and Toledo on toward Detroit (just some few miles still to go), he'd been reading the book he held now closed on his lap. His father's book. *William Herschel Cobb, Turning Points of His Life, Commencing With His Coming into His Profession.* It was the running story of his life that his father had kept up for over twenty years, marking what he called those turning points, beginning with the beginning of his teaching career in "The Narrows" of Banks County, Georgia, where his first son was born. And now that son, with this book on his lap (his finger held for near forty minutes to a page he couldn't get past, one he knew was close to where the writing stopped), was coming into his own profession. And the ironies in every one of his father's words of hope and expectation, for Georgia education, for the South's rising from the dead, for his *son Tyrus*, almost made the boy laugh out loud, or break down crying. Only he wouldn't let these Yankees riding now with him, crowding him, on the Michigan Central's late-night Toledo-Detroit, get the chance to think of him as crazy. He was dead certain someone would use that to deny him the opportunity of his life.

And let him spit at the damned, cheap neatness of irony, it made it hurt so much more that right now was *supposed to be* the happiest moment of his life. His father had done everything to talk him out of becoming a ballplayer, to get him to go to university and make himself ready for one of the learned professions. But, as his mama knew, there was no talking him out of it. He was born to be a ballplayer. And when you've heard your calling—when you know that difference between how dead and small you are when you're doing what somebody else wants for you and how alive when you're going your own way—well, then, there's no stopping you. And now he was just a handful of hours from putting on a major-league uniform, though he was still only eighteen. How many had made it so far, so fast? You could count 'em now maybe on a single hand.

But no good—such sweet, dream things. With all the other sad and godforsaken horrible things that had happened these last days, Jesus Lord help him, please, *Jesus*, he was feeling not just shattered in his heart but confused far down in his mind—to the point of something strange. Like the way he felt now—as if he were on two trains at the same time. The first—the one now speeding him to the end of his father's book, the last two words of which story he knew were a sick-ominous, darkly scrawled *BURN THIS* (and he knew this because among the hundred guilty temptations to be curious that he'd felt in the last twenty days, going ahead and looking at those last words was one more he couldn't resist). And the second—the train that was actually now carrying him to Detroit, driving him on and on through territory more and more foreign the farther north it went (for he'd never in his life before been north of Chattanooga). But this second train he couldn't really feel. Couldn't, hours on end now, sense the real motion of it much at all, even though for a ballplayer there is no time in his whole life like the time of his call-up to the major leagues. It was as if this train to Detroit, impossible but true, ran only alongside the one he was really on. And, *Christ*, how could it be that he couldn't even much sense the dream of his life coming true? Right this instant, though, he thought that the reason he couldn't much notice the motion of the Toledo-Detroit was that it ran exactly parallel to the train of his reading his father's book, and at exactly the same speed—in that way trains have of seeming not to be moving when they are moving right with us. And somehow, which was strange too, he suspected that the moment he arrived at the Tigers' Bennett Park would be the moment that he came to the end of his father's story, and that the two arrivals would be at the same place. Don't ask him what that place would be.

It tore him, too, though, made his heart feel still more sadness, to think back on how he had killed train-time and distance when he was playing in the South Atlantic League, before the accident. Just Charlie, that's all it would be, just his beautiful girl, Charlie, Charlotte Lombard—he could think of Charlie for hours, and hours, and hours, nonstop. And he wouldn't know that he was on a real train, then, either. Easily he could spend two hours on a word he might say to her and how she might laugh or smile when he said it. That soft turn of her lips, so wonderful. Or all the way from Augusta to Chattanooga, just on the kind of day it would be, and where they would be, when he asked her to marry him. Or on how gentle he would be the first time he made love to her. On that he could spend a day. And on the kisses they'd begun to share now, not clumsy like that stupid first one, but cool as the clean taste of her soft lips and then warm with their passion, and tenderness. Hours and hours on that unbelievable feeling. And on how beautiful she looked on her chestnut, Highlander, when they rode together at The Oaks, her family's home outside Augusta. And could the girl ride! It had made his eyes tear up with warm pride to watch her.

He had confessed to Charlie now that he loved her, and she had told him that she loved him. And she would move heaven and earth, she said, when they parted three days ago, to get the schedule of her and her mother's upcoming junket to New York matched to the schedule of the New York games between the Highlanders and the Detroit Tigers. "Heaven and earth." She told him this again when they held each other and kissed good-bye on the platform in Augusta, with the locomotive vibrating on the track, the roar of its whistle about to sound its impatience with their tender farewells.

But this whole northbound journey now, and these last two and a half weeks of hell, he could only rarely think of Charlie the way he had for months and months. It could only be for the briefest moments now, because everything seemed to be another version of this present turning point of *his* life, the point at which he became the son of a mother rumored to be unfaithful and facing twenty years in prison for the voluntary manslaughter of his father (who may have been, when he died, intending to kill her, at least). That is, everything best seemed so close to something worst, to be *infected* by it, to *become* it in some bitter irony. So he had to put the good things of his life on some other train. And he knew he had reason to fear that if this kind of thing kept up it might drive him insane (a word he didn't use as just a word). That he might find one part of himself talking in some strange way to the other part of himself, as if he were two different people. And in fist-gripping anger, right now, he wondered what mood of the Prince of Darkness made it happen that the best and the worst times of his life would be the same time?

But, his hand still tight-gripped, now sweating hard, he thought that some *use* had to be made of bad things. Or maybe he'd end up with nothing. He had to use the threat of shame to the Cobbs, even keep the idea of this threat raging in his heart, to give himself enough power to shut shame's mouth.

Of course, Charlie knew about his mother and father. Everyone in the state of Georgia had to know, thanks not just to the *Royston Record* but the *Atlanta Journal* (and if the boy understood that it would be newspapers that spread his fame, if he ever came into fame, he hated newspapers right now to the death). And the *Journal* picked up the word from the *Record* and spread it statewide, because his father, former mayor of Royston and, when he died, prestigious member of the Georgia state senate, was a very-much-celebrated man. But though Charlie obviously had to know the full word about his family, the boy never fully opened his heart to her about what happened.

He broke down in her arms, the first day he came to her about it, after returning to Augusta from Royston, and the funeral, and the *arraignment*. She held him like a pitiful little baby. For a long time he didn't move his face from her shoulder, and he didn't care that she'd seen him cry. But he never confessed to her his real misery and fear. The Lord knows he wanted in the deepest part of his soul to admit things to her. Say the words. Confess all. Every fear. Every shame. Say it *all*. And he was so sure of a certain feeling he had that he believed truly it *was* the Lord who put the feeling in his heart: bad things would go out of him if he just spoke them out to Charlie. The flower-smell of her dress, too, when he broke down on her shoulder . . . Till the day he died, he would remember the way that flower-smell softened him.

But the same way he did with the team when he played his last ten days' of games with the Augusta Tourists, acting before them all as if not a first word had been said anywhere in the world about how his father died, he kept the center of himself silent, closed down tight, and separate from Charlie. The accident, in their closest conversations, for all that warmth and tenderness, was never anything but an accident.

He never once said even that his mother had been arrested.

But then those last eight games with Augusta—he played them like a man driven by the terrors of the earth, leaving all his rivals for the batting title of the South Atlantic League in the damned, sorry dust, hammering out multiple hits in all eight games, stealing bases to a point near insanity (proof of which he had in a five-inch spike gash on the back of his right thigh, the only thing in this call-up journey that did keep on reminding him that his calling was a ball-player's). So as a ballplayer he *had* made fine, burning use out of shame. It set him going hard as hell—hard enough to prove the righteousness of the name Cobb. And when he broke down soft with Charlie, he sensed it as deep as any other feeling in his heart, that if he opened himself up completely even to her, who would be the one he'd talk to first in the entire world, he would lose all use of his anger and he'd have nothing, no power or energy, and he would die. As a ballplayer, he would die.

But always with him now, there was that fear that he might make himself sick, too, keeping things in. And not just keeping things in but now waging an hour-after-hour battle against anybody who might want to get him to open up. Because if he broke down and opened up, it would be like surrendering to that whore called apology. And, yes, it energized him, like fire, this warfare against accusation, or even the hint of accusation. He found himself even liking it that words could spread as fast as they had through Georgia. But in himself alone, he knew he'd been at times terrified that he could lose control of his mind.

He looked around the train car. Yankee faces. Cold. He felt the train rock. It was moving all right, high-speed north to Detroit.

And these Yankees. All his thinking life he'd known deep, deep bitterness over North and South. He was brought up on it. Fed on it. But especially now, since he'd waved good-bye to Charlie and begun this, his first-ever south-north journey, if he had a moment free of the book, or even when he was in the book, since his father's life was so passionately devoted to the South's rising from the grave, he'd been thinking that what Yankees want most in the world is to hear exactly that last surrender of apology or confession from the South. He could admit to himself, and why not, that his own miseries probably made him crazier right now with this particular thought. But he looked around and he did think sure enough that what these people would all love is just for the South to get down on its knees and beg forgiveness for all its so-called sins and shames. To admit and admit, until it couldn't admit any more. But dam*nation* to hell on earth, he'd been thinking, the South would rather go insane than say words that somebody else had thought up for it to say, as if they came out from its own true conscience.

He withdrew still further back inside himself. And he let himself hear now his father's rebel yellin' in the Georgia senate, where they were dead set, in these first years of the new century, to give the Solid South some iron backbone and establish by state law the supremacy of the best. And history—Yankees ought to know from their good luck in it—is as full of accidents as anything else. So the hell with confessing to what somebody who loves tragedies would just love to call a "crime," and have you call a crime. Think instead of Atlanta on fire. Think of that, his father would say when he departed from the Yankee-written American history books he had to use in his schoolmaster days. And still again before the senate. Think of the pillage, of daughters and wives taken in rape. Think of being invaded. Think of being occupied and sullied for years and years by a half-breed militia and the money-grubbing minions of sordid vengeance. The boy saw also in the newspaper, and he put to hard memory sometimes, the words of his father's speeches. He could see the man at the podium, hands gripped to the lectern. And hear that voice: "Indeed let this be the whetstone for our sword. Let grief convert to anger, blunt not the heart, *enrage* it." So don't apologize, he thought now. Don't ever, Tyrus Cobb. Because there is nothing to apologize *for*, or to confess *to*, no matter what every self-satisfied mind in the world might love to think.

But why why why *why*, if his mother was innocent, as she was, did he feel like he had so much to be ashamed of, and apologize for?

False conscience. He knew all about that. We're all such sorry suckers for guilt. You have to fight hard against idiot guilt, which would make a pure sucker out of you, to the point of draining your energy dry. Making you pure soft. Crippling you with weakness so deep that you could never find the hard grit it takes to vindicate your name, when you need to. And then you'd never walk a triumph over that filthy world of words spun out against your family. And maybe to walk that triumph someday was why he was on this Toledo-Detroit right now—and there was, maybe, even some deep destiny in everything that had happened to him. And wouldn't irony have to swallow some of its own medicine if *that* proved true.

He felt the train once more. It was moving into a bend, and he had to catch himself to fight off a lean into the man next to him. Some time back—how long?—when they pulled out of the Toledo station and there was this huge body of water, like an ocean, to the right, this man, who seemed like a banker type, had caught him gazing. The big water was beautiful in the sunset light, streaming from the left. It was one of the Great Lakes (the boy didn't know which one). And he had had no idea they were so big. He saw a number of huge, long steamers passing, too, maybe as big as the ones in Charleston Bay (though he didn't think so). Then the bankery man, who must have known from the way he was gazing that he wasn't from these parts, sort of leaned over him a bit, pointing, and said, "Mostly ore or wheat, heading south. Coming north it's coal, up from West Virginia."

And he was being friendly. That was all. So the boy felt

a natural inclination to be friendly, too, and start up a conversation. But he didn't go soft or start up any conversation with the friendly Yankee, whom he kept himself from touching now. Nor did he when the man tried again later, as they saw what, for the boy, was a true, true rarity, that is automobilists. There were two of them, in long white coats and goggles, stirring up dust into the rows of high corn along a dirt road that ran along the tracks. And the man pointed to one of the automobiles and said, "Oldsmobile. Gasoline engine. And word's all over Detroit—Olds just sold his company for a cool million. Just this past week. Not bad, eh?"

What was that but again just plain old friendliness—North, South, what's the difference. It's the same everywhere. The boy knew it perfectly well. He wasn't a fool. And the subject of a cool million, coming out of Detroit, interested the hell out of him. You could get your hands on court records and even buy the silence of newspapers with that kind of stock. But he didn't respond to the man, not with more than a nod. He just thought again what he thought when the man first boarded and asked him, as he stood at the two seats the boy was occupying, "Mind?"—which was "Mind *plenty*," though he didn't say this then, or when that gasoline-driven Oldsmobile was raising those dust clouds that fell over the high green corn.

The train now pulled straight once more, so he was free of its listing. He looked out on the dark. The North. He was feeling differences, all right. And he thought now of last night when he crossed the Ohio, which was one point along this three-day journey that had sure awakened him, and not just because he would have to stop in Cincinnati and spend the night.

It was late, and full dark, like now. And from the Covington station, on the south side of the big river, the lights of Cincinnati, all spread up and down its seven hills, were to him, he had to confess it, beautiful. And thrilling. For what was Cincinnati but the home of Mr. Ban Johnson, founder of the American League. And of the great, great Cincinnati Reds. Harry Wright and all those Yankee boys had gone 76-0, and when they did, they made possible professional baseball. They made the market that made it possible for Tyrus Cobb to come into the profession he was born for. Sweet gratitude he felt at that moment for those Yankee boys, and sweet admiration along with the sincere thanks. And even for a second actually just to stop in his heart the damned War Between the States felt good, as it had to smell the soft, beautiful flower-smell of Charlie's white sundress. Good even like a kiss, he had to admit. Or like listening to those words of the Lord in his heart. Healing words—he knew why they called them that. He knew the difference between right and wrong, as well as any Christian.

But the energy that came to him with refusal to surrender brought more weight to the balance, as he knew it would. He began watching for the black-glimmering river's midpoint, as the train slow-chugged and clanked in its tremendous weight across the black-iron railroad bridge. He fixed his eye on what he figured to be the exact line where the South ended and the North began. He let himself hear the five-hundred-drum drum corps from his father's description of the great Confederate Reunion in Atlanta, which he had been reading just moments before in the man's book. He let himself be Caesar, of whom since his last days of school he'd been a student (and so he carried with him now a volume of Plutarch's *Lives* that he'd taken from his dead father's library, and in which he knew there was the story of Caesar's world-famous accomplishments that went back to revenge for things done to his family). The Die Is Cast. He let the Ohio be his Rubicon. And then for even more and even hotter fire, he let himself be Stonewall Jackson. He let himself be Nathan Bedford Forrest, with all nineteen battle horses shot dead beneath him. And he let himself be Robert E. Lee, the Christ Savior of the South, which would rise again because it was baptized in the blood, a fact known by every single soul south of the Kingdom of Mammon, which began at the Ohio River.

"Know ye not that there is a prince and a great man fallen today?" His father taught him these words and made him put them hard into his mind, for these were the words said by General Lee himself over the grave of the brigadier Thomas Reade Cobb, one great name among a number in his ancestry, who died at Fredericksburg at The Stone Wall, who was *facile princeps* at the University of Georgia, who was first to codify the state's laws, and who in the War Between the States was the wildly brave and famed commander of Cobb's Legion.

Always the thought that Robert E. Lee had said those words over the grave of a member of his family stirred him deep in his heart. Time would pass, and some place—on the way home from school, or in the woods—it would make him cry. He was sure it would still make him cry some place when he was old.

He felt pain from the pressure on his finger as he held it still to his place in his father's book. But he took a newspaper clipping that he'd tucked in the book's beginning and set it at his reading place. Then he put the book away in the leather grip that he'd set beneath his feet. It was—in truth—some kind of real and deep sin to read this book in the first place (for the book was as private as the drawer of his desk that his father had kept it locked in till the day he died), but to read its end in front of these cold foreign faces would be an unforgivable violation of the man's privacy. And he intended to lodge as close as he could to Bennett Park, so if he read the end of the book from where he could see the park, he would still be arriving on both his trains at the same place and the same time.

There was a long, loud roar of the whistle. But just another hard running then through another small, darkened Ohio town. He looked only a moment, without really looking. Then, letting his mind drift where it would, he found himself back in his father's library—back now at that day when he was twelve and his father read to him from a history writer named Grote the story of the ancient Tyrians' defense of their city against Alexander the Great, when not a single Tyrian dishonored himself by cowardice—or surrender. He let himself hear again his father's question as the man sat in his old green morocco, reaching out his huge hand and setting it warm on his boy's shoulder, squeezing it gently as he asked, "Can you think, son, of anyone whose name sounds like *Tyre*?"

The boy remembered, or *felt* perfectly his own smiling, and felt the returning warmth of his father's smile. The bravery and honor of those ancient Tyrians. Such courage to do right. These were the things his father wanted him to think of whenever he thought of his own name, which he whispered silently to himself, as the northbound train drove on through the dark.

But not a month later, his father off in Athens at the University, the boy stole into the man's library and took, from right next to the Grote, a copy of Homer's *Iliad*. He went then and sold the book to get money for a ball glove.

"Lord God Almighty! Doesn't this just write large and spell out clearly the point I've tried to press on you." His father, having detected the crime not an hour back from Athens, hurled this chastisement at him in bitterest anger. "Do you know what it means, boy, to forget what's right and what's wrong? Do you know what you're left with when you move away even a small, first step from doing things right? Well, I'll tell you what you're left with. You're left with nothing but your own selfishness. And that's small, boy. That's very, very small."

He never would have forgotten this, so it needed no repeating. But over the years he heard it in so many words again and again and again, not a few times to the tune of birch whips in the woodshed—because it was hard to be a schoolmaster's son and not be any slick achiever in school, to be, truth to tell, bored stiff by school most times. He re-called now sitting in the cellar stairwell of the house when they lived in Harmony Grove, so when he was maybe eight years old, and repeating in that damp place sort of like a cave, till he almost hypnotized himself with his own words, that the son of a teacher should never, never, never, never, never, never, *never* have to go to school where his father was master.

He could see, clear to the small scratches of black ink, a certain page of the man's story—the one dated "December 18, 1886, The Narrows." It was the day he was born, and the place. And he now read that page verbatim with his mind's eye (for he had that photographic capacity, almost as weird, Joe Cunningham said, as the spooky-blue stare of his eyes—though it was a gift that sometimes frustrated his father, be-cause it made easy for his son things that should have taken discipline and time). "Bright sun today, but bitterest cold and wind. Great limbs of pecans, heavy with ice, can be heard groaning and then cracking. But in our cottage a warm stove, and a cause for inexpressible joy. Today, this seven days be-fore Christmas, a son was born to us. And if there could be a day more wonderful with promise, then I cannot imagine it. I have named our wonderful boy 'Tyrus,' for the honor of the ancient Tyrians, defiant against Alexander to the end. Un-surrendered. And I have dreamed. I have dreamed for my students—but they are not my son. I have prayed for my students—but never in a lifetime as in a single hour for my son. Not ever like this. Never have I cared like this for anything, or anyone. Or hoped like this. He will be a truly educated man, my son. He will be a free man who finds God in the truth, as no other child I have known. Lord forgive me, but I dream of a doctor. Or of a West Point commission and degree. Of a life of ennobling, fulfilling labor and just fame: a life that knows and never loses its point. I have dreamed of professional fulfillment for my students, too. But I am not their father. And they are not my son."

If he just closed his eyes and thought *appear*, the boy had this page right with him, immediately. But now here he was, heading off not to university but to the life of a ballplayer, which his father so much despised, not just for what it was itself, which he indeed despised, but because it so deeply disappointed him that his son would choose *this* instead of a calling to his honor.

His mind went back again to the man's library, and now to their night of argument, lasting nearly till the dawn itself when he would head off for his first assignment in the minor leagues. With his fingers and palm pressing hard against the edge of his father's desk, Tyrus had pleaded with him to see that he wasn't going wrong, at what his father called "the absolute crossroads" of his life, in deciding to be a ballplayer. "It's the toughest go there is, Father. It's the toughest go there is—and so maybe the best way to test one's worth, if the best test is the toughest competition there is."

His father had dismissed such a notion as "a preposterous falsehood," adding contemptuously that a ballplayer was "a synonym for a drunk and an ungentlemanly, brawling rowdy, the whore's game, and the gambler's easy touch."

But with his hands continuing to press down hard on the man's desk, the boy kept insisting: "Maybe sometime in the past. But what the game may have been in the past, Father, doesn't change the fact that what it is now is the toughest go there is anywhere around. People in this country look to great players not as tramps but as heroes because they know how much it takes in brains and guts and character to play the game right. And what it takes to get to the top. You've always wanted me to understand that doing things right is everything, and doing them wrong is worse than nothing. But I want you to believe that I'll never know this as well as I could if I go into something that has only half my heart in the first place. That's what's been wrong. Everyone's different, Father. And that's what's been wrong all along. I've been in things for you, and not for me, and with only half my heart. But this game's got all of me. It's got all of me, and I'll find out who I really am only if I play it. You talk about discovering true individuality, because finding *that*—it's what makes your soul come alive. But here I am pursuing things with only half my self. And *this* . . . It's living in a cage! A *cage!*"

And the boy now felt again his passion. It was as if his fingers pressed down hard still on the top of the man's desk, and felt the pain, because he knew that his father had not been persuaded, for all his sincere pleading to him, and that he had not run out of bitter remonstrances and warnings. The man was well aware of the war between the National and American Leagues, which had just been fought, and just set-tled—an agreement between the "Senior Circuit" and the "Band of Upstarts" having been fixed on what looked like a solid and permanent basis.

"You'll be a purchasable and tradeable *commodity*, boy," he said. "A *property*. A property of men with money, which isn't so fine a thing for a white man. This contract, which you say gives you such a feeling of self-esteem, have you *read* it? Do you understand this business of their 'reserving the rights' to you? They'll give you a hundred pious reasons for it. They'll tell you it's for the good of all, and for equity in their league as a whole, and for unity and loyalty forever and ever amen. But they'll beggar you with it, my fine young man. Trust that: They'll ply you like a slave. They're not Christians dealing with souls, but businessmen dealing with properties. And if you think you can alter *that*, they'll black-ball you forever and sixteen days. You'll wish you were some sorry runaway nigger with the hounds at your back. That's what you'll wish."

"Monopsony." A strange word that the boy would now know forever. "It's from the Greek terms," his father told him, "meaning 'one' and 'buyer of food.' One buyer of food. When you're the farmer, one buyer doesn't make much of a market, does it?" The boy shook his head. And his father said, "Right you are, sir." And, once again, he explained to him that with their war over, with their monopsony in place, which was their own peculiar little institution, "those rugged-individual, blaring hypocrites of silk-hat Yankee moguls of this game that you so love will have you at their mercy. And all that," the man said, his fist clenched hard, "would be fine if you were ordained by the Almighty for service essentially, but *you* are not. *You* are not some peon, Tyrus Cobb! You are my son!"

But when the dawn came, the boy was gone. And now he was still going, because, as his mama told him, it was his truest, deepest happiness. That, she said, was why he would be a great, great ballplayer. The greatest ballplayer who ever was, she whispered to him, as she held him a last time two weeks ago at the Royston whistle-stop. Her eyes were swollen and raw from her days of tears but still blue as his (blue, Gramma Chitwood had told her, as the wings of bluebirds). But so strange, oh, God Jesus, to see those eyes looking out from behind that black veil.

And what possibly on this damned and rotten earth could break his heart more than his so-called "truest, deepest happiness?" What possibly, Lord. What on earth could more rip open his heart. Tell me that I can make her words about greatness come true, tell me how I can make those words come true without anger. And I will. But you tell me how, because I have *got* to make those words come true. Nobody on this sorry earth knows how much.

He bowed his head and squeezed his temples fiercely tight with his forefinger and thumb. For some time he pressed his temples. Some time. Hard. And harder. But he wouldn't let these Yankees catch him breaking down. He stopped, looked right up. But then instantly he seemed to want more grief to weigh him down again, because he just *let* his mind's eye, for the hundredth, for the thousandth time, these last eighteen days, start to picture himself in the telephone office at the

Augusta station, when he'd had to make a call home. A call to his father.

A call because he had failed in that first test in the minor leagues, with the Augusta Tourists. They cut him right out of Organized Ball, in about no time flat, which memory made his gut tense hard now and made him feel the rumble and hear the clacking, clacking, clacking of the Toledo-Detroit. Detroit, where he could fail again, this time for good. But still now, with that thought and fear tensing his gut hard as if readying for a brutal punch, he kept picturing himself in that phone office in Augusta, from which he had had to call Royston to give his father the word. And to tell him pitifully that he was going to Anniston, Alabama, to see if he could still find life for himself on some outlaw team that somebody said needed an outfielder.

And what would he say, the severest critic of "the dead end and damned waste of *mind* that baseball was?" Wouldn't he seize his advantage and insist that the pink slip was a dead, cold sign that the boy was pursuing some false and worthless calling? As the phone rang, the boy felt a total fool and wholly shamed. Truth was, he'd been cut just about clean out of existence. But (and if he ever wrote his own story, *here* would be a turning point; or he prayed now that it would be *the* turning point, as the Toledo-Detroit sped on), his father did not take the advantage. So easily the man could have. But he didn't. Rather over that scratchy phone line he made just a few quiet inquiries about what remained of the six fifteen-dollar checks he'd written when, after that night in the library, he knew that he couldn't break his son before he started, which is what he'd wanted to do. And now, when he heard that forty-four dollars and some odd cents was still left, he surprised the shut-out seventeen-year-old "free agent" even more, and breathed the spirit of life into him, for he gave the boy's dream his sanction. He told him he should go to Anniston, that there was "a clearly perceivable worth in the quality of the *ambition*." "I cannot say, son, that this is what I wanted. You know it isn't. But I respect your desire. You've proven to me this: It comes deep out of your heart."

The boy hadn't known what to say. He just trembled. There had been so few times when he felt that his father had bought him as his son. He turned away from the faces in the phone office and, pressing his eyes fiercely with the cuff of his shirt, he said, "Thank you, sir. Father . . . Thank you. . . . So much."

There was silence for a moment on the other end of the line. Just scratches—then—"I know how much this means to you, Tyrus. I do. So now, whatever happens . . . Whatever happens, Son . . . Don't come home a failure."

The boy couldn't say good-bye. And after some moments, at the other end, there was a click. But with this it was started, truly. And yes, let his mama whisper her prophecy about the greatest who ever was. Let her say it out loud. Make it a binding contract. For when his father gave him this inspiration in his hour of defeat, he created more determination and new will in him than he would ever know. And— he wouldn't let these Yankees see him damn cry—he was sure that every thought he had of his father's beautiful distance and iron reserve was one of love so deep there weren't words for it. And gratitude every bit as deep. For rare approval made Tyrus Cobb exactly what he was. Not no approval. Just rare, kept back the way diamonds are hidden deep. And for those rare diamonds, thank you, sir, so much.

He thought now, too, with fiercest satisfaction and pride how a certain educator and senator's son then tore like hell on earth through the Alabama-Tennessee League, leading it in hitting every day of the three months and nineteen days that he was there. And how with this he found himself in one very great hurry. Even those hundred and ten days, he didn't want to wait. That league, too, was no more than a mayfly. "A quick bug to die," he warned his roommate. So before he could *be* somebody or rise, he had to get noticed again and get back into Organized Ball. He had to scheme, fast. He began to write letters and cards under various and sundry signatures, all of an "interested following," to Grantland Rice at the *Atlanta Journal*. "Elmer Smith" and "Harper Jones" and "Finley Brown," *et alia*, each in his individual and distinctive script, would extol "the phenomenal eye," "the unmatched speed," "the uncanny power of the rapid-thinking mind" of a player over in Anniston named Tyrus Raymond Cobb.

And even now, in all the tight grip of his pride and heartbroken pain, Tyrus was able to smile a moment thinking of what pleasure there'd been in making a whole world of different people sing through those fabrications and forgeries just exactly the tune he wanted them to sing. Real and true reputation-building, which he was praying every second now that his father would be watching from the other world, would depend upon the real measure of magic in his black ash bats; nonetheless, he had learned with a kind of wicked joy the power of advertising and of tactic—of (by hook or by crook) making, rather than just letting things happen in other people's minds. Granny Rice eventually responded with a notice in his column of a "young fellow over in Alabama named Cobb who is showing an unusual amount of talent." And not three days later came the telegram from the Tourists offering the contract that would bring him back to Organized Ball and give him life once more.

He remembered in hot anger now, though, his covering the bottom of that telegram paper tight with his thumb as he read the good news. If, at the end of that paper, he saw that the invitation back into The One and Only, Holy and Great Baseball Organization came from Mr. Con Strouthers, the one who'd cut him, he wouldn't go back. He'd tear the invitation in a million pieces. He'd tear his damned life to shreds before he'd go back and play for that sonofabitch. "Truth is, Cobb," Strouthers had said, so high-and-mighty-like, taking a God-the-Father attitude, "you're just not made for it. You're just not professional material. And that's all there is to it. I'm afraid it's something you'll have to swallow." But he wouldn't swallow it. He'd spit it out—and spit it out because denying so-called God's truth until it became a goddamned lie, he'd discovered, was sometimes the only way to keep on living. But he'd give up any life in baseball whatsoever, any life at all, rather than breathe a whisper of gratitude to Con Strouthers. That he knew. He'd heard word, though, that Strouthers was no longer managing the team and was gone. That's why he'd read even the first line of the telegram. And as he came to the last line, and slowly lifted his hard-pressing thumb, he felt a joy about as sweet as anger to see it was from a new manager, Andy Roth.

The deep gash on the back of his right thigh was starting again to call steady attention to itself. He could feel an ache and a pounding. He wore lead weights in his shoes because with that dead weight he could make himself fly, when he took the weights out. And there was the good building of muscle, day after day, that came from the weight, too. But he lifted his heavy, leaded feet now, deliberately to put more throb into his pain. And long enough—what?—to make the blood drip? Nearly. Then he set his feet down again and checked his wallet, which he'd done maybe a hundred times on this three-day journey. He arched his back against the seat, to dig his watch up from his front pocket. And as he was fingering out the timepiece, the sound of the train broke into his ears. Then he sat straight and snapped open the brand new gold watch. It was the trophy he'd received from the mayor of Augusta and the brass of the Tourists for winning the Sally League batting crown. And what the watch said— as the black-arrowed second hand moved one, two, three ticks more—was 11:15. So exactly a half hour to go, if this Toledo-Detroit, whose *pocketah pocketah* once again now broke in on his ears, was on time.

He read the inscription on the watch case, cupping the gold in his hand so it wouldn't glitter in his seat's sconce-light. The date, AUGUST 26, 1905. And the words, LET 'EM

KNOW WHERE YOU'RE FROM, TYRUS COBB, IN THE BIG SHOW. But quickly now he snapped the watch back shut and stuffed it again in his pocket, for he had the feeling that some of the Yankee faces in this car might think he'd stolen it.

Having thumbed the timepiece deep and safe, however, he let his mind ponder those words cut for the inscription. Where he was from? Royston, Georgia. That's what he'd let 'em know, in the Big Show. But *what* he was from? It was to find out *this* that he'd broken into his father's secrets.

He'd come to despise secrets. Like deep hell despise them. But then who knew more about the need for privacy than someone whose family name was a dirty newspaper word? Nobody. And what is it, *privacy*? What but the chance and the damned *right* to keep secret so-called truths that could murder you? Who isn't a sinner, after all is said and done? And a criminal? Who hasn't in his thoughts, at least, been a killer or a thief? Who isn't a failure? But we have a *right* to keep these things secret because every one of these so-called truths, given time, can be proved a lie. Or turned into a lie—because we can trample them over with other truths. Stronger, better truths. Batting titles after what that fool Strouthers said was the truth about Tyrus Cobb, who'd put a lock on Con Strouthers's yap, all right. So no so-called word of truth gets to be the final word about a free soul, no matter how many curious little readers of that so-called truth might like to have it so.

But how much he'd failed, himself, to resist curiosity, and not to break into someone else's privacy. Just as he'd leapt to the end and read, so eagerly, the last words of the man's book, he'd leapt in in the first place, weak before his own temptations, and sought the key to his father's locked desk drawer. And this drawer was the man's closest privacy, no matter that he was no longer in the world. Even more cheap and sinful to play detective on a dead man. Or to read his private words, which the boy was beginning to think was like killing the man all over again.

It was in the quiet time before the visitation began. They'd placed the coffin in the library; and the boy would always remember the odd situation of the green morocco, which *Cunningham and Son*, Joe's father and Joe, cabinet- and coffin-makers, had put the chair in—in the back left corner.

"The only man whose bidding I'd ever do." "The only man I've ever loved." These were his two phrases for his father, as Joe knew well. And Charlie now knew the second. But he didn't always do the man's bidding. And in that library become a tomb, though he thought the man might rise out of that coffin and like the old, blind prophet call him fool and warn him to stop looking, he didn't stop looking.

He sat at his father's desk a long, long time—but then took in his fingers the rolltop's oaken knob, and slowly pulled up the wooden desk cover. He found nothing on the green-leather writing surface but a half-empty bottle of ink. The pigeon holes held nothing except a box of envelopes and a few dry pens. He tried the brass-handled drawers beneath the pigeon holes and saw only boxes of clips and bands, and an old punch. But when he lifted and moved the punch slightly, he found the small copper-colored key that he was sure fit the side drawer below.

Temptations. Hell, yes, they bring on feelings of guilt and sickening shame. But they, too, can bring on a feeling like a destiny. And what all was waiting to be born out of that drawer of secrets, which was heavy and sagged down hard on its runners when the boy had it freed? There was the book, which he knew would be there, but which seemed then—as he saw its worn, brown-leather cover actually appear—to have been waiting mysteriously in silence for this exact time when he would come for it, and to be intending now finally to speak. It was thicker and heavier than a Bible. And his hands were as nervous on it as his left would be on the Good Book in a court of law, if maybe he'd come to that court to tell lies.

But, still—even with the man coffined not ten feet from

him—another sin after a sin—he opened the book's cover, wishing as he did, that this was one of those books that itself had a lock on it, like a secret diary, which it was (though not of day after day, just of *turning points*). And there, beneath the cover as slowly he turned it back, was that title in his father's strong hand. And then, right there, the first entry, "November 8, 1882, The Narrows." So, yes, from that time when his father began his first school, in Banks County. And from the time, too, that he met his wife-to-be; for the boy's mama, still then a child of eleven, was a pupil in his father's first school.

But the boy wouldn't read a word more now, not where the ghost of a slaughtered man might rise up and say things to him. Or not read more than what his eye, in a single flash, caught beneath the entry heading, his father's first words: "Today is a day that will mark things off. There'll be the time before it, and the time after. Having waited for years, I feel now that I *am* someone." Just this. Then a quick closing back of the cover, which the boy would not open again until he was alone at the Inn of the White Camellia, in Atlanta, nearly two weeks later, sometime past midnight on the first night of this three-day journey.

But in the drawer, having lain buried between his father's book and a heavy stack of what the boy would see were Georgia-senatorial papers, was a newspaper clipping, pasted on a blue backing. It was indeed that clipping that right now, still pasted to its backing, marked the boy's place near the endpoint of his father's story. And were it not for something *else's* having been hidden in that drawer, he might need again now to press his cuff hard into his eyes to keep back tears, no matter who on this train might see. For where was this clipping from but that *Atlanta Journal* article, by Grantland Rice, that gave notice of "a young fellow over in Alabama named Cobb, who is showing an unusual amount of talent." And what was penned in the clipping's margin, in the same strong hand that wrote the book of secrets that sat now in the boy's grip, beneath his seat, but the words "My son."

But that "something else" was hidden in the grip now too. And what it was, was his father's loaded pistol.

The boy didn't know if he'd ever get over any of these things that had happened to him. Ever in his life. But sure as he was alive at all, he couldn't get past his father's handgun's lying hidden too in that locked drawer, in a cloth sack behind the senate papers. It shouldn't have been there. But it was. And somehow—by the fact that it was—the boy was not surprised. The gun too seemed to be waiting for him, like another part of his destiny. Even before he loosened its pull string, finger-spread open its mouth, and felt inside it, the sack did not fool him. As he'd taken the sack up, the weight of the hidden object inside had let him know.

But why—*why* would the gun be there, when it *shouldn't be*? His father always kept his revolver high on a shelf in the library's closet. Always. Nor did he *ever* carry it with him. So what was it doing there secreted away in the drawer? The boy couldn't help himself. He rushed ahead and damn sinned himself into an imagination—a *picture* of his mother actually stepping out on the roof where her dead husband lay twice-shotgunned, as much as decapitated and in a godforsaken *lake* of pouring blood, because of *her*, and retrieving from the man's pocket the gun that protruded from it. For what would that gun be but a dead cold sign that there was some shameful tragic *hell* at the heart of the Cobb family. That gun in the man's pocket didn't say the first word about any accident. It spoke the word *intent* and the word *murder*. So it was the gun of dead solid disgrace. His mother never said a word about self-defense against a husband with a gun. For that would be an admission of pure shame. So she made the man a housebreaker, whom she couldn't see and who never identified himself, or showed a gun.

Or that was what he *did* appear to her as. He *did* appear to her as a housebreaker. So easily this could be pure and complete truth. So damned easily. And Royston would never prove otherwise, for all its hot desire to put some stir into its dead life.

The Cunninghams lived next door to the Cobbs, and Joe was the first to come running after the shotgun blasts broke the silence that night to all hell and gone, sometime after midnight. Joe was the one who first looked at the body. And *why*, the boy wanted to know, would he be *jealous* of Joe Cunningham's being the one to see that godforsaken horror of a body? Why? Joe, who could barely make sense when asked, just said over and over again it was "the worst thing I ever saw." But it must have been Joe—when he went running back then to get Joe, Sr.,—who said he'd thought he'd seen a gun on the dead man, for it was Joe, Sr., who mentioned the gun to Constable Crichter but who said that when he went back to the roof, there was no gun to be found.

The boy imagined his best friend on the witness stand. And he imagined himself carrying under his coat at that trial, as he carried it in his grip now, the handgun that Joe would say he saw. He'd show Joe Cunningham that gun all right! Full loaded. But no, Jesus, he didn't want to hate Joe Cunningham. He didn't want any sick, filthy jealousies either. And what *explained* those feelings of envy! He wanted to vomit the filth of them out, for good, and spit his mouth clean. And he wanted what he always had with Joe, which was the warmest, best friendship there ever was anywhere between a cuss and a saint. For who was Joe Cunningham but the one the Lord had in mind when he said the meek shall inherit the earth. But do the meek inherit the earth because they tell lies?

He thought of the three black ash bats, so beautiful with their black shine, resting on the rack above him now, in his canvas bat bag. Joe had milled these true, pure black angels as a gift for his friend. And his friend had a superstition about these ashes—that when he touched them he'd get the good luck to be a touch like Joe Cunningham, or a touch less like him*self*, which would be a pure relief once in a while. Another thing he knew because he was no fool.

But it must have been Joe, too, who talked about the interval. The damned *time* between the two blasts. Long enough "for someone to walk back and forth across a room." These were the words in the *Record*. Whose words could they have been but Joe's? He pictured himself in that courtroom again, wearing under his coat the gun that, yes, he'd *taken* from the locked drawer. Taken it, no stopping him, no matter what his mama might think—if she was the one who hid it there. Which she was *not*. Which she could not have been. Couldn't. She could not fit that picture in his mind, of the woman on that roof, reaching into the pocket of that worst thing Joe ever saw—that blown-apart, bleeding, dismembered thing that used to be a man. A father. They're all *liars* who said there was a gun sticking out of his pocket!

But time. *Intervals*. Long enough to walk back and forth across a room. How long is *that*! Long enough to take the accident out of things. That's how long they all want it to be. Long enough for her to have seen exactly who was in that window. To have gone up and looked, hard. God damn them all forever.

And their intervals. If he'd learned one thing on this three-day journey with its two godforsaken trains it was this: If time makes us, we also make it. The clock keeps ticking, all right. And the train north keeps moving. But hours and hours we don't know where we are, or anything about any clock or gold watch. Heaven. Hell. That's where we are. And I guess that proves we have a mind, Father, eh! That proves we have a soul, all right! And isn't that a sweet little joke on us. We're not just *bodies* that can run out in gutters of blood, and have our heads taken off, and our guts all shot wide open. We have souls that know the story of heaven and hell, and how the trains run on strange, strange time between these two places. Quick time—accident time—heaven. Murder time—long enough to walk back and forth across a room—eternity in hot, burning hell. She knew perfectly who it was, because she had time to look hard. She and her lover, who, if he existed, which he didn't, Tyrus would damn find someday for a deadly pistol whipping.

He bowed his head again and vice-squeezed his temples. He thought why. *Why* any of this? And if there were turning points what were they? He had read that book searching. Damn him forever for a sickening detective. But he was searching for those points of time when he might have been able to go back and whisper some word of warning, if there *needed* to be any. But not, goddammit, watch your house! Not *that,* whoever you are! And I'll find you, too, someday. You can be dead sure of that, if you exist, which you don't. Those so-called words of warning, as Uncle Chitwood said, just some sick spew from the *Record*, hearsay passed along from a dream.

But what would they have been, the turning points and the right words of warning? As many times as he'd counted money in his pockets he'd counted in his life the number of years, the damned *interval*, between the time his parents were married and the time he was born. Because his mama was only twelve years old when she was married. That's why he let in the sick curiosity of ever even thinking when his father first . . . God Jesus, why did he ever have to put his mind on this? And why did his mother have to say so many times— how many times?—ten thousand?—that she would never, never, *never* let a girl of hers marry as young as she had?

And why had she? Girls back then did, sometimes. It wasn't the most unusual thing in the entire world, back then. But why? Why his mother? What was the cause? Forever, he would remember the picture of his mother's last two fingers on her left hand. Both of them locked into a severe crook because they'd been broken and the tendons, which had been torn, had frozen rather than healed. And in itself this was a thing one did not forget. But the reason he would carry the

picture of the hand even past his grave was that she'd told
him a secret about it.

For years she'd said that her fingers were mangled in a
fall when an old rose trellis she'd often used to climb from
her childhood bedroom broke (and five hundred times in
these last weeks the detective in him had connected this trellis *insanely* with the one his father climbed the night he died).
But one day, when he was twelve, his mother told him that
it was no broken trellis and no fall (so only an insane thought
would make connections with the other trellis, for there was
no *first* one). No. Not a fall. It was her own father, who deliberately, even though he had no reason on earth to do so,
took her hand and wrenched it with enough violence to half-
cripple it for the rest of her life. That was the real cause.

Captain Nehemiah Pylades Chitwood. His mother's father. The man served under Lee from Antietam to the end,
after which he walked the hundreds of miles home with only
calluses and blood for boots, and almost totally without food,
a huge, powerful man brought down to an unrecognizable
ghost. So no one was supposed even to think a word against
him, not against one who for The Cause had taken bullets on
two different occasions and, on a third, at Gettysburg, when
things, as he said, "got mighty tight and narrow," a stab
wound deep in the back. The boy remembered a sudden instant of wishing, after his mother told him about her hand,
that the Captain had died of that stab wound. This even
though a war death for the man meant Tyrus Cobb would
never have been born.

His grandfather's battle grays, wearing the same scar-
stitchings as those of his flesh, were hung in a huge oaken
wardrobe at the Chitwood plantation. The wardrobe had a
large, black, circular lock that his father told him, proudly,
was "embossed after the shield of Achilles, in Homer." His
mother, though, told him that one time the Captain locked
her inside the black dark of this oaken coffin for the better
part of an entire day. And when he asked her what she'd

done that made his grandfather do that, she sort of smiled and laughed, in a nervous way that made the boy, maybe ten at the time, think she wanted to take back the secret she'd just told him, or was anxious to make it seem not to be that much of a thing. But when, her smile turning down a bit to a frown, she said she'd done "nothing," the secret settled in hard again, and for good. And maybe two years later, there was the revelation of the real cause of her broken and torn fingers (which revelation, as it turns out, she shared with the boy after one of those hard visits to the woodshed: a coincidence that his mind had lately recalled, and had kept recalling).

It was, then, odd that his father never said a word against the Captain. It always seemed in fact that his father would rather knock a man down and break him than hear him say a word against Nehemiah Chitwood. The boy could recite the litany of praise: Besides the heroic battle record, there was, after the war, the Captain's fierce, unyielding determination to overcome the degradation of carpetbagger tyranny, and to get past the Yankees' filthy thieving of his cotton stores, and the Yankee tariff gouges, and their banking gouges, and their rail transport gouges. And then the misery of the financial panics, and the rock-bottom cotton prices, and the tired soil.

His father had it, always, in fact, that his wife's father was nothing but a powerful and true knight-hero of The Cause, for which he three times nearly made the ultimate sacrifice. And so the boy always thought—after he found out things himself—that his father must never have found out the real truth about the Captain: that he must just never have questioned that story of the rose trellis, never having been told any other. Secrets about them, after all, get kept for the great and powerful. The boy knew this, even young, from how strange and surprising, even weird, it felt when his mother actually told him the secret. And, as time passed, he knew it from the fact that he himself never breathed the secret to another soul, which fact helped him understand "false conscience," the first time he heard that term. For how in God's real world could he *be* as guilty as he knew he would feel if he ever exposed such a man?

But his father's stubborn reverence for his father-in-law turned out to be not just odd but disturbing, truly, truly disturbing to the boy; for in his book his father made it clear he did know—that in fact, not believing the story of the trellis at all and seeing numerous danger signs, including other physical wounds, he was moved to propose as early as he did to his future girl-bride because he felt he needed to get her free of a "hard and very real peril in her home." And there was a grim night of the Captain's drunkenness that his father witnessed, the two of them alone at the plantation, the others all having gone to bed, and that his father recounted in his book with rage and revulsion. Tyrus almost stopped, but he didn't stop reading about the Captain's, his own *grandfather's*, leering, drunken confidences about his "understanding" how schoolmasters must be driven by a need to "mold" and "control" young life, especially when that young life had such a "fetching woman shape coming on." And then a sickening, laughing-drunk prophecy about the schoolmaster's no doubt finding it too hard to "wait the fair time" once he had secured his sweet prize by a marriage contract, which made the boy count *once again* that interval between his parents' wedding and his birth, which was a safe two and three-quarters years, but as if numbers could change and get better, or worse, if you kept counting them over and over and over.

For pages after, his father referred to his grandfather in such terms as "that miserable, pathetic grotesque." So odd, then, and so painful, that his father would never cease to hold the man up as the kind of "solid, self-sustaining force" that the South so desperately needed to raise itself up from the dead, no thanks to anything on this earth but its own independent strength.

It was no doubt not just love but salvation from this

"force" that his mother sought when she married. His father told, too, in his book, how his child bride, after their marriage, revealed to him what it was like in the house sometimes when the Captain had been startled, which was a very peculiarly frequent thing. How the man would sometimes turn violent in an instant and maybe rage through the plantation house. And then, after the rage was over, quite likely seek his chair to sob in (sometimes with his war rifle—which would always be returned later to its set place against the hearthstones—resting across his knees). And sometimes, finally, seek the bourbon bottle, which meant the house could go seas over in terror for who knew how long. And how it was particularly his youngest, and his only girl, who seemed to bring out a strange character in the man, especially when she'd committed such grievous sins as smiling, or laughing, or moving, or making a sound, or breathing, or being there at all. She recalled for his father one time when the Captain raised his rifle and pointed it at her as she stood in the parlor doorway arch, some long time, and then, not lowering the gun, made the sound of a click with his mouth.

But almost worse than these nightmares—something that plain stabbed the boy as he read—was his father's confession that his young bride's bitternesses against the Captain were things he "could not like" after a while. "Could not like at all." The boy would have whispered warnings right then. Strong warnings.

And it seemed to be so fast that things changed. His father's words about his mother before they married were all like love poems. From the moment he saw her, young as she was, he knew. And if he thought she would have him, after a time of waiting, he would *wait*, no matter how long. Five years. Ten. He had never in this world seen "so great a power of beauty, deep, deep as the blue of her miracle eyes." Nor if he walked the world over and lived all time would he find a gentleness, "a putting of herself out of the way," that so touched his heart. Tenderest love words, beautiful pages of them. And this language, which did not surprise him, not one bit, made the boy think of those things about his father that he so deeply loved himself. For he never doubted that his father was hard on him *only* out of love. And the reason he never doubted it is that his father would never not soften in time. It would be so long coming sometimes that the boy felt tensions he thought would just about tense up his entire life and future. But then there would be the smile, the kind word, the encouraging word. Gentle, healing words. "My son." Those words of acceptance and warm pride in the margin of that clipping wouldn't have stayed silent secrets any longer than was needed for the man's purposes. The boy was *sure* of this. And maybe he loved most that those purposes were to make his son not stop until he'd found real and true greatness, which might be the hardest thing.

But his mama—and, if it was just in his *mind*, just to himself, he could whisper this—maybe didn't share such a faith in the man. Maybe not for years. For things seemed, as the boy read them, so quickly to change after the marriage. No more tender words, almost just like that. And why? The boy thought about a strange, sharp turnaround the Captain, his grandfather, made. The man had been shocked, indeed outraged by the schoolmaster's asking for his child's hand in marriage. But not a month later he was all for it. Wanted it to take place, his father wrote, "Soon. Soon as possible." What explains the way people go from one extreme to another? Had his grandfather suddenly found some satisfaction in Herschel Cobb's marrying his daughter? And did his father fall in love with his opposite (which the boy knew could be a deep need) and then find, just like that, he hated his opposite?

He had seen his parents fight. Why not just say it! He'd seen them fight for years. Go ahead, say it! Don't keep secrets for the great and powerful forever! And he knew his beautiful mother, though gentleness of heart was her *name*, was not always likely to put herself out of the way.

But how could he let his mind not love this—for how many times had it been for *him*. For *her* son. He couldn't count the times she'd been his comfort after one of his father's disciplinings. Or how many times she'd actually prevented one of those disciplinings, though she had had to hear it more than once that it was never to be her business to stand between a father and his correcting of his child. And he had thought that maybe he'd remember forever the flower-smell of Charlie's dress because it was like the perfumed smell of his mama's dresses, which it was.

In his private silence, riding only the train of his thought and recollection, the boy was now sickened by himself. He couldn't believe what he was doing, what he had done and was *still* doing. Trying to find a tragedy. A story. Just like all the Royston rumormongers. Playing detective. And why? What was all this dreaming of his about finding points where he could have whispered words of warning? You don't stop a pure accident with warnings like the ones he was thinking of. Accidents don't hang on people's feelings and damned sick motives, those things godforsaken Royston wanted so much to see. But why did *he* want a story, too? Why! So it would kill his heart and end his damned life? So he could *not be*? Not being—that was our opposite all right! And don't we feel a sort of love for it. And then a *hatred* for it, just like that. Or maybe he wanted enough godforsaken grievance so, like Caesar, he could imagine for himself a great destiny, a story with real train-drive, which no doubt needs more pain and misery than accidents can provide. You don't avenge an accident, or blame the cause of an accident. He felt so worn out he could die. He thought he might be dead already. So maybe he was seeking energy wherever in sorry desperation he could dig it up from. Because he so much needed it, if he was ever going to prove a thing.

And what had Tyrus Cobb made it all come to now in his imagination, but Tyrus Cobb in the middle. *Casus belli.* More fancy words of his father's. And he knew their meaning. "Reason for war." That's what his father called his first son in his account of the night after this son had left for the minor leagues. His mother and father had fought when the boy left. And fought hard, over Herschel Cobb's son's following his own dream. And his father wrote it all out. Every bitterness of the argument. The man was writing everything out toward the end. Their fights. His suspicions. Why? Why do you *write out* horrible words? It tends, like reading horrible words, to give the things described a life that they wouldn't otherwise have. Why in hell do you want to give them that life? But shouldn't *he* know, the son who put his father's words in his mind, and for himself gave them a life, by the hardest reading he'd ever done. Better not to read words. Or write them. Or say them. Just forget them, or let them die before they get started.

There was this boy named Cutty Hayward his mother had known in school. His father, spying through a window, had caught them kissing once. And the boy thought when he read this that if he'd been there in that schoolyard he'd have whipped that kid himself. He and his mama were playing catch with a baseball. He'd have whipped that kid himself. Kissing his mama. But his father took this boy from so many years past and brought him back into his mind. He thought he'd seen this Hayward in Royston, after all the years, and he put the boy in his mind, as if he were a present rival. He didn't know if it *was* the boy, now a man. He just saw someone on the streets of Royston who reminded him. No more. There wasn't anything else to go on. No words exchanged. No proof. It was crazy stuff the man was writing sometimes. Stuff he just imagined. And angry as crazy; for he considered this Hayward, who never showed "even the rudiments of respect for true culture," his natural enemy.

And if it was war now with his wife, his son was the *casus belli*. That's what the boy had been reading when he closed the book's cover and for a long, long time just held the mark hard with his finger. And tried to recover himself.

To regain his faith, which he did, and always would.

But there was another strange truth. For hadn't he, for some long time before he came to those words, imagined himself, already, to be the cause? The *casus belli*. The one to blame for all the trouble? Hadn't he been blaming himself already, maybe from the moment Uncle Chitwood called with the news of his father's death? And so those words, didn't they hit him like something he'd long suspected? And wasn't his suspicion, by his father's words, proved true? As true, say, as his finding a gun in a locked drawer? Imagination may *know* something then. What? What did it know? He thought of his imagination as itching for a target, the way we get a crazy, haunting itch, when we carry a gun, to use it on some target.

His mama, who wanted salvation from her miserable, war-destroyed father, wanted no gun at all in the house. She told her husband that she feared deeply what kind of things a gun in the house could do to a mind. But the man who came to imagine and fear that an old ghost out of his wife's childhood was haunting their town—he brought a shotgun into their first house. And it was no long time, not a month, after their marriage. The boy could picture that house perfectly, the little white-clapboard cabin down the road from the school, in The Narrows. He could imagine his mother as his father described her. He could see the beautiful, blue-eyed girl crying and pleading with the man not to bring a gun into their house. And then, when he just did it, not even waiting for her to come round, her not crying another tear. Maybe this was the point, the boy thought, when his mama's childhood ended. And with a true hatred of himself, he now took satisfaction in an irony right out of hell's own story, regarding the Cobb family gun; for it was his father, once his girl-bride's tears had dried, who had taught her how to use it.

Chapter Two
WATCH YOUR HOUSE

He let time pass. And more time. But suddenly then, motion among the seats. People beginning to stand and take down grips and valises. In the next car, the conductor calling something out. *Detroit.* It had to be. He looked out ahead. He saw what looked like tall buildings and a huge light on top of a tower, not that far in the distance. The car door opened, letting in the full roar. Then, "DEE-troit! *End* of the line! Four more minutes to *Dee*-troit!"

He felt all leaded and held down. He thought of his body as made up of hundreds of birds that wanted to fly and struggled but had lead balls attached to their feet and couldn't. And sure that *was* a light tower of some kind. And those *were* buildings, huge. He wanted to go home, wherever that was. The banker man stood now and left the seat without a nod and moved up with the men standing near the end of the car. Everyone was rising and moving forward. Why hadn't he asked that friendly man about a place to stay. Why *not*?

He had a sudden superstition that when he rose, his bat bag would be gone and that this would be a sign he had no right to be here. That he'd fail, if he tried to make it in this place. He'd damned disgrace himself. But no—he saw, as he stood on shaking legs—the bats were there; and as the whistle blew now in a vibrating, ear-shattering blast, he took them down, trying to be careful, his hands trembling, strengthless. The whistle blew again. He picked up the grip and, feeling its heaviness, laid it down quickly on the seat. He forced shaking fingers into his pocket and somehow dug out his watch, which *he* now felt that he'd stolen. Eleven forty-four. The wheels began their screeching. Right on time. God damn. LET 'EM KNOW WHERE YOU'RE FROM, TYRUS COBB, IN THE BIG SHOW! What a sorry laugh!

The screeching—screeching—screeching—of steel on steel now ended. And the train jerked to its final halt. But as the crowd moved him out quickly from the car and onto the station's huge track area, he was afraid he'd fall. His body felt so weak. But his leaded feet he thought balanced him in the motion—onward—through a lighted, triple-arched entryway. And the high, gilded cavern of the Michigan Central Station, when it opened on his eyes, reminded him closely enough of Atlanta's Central. Similar look. Same smell. He began to look around. But he knew it was a good laugh to think anyone would be there waiting for him. And he'd lost the banker man completely. The crowd moved faster than gun-spooked rabbits, so *not* like Atlanta. Where the hell were they all going so fast? But all were moving in the same direction, so he kept moving along with them, his grip in one sweating hand and his bats held hard, almost bruisingly, against his ribs, until he found himself moved right out the door and onto the street, where, hit by a shock of cool air, he now saw a good eight or ten lamp-lit, smoking automobiles as well as a dozen or so horse-drawn cabs, all of which were taken immediately—and gone. The walking crowd was scattering fast in all directions, too, so he asked the first person who looked like he might be a Tigers crank, a man about thirty with an athlete's frame, "Pardon me, sir, can you tell me where I'd find Bennett Park?"

"Michigan and Trumbull, edge a Corktown. But, say, mister, where in the not-too-close might you be from?"

So there it was—in no time—rude Yankees not letting his Southernness *alone*. But he saw the man smile, so he smiled back.

"Royston, Georgia."

"Well, Rohiyston Gowidga, it's about two miles, er mahls, *that away*." The man pointed down a long street of shop signs and gaslights. There were some five or six automobiles, at various distances, moving their bobbing lamps along the way the man pointed. "Follow the crowd," he said, nodding, then turned and walked the other way. And that fast, the boy found himself alone. Alone in this foreign-as-hell place that he couldn't much make out at all now, besides the one street he looked down, not finding even that light tower as he turned slightly about. And it gave him a sick feeling that it was on this strange city he'd depend for praise, if he ever was to hear praise again. That if he ever was to become a hero, it would have to be to *these* people. Could he ever power them into accepting him? Could he ever make their embracing him something other than a complete damned lie?

His muscles had tightened hard almost as in spasm, but he began now walking down the gas-lamp-lighted street, grip in his sweating hand, his bag of ashes hoisted to his shoulder. He felt the weight of everything—of his leaded shoes; of the fatigue from days of no sleep; of the weariness in his eyes, which the glare of the extending row of gas lamps made ache and burn; of the pain spreading out from his wound, which now beat and showed no sign of itching or healing; of the bag of bats, which immediately made his shoulder ache with every roll and new touch; and of the grip, with all it contained. And he thought isn't that how it worked, all right: When he was supposed to leap for joy, he could barely walk a step.

He walked on, in all his heaviness and ache and tight cramp, not even wanting now to look or imagine beyond the street of two- and three-story shops and other emporiums he saw before him; for this Detroit might become more strange and disappointing than he could take.

After some minutes, though, the streetcar came up behind him, rocking, rumbling on its tracks, clanging its bell. He thought he might allow himself the lift. Streetcars and ballparks, he thought, must surely go together. That would be logical. But he didn't know. He didn't know—and he let it pass.

God *damn* me! he swore then as he kept on walking, coming now on some night action—signs for taverns, and men in the street, talking and laughing. He saw no sign yet for Bennett or Michigan or Trumbull or Corktown. But he didn't want to ask, and wouldn't. Wouldn't look an ignorant fool, or a sucker for some night-working Yankee thug. But what if that athlete-Yankee *did* lie and he was headed in the wrong direction, into real trouble? He saw now, though, a horse-drawn cab, empty of passengers, at street side just ahead. Every effort was sharply painful, but he walked up quickly and asked politely if he could be taken to "some maybe not too expensive place . . . maybe not too far from the ballpark?"

"Got the nickel, stranger?" The cabby wanted to know. His smile in the gaslight revealed a missing eyetooth and a scum-blackened row of what was left.

The boy nodded, but determined immediately that this rude Yankee tramp wouldn't see a red cent till they got wherever they were going.

"Hoist yourself on," the cabby said; then, when Tyrus settled himself and his things, the hackster flipped his reins, clacked his tongue, and drove straight, the way the athlete one had pointed. Several more automobiles, lights bobbing, horns croaking, passed them by, and, even at this late hour, numbers of men on bicycles with jangling bells. Traffic started thinning, though, as the buildings began to change from the two- and three-story kind to six-, seven-, and eight-story factories and warehouses with docks and wagon hitches. And in this darkening canyon of brick, from which a wide view of the city became even more impossible, the shoes of the cab's horse clopped loud and hollow on what had turned to a pavement of cedar blocks.

Then no other street traffic. But in the canyon darkness, as he looked down cross streets they passed and alleyways— here, there—he saw maybe a half dozen red, blazing night fires of what he guessed must be iron forges, much too busy at night to be blacksmiths' shops. He could now and again hear, too, come out of the silence, the banging and pounding of what must have been powerful machines against metal. And at the end of one blind alley he saw an aproned iron smith, his black outline set against a tremendous fire, swinging off on a chain-trolley what he felt certain was a side panel for an automobile. He felt an excitement—then checked himself, thinking with bitter contempt that this, and all these blazes in the dark, would be a perfect portrait, all right, of damned sleepless, burning, metal-pounding Yankee hell.

But now the cabby pointed up ahead, past a corner where the gaslights no longer shone. "See up there, my good friend. That'll be your Bennett Park. But I'll take ya past, a block or so, to the Union House bar 'n boardin' house—won't hurt your stash too bad and good eatin'. How's that sound?"

Tyrus said, "Sounds fine." He actually didn't like the sound much at all. But so near the park he liked. And *goddammit*, this was really *it*! Bennett Park! He felt a sudden indomitable throbbing of energy in his heart and soul that no dead weight of alienated disappointment and exhaustion could kill. He was all eyes for Bennett Park! And in the lampless dark, but under a good disk of a moon, which clearly silvered things now that the gas lamps' glare was passed, he began to make the park out. At ground level, though, it looked, as they came closer, and closer, to be just a wild mess of cross ties and scaffolding, supporting a stack of makeshift, rigged-up bleachers.

But, gradually, as they came out past a last, dark, hovering building, the boy could see, with space now opening wide, the real park walls—and then the grandstand's overhang, rising high in the moonlight. Against the blue-black sky, the grandstand looked sure enough like a huge steamer coming on a clear night, under a full moon, into Charleston Bay! He hadn't seen a park like this before! He held his bats tight between his knees as the cab clattered over the cedar-block bricks and a rail crossing, right under the weird bleacher riggings. As they rode just under them, the moonlight came down through the benches and crazy cross ties, and it made them spooky, like something that came to the devil in a bad dream. But it was the good angels who built that grandstand—the boy thought so—even when seeing the moonlit pavilion made him wish suddenly, again, that he'd never made it here, to this situation he'd always wanted. That he was born wanting.

The horse's shoes kept clopping loud on the cedar blocks as they rode under the high park wall. But when the cab passed out beyond the wall's end, the street became smooth and quiet again. As the wheels rolled on in the new smoothness, the boy turned back his head. He saw then, at what must have been the home-plate entrance, a broad, towering, convex sign that read

HOME OF THE TIGERS
PRIDE OF DETROIT

Paradise. But suddenly a hard confusion of emotion. He wanted to go home, back south, rather than be part of any Yankee-kind of "pride." But home? He imagined a train-car door opening and heard in his mind another loud roar of motion. His other journey, the one inside the book that lay inside his grip beside the loaded gun, took him up again and ripped his heart. Home! *BURN THIS!* That was home!

The cab kept rolling. And as he looked back from a lengthening open distance on the white, dark-lettered sign and up at the full, high grandstand, with its pennants—some rippling, some floating slow in the moonlight—he admitted a measure of respect for the enemy, these damned Yankees. And his heart, sick and torn, still felt a throbbing of wonder.

But the Union House Hotel and Restaurant wasn't far. He turned forward at last and saw it where the gaslights began again. He reached in for his nickel and had it ready as the cab rolled back again onto cedar block and clopped on up toward the "hotel." The more he saw of the Union House, the less he liked. The "restaurant" looked like a jumpin' joint for sure. There were shirtsleeved characters in floppy caps and ladies with some real wallop in their Yankee lungs, parting ways out front. But it was too late for any place else.

He handed over the nickel. That bastard of a cabby held it up under the gaslight. Then, as he pocketed the coin, he showed his rotten teeth in a smile. Tyrus was already out and on the ground, his grip in hand and his bat bag up on his left shoulder.

"Chesbro for New York tomorrow, in case you's wonderin'," the cabby said. "Keep your money off them Bengals."

The boy tightened his hold hard on the bag on his shoulder.

"But say, are them *bats* you's carryin'? You a ballplayer er somethin'? You with the Tigers, my good friend?"

"Maybe."

"Well what's your name, *maybe*?"

"Tyrus Cobb."

"Ain't heard that one yet." He turned his nag out and back around. "But I'll look for ya, Cyrus, in the spreadsheet gab. Fred West's the name. Mr. Freddie West. And I watch the game real close, with a perfessional innerest, so t' speak."

He pulled up his reins, stopped, and leaned out. "Them Brahmins ever make ya feel like they don't know Cyrus's worth 'n merits, just whisper the words 'Freddie West'—and see if I ain't close by." He smiled, clacked his tongue then, and pulled away down the wood-block street in the direction they'd come.

Tyrus asked himself if what he thought just happened, happened. He stood a moment staring at nothing, then looked to watch the cab in the moonlight as it rolled on past the park sign out of sight. He tightened his fists in fear and anger. And he could see his father, seated in the chair at the rolltop desk, and hear the prophet.

"I'll make a sure set of predictions, Tyrus Cobb," he said. "A sure *set*. You'll be with those who passed by 'hells' and 'damns' in a quick enough hurry and kept on till all the real degrading four-letter filth became their common parlance. And with those who may have swatted away gamblers for a while but who one day got weary of it, and gave in. And with those who, underpaid and overworked, every night drink away their feelings of worthlessness with hard liquor. And with those who don't even consider what their bodies, let alone their souls, might pick up from filthy road whores. Day after day, year after year, *these* will be your companions. Cause, Tyrus, and effect. Don't be surprised. Don't you be surprised, boy, if my words of warning come back to haunt you some day. And pray it won't be a day too late and that you won't be too much a *ballplayer*."

He heard a girl's sharp cackling laugh and a man's guffaw. He turned, and glanced at the riffraff smoking and drinking on the sidewalk. Then he faced the green, latticed door that read UNION HOUSE in gold letters across the top, and with a tight, angry clamping of his jaw, his temples aching, he walked in.

The lobby was a blaring-loud, smoke-filled barroom; and the boardinghouse desk clerk, he got told, was whichever bartender had the first free moment. He wedged his way up to the brass rail, set his elbows on the bar, and waited for his chance to inquire. He heard a tinny piano and could half see, across the packed saloon, through the smoke-haze, a little curtained stage with a trio of red-gartered dancing girls lifting their skirts off their thrust-out backsides. He hated that filth of a cabby, the sonofabitch; but now a brawny-armed, mustachioed barkeep came up and interrupted this bitter little reflection.

"What'll it be thar, *sonny boy*?"

He recalled Cincinnati voices and wondered how many strange-as-hell foreign *jabbers* he'd hear before he got back south again, but he just said, politely, "I'd like a room, if you have one."

"A duller sivinty fyve a day. Or ten boocks a week, American plan, threy squarrs inclooded."

"Can I get a room high enough where it's quiet?"

The man took a key down from a hook on the bar-mirror's frame. "Thard floor's like the pravarbial Cave a' Marpheus, *sonny boy*."

Tyrus, who knew what the Cave of Morpheus was, if this wisecracker Yankee might not think so, paid the ten, figuring he'd demand it right back if the racket was a fraction too much, though he didn't want to be taking any more cab rides. And he figured, too, that he might be close enough here even to see those floating pennants out a decent high window. So, yes, his two journeys—same place, same time. He took the key and followed directions—"Right oop them stars, till ya can't hear us n' mar."

Up the two tight, dim-lit flights, when he closed his room door behind him, it surprisingly wasn't too bad—quiet and well-lighted by the overhead, and fairly clean (if the walls showed the rusty wash of water stains in a dozen or so places under the moldings). He dead-bolted and latched the door, then set down his things at the foot of the bed. There was a ladder-back chair with a woven-straw seat, and he pulled it to the window to look out. And sure enough there was Bennett, all right! "Home of the Tigers, Pride of Detroit," with the moon hung behind the grandstand, and the high, slow-floating pennants . . .

He took out his watch: 12:14. Reading far into the mornings, he hadn't slept more than a few hours the first two nights of this journey. But he thought it might not be too late, if he got a good sleep now before he played. He'd need to go out soon, though, or else. But right this minute he was cocked and loaded, with the park's being *right there*. So incredible, that it was no lie! And he knew about Jack Chesbro, all right, "Happy Jack," who just the year before won forty-one! Forty-one! What if he got put right in to play tomorrow, against Happy Jack Chesbro? They didn't bring him up because they didn't need him. He hated like hell that he'd never seen that famous spitball all slicked up and dipping at the plate. Because if he had seen it, he would know it. And then he'd make a plan for how to kill it—and then he *would* kill it—and then no more happy in "Happy Jack!" But maybe (chances tripling if he didn't sleep) it would be no more Tyrus Cobb. *Cyrus* Cobb. Let 'Em Know Where You're From, *Cyrus*, in the Big Show.

August 27, Atlanta, The White Camellia. August 28, that pukehole in Cincinnati. August 29, The Union, Detroit. Tomorrow . . . August 30, 1905, Bennett Park, the first day of Tyrus Cobb in the major leagues: ". . . a day that will mark things off . . ." He remembered the words with which his father had begun his story. "There'll be the time before it, and the time after." He thought only a moment, then stood from the chair.

There was a small, shaded lamp and a table by the side of the bed. He got and moved them, set them up by the window and pulled on the lamp. He went to the door, double-checked the latch chain and dead-bolt, and turned out the overhead. Then he went to his grip, thrust in his hand, feeling past the loaded gun, and took out and opened *William Herschel Cobb, Turning Points of His Life, Commencing with His*

Coming into His Profession. He sat again at the window, and, in the darker room, but under the shaded lamp, looked again at the first entry.

"Having waited for years . . ." Yes. "I feel now that I *am* someone. I've been given a place, and I am in it." But maybe more than ever because he was here, in this strange Detroit, Tyrus didn't know if he himself had a place at all, anywhere. Or if he would ever *be* anybody.

BURN THIS. It seemed that a voice outside and above him—but somewhere in the room—spoke the words. In a pulse of true terror, he felt that fear for his mind again. Or that he already *was* crazy. But something in him was also sick-glad (as if he saw that some gun he intended to kill with was in fact loaded), because he knew now he would be matching up his two journeys and their arrivals, no matter how late it got.

He looked out at the moonlit park, which from his darker perch he could see now even better, the pennants rippling in a stronger wind. He would not stop reading till he reached the end. But now what—some kind of game first? Without looking at it, he slipped the blue-backed clipping out from its place and set it back under the front cover. He worked his forefinger then between pages, into a place which must be near where that clipping had been set. He opened the book slowly, where his finger had made its crack. He was right. More than right. He'd come *exactly* to the place—to the *exact page*—which made him think a moment "No accident" and believe he'd received some further sign from destiny.

But in just one more moment, perhaps, all the weight of his pains and no sleep, his raw-eyed exhaustion, might stop him dead. He thought he might keel over. He could feel the pulse beating in his thigh, the hard pressure of the stiff chair against it. He would tear and bleed if he didn't lift his weight some from off the spot of his wound. He could hear a ticking. Was it a hallucination? He was that tired. But, no matter, it was time. Time to satisfy his curiosities, by this window over-looking "The Home of the Tigers."

He squinted his burning eyes and began to read. But in the next entry he didn't find his own name. Instead, passionate expressions of his father's determination that "the liberating fact" of "the organizational capacities of the white *male*" should be established "as firmly in the state of Georgia as it is in the Holy Bible." Also of the man's hopes for "the populist/progressivist evolution of Mr. Hoke Smith . . . and possibilities of a truer white man's unity . . . a coming together in essential principle: in the idea of the Southern Democrat."

And having read as many pages as he had on his father's public commitments, all the man's countless recollections of his battles for public education and to secure the franchise (battles that began as far back as the earliest days of his marriage—when the love language stopped), the boy thought that this is where his father went—and, forgive him for thinking it, went *wrong*—too far into politics, and *out* of his marriage. The fact that his mother didn't see eye-to-eye with the man, either, on how it was that the South should recoup its strength: this, the boy was positive, was part of the story. But if there *was* a story, which there wasn't, he couldn't help it: He wanted again to find himself at the center of it. So he turned back now to that place of violence that on the train stopped him from reading another word. And he thought—what? That he wanted to bring a gun into the house of his own brain? That's what going back deliberately to reread the passage felt like. Or like loading his father's pistol if he hadn't, in the drawer, found it with the chamber full already. He came to the place.

> March 30, 1904, Royston. There are inconceivable
> dangers in hoping, and expecting, too much. What
> possibly on this earth could have meant more to me
> than my son's completing his schooling? The whole

point of my life has been the promotion of learning—
the whole *point*. From the *day he was born* I dreamed of
my son's being a truly educated man. I prayed from
the bottom of my heart that he would enter one of the
learned professions—and achieve the highest eminence—
which I know he could have—which I am absolutely
convinced he was *born for*. And now he leaves home to
become a *ballplayer*. What is the beautiful *summum
bonum* of the Southern imagination but the true
Gentleman? A man of proportion and harmony,
Castiglione's man, a Sidney, a Galahad. And what
would be the perfect opposite of all this but a
godforsaken *ballplayer*, not a half-step above a nigger,
not a half-step.

So what a damned fine conclusion! His animal
body usurping the place of his soul. And the
companions! And the life! Indeed the gods are
laughing at me, with all my expectations. They're
laughing at me. Roaring with damned laughter! Whom
they would destroy, they first make mad. Of course
I've seen the signs for years—years of resistance and
opposition, encouraged every step of the way by his
mother (a problem in my life that I *will* solve). But this
does nothing to palliate my indescribable,
heartbreaking disappointment. When one sees that *this*
is the end of all his cherished plans.

The boy stopped, sick again with so much proved, and
proved against him. He felt his imagination's getting crazy
again to find some target. What? Who? He put his finger hard
on the point where he stopped and looked out once more,
for some further self-whipping, on damned Detroit—where
he was supposed to prove himself righteous. In the increas-
ing dark, the moon having sunk now below the roofs of the
factories and warehouses, he could see again all those red-
flamed forge fires. God Jesus. The place he'd make himself

great in, because he followed now his "true happiness." In pain and misery, as far from true happiness as he was from Georgia, or from some home he maybe never had known at all, he turned his eyes back down to the book, lifting his finger from the point where he'd stopped.

And so my son is gone, to God knows where. And I, set free, as his mother would now put it to me, by the truth, will try to love him. I will try to change myself. Change all my hopes. It's like dying, and *not* to rise again! A *ballplayer*—what a world-sized *laugh*! I prayed I was dreaming, prayed that the sleep-god had just sent me a nightmare. But it was the truth. And so the perfect laugh on me: the great lover of God's living truth. I tried to convince him they'd make a peon out of him, with their "reserved rights" to him, a damned *insult* to the American Constitution! And God knows they will: they will make a *nigger* out of a *man*, as he will out of himself, giving up his education. But I'll try to make the best place in my heart that I can for this ending of a dream. I know he has a hotter fire in his gut than Hephaestos in his forge, of which something good, some kind of achievement, still may come.

But his mother can go to *hell* if she thinks she can shame me into anything! I've had *enough* of her attempts to make me feel guilt and shame! Of *her*—making *me* feel guilt! Now there is a *laugh*! I like *that*! And I heard it all again last night, after the boy, our *casus belli*, was gone. The more bitterly I lamented his choice, the more *mindlessly* she praised it. I told her I knew why she favored his following his, must I call it his *dream*? I said I knew what her words meant. The revolting boldness of her. She walked up to me. She said to me, you think you know, Herschel. But you don't know. You think you know what I feel. But you haven't known me in *years*. If it's your *expectations* that

make you turn so hard, then shame on you, sir, for
your expectations! And your disappointments! And
now I swear I don't know if you could even give an
account now of my days, Herschel Cobb, so little do
you seem to care! You know nothing. Absolutely
nothing! You see only what you want to see. But what
do you really know of me anymore? Could you say
what I *do* when you're not around? Could you say one
thing that I *do*! She stood not three feet from me. I felt
so many things coming to a perfect point in her
question. My suspicions. All of them. What does she *do*
when I'm not around? What does she do with her
time? But she'd know no more from me! I said only I
have a mind, Amanda! A mind! And I know enough
of what I need to know about you!

There was noise down in the street. Drunks and drunk
women. The boy wanted to shout out at the top of his lungs
that the next bit of squalling would be somebody's last! Godforsaken goddamned Yankees! But he wanted to shout loud
enough, too, to his father in the grave that he had no reason
to believe what he seemed too ready to believe! What he saw
that day in town meant nothing. Nothing at all. Why so hun-
gry to make it *mean* something? Was he trying to drive himself insane? What *causes* this?

He heard a heavy tread on the stairs. But it seemed, somehow, no interruption—rather a connection. Someone was
coming up. Closer. Yes. To the top. Walking now down the
hall, to the door. Closer. But no knock. The steps passed by.
The door of the next room opened, and closed. He could hear
footsteps on the creaking floor, then shoes drop, and then
someone's falling heavily onto the bed. But he rose now and
set down the book, face open to keep his place. He went to
his grip, reached in, finger-spread open the cloth sack, then
closed his fingers on the handle of the gun, which he drew
out and took back with him to his table by the window over-

looking Bennett Park, and this so-called city of Earth that at night could pass easily for the dead center of Hell.

He closed his eyes and imagined that if he knew his target he wouldn't hesitate. He shut his eyes harder, thinking if he pressed them down tight enough he might be able to produce a picture of whoever it was. But nothing came except darkness and, in pulses, floating blotches of gray. He opened his eyes again, looking once more out the window. And what would it be like, he wondered, to trust nothing? To live in a world completely, everywhere, rotted? That's the question he was asking, right when he was getting all he ever wanted!

He turned his eyes back inside. There was the gun. He reached his hand to it and tapped, and tapped. He set his fingers round the handle. But it would never stop. Till it *stopped*. Not till then, would this reading stop. Then he would follow his father's instructions and *BURN THIS!*—if he lived.

He took the book by the fold, his thumb under the crease and his fingers over the spine. He turned it over and then held it open in his two hands. He hadn't looked ahead (only once had he done that), but, somehow, he was not surprised by what he found now. Not at all surprised. Amid the endless detail, all the politics and politics, of his father's book, he'd had to wait long times for word of himself. But no wait now, which didn't surprise him. It all made sense.

April 23, 1904, Royston. And so I had my chance to bring my son home—and I did not take it. *Why?* I had a chance to restore my own hopes. I could have made him. But I did not. Why? I know he would have come home. I know this. I could have made him. And not to make him was like *dying* for me. And I think what he's doing is so completely *wrong*. I could not possibly think it more wrong. Never will this change. But I never heard such misery in that boy's voice—when he told me he'd been cut from that ball team—when he had to *admit* this. It was the misery of all the ages. I swear it was. And if it killed me just thinking it, I did begin thinking, when I heard him, that maybe all I've ever said about freedom was at its true point of trial and truth. My fine words. He has turned them back on me. Our last dispute. He turned them back on me. Individual free choice. My fine, fine words. I confess here on these private pages something I cannot—if I wish to live—admit openly to him. I confess it—there is a great weight of guilt that I have borne—the way I do a kind of violence to myself, and others—Lord in heaven how I know this—showing never enough latitude and forbearance with those not of my mind. Or enough *mercy*—to use my wife's word. Forcing myself. The voice of conscience—another thing I like to talk about. But what my conscience said now, as I heard my son's voice over that phone line, was that I'd be a dead cold liar if I was too cowardly to let him go— or to *encourage* him to go. His having to admit to me that his contract had been canceled. How much that must have killed him. I know him. We're the same— though the gods for their very deepest laughter put in a large world of difference, too. He told me of some team or other in Alabama, with whom he had a chance to make a beginning. I'm sure I could have ended this. And made him come home. I could have ended it and made him. But I told him to go. And not to fail, the lasting effect of which words I can easily foresee. And how much it makes me regret I said such words. But then I was overcome, or released. In the silence that followed, I had a sudden tremendous, proud conviction—I heard a voice somewhere crying in my heart—louder than my pain—that if they ever do give my son his chance, he'll be the greatest ballplayer who ever lived.

The boy's tears, as he'd read on, had welled. Now they overflowed. He broke down sobbing, his shoulders heaving.

His sorrow so overcame him he almost wished these last words had stayed secret forever, no matter that they would drive him so hard on the diamond. No matter that he *knew* how hard they would drive him. He bowed his head, placed the book on his lap and, still sobbing, pictured that dark coffin, never opened, being lowered into the grave, in that burning Georgia August heat. He could see the black, sweating funeral horses, the feathered heads bobbing. The black coats of men from the town. "The only man I'll ever love." He'd whispered his phrase as the ropes played out, and the casket went down, and—before letting it go—he had squeezed hard his fistful of dirt. Oh Jesus God in heaven how he loved the man! How he understood and loved his father, who *never* forgot his son! He *never* let too much time pass before he gave him encouragement. Reassurances. He *wouldn't* wait too long. He wouldn't ever break his son's spirit. Again, the boy's shoulders heaved. He bowed his head again, and, sobbing, thought of how for everything he was, or ever would be, he was grateful to his father. How he owed, everything.

He kept then whispering prayers of thanks, and payment. But eventually, as his sobbing and praying grew more and more quiet, he heard a noise, from the next room. What? A rustling and squeaking on that bed? Oh God damn! He'd kill before he'd be shamed before some drunken Yankee lout. Never! God damn *never*! He pressed the heals of his hands against his eyes. He dried his tears hard. Then pressing his thumbs against his forefingers so that he made bright crescents of blood beneath the nails, he looked at the page—and made a vow that every day he played, he'd leave the field with nothing left—that he'd give everything he had, down to his last drop of energy and life!—and that on the diamond he'd fight for records never to be broken till the end of time! "As much as it takes to bring the word to the other world, Father. I'll *get* it to you! I swear I will. There'll be total vindication, I swear to God Almighty!"

He was trembling, his eyes blinded by more stinging

tears. But he wouldn't be shamed. He wouldn't be heard by any Yankee. He breathed a deep breath, once more brutally dried his eyes, and tried to calm himself. But when he let his eyes fall to his book, he thought—guessed—it must be!—that he had come now to within *pages* of the end! These dates now, coming fast to the end. He was shaking again, but he couldn't be stopped. He lowered his eyes.

"July 16, 1904, Atlanta, Stump Street." His father's in-session lodgings. "I have received a communication today. A letter. Oh so very, very interesting." Then, next page,

WATCH YOUR HOUSE! Watch your house, Herschel Cobb. Just that warning. Unsigned. But it can mean only one thing. ONE THING! Who'd hate me enough to lie? Several perhaps. So many wars in my time. So many. But I have telephoned home—to find what? To find what I expected to find? Which is what? That Paul and Florence are at the farm. That they are taken there by Ezra. That he and Mama Mary will stay with them for tonight, tomorrow, and tomorrow night. How am I to read this? I confess it is only the first time since I began my vigilance in this matter that I've heard that the children were gone and she was at home alone. I won't let this news alarm me. Her voice was calm. She answered on the second ring, so she can not have been in our bed. *Not* in our bed! Impossible. Too far. Too much time. *Facts*, not imaginations. And I'll stop myself because—God knows this—I am most accomplished now at reading into things. Don't I know that to be the last insane delight! I'll stop myself. For oh God! do I not know how vague words (spoken by what demon force?) can get a sick imagination to create tales. And so elaborate we make them—detail, detail, and detail all connected, and so rich with plot and *sickness*—most accomplished goddamnable tales that will destroy and end lives—ours, or others'. I

swear we hate ourselves and want to *kill* ourselves
with certainties that go against us.

The boy read on, glancing quickly, seeing all the turning
points beginning to lead in a straight line—of heartbreaking
confirmation.

> August 1, 1904, Atlanta, Stump Street. Once more, the
> children let go to the farm. But still that only makes
> twice. I've spoken to Paul and Florence, not Tyrus, he's
> gone. Do they enjoy the farm, spending time there?
> Yes! Yes! But I will put a sharp eye on that nigger. If
> he's complicit. If he laughs. I'll watch, and I'll know.
> August 10, 1904, Royston. I knew. I *knew* this
> would happen. I knew the boy had it in him, so *deep*,
> and it is an *ecstasy* for me to be torn and shredded by
> the gods of *I told you so*, for they make me glad in my
> conscience as they shatter my dreams. It seems there is
> a young man over in Alabama who is showing an
> unusual amount of talent, a young man named Tyrus
> Raymond Cobb. So his story is begun. I will watch
> him. I don't know from what distance. The one that
> best will make him burn with ambition. Let fools write
> my son's story as if God really wants us content! At
> peace, rather than war! Let them write it a million
> ways and a million times wrong so long as Tyrus
> Cobb knows that heaven is God's *deliberate* hiding
> place from us.

The boy heard a knocking. There was a knocking, but
not at his door. The next room. A knocking. Some stirring on
the bed. Someone rising and walking to the door. Whispering. The door opened. A woman in the hall, giggling, laughing. The door again closed, and again in the room a giggling
and laughing. The woman, or girl, laughing, and a man. The
sound of them falling on the bed, and her laughing.

October 11, 1904, Royston. I found out from the
children some days past now that there were several
more times—maybe three or four—that I didn't know
about, times I didn't call! And I am good to my oath
and word. I swore if I ever saw her laughing or
whispering with that nigger, I'd find out what it *meant*.
And two days ago, SURE AS HELL, there they were in
whispering confab and laughing. She touched her
finger to her lips, and he to his! And she gave him
money. I didn't wait. The minute she was gone, I
called him to me. I put my eye on his face and asked
him what he and Mrs. Cobb found so amusing. He
couldn't answer. He said he couldn't recall. I said it
was but a moment ago and so he MUST BE a liar! I
said I wanted the truth—the whole truth! I said I had
an idea of what it was and that he couldn't fool me. I
demanded that he tell me. He couldn't answer. I think
I was near madness. That I was forced to expose
myself before such! That a nigger would see me fall
apart! Fail in my marriage! That he would know
anything about me! That I would ever have to ask him
about anything that might affect my life! I hated *him*
more than I hated *her*! I told him if he didn't find an
answer soon enough, he'd have to find another place. I
wasn't going to wait for the truth. I let him know that
if he didn't crop for me he'd end up working *no place*.
That he'd end up scavenging in some damned Atlanta
alley camp. He started nervously to concoct some story
about Mizrus Cobb jes bein' kind t' Ez. Thas all. She
jes bein' . . . She *jes bein'* . . . But I cut this off! I could
tell by the way he shook and worried he was lying. I
know the rotten stink of a *story* when I smell it. I said,
Damn you, you pitiful, sorry nigger! I can tell you lie
to me. You just tell me now how many times my
children have stayed out at the farm with you and
Mama Mary this year! You tell me true, or so help me,

I'll flay your black hide! He looked terrified—and the look spoke volumes. I don' rightly know, Mistuh Cobb, suh. Twicet er three time? I don' rightly know, ah swears d' troof. He looked about him in terror, as if for some partner in crime. I was enraged. So much readable in a face to an eye that looks hard enough. I said, You liar! You filthy black nigger liar! If that's your record of things, I don't know you. As of NOW, I don't know you. You get your things and clear yourself off that farm and go. And don't you dare think I'll say more. And don't you dare try to say more. Or play your game of goddamned *I don't know* with me. Don't you think to shame me, or that I'll shame myself. You just GO! And now this morning my wife has looked cold, murderous steel at me but said nothing. I'm sure she's seen the nigger and gotten word of what happened. But she doesn't dare bring it up. She wouldn't dare. I'm certain.

The street below the boy's window was now all quiet, and the bar crowd gone. A hush had fallen over the entire place, except for the room next door, where a girl's giggling and a man's deep voice could now be heard even more clearly, though not enough so that words could be made out.

And now sessions in the General Assembly dealing with the need to extend the segregation of the races in a manner more minute and particular, "for the sake of the clearest possible and most heightened awareness, understanding, and *knowledge*—as this will lead to the fullest possible contentment and peace in the end. Supremacy is regarded by some as a filthy word. If the Lord God agreed, he wouldn't have made the contemplation of it so profoundly liberating and pleasurably akin to the joys of religion. It is a key to peace. And a form of the contemplation of God."

Then another entry from Atlanta. But it was not the last, the boy could see.

Atlanta, Stump Street, July 25, 1905. This very hour I
have received a telephone call. From *Royston,* but more
truly from a *nightmare!* The voice came muffled. He
wouldn't say who he was. A friend. But I'd heard
from him before, he said. I tried to warn you, he said.
He couldn't bear to see me deceived. Who are you! I
shouted. He didn't tell me. Just that I must *watch my
home.* Tonight. He said *tonight.* I shouted Who is it
she's with! Tell me if you care for my manhood! Give
me the opportunity to avenge myself like a man! Give
me his name! Is it Hayward! Is it that no-account
goddamned worthless tramp! IS IT?! He wouldn't say.
Just that I should let my judgment be my guide. That I
am a man of keenest intelligence and clearest
discernment. No more. Just my intelligence and
discernment, that's what I was left with, but I put
them instantly to the task of goddamned *knowing.* I
thought possibly Reeve. That tone. Was it Reeve?
Could I trust? Or was it some filthy liar? Was there
anyone who would so hate me and want to do me in?
It would be a fiend of hell. No *friend.* I called home.
Fourteen rings! At 10:05. What in hell was I going
through! What in *hell!* She wouldn't be out. She could
only be home! That's all that's possible! And was I
standing here a pitiful cuckold fool, while she spread
her rotten, filthy legs for that cynical, irreverent tramp!
In my room and my bed!! On the *fifteenth ring* she
answered! And what was that tone? I wanted full
secrecy, to give away nothing of my plans. I asked if
Paul was home. I'd seen the chancellor of Tech about
medical school. Could I speak with Paul? But *too good!*
The children were at the McCallums'! And where was
I? She wanted to know. Could it get *better!* I wanted to
say I was right down the street! But I told her I'd be
home tomorrow. I didn't sound *myself,* she said. She
wondered was I all right. But I'm sure she feels safe

still. A guilty mind can suspect just about anything. But she can't suspect I can know things across impossible distances. But my running off of the nigger. I believe—I think—that she spoke with him and heard my reasons for dismissing him. She might know why I did that. She must. And so she'd know I could never be *at all* calm about the children's being away. But I'll wait my moment. If things are going the way I know they're going, my time will come. I won't rush it. Is it not nice, too, how I enjoy the laugh against myself! A little freedom, dear, yes, good for you, with the children not there. And you must have been in bed, dear. Were you in bed?!! Do you lie in my bed, dear, and open yourself up for that dishonorable, worthless tramp. Did I disturb your great *happiness* with him, dear? Have you gone back now? Are you kissing him now? Go at it! Go at it, you mindless, unprincipled, treasonous whore! But I'll see, and I'll know. I'll bide my time. I'll lay the trap for you. And then I won't wait. I'll bring it all to a close. But I want to see it! I wish it were tomorrow that I could see it and then end this marriage. But I'll bide my time. I'll take my damned sweet time.

The boy was groaning and rocking. He let the book fall to his lap and rocked back and forth convulsively, his eyes now shut tight on the bitterest tears he'd cried yet in his life. A life that was over. Over. He already knew. But now he knew. He knew. He knew it would end this way all along. But to know. To see. The complete nightmare. His father at the window. It had been a plan. His father set the trap, for murder. Murder! And then his life ended. His head blown off. His blood running like rain in the gutter! His life! It was his own home!

And who was his mother?! A man in the house with her. No! *No!* But he pictured a man there. And he pictured his mother in bed with him. Yes. He couldn't stop picturing her and picturing her and picturing her. Hayward—who could *he* ever be, compared to his father! Nothing! The shame went deeper than any pride he'd ever felt. So deep—there'd be no words ever. But if the friend was a liar? If it was a mistake! And she was innocent! His father never spoke clearly with her. Never had it out in clear words. Why? Oh God. Hell. He would kill that voice! That friend!! But did his mother *see* who was at the window? What time between the blasts? If he could count . . . and know it was an accident . . . So bad to want to know . . . but so bad *not* to know . . . so bad . . . not to know . . . not to know . . . He couldn't not know. . . . But so bad every way.

He ripped a sleeve over his eyes, then gripped the book as if it were a living thing and he wanted to kill it. The last entry—it had to be, Christ—oh Jesus—was for the last day of his father's life. And the boy knew there was no resisting the conclusion. It would be one of the things he'd know as well as anyone can know anything. He heard laughter coming from the room next door, and he wanted to raise his gun, and kill. But he read.

Royston, August 9, 1905. I'll kill them both, and my
life will end. I'll be caught and maybe I'll be hanged.
Strange how this has its appeal. Hanged. All my life
I've been impatient for things to happen and be done.
And now this. I'm summed up. Strange how I felt such
a thrill of excitement when I told her I would be going
this evening to the farm and, after two weeks of sharp
looking, I at last detected clear signs of treason, yes. I
said that I'd need to spend the night at the farm, and
perhaps all day tomorrow and tomorrow night as well.
I was setting my trap, and I watched her face for signs.
I could detect a slight abstraction. She was thinking to
herself. Was she thinking of how good it felt with him?
I felt a hot stirring in my loins. I waited and watched.

She asked me what time I would have to go, and I
watched her face. I saw what I wanted to see—a slight
lowering of those eyes and a twitching of her sweet
mouth. Then the next hour I got all I could want. I
saw her talking to Paul and Florence. I didn't see who
initiated this conversation. But I didn't need to be told.
I knew. And sure as hell I knew what I would hear.
She'd given them permission as they'd *so begged* to
spend the night again at McCallums'. I was thrilled in
every nerve end. I'll give her time, give her rope to
hang herself, and then I'll come back to the house and
get the *truth*! So it won't matter that I didn't question
the children. And how could I involve them, my
children? I can't think—not of that. And she—they've
left with her. No doubt she'll be parting from them to
get word to him. How does she get word to him? The
phone office in town? I could have followed. No
matter. Tonight, I'll know all I'll ever need to know.
But if I must admit I'm wrong, it won't be fired—this
gun, which I have *loaded*. If my scheme is foiled by the
truth: if she's *not* there with him! I'll admit what I
have to admit.

But I might now have ruined my plan utterly!!
An hour has passed. She returned. And we have
argued violently! I can't believe myself! I struck her
and knocked her down with the blow! God forgive
me! But I know I'll *never* be forgiven. And good! So BE
it! Christ Jesus! But Why! Why *now* would I show her
so much! I asked her what took her so long in town.
And *why* would I reveal myself? Why couldn't I just
silence all incautious words! Why give her the damned
advantage of a warning?! She couldn't account for her
time, not all of it, not to my satisfaction. She said she'd
seen some of the men folk and talked for a while
about Tyrus down in Augusta. That and *what else*,
gone as long as she was!! But I wasn't fool enough to

ask her this, or *which men folk*! I wanted to know which
men folk, or *which MAN*, more than I want to know
anything on this earth! But I didn't let her know this.
Which men folk! God damn her forever! She said she
was so proud to see people following the boy's
progress. First in his league. The best player of all! But
I didn't respond, nor, I'm sure, did I look as if I liked
what she was saying. For I despise her taking credit
for my son, with all her forgivenesses. Oh the sweet
mindless mysterious heart, as opposed to hard, hard
principle and *measure*! Her with her lawless happiness
and her love of freedom—in *MY BED!* She frowned.
She told me—again!—I needed to *forget* myself and
just plain admire the boy, for *heaven's sake*. That he is
so wonderful *as he is*, coming into his own now. I
needed to forget myself! I wanted to say couldn't I
learn from *you* what it means to forget oneself!! But I
kept my feelings to myself. If you'd only seen him, she
said. If you'd just gone out *once* to watch! He hits it
where he wants. He runs like a deer. Faster! They
never know *where* he is. But *he* knows. They're all so
lost when he gets them shaken. But he *knows* what he's
doing. They complain he's lucky. He's *not* lucky. He
knows what's going to happen. Before it happens, he
knows. I said, Don't do this to me, Amanda! I won't
have you do this to me! He *knows. I KNOW! I know
your game!* She told me to get a hold of myself!
Someone might hear, she said. I said, I don't care who
might hear! And don't you tell me to get a hold of
myself, you fool! Don't you dare! You remember your
place with me! And you'd better know I understand
what all you *mean* in your games with me! She
wondered had I lost my mind! And God bless us, she
says—am I to maintain a perpetual *silence* on the
subject of our boy's ball playing? She looked at me
with vicious defiance. Am I, she said. Well, I can tell

you I will *not*! It gives me joy to speak of it! And I will
not cease. And I have no idea what you *mean* when
you say I play some game with you. Then she fires me
that look of cold steel. I've seen that look more than
once. And *she* had limits to her patience, she said. *She*
had! You haven't loved me in so *long*, she said. A
thousand, thousand years! And you cruelly criticize
and belittle everything I do, or at least what comes to
your attention. No words of any meaning pass
between us. My whole life is a plea for responses and
you communicate *nothing*! You think you're God who
needs to send no Jesus, ever! Ever! But I have *not*
forgotten what happiness means. I promise you. And
while you may not want me to live or breathe or
move, I promise you I will. I *will live*, Mr. Cobb. And I
will *not* stand for your taking my happiness from me. I
promise you, I will come to that point! And she shook
her sorry hand at my face!

The boy couldn't turn the page. But there was no possibility of his not turning it! He wanted to take up the book
to see if in this place there were traces of his mother's per-
fume, the smell of her skin and hair and dress! But no. He
turned the page. And there it *was: BURN THIS!!* Yet still
clearly the words beneath the hard scrawl:

But I took *her* face in my hands and pressed my
thumbs up under her chin. I would shut her damned
mouth out of hell!! But she began still to laugh! Her
strength surprised me! Her laughter made me rage!
Her beauty! I never felt such anger against a thing
ever! I would have killed her right there if I didn't
want to see the final truth. I want to be on the side of
right when I end her life! I want to see her betraying
me! No pictures of my imagination! All with my eyes!
But I might have ruined my plans! She kept laughing

at me! And I struck her! I knocked her to the floor
with the blow! I shouted, Look at me, you mindless,
worthless bitch! But she only knelt on the floor
weeping with her head down. She wouldn't look. She
said, It's come to this! I suppose I knew it would!! I
suppose I knew you were no different!! But I can tell
you I won't stand for it!! I shouted, You'll stand for
whatever I tell you to stand for! And not just now, but
every time always!! I reached down then and grabbed
her hands, *both* of them, as she knelt on them. I
wrenched her up without mercy. But she laughed at
me. Laughed, and said, You're no different! Just an
insane, morbid brute! You know nothing about
happiness. For all your dead pride, you know nothing!
You'll never know!! You'll be ignorant forever!! But I
am not! Do you hear me, Mr. Cobb! *I AM NOT!* I put
my face up against her face. I said, I'm going to the
farm. I won't be back tonight. Expect me no sooner
than tomorrow night. She lies up in the bed now
weeping. I can hear her. I know that sound. God
forgive me, though I know You will not, Lord. And
cannot forgive me. Forever and ever. But *I AM NOT!*
What is this except a bold confession of her treason, in
my teeth. What is it, Lord God Almighty Father! After
tonight I will destroy this book. I will burn it. But I
will know the truth. And I will place this gun in my
pocket.

The boy rose in a nearly mad stupor. He stared at the
gun on the table, then began to pace, away and back. He
came back toward the window and saw the flags over Bennett, whipping taut in the wind. He saw the forge fires. He
took the gun and paced back, now slowly, staring at the
weapon—and then, in the middle of the floor, dropped to his
knees. In the dim light, kneeling, he stared at the loaded gun.
Then there were sounds—the sounds of the man and the girl

next door. He heard their sounds. He began sobbing, and he kept sobbing. He couldn't stop. He looked at the gun and groaned. He wailed, looking at the gun. He was groaning and wailing.

There was a pounding now on the wall. Again a pounding, and words shouted. But the boy kept groaning. He was rocking back and forth on his knees and groaning as he kept looking at the gun. He didn't stop. For a long while, he didn't stop. Then there was a fierce, loud pounding on the door of his room. But he didn't stop.

He heard shouting at the door. "Hey! Shuduppa da fuck in dere, ya fuckin disturbina da peace. Ya hear me!"

He heard the pounding. Louder and louder. He took the gun in his hands. He looked at the door but was still groaning.

"Ya crazy sonomombitch. Shudda da fuck up, ya sonomombitch!!"

The boy, at last turning his mind to the voice, stopped his moan. He got up from his knees, his sense of shame returning. He looked at the door. He walked to it. And opened it. A powerful, dark-skinned man was standing there shirtless. And a woman, or a girl—it was a girl—standing behind him half-dressed, beautiful, holding up loosely over her breasts one of those dancing outfits he'd seen through the smoke across the bar.

The boy held the gun down behind his leg, pressed against the gash. He looked at the man, like some big half-nigger, and at his girl whore—at the beauty of her dark eyes and rouged skin—and, right that instant, he *knew*. He *knew*. He looked at the two of them and was dead certain where he'd be tomorrow and the day after and the day after! It wouldn't be Tyrus Cobb who died. He *knew*. If it was a pact with Satan he made, he wouldn't be the one. He'd live. If the whole rest of the world died, he'd still damned *be*. With a destiny like a weapon.

"You say something, mister?" he asked with the gun still concealed and pressed hard against the gash.

The beautiful girl whore was staring strangely into his eyes, holding the untied dancing outfit half over her pale breasts. The man bent down his dark, whiskered face. "I says you keepa disturbina da peace and I shudda you uppa real good."

The boy looked at him and, pressing his fingers tight on the handle of the gun, said, "Nobody tells me what to do."

The man, with his face still down, said, "Oh yeah."

The boy now took the gun from behind his thigh and raised it to the man's face. The man stepped back in terror, the girl behind him still looking strangely into Tyrus's eyes. "Yeah," the boy said. And with the gun still pointed hard, he stepped back into his room, then closed the door.

He held the gun down at his side and with his free hand relocked the dead-bolt and fixed the chain, then stepped to the chair and lamp. His father's book was on the floor, open, facedown on its final pages, dead. He knew how he would bury it, but not tonight. He picked the book up now with his free hand, by the crease, and let it fold closed, slipping his hand out from between the pages, and then holding the book tight shut, his hand clamped hard over the back binding. The last page of this book, he thought, his hand clamping still harder over the spine, was *not* the last page of his life. He set his jaw, and with his gun hand, freeing his forefinger and thumb enough from the gun to pull the lamp cord, he turned off the light. Then in the dark, the shut book in one hand and the loaded pistol in the other, he looked out on Detroit, with its red burning forges glowing still like the stars of hell.

He almost died in this place. But he didn't die. Another few seconds and he might have blown out his brains. Fool kid. His heart leapt and beat hard at the admission. And he still held the gun. But he did *not* die. Maybe it was just an accident that what happened, happened. That he lived. But looking out now at Bennett in the dark, the moon fully gone, he didn't think so. In fact he was sure not. And nobody—nobody was he going to *thank* anymore for Tyrus Cobb's life. He would make his damned *self* into the best ballplayer who ever lived.

But something in him asked: Could he owe nobody even the first thing and at the same time feel *chosen*? Who chose him, if he owed nobody? He smiled, as he knew suddenly that shutting up this exact question, tight as hell, would be the best way of bringing his life to the explosion point he wanted.

But did that point lie the other side of madness? Jesus! Or out into hardened sin and true evil? In the turning of an instant now, he could see his whole life cracking and breaking with shame, fear, sorrow, and insanity. But with some tremendous surge of deep energy, he did not break, or cry.

He held himself hard. Tight. Then he smiled, satisfied he had the look of somebody who could gun a man down. Just ask that Yankee half-nigger and the beautiful young mystery girl. Feeling all the tremendous, hard energy it took to keep himself from breaking down, he thought, yes, that would be the way he played, with that look that terrified those two—and with that *truth*. Being able to kill a man was crossing a line the other side of which you stood by your pure lonesome. Amen. And the hatred of the billion sobsisters who would never cross such a line would energize his days. Total damned independence, no debts to *them*: they'll hate that with everything in 'em. They'll call it treason! Secession! And *good*! Because their every hot wish to see him fail would make him work harder *not* to fail. He'd scorn 'em all, and then prove them all dead wrong. He'd draw a hard as hell line. And another. And another. Farther and farther off from them all and from his own pasts into greater and greater intensity. Let 'em call that sick, or damned, all they wanted. And if in some possible pain or terror, far far out there, any voice said if you keep trying to go it by yourself,

Tyrus Cobb, even one more step—you'll die—he wouldn't listen. He'd shut his ears hard as hell.

He wanted to unload his gun through the window into the air—to let this Detroit know he'd arrived. But he wouldn't give these people any easy excuse to collar him. He closed his eyes and in full darkness meditated on his debt to nobody. For the length of his career, maybe twenty some years, he'd deny every obligation but the one he had to Tyrus Raymond Cobb. And if after a point it really got to be too late—and he could never repent and get back to goodness . . . ? But he'd be above *that*, too! He'd come back and be decent the way people expected, when he was good and ready, which is to say when he'd set so many records he could afford to turn soft. After all, it was when he knew that he was *God* that Jesus Christ was able to give up his life. And not before.

He smiled, his eyes still shut. In the deepening quiet, he heard the ticking of his watch. He kept smiling. Maybe twenty plus years. Starting right now. He flexed tight his whole body to bring back the pounding of his wound. Good. There it was. And this was the pain he'd play through all his career. Pain. It makes you cry out for help. Cry out and say you're oh so helpless. And that you need someone. He'd goddamned play *through* that! Run right through the signs! He'd give *himself* signs. And if his entire body became one spread of scar, so be it.

He set the book down on the lamp table and the gun on the window ledge. He took off his shoes, lifting one and then the other up to the chair seat, each time feeling the pull of the lead weight on his wound. He undressed, then took out and set now his presentables carefully over the ladderback. He couldn't have guessed the time. But he figured it maybe wasn't too late to get at least *some* good sleep after all, a break which he felt now was prepared and waiting for him all along. He smiled, then picked up the gun and, feeling for the moment wing-footed, the weight of the lead all gone, he stepped to his bat bag, beside his grip. He reached into the bag with his free hand and set his ashes in what he'd for some time believed was his magic pattern, the second handle crossed over the first and the third over the second, with the three heads fanned out. Placing the gun, then, loaded beneath his pillow, he pulled himself up and stretched out facedown on the bed. He held his arms raised and apart, like a man being arrested. And soon he slept, under a dead weight of exhaustion.

Book Two

THE SHOW

Chapter Three
PRIDE OF GEORGIA

At some time during the night, he dreamed of the painted young beauty with the mystery stare. In the dream she came to his door unaccompanied, and no loud knocking, nor any warfare in her voice. She asked him that question: "Where in the not-too-close might you be from, mister?" Though now as he looked into beautiful sloe eyes and at the smoothness of the girl's cheek and pale bare shoulders, at the wisps of dark hair that strayed and fell from the binding that held it, he didn't hate but loved this question. He told her he was from Georgia. Royston, Georgia. She smiled. She asked if he minded if a Yankee girl brought him some welcome. He said he didn't mind at all and asked her wouldn't she please, please come in. And when she came in on soft bare feet, she turned to him and stared at him with that mystery stare, which reached now to the depths of his soul, and said, "Would you like to kiss me?"

He closed the door, forgetting the bolting of it, and put his hands, trembling, on her shoulders and white neck, and kissed her. The softness and sweet taste of her mouth made him want to tell this stranger not just where he was from but every secret of his life. He said that his father had prophesied that he'd fall to women if he followed his dream of becoming a ballplayer. "And here you are," she said, reaching to him with a soft touch and bringing his lips to hers again. And after a kiss that made him want once more to unlock his heart to her, completely, she said, "And you are happy."

But he said, "I've never been with a woman. I have a girl at home. Charlie. I want to save myself for Charlie. I want to save myself."

"No," she said, as she reached her white hands up into her hair for a pin, which she loosed and, out of a slack hand, let drop to the floor. "No," she whispered, now raising her soft hands again, to run her fingers through her hair and make its thick darkness fall. She took his hands, then, in hers and led him to the bed where she stood and touched his face. "You've waited so long. Too long. I can see all your sorrows and pain in your face and your eyes. And I want you to wait no more." And she kissed him and took him to her on the bed. Nor did he wait. He made love to her—his first time with a woman—and as he made love to her, he whispered to her his secrets—told her his sufferings—and felt the flow of life come from him as he confessed to her all.

It seemed to him that it was only seconds later that he felt the sun hot on his face. He reached his hand up under his pillow, and he touched, beneath the back of his neck, the wooden handle of his father's pistol. He opened his eyes. In the hard morning glare, he saw beneath the moldings all the rusty smears of the water stains. He turned and looked at the door. Realities now came rushing back—that knocking and pounding. His blood began to race. He was coming awake all right. The words "disturbina the peace" came to him. Goddamn! Yes. That had happened. And he would disturb the peace, all right! He would have goddamned killed that half-nigger Yankee sonsofabitch and his little girly slut, too.

He reached up again, took the gun from beneath the pillow, and sat up, feeling a ferocious throbbing agony in his thigh. When he threw off the top sheet, he saw that his gash had broken (it must have been when he held the gun pressed hard behind him) and that the blood had spread in a pool and left a broad, red-brown stain on the sheet. But the *hell* with it. Nothing to do. The stain was in. And that other, too. The warm sweetness of his dream came back to him, but he fought off the pleasure with a hard resentment over the loss of energy. And he promised himself that tonight, after he'd gotten himself past the start, at least, of a certain trial that began just hours from now across the street, he'd write his first Detroit letter to Charlie.

He got up and walked to the chair by the window, where he'd hung his good pants and jacket. He held the gun pointed to his lapel and, like a thief in a stickup, reached in his coat pocket with his free hand and took out his gold time-piece, which, when he clicked it open, flared bright in the sun. He read the time. Already ten, now . . . eleven, past nine. He'd need to eat soon and dress his wound.

He stood at the window, holding the handgun and the gold timepiece. He looked out on what was a city all right, bigger than Atlanta by a good stretch. He could see the trolleys clear now, running both ways along the street the park was on. He could hear the clang of a car approaching. He also saw what must have been forty dray-hauled wagons, loading and unloading along those warehouse docks, and people moving all about on the cedar-block streets. Bennett in the daylight had shrunk down among a dozen surrounding factories, several already spewing from their blackened chimneys. In the harsher light of day, the park seemed, too, to take on the soot and dust of the neighborhood.

He heard a deafening mechanical whine. Was that a sawmill over there, across the street? What the *hell*—this place was filth! But this morning maybe he liked his paradise raw, filled with the sharp whines of some huge saw blade, and all the moon glow cut out.

He closed his eyes ... then looked down and saw his father's book, its covers shut, lying at the foot of the chair. But the book would remain shut. It tried to murder him, but he didn't die. And the only words of it he let himself think of now were his father's saying he intended to set it on fire. He'd do it himself—tonight. And so destroy evidence: a crime. Obstruction of justice. But so damn be it. Destroying evidence was the only way *anybody* survived.

He held evidence too in his hand. Someone knew the gun got put back in the drawer. Someone did, obviously. But no one would know who had it now. And if no one inquired further, he sure as hell wouldn't offer. Whatever it took to bury shame in the grave, he'd do, even if that meant he'd never have another easy day in his life. And *good*, if he didn't.

He set the gun down on the chair and put his watch back in his pocket. He walked to the foot of the bed. He reached down and, opening the canvas bag, disarranging their magic alignment, took out all three of his black ashes. He stood then and began to swing them like a pendulum, back and forth, first low toward his feet, then higher and higher till he was rotating with them back and forth through his normal swing. Then he dropped two on the bed; but the third, which he'd now made light, he gripped with a two-inch choke, splitting his top hand from his bottom by another three inches. He looked back at the window, with the park in the distance. He set his feet close together and square and his hands away from his body. He went into a slight crouch, knees bent, face jutted forward, his spooky-blue hawks set hard on the imagined enemy. "Give me a little chance to know you, you Yankee sonsofbitches," he whispered, with his teeth set, "and I'll make you *real* sorry you ever knew me."

He carried his gun to the tub in case of half-niggers or whores. And he kept it under his jacket, stuck in his belt, when he went down and ate in the little dining nook, just off

the bar, where two white-whiskered, red-faced flies were already dimming their sorry brains. But while armed and on
the lookout, he couldn't have been more polite, because he'd
show these Yankees what the word *polite* meant. And if they
didn't respond, he'd give them the look that would let them
know what he could do.

Back in his room, he stripped and then five times
wrapped his wound, so if he played today and tore it, only
he would know. And in the locker room, he'd dress with his
back to his locker, so no one would see he was hurt. The hell
if they'd find *any* cheap excuses to take away the opportunity
of his life.

He had a tin of wax blacking stuffed in the toe of his
right spike. He took it out now and dabbed up his chamois
and began to polish one of his spikes hard. And he would
work the leather to one damn sharp shine, because if they
thought he was going to come in some modest, don't-look-
at-me piece of sweet cooperation, they had another think
coming.

He heard the sound of something sliding under the
door. He dropped the chamois and reached for the gun in
his belt. But he saw that what had come through the crack
was only a newspaper. He relaxed. Friendly of 'em, he had
to admit. He set down the spike he was shining and put the
gun back in his belt and got the paper. He sat with the *Free
Press* then and turned quickly to the sports. Tigers lost yesterday; but that was nothing to him, as would be all the time
before he got there, with everything in it. But was there any
word of his arrival? He ran his finger up and down the columns, his eyes raw but still sharp as hell. He thought of how
sometimes he saw a thing in his mind and then, next thing,
when he looked, there it was. He had a similar feeling of
strange strength now in his anticipation. But nothing. And
still nothing. Nothing. Nothing. But then—this—which made
the hurting pressure beat in his eyes again.

Bengals might receive today a bundle from the Double-A Sally League (That's South Atlantic League—ever hear of it?). A child goes by the name of Cyrus Cobb to be left on their doorstep. Rumor has it young Cyrus isn't ready for much. And haven't we seen our share of September's ephemerae? But, as we know, there's that hole in the Tiger outfield. And so Frankie J. has thumbed out his plug nickel to plug it.

He closed the paper and tossed it down. Newspapers. He picked up his spike again, and the chamois, and began to shine the black leather. He stood up and looked out the window at the park, still working the glowing leather hard with the wax blacking and the chamois: to get a shine as sharp as his pride. And he found himself now wishing he had a file for his steel because by God Jesus Christ in heaven he would tear the earth in this place. And they'd know the name his father chose for him, all right. They'd know it and they'd never forget that it was *Tyrus*.

It was eleven sharp when in a hot, bright sun he stood under the PRIDE OF DETROIT sign. He had his bag of ashes slung up on his shoulder and, firm in his right hand, he held his grip, lightened of its books, but not lightened of the loaded gun. He looked all around, peering hard into the dark of the entry passages beyond the turnstiles, but could see no one anywhere. He could hear, though, not the ticking of his watch but the sounds of cracking bats in the enclosed park; and when he did, the weight of his own bats seemed instantly to sink down harder on his shoulder. Good, he said to himself. Good.

He'd seen no other entrance, so, while trying hard not to look like some sorry damned crasher, he began lifting his still lead-weighted foot over the main-gate turnstile. But as he straddled the stile's arms, a ruffled, white-whiskered old gnome in a greasy, skewed ball cap, limped out from the shadows. "Hey, bub, what's your game?"

It was as if he'd been watching Tyrus every second and was just waiting for his first move to nab him as if he were a housebreaker or something. And the boy took some satisfaction in thinking this scruffy, crippled runt a perfect summary of Yankee hospitality. But the more powerful feeling was *resentment*. Still he said politely, in this first moment of greeting, "I'm Cobb, come up from Augusta to join the team."

"Cobb *who*?"

"Tyrus Cobb." He shot this back with a good deal less politeness and, lifting his weighted legs fully over the stile now and, tipping his bats to make his point clear, said, "I'm a *ballplayer*."

"I ain't heard nothin' about *that*. Who you supposed to see?"

"The owner, Mr. Frank Navin, or Manager Billy Armour."

The old gatekeeper preferred still to look him over as if he were some uninvited and suspect nobody for whom he sure as hell wasn't going to hurry, not in this life. But, finally, he pointed with a backward twist of his head. "Clubhouse," he said, "is through the fence in center." No more then, before he limped off.

Tyrus, guessing this old scab was maybe some figure he would be supposed to feel affection for, or veneration, spat at the notion. But he followed the old man's nod into a high, dark portal leading to an ascending, ramped vault, which, with no crowd around, had the hollow feeling and damp smell of a cave. But there was a glowing light at the far end— and beyond that—he could hear now more clearly—louder— the call of those cracking bats. But he waited to ascend, leaning now against one of the side walls of the vault.

The game! The Show! Jesus Christ, with everything else these past days, he truly had, at times, just about forgotten what he'd come for! But as he listened now to the cracking of bats and the snap of balls into leather and the voices, men's voices calling names he couldn't make out yet but which he knew he would know—he thought maybe his journey here was like the three-day descent into hell. And it was always opposites, wasn't it? Always the fire or the blood that was needed for the baptism.

And the smokestacks and sawdust and carthorse dung and this damp stench here and all the idiot rowdies and drunks and gamblers, who would be here, Christ, let him admit it all to his father, they couldn't bring down the sound of bats and of the snap of the ball. And it was now. His calling. His real life, not that dream of death he'd just passed through.

He'd begun to tremble, but he firmed his ashes hard on his shoulder and tightened his hand round the handle of his grip. He lifted himself off the wall and began to ascend the ramp. In his mind as he stepped up, shaking now till he feared he'd stumble, he scored hard over his nerves that it would be no sobsister's or mollycoddler's dance with Tyrus Cobb. Not a single goddamned second. Rather (and as he stepped farther into the light, there was fresher and fresher air to breathe and fill his lungs) it would be war.

Crack! Snap! The sounds were beautiful to him—but they were war music: drums. Sure as hell. But now the last steps, yes, and the full light and the fresh air and warmth. And there it all was—actual, real, the green, sunlit field and fifteen men in what he knew must be New York uniforms. The grass! It must be he'd never seen a field in his life before! Because this green grass seemed to spread out before him forever. And the grandstand to tower up again high as blue heaven.

"Hey, ya *busher*!" He heard the cry and looked. But it wasn't for him. He was angry at himself for thinking. . . . He felt an urge. But no. He wouldn't damn prove himself now by strutting onto the field with the players there. He made his way through the rows of grandstand seats—at times almost tripping—as he kept looking and wondering which was

"Prince Hal" Chase, and if Chesbro was out yet. He saw a small man who had to be Keeler. It had to be Wee Willie!

He made his way deep enough down the line in left to be out past the action. A green metal door, which must be the door to the clubhouse, was just his side of straightaway center. He stopped and looked—then thought, "All right, here she goes"—and leapt the left-field-line barrier onto the grass, which felt and smelled like ordinary grass, though he was glad he didn't fall when he landed on it. He set his bats now tight under his left arm, keeping the grip in a sweaty left hand, and so had his right hand free for knocking. He walked to the door as fast as he could without breaking into a run. And then he was there, before the green sheet of metal, wondering how much of a black and red and bloodshot crazy man he might look, after his three days' descent to the underworld. And he wondered if he'd be able to dress out of sight of the others. Or if he'd have to *talk* to people. But goddammit he had to leap into the dark and keep on damn leaping. He couldn't just stand here.

Bang! Bang! Bang! He knocked on the door to break it down, rattling it hard, all right. But nothing. He waited. And what would be polite? How long? He waited what seemed like a *long* time, and then did hear some voices. Who would be there? Wahoo Crawford? Wild Bill Donovan? George Mullin? Germany Schaeffer? Matty McIntyre? For all the dark, hard resolve he'd formed in the solitude of his room, he hoped now like some pitiful little kid that the team would be friendly. Christ. He despised himself. And what was he doing here just standing like a goddamned, naked idiot?

He'd heard those voices, and could still hear them, but no one opened the door! He knocked again, *Bang* . . . and *Bang!*

"It's *open* for Chrissake! Just walk the hell in!"

Immediately, his heart went ice with *that* (and why in hell was there nobody to greet him anywhere in Detroit so far, outside of a dream girl! A resentment, which must have been gathering all along, sprang up and rushed back to the first moment he'd arrived). But he opened the door, politely. He saw two men, who must have been those voices, facing their lockers, talking. Neither looked up. But finally, after he'd stood there some time in clear need of assistance, one turned to him. He looked to be in his late twenties and had a long, fleshy, horsey face. "You lookin' for somethin', buster?"

"I'm looking for Mr. Navin or Mr. Armour, please." Still standing in the threshold, Tyrus was flushed and shaking. He nearly stammered. So he despised himself even more. He couldn't believe he took this Yankee treatment, any of it, politely, nervously. But he could feel now some of his fatal resolution to *live*, to *be*, reasserting itself—and pushing him toward a leap. Already, he had dead hard feelings for both of these two, this horsey one and his even less friendly friend, who was a pale-skinned but dark-haired and muscled-tight package with an unclearable shadow of beard, the stain of which mixed a blue-black undercoloring into a ghosty-white face.

"And who in the hayell mahht be callin' nahhh? *Ginral Lee* his*sef*?" The horse face, grinning, biffed with his forearm the shoulder of the other one, who now turned to Tyrus, but without smiling.

Tyrus felt an immediate hot urge to do something that would end his career before it started. He had his gun still in his grip. He might take it out and wave it a bit! But no—he wouldn't let these Yankee bastards push him over any line—and take his chance away. That's exactly what they wanted, he knew *that*. He had only stared, saying nothing, although he hoped they somehow could tell that last night he nearly killed a man. Then, "I'm Cobb. Tyrus. I've come to join the club, from Augusta."

"Oh, is that so?" The big horsey one only half held back a laugh.

"Yes it *is so*," the boy said, feeling that with these words he just wrote a steel contract between himself and him*self*, that for his career, no joke on Cobb would ever make Cobb laugh. And he found himself liking this as a start, standing up to the one here for the smart remarks and to the other, who was younger, maybe twenty-four or -five, for what he was dead cold certain was an I'll-get-*you* look in his unwelcoming Yankee damned eyes.

This other, Tyrus now saw as the man turned fully to face him, was fine-cut, handsome, facially as well as bodily tight-compressed. "Matty McIntyre," he said, nodding. But he extended no hand.

"Ed Killian," the horsey one then said, adding, "Navin and Armour are in there." He jerked his thumb backward to point to a low, vaulted hallway that led off from the locker room behind him.

The boy nodded, and slung his bats back up on his shoulder, showing no sign of gratitude, and making it clear that if this rookie was supposed to be afraid a bad first moment might lead to a bad whole career, or no career, he *didn't* fear it. As he walked off, he could hear the two veterans (for he knew who the pitcher Killian was and McIntyre, the outfielder, and so rival, and natural enemy) whispering. What were they saying? That it looked like this busher didn't understand the way things were done? Good. This was one busher who didn't give a *damn* about the way things were done.

Strip yourself down to nothing, rookie, and then we'll let you into the Holy of Holies. He'd been asked to play initiation games before: to let one cheek be hazed, and then the other. But he let 'em know in Augusta and he'd let 'em know here that the only game Tyrus Cobb came to play was baseball. And if that played hell with their holy rites, then so be it. He'd have his own holy rites; and the only ones baptized would be the ones who wanted to win as badly as he did, which, besides himself, meant nobody.

The office door, above a standard-lettered OFFICE OF THE

MANAGEMENT, had stenciled on its smoked glass the team name with the famous Gothic "D." So it kept getting more real, all right. But he thought of that odd "Pride of Detroit" out at home plate and then, angrily, that the Pride of Georgia wouldn't be intimidated by any damned Yankee. With his free right hand, he knocked hard and loud on the glass.

"It's *open!*" somebody inside barked, annoyed.

Tyrus quietly turned the handle, pulled back the door and saw, seated at a desk, a dapper-dressed, mustachioed, middle-aged man with a fancy boater pushed back on his head and a half-smoked cigar in his mouth. He was a tough-lookin' one, but a bit of a dude, too, with his snappy lid and an expensive gray suit and a perfect wax on his handlebar. Immediately, the boy noticed also, in an inner office beyond, a big, lumpy-looking, expressionless bag of a man, bald as an egg, sitting at a desk, looking over what must have been a ledger. Armour. And Navin.

"Ya got a tongue, young fella?" the dapper dan said, spearing an envelope with a pen knife, not looking up.

"I'm Cobb, from Augusta."

"Well . . . well . . . well." The manager, after a little managerial pause, looked up and nodded to a chair in front of the desk. "Bill Armour," he said. And then, as Tyrus sat, "Cobb—the nut from Augusta. Just keep on runnin' until somebody tags ya out. Ain't that the philosophy?"

"I stole forty bases."

"Don't be so sensitive, Georgia boy, it'll undo ya. What'dya end up hittin' down there—in the whatd'ya call it? Sally League?"

"Three-twenty-six."

"Think that's beat all and just the beginnin' a great things, don't ya, boy?"

Tyrus, though he was thinking in fact of his gun and his bats, began to offer politely some modest rejoinder. "I guess I just hope. . . ."

But Armour cut him off. "You a fast liver, Cobb? Cigareets, whiskey and wahld, wahld women?"

"None."

"Good Southern Baptist boy, hunh?" Armour smiled as he bit down on his cigar.

"I hope so."

"*Your* mama and daddy raised *you* right, didn't they?"

"They did," Tyrus said, gripping through the canvas one of his bat handles and squeezing it hard.

"Well . . ." Armour said, leaning forward over his desk and setting his chin on his fist, ". . . suppose you tell me true, then, Georgia: Why are you lookin' so much like a damned dope fiend? You should see the rings around your eyes, sonny."

Not that he would let on the first thing about what he'd really been through—but Tyrus stopped the possibility of *any* explanation about sleeplessness costing him a chance to play. "I don't know," he said. "I feel *fine*."

Armour sniffed a laugh. "Well tell me this now," he said, "you think ol' Bill Byron knows how to call 'em?"

"The umpire?" Tyrus was sure he didn't need to hide his contempt. "No."

Armour smiled, took his cigar to his ash tray and tipped off his ash, popping the butt twice with his thumb. "Reason I ask," he said, "is Byron the umpire—he told our Heinie Youngman that if it was Tyrus Cobb or Clyde Engle, to take ole Ty Cobb any day this century or next."

Tyrus smiled. "I always said Mr. Byron had the best eye in baseball."

Armour smiled, and stuck his cigar between his teeth. "Papa Leidy thinks you'll be some kinda legend some day, too. But what about you, Mr. Tyrus? I'll bet you'd be satisfied with a little ol' bingle now and again, wouldn't ya?"

"No."

" 'No.' He says just plain 'No.' Well, maybe not. We'll see, won't we? You willin' to work, Cobb? This ain't all fun and games, ya know. It's hell's own ditch diggin' a lot of the time. Fifteen places on this team. You want one of 'em, you're gonna put out like a goddamned sweatin' devil.... And ..." He reached now down into his desk drawer, pulling out, after a moment or two, and then glancing over, a one-page, already-completed form. "... Says here you'll be willin' to do this puttin' out for fifteen hundred a year. *Proratum*. And with forty-one games left ... Let me see...." He picked up a pencil and licked its point.

"Four hundred twenty-two dollars and eight cents." Tyrus had it cross-multiplied and divided before Armour finished setting the problem to paper.

"Well ... well," the manager said, looking up, stopping his pencil. "Ain't you the ..."

But even more quickly than Armour, the large, bald figure in the inner office had raised his head. And Tyrus, expecting that this would happen, didn't look at Billy Armour—rather straight through the inner door at Frank J. Navin. The club president and owner, though, appearing, when his face was raised, like some kind of water-bloated Chinaman, said nothing, showed no expression, and lowered his eyes again soon to his ledger. In the brief moment when their glances had met, however, Tyrus, to let this owner know exactly his new hire's philosophy of gratitude, had given him a dead cold nothing for his nothing.

"So what the hell, Cobb," Armour said, tapping his pencil, "if you're as quick on the field as ya are with the amounts, ya just might be worth a little fraction or two of what we pay ya." The manager then reached for a pen and set it on the contract as he turned it to his new boy.

Rather than just set the pen to the paper and sign with it, however, Tyrus took the pen and held it poised—as if to make notes, or corrections!—and actually began *reading* the contract, moving the pen and hovering with it like a hawk over every word.

Armour smiled, shook his head at this oddball behavior,

then rose from his desk and went out toward the locker room. Tyrus then, with his manager gone, reading *hard*, was certain that the eyes of his owner were on him. He felt them like a heat covering his skull. And he now hated wanting, as much as he *wanted* it, something that no one could provide him except this Navin—who thought him, no doubt, worth a plug nickel a dozen. So much now did he hate it that he thought rather than give *any* of himself to these sonofabitching goddamn Yankees he really might end his career before he started it. To hell with the whole lot of 'em. That horse-face Yankee, Killian, and that white-rat Yankee, McIntyre, and that dapper-dan Yankee, his manager, and, in the next room here, this goddamn Chinese Yankee egg, who was making his skull steam. Did they think he *couldn't* clear out of here right now? Did they? He'd take his father's pistol out and blow a hole right through this contract. Just one slight provocation and he would, he swore. Just one. And his father, and those predictions. Prophecies! He'd fire a bullet through those, too.

But on his face he tried to give away nothing. And he read, and read tight now, the familiar clauses reserving him for Detroit for a year after the contract's expiration date (which he, of course, knew with "gentlemen's agreements" and the black list, call it the *nigger list*, meant forever and a month of Sundays) and empowering the Detroit Tigers Baseball Club to release him essentially any damned time it felt the itch, no compensations for career-ending or crippling injuries. Were it not for the fact that he was every inch as angry at his father for all those complacent forecastings and fancy Greek etymologies, he might have walked out.

But now Armour had gone and gotten something, which he laid out across the desk next to the contract. White with the black collar and the black Gothic "D" on the chest: a Detroit Tigers uniform. And as the manager, smiling, sat back down at his desk, Tyrus let his pen hand relax. God knew how all his thinking life he despised any soft capitulations, and how in any bargaining like this he really enjoyed putting his life at risk with a nice, rock-hard demand. But that uniform seemed to him suddenly the most beautiful thing he'd ever laid eyes on, even if it was a management ploy, this laying it out here now. And God damn them. But he admitted now to himself that he was going to sign for the $1,500 after all; so, in *this* case, *this* time, he was going to go ahead and give himself away soft. But he showed them nothing, just as a good gambler with a losing hand would *never* show what it was. He only nodded, as if him*self* satisfied, and fixed his Tyrus Raymond Cobb on the dotted line. Then he turned the paper, with the pen back on it, and slid it, slowly, across the desk.

But suddenly now, firing at least one belligerent shot, he said, "I assume I get a copy." He knew that no ballplayer ever received a contract copy from any owner (the secret-keeping, mystery-guarding bastards!). But he found himself asking for one for Tyrus Cobb and becoming very quickly glad that they wouldn't like this at all.

Armour, after blowing dry the signature, buried the contract into the desk's side drawer, which he locked with a key. He put his cigar back between his teeth. "Maybe in Your Aunt Sally's League, Cobb—but that ain't the way it works up here. Up *here*, ya see, we believe in safekeeping. And in keeping *you* safe. But if that don't satisfy ya, then don't put this on."

He handed Tyrus the uniform, hanging from its hanger. He smiled as he puffed on the cigar between his teeth. Then he sat back, watching the boy as he stood and held the fresh white uniform out from him and looked at it, as if at his own fondest dream of his future self, hanging there before him.

"And if that ain't enough to satisfy ya, Georgia, then maybe you'll settle for startin' in today's ball game."

The boy, though still holding the uniform hung before him in the air, now turned his eyes from it to his manager, this fancy dan leaning back, smiling under his tipped-back boater. Was he saying what Tyrus thought he was saying?

"That's right, Cobb. My center fielder, Cooley, he's sick today, so it'll be you in center, though I swear ya look as sick as a spook yourself. Christ! I'll put ya fifth, behind Wahoo, kid. Griffith's got Chesbro on for today, but don't let the big-name horseshit scare ya, hear? Just stay calm and you'll be fine. Battin's in an hour; game time's two. I'll see ya out there." He leaned forward in his chair and, without getting up, stuck his hand across the desk. Tyrus took it and shook it, warmly. "And by the way, son," the manager said, looking off to the side, "it was me who pushed for ya, figurin' Billy Byron's a friggin' fine dopester and *knowin'* Leidy is." The manager now half looked back. "You'll get your chance, Cobb. Trust we're gonna look ya over."

The boy warmed still more when he heard this! He smiled and nodded, then took the Tigers shirt and held it to his chest. "Mr. Armour, sir," he said, looking down at the "D" (and suddenly *liking* the feeling of playing for this Yankee town, feeling warmly proud to do it), "I won't let you down, sir. You've got my word. I swear I never feel right . . . until I give it everything I have." He looked up. "And when I do— then I feel like I can go home. . . . But not until."

Armour bit his cigar as he grinned; and, behind him, Navin continued to figure.

When the boy headed back down the corridor to the locker room, holding out the brand, spanking new uniform on its hanger, he saw three or four new faces gathered where he'd first been met. He thought sure that a big, tough, square-jawed one there was Crawford, "Wahoo Sam," major-league king of the three-base hit. He was sure. Man, oh man, he was really sure. But they were all talking with that horse-face Killian and that McIntyre. And what were the chances that it wouldn't be about the damned sorehead Southern busher? the swell-head rebel kid? Tyrus, as he passed them all, said nothing and didn't look, hoping no one would say hello— and also resenting it that no one did. Keeping to himself, he took his bats and grip and white uniform to a quiet corner out of the way and began putting his things on, at an empty locker. He guessed, hoped, the locker belonged to no one. There was no locker around it with things in it. God damn, he'd bet that whole fifteen hundred they were talking now about the "nut from Augusta." He was sure; but he wouldn't give them the satisfaction of looking up, as if he gave a damn. And where was the decency and cordiality when they'd *let* him slip by like that? Was it *his* job to make his own welcome smooth?

He saw now, as he hung the uniform in the locker, that beneath the shirt there were stockings. Good. He wouldn't have to go back and ask. He could stick right where he was. He felt angrily in his grip for his spikes, touching the gun as he took out the shoes, wrapped still in the chamois. He was glad, as he unwrapped the cloth on the bright, black-burnished leather, that he'd shined his spikes to a spit polish, in which he could damn well see himself. "Let the rest of 'em be sheepish and shy when they get to the Bigs," he thought. "Not this particular individual."

But would he look like an overanxious jackass if he dressed now? Hitting wasn't for an hour. So 12:30? He took out his watch. Fifty-seven minutes. Hell. He didn't read the inscription, rather put the watch back in his pocket, not wanting to get caught with it. And now hell, what was he supposed to do? Go talk? Introduce him*self*? If these Yankees were decent. . . . He took off his jacket, laid it on the locker bench and began to unbutton his shirt. He found himself wishing he had more weight to him. Sizing himself up in his mind, he was sure he was taller right now than most, if not all of 'em; but also right down the line he gave away anywhere from ten pounds to fifty. Damn his skinny bones. But that would change, if he lasted.

He continued to undress, stuffing his street socks quietly in his shoes so no one would see his secret weights. Nor could he show the wrap over his gash. He changed as quickly out of his shirt and pants and into his uniform as he could. Then, glad, relieved, he turned his back on the room. But a uniform was supposed to make you feel that you belonged— and this new, white thing, warm and soft to the touch but cold as hell and stiff on his back, made him feel ten worlds off from his "teammates," who were talking together still across the room. What would they think when they saw him in this thing but that he had no right? And him now the only one dressed. What a jackass.

He laced tight his spikes, trying to warm himself. He hadn't looked at the room around him, just felt a vague satisfaction that its several hanging lamps were well shaded and dim. But as he finished tightening his laces tight, he noticed a bat bone dangling from the training table not too far from his locker.

He took out one of his ashes and, clacking his spikes as softly as he could on the concrete floor, feeling as if he walked on ice, he lifted a bench-end up quietly to the bone. He still hadn't looked up to see if anyone was looking his way. Preferring the lonely exercise (and if he could have set up a solid wall he'd have been happy), he sat and began to stroke the black ash with the bone. He always wanted his wands tight solid for the kill. If they cracked, what would that mean but that the gods had turned away their favor? He wished he'd seen some little nigger boy, to rub his pate for best luck. And if he got hits today, did he remember the exact places he'd stepped between the Union House and Bennett? God dammit, maybe not.

More of them were come now—more Yankee voices yapping and barking—and still none of 'em had come by to say a word. He could hear the voices growing louder; made out friendly tauntings, ribbings. "Hey, Schaeffer, ya krauthead muckitymuck, ya think you'll get a bingle this month!" "Ahhch, you freckle-puss Irish potato. Listen to you! Won't Mr. Chessbro be just shivering in his shoos when you step in!" He knew who these men were, all of them—although he might not let that be known. For if they liked each other just fine, it was as if Cobb here didn't exist. But good to that, too. He'd rather be a filthy chaw in Satan's mouth than get his nose brown in this goddamn clubroom of the Union League.

But now a voice. A friendly voice. Someone had come up behind him. "Say there, you must be the kid from Augusta."

His private meditation thus interrupted, Tyrus looked up and saw a dark-haired, handsome man, maybe thirty, with a friendly face and smile.

"Yes I am. Tyrus Cobb," he said, hoping instantly that this one, and he had a good guess who it was, was as kind as he sounded and looked. A hand was extended, and Tyrus rose and shook it warmly.

"Bill Donovan. Glad to meet ya, Tyrus Cobb."

Chapter Four

A SOLID DAMNED DEBUT

So he was right! Wild Bill Donovan! Best pitcher Detroit ever had! And he did seem like a fine fella! Tyrus wanted to say, "I've heard of you, all right, Mr. Donovan!" But he just smiled shyly, and confessed, "Glad somebody's glad to meet me."

The veteran star smiled. He said, "Gettin' a bit of the treatment, eh?" He put his hand on the boy's shoulder. "Well, the thing is, kid, not to make too much of it. Or just to remember it's called the fear of losin' your place, and that it's only natural." He put his head a little closer. "And I'll be honest with ya, Tyrus Cobb. These boys, ya see, most of 'em had to wait a time, so they're figurin' you're in the startin' lineup a little quick. But that's not your fault. And they know that. So just give it time. The only thing it takes to be one with 'em is lettin' 'em know you *are* one with 'em, which shouldn't be too hard, eh? Take my word, it'll work if ya give it a little time." Donovan gave him a smile and a friendly pat on the back, then, and left the boy to contemplate his situation, while he boned his ashes.

He worked the bone over all three bats a

good time. Some good time, thinking back and forth on Donovan's advice, which he knew wasn't just friendly—it was good advice, from a good fella, who happened to be a true star on top of it. So there were no walls put up against him on that account. At least not with Bill Donovan, which would be a start. And he could see an all-right future, if he just listened. But now what time *was* it? He wished he knew. It could have been ten minutes he'd been at it. Or an hour. Did anyone want to use the bone? He was sorry. But well, why in hell didn't they come up and ask him? It wasn't his fault they didn't get a chance. He kept rubbing, not looking up, determined he wouldn't get caught nervously checking his timepiece. But now he noticed things had gotten quieter. What else could that mean but that it had come time for hitting? He still didn't look up—but now it was—Christ—*all* quiet. He raised his eyes carefully—and found himself alone! Damn *all* of 'em, and Donovan, too. The Yankee bastards.

He jerked himself up, feeling like a complete fool in his brand new suit. And damn his damn clacking spikes. He put two bats in the bag, which he hung then quickly in his locker, and took with him the first he'd boned, then made his way to the door. But then back. He'd forgotten his glove! Then again to the door. But they'd all gone, and it was closed. Would it be locked? He went up to the metal, hearing now, beyond the panel, voices, then the snap of a ball into a glove! He gripped his bat handle hard enough almost to hurt himself and then pulled at the heavy door, which, nearly to his surprise, swung back.

And in a light that nearly blinded him as he came out of the dark, there it was again, spreading wide before him: all Bennett's green. His eyes adjusted as he blinked. When he could focus, he thought it was from center, just like this, that he would see this incredible field. But for how long? Just these five weeks? Just today? He'd get his chance, Armour said. But would he make good on it? Christ, he felt right now as if he'd forgotten how to walk.

He took a quick, nervous scan and saw not far to his left the big square-jawed one he'd figured was Wahoo Crawford. And then to his right, McIntyre, who made the watchdog in him want now to run teeth-bared to his fence. It was these two he'd heard talking, and now he saw the ball that he'd heard popping into a glove, sailing over his head. They were playing catch right over him. He stood there now in a cold, painful awkwardness, his uniform like a hair shirt. Would they ask him to join? He waited. And . . . waited . . . No? Not a single word? They'd just act as if he weren't there! Just let him goddamn *stand* there! The *hell*, then. Cold, but burning too, he started to walk in under their game, to go and hit, and maybe send the sonsofbitches out a nice hot bullet or two.

But now he felt, and saw, a hard grounder ripping past him, just before him, as he walked in. It came right to left: so McIntyre, the smart sonofabitch. Tyrus looked over and gave the left fielder a hard glare. But he saw McIntyre was now eyeing something coming back his way on the ground. Then there was the ball ripping past him from the other direction. So Crawford, no different. The big dog in the yard. The big sonofa*bitch*. And damn my pitiful skinny bones, the boy thought. Then in his mind he heard that good advice again: the only thing it takes to be one with 'em is lettin' 'em know you *are* one with 'em. Just take Bill Donovan's word, and give it time. The *hell*. He walked on over the green, figuring any second now he might have to skip a rope. But no— not that. Rather something else. Laughter. He heard them laughing. The two Yankee bastards he would share the outfield with, sniggering at him. That was their Yankee welcome. But maybe all he'd have to do to be one with 'em would be to laugh at himself. Take a little joke at Cobb's expense. But there'd been his *decision* that he'd be torn limb from limb before he would let jokes be told at his expense.

He made his way in, wearing what he knew must be a death-gloomy scowl on the face that had made Armour want to send him off sick. But to hell with it all. He took his place, wordlessly as he was treated, at the end of the batting line. The line, though, would never shorten for him. When he would move up, someone would cut in. And next time, someone else. And after that, someone else. Till—what? It had to be near the end of the time. He'd determined not to say a word. But now he despised the idea of *not* talking as much as he despised the idea of talking. And now McIntyre and Crawford were picking up bats, for what would be their *second* shots. And he hadn't gotten his first.

There was Armour. "Mr. Armour," he said, and noticed immediately that not a single one of 'em didn't catch his first sounds. "What does an individual need to do to get a break here. I don't find any room getting made for me, and I'd like to hit."

"Back it off there, Matty," Armour barked. "Give the kid a shot, for Chrissake."

So he got his chance, and stepped up in his ice uniform past that rat McIntyre for his twenty-five warmup swings. Germany Schaeffer, who'd been hitting, tried for a little laugh, making a sweeping bow. "Mein Meister," he said (and this was the first thing *any* of 'em had said to him), and made way, taking dainty little backward steps out of the batter's box. But Tyrus decided against putting even the beginning of a smile on his face. Nor was he going to let these Yankee bastards see much from him now—just a little bit of a signal maybe as he hit the first ten puffballs (no real test of anything) within a foot or two of the third-base chalk and then the next ten the exact same way down the right side, and then the last five straight up the middle, the twenty-fifth like a bullet right over the bag. And so *done*.

"Oh so very, very fine, Mr. Shiny Shoes."

He heard this damn crack all right. But he wouldn't give any of 'em the satisfaction of his looking around. Not the first one. He'd decided. And when the team went in, now before a small but growing crowd—he hung back by himself, maybe twenty paces.

Back in the locker room, too, he hung by himself, glad only for the lather that he'd worked up with his swings, as it made his suit with the "D" for *damned* a little less irritating on his skin. He heard their voices. He was sure they were talking about him. He thought of his gun in his grip. Just enough more of a provocation, and by God he'd end this whole thing before it began. But he wouldn't satisfy them by listening. He knew their theme. And hell now if he wouldn't do whatever he goddamn well pleased. He rose, clacked in his spikes to his locker, and took out his championship gold. One-forty-one. They'd take the field any moment now. He read the inscription. LET 'EM KNOW WHERE YOU'RE FROM, TYRUS COBB, IN THE BIG SHOW. He thought, however, now, suddenly of his three-day and -night journey. He went dead black empty—felt a sudden draining of his life right out of him. But at that exact instant Armour came in, clearing his throat, and gave it a "Listen up!"

The manager held out and would read now from a sheet of paper: the starting lineup! The boy in his black emptiness was sure suddenly that it had all been a lie, and that he wouldn't play. He felt so heavy on his feet he thought he'd put the lead weights in his playing shoes! He heard, "McIntyre, left, one. Lindsay, first, two. Schaeffer, second, three. Crawford, right, four." Then, "Cobb, center, five." So again, real! *Real!* But before he heard the next name called—right after "Cobb, center, five"—he heard a loud spit shot out, and then its dropping into a cuspidor. And he noticed out of the corner of his eye McIntyre wiping his mouth with the back of his hand. Strange and weak as he felt, he still wrote that down in his mind as he took out his second and third bat.

Then it was time. He took up the rear, but he moved with the team out the open metal door into the bright light again. His eyes adjusted more quickly now, though he wanted to check his spikes to see if he *had* put that lead in-

side. He feared he'd stumble, as the team jogged to the bench and set down their bats. His head was down, but still he could see, as he laid down his ashes, that the crowd had grown to several thousand and that the rigged bleachers in right and center were packed. Then the team broke to positions, and on trembling legs he took off on his separate path to center. Faces, as he came up, immediately stuck themselves out. "Hey, whoever ya are, we're for ya! 'Less a course yer a bum! Then we ain't!" "Yeah, them's the rules, September Baby."

He found himself immediately despising these Yankee sounds. With hard scorn, he looked back and up. "Aww look, for criminee's sake! A *sorehead*! A sorehead *kid*! Everybody loves *that* all right! Go on home, if that's your game, young fella!" "Yeah, sourpuss!" "Yeah, *you*, sourpuss! We're talkin' to *you*!" He looked back over the wall again, with a fierce scowl.

But in no more than a moment it was Mullin, the Tigers' pitcher signaling he was ready. And then, audible clear out in center, the shattering bark of Mr. Francis "Silk" O'Loughlin: *"Play Ball!"* So it was begun. True and real. The Show! But, his lather dried, the boy felt cold again in his ice uniform and hated his damned spit-polished shoes.

"Hey, Matty, straightaway and three quarters!" The cry came over his head from the left. And then from the right, "Let's take 'em, Wahoo!" Just like that ball, their words flew past. But once more now his embittering situation struck the boy as just the thing for the beginning of his career. He felt a warm flow of energy. And, as he looked in, watching with his blue hawks for the pitch's type, and speed, and location—and as he coiled himself tight as hell to spring with the batter's motion, body turn, and bat speed—he found himself renewing his vow that for best energy his baseball life would be a war from beginning to end.

He could see in a second that Mullin (while he was sure from his guesses about locker-room murmurs that the pitcher was another sonofabitch of the McIntyre crowd) had stuff enough for Wid Conroy, New York's lead-off man. *Snap!* The ball sounded in the catcher Drill's mitt. And just that fast, the Silk's calls let Conroy know the sad truth. Four pitches and the man was gone. Tyrus confessed an admiration for his pitcher. And the admission felt good. He let, though, friend McIntyre and friend Crawford make the noises: "All right, Georgie! They're all yours, boy!" "Lookin' fine, Wabash! Lookin' sweet, and very fine!"

But now what? The Detroit bugs were clapping, some even standing—for the enemy. Why? The boy now saw why: It was Keeler! Oh yes it was. Wee Willie, the great little man, who'd go down in history both for saying he hit 'em where they ain't, and for *doing* it. Immediately, forgetting he was a first-minute rookie and a nobody, Tyrus was close to crazy with rivalry. He wanted to turn the famous little man's name-phrase into a lie—and to be exactly *where* this Keeler hit it. He watched Keeler as he'd never watched another hitter in his life. And what would his father say to this! Let him find a calling that brought out more in him than *this!*

Keeler was closing his left-side stance. The pitch, Tyrus saw—saw even before it left Mullin's hand—was a fastball going low and away. And now he saw that Keeler wanted it. But the little man waited on it. He *waited!* And now! The swing. No turn! It would be a push! Tyrus had a terrific jump; and though he knew he wasn't supposed to, he charged on and, from center field, almost had Keeler's slash over short picked off—though he failed and the ball ran past. But who couldn't see all along where Keeler was going? That thickwit McIntyre, that's who! If the left fielder had *eyes*, he'd have charged up for it, and nabbed it. But all McIntyre used his eyes for now was giving Tyrus Cobb a stay-the-hell-out-of-my-territory look. Then, with his rat mouth: "This here's a team game, ya redneck peckerhead. Ya cross my line again, and I'll knock ya straight back to whatever sorry little cracker burgh ya come from." And Tyrus thought he'd go and take this rat's throat, right then. But Christ, if he'd stood as much as he'd already stood, he wasn't going to finish himself off now. And yet God *damn* his skinny kid bones. Burning with suppressed fury, he just looked at McIntyre hard in silence, and then—exactly as McIntyre had when Cobb was named to start—he spat in clearest contempt. And as he wiped his mouth fiercely, he raged all the more, thinking that this son-ofabitch can say anything and I'm supposed to shut up and *swallow* it. The *hell*!

But now Kid Elberfeld, also having received a star's po-lite welcome, got immediately doubled up: Coughlin to Schaeffer to Lindsay. And no time for reflection on how even great ones like Elberfeld can go down so easy. For it was Ti-gers up. Right now. And if this McIntyre, from whom Tyrus would sit as far away on the bench as damned possible, and the great Wahoo, or a couple of others, did anything, there would be Cobb, his first time up in the major leagues, against the Happy One, Jack Chesbro.

And sure enough the Bengals got on Chesbro fast. Tyrus was wishing failure on the white rat bastard, but McIntyre led off, first pitch, with a stand-up double; and then, just like that, Pinky Lindsay rapped a hard one up the middle and brought McIntyre home! So, bang!—no double plays and Cobb would be up! And now there it was! Mr. Smart Aleck himself, Germany Schaeffer, moved Lindsay to second with a sweet little bunt. So it would be "Cobb, on deck!"

The boy, as he rose to the circle, listened to the chatter from the bench. Just "Give it to 'em, Wahoo!" "Come on, Sam, boy, let 'em have it!" "Make 'em hurt, Wahoo! Make 'em feel the pain!" So not a word of it for him. But the hell with their silent treatment. He didn't need encouraging words. This was it. This was his life. Leidy had lied about the crowds. Truth was, the boy had seen bigger turnouts for games in Augusta, lots of times. And this park was no par-adise, after all. The grass in truth felt like a cheap blanket thrown over a bed of rocks. But it was real ball here; he could

see *that*, every pitch. There was no bat in Augusta like a Keeler (who, Tyrus admitted now, would have turned him
around in a second if he'd caught him cheating in) and no
snake man like this Chesbro. They were getting to the Happy
One. God Almighty, though, the sonofabitch was clever.

And this was the kind of real, he knew already, that
would demand everything from him: every second, the deepest, downright damnedest he had. There'd never not be
enough here for his war. He knew it already.

"But ain't we got *somethin'* here!" "Must be fuckin' Hercules or somethin'!" "Yeah, if Hercules is a swell-headed
bush baby lookin' for a quick trimmin'."

Tyrus heard everything now faintly; but, when he heard
the last, he recognized that these foulnesses and cuts had
been for him. He'd walked to the on-deck area with all three
of his ashes slung up on his shoulder and now swung them
all together to make the one he'd finally use, *light*: in the same
way he would drop the secret lead from his feet. But using
weight to get lightness in these ways was an innovation of
his. And nobody in The Show had ever seen anything like
this act with the three bats.

His eyes from the first pitch to McIntyre had been on
Chesbro and Chesbro only, watching hard as hell the
pitcher's face, his motion, his hands—looking out for any
tipoffs at all of pitch type and speed (patterns, consistencies,
alterations, eccentricities), trying to record as much as he possibly could in the almost no-time he had. But now he saw
Crawford staring and scowling at him as the right fielder
stood out of the batter's box. And he had it all put together:
this scowl of Crawford's and the derision, the cutting remarks. He turned back and saw the whole bench giving him
the once over, and now heard the full razz chorus: "Ya
wanna get all your strikes over with in one fan, is that it,
Georgia boy." "Don't worry, bush baby, strikin' out with one
bat don't take that long."

He'd have said something, gladly, but now Crawford

took a backbreaking rip at a sharp-dipping curve (*God dam-mit*—did it come after the same higher knee bend that this Chesbro had shown when he threw the first curve to Lindsay? God *damn*, he wished he'd gotten at least a little past guessing! But no more time for study). Crawford topped the ball and hit a slow roller out to the right of the mound. Chesbro's only play was to first, Lindsay having broken quick and hard for third.

So it was time. Really time. And now an announcer with a megaphone paced the third-base line and shouted out, "Attention! *Attention*! Now batting for Detroit, center field, Tyrus Cobb. *Attention! Tyrus Cobb* now batting for Detroit! *Cobb. Tyrus Cobb*, batting for Detroit...."

The boy shut out the hoots from the benches, the polite claps from the stands; shut out everything, and dropped two bats behind him. He held the third tight and walked slowly over the hard, rocky dirt toward the left-side batter's box. He whipped the lightened bat three times quickly, to feel its lightness. He tapped his shiny black leathers, first one foot, then the other, to free the steel, and stepped in.

Then he heard it. "Well now who in *hell* might this be? What's that name the bugle was shoutin'? Corn Cobb? Soon to be out of a job Cobb?" McGuire, the Highlander catcher, now shouted out to Chesbro, "Hey, Happy, what'd they say this busher's name was?"

Chesbro was licking his fingers while he looked over at Lindsay. Then, black-eyebrowed, dark and big, his cheek bulging with a plug of slippery elm, he faced the plate. He didn't answer McGuire. He just spat and said to the boy, as he looked in, "You come up with them three bats too often, ya baby shit, and you ain't gonna live long."

Tyrus said nothing; but, as he set his feet and split his grip, he determined for his life that he'd never bring up a single bat less for any sonofabitch on his own team or any other. The ignorant Yankee bastards. God damn them all. And let 'em bring it on, now. Let 'em bring it. He thought this in fury as with his hawks he scanned the field—closed here, closed here, closed here—but open *there*, in left center.

Chesbro peered in, glanced to third, peered in, nodded slowly to McGuire, and began his motion. Tyrus watched every slightest movement of the delivery—from the placing of the ball in the glove and the first rocking motion to the taking of the glove to the chest, to the rearing back, to the tilting of the head, to the raising of the knee. The knee raised high. Yes. So he guessed curve. But he guessed wrong. The pitch was a sweet high fastball, which still, God dammit, he had to have! He choked his grip in the fraction of a fraction of a second that he had. He tore into the sweet offering— but was a full day late.

"Str-r-r-r-rike one!" The Silk let the word go forth, quick as the pop in the leather.

And McGuire wasted no time. "Well, *hell*; and this sorry bush baby thought he was somethin' special. 'I ain't no sucker rookie who can't lay off them high fastballs,' he says. 'Not me. I'm fuckin' Corn Cobb. I'm here to stay.' "

The Silk was amused. Impartial umpire justice, but he couldn't help a smile and a sniff of a laugh. In this moment, though, the boy had even less than his now-characteristic zero humor about himself. Goddamn *less* than zero. And he found himself suddenly wild for a noisy, crazy boast. "That's *Tyrus* Cobb, mister," he said, "and I'm getting to know your man out there." Then, leaping into his brag, he shouted out to Chesbro. "Ya *hear* that? I said I'm getting to know you. And that'll be all I'll need. So you serve it up, *Happy*."

"Well, *hell!*" McGuire roared when he snapped the ball back to the mound. "Ain't we got us a loud-mouthed little cracker turd from down in beat-to-dirt Dixie!" He got down in his crouch. "And won't you be skiddin' on your fuckin' bony bum into Cotton Ball County sayin' 'Mama! Daddy! Y'all, ahhm back!' "

O'Loughlin couldn't keep his face as straight as he needed to. He looked away a second. But the boy looked with no smile out at Chesbro. Just stared, watching. He watched the pitcher's spit. Watched his nod. Watched his dip and rock. Watched the swing of his arms. Watched everything he possibly could in the time he had. And thought, relax never. Relax never. Never. Never. And never forget one single thing. Goddamn *never*!

He again figured curve. And he saw Chesbro exaggerate his rearing back. The knee-bend gave no real read. But *this* might be a sign. And sure enough it *was* a curve—but the boy had at no time ever experienced a hook that bent so mean.

"Str-r-r-r-rike tuh!" The Silk shrilled out the pronouncement.

And McGuire loved it. There was something about this particular busher that made him really love it. "Oh Mama Cobb, Oh Daddy Cobb, y'all come take me home!" he cracked with sheer raucous delight. "It's so powerful turrible up here! For all my hopin' and dreamin' and *talkin'*, I cain't hit *nothin'*! I ain't worth a durn turd. Your Corn."

Not that he didn't love putting himself out there with his mouth, but the boy said nothing this time. He shut his ears—ignored—shut out every sound that this Yankee funny boy was yapping. And he watched. He watched Chesbro. The habits. The spit. The nod. The arm swing. The rock back and forth. The hands coming up and the rearing back. The rearing back not so exaggerated! So bring that *fastball*! Bring it now! Tyrus slipped his grip into a choke in anticipation. He drew a line from his heart to the green void in left center. And then the heat came—right on the outside quarter.

And you bet your goddamned life—he got it *all*! *All*! And that he was gone from the box so spooky fast he had 'em drop-jawed and blinking!! The center fielder, nervous when he saw the boy's lightning break, tried to close the gap. But not a prayer. The line-shot fired right past him. And Tyrus, as he tore hard around first, had his hawks on the man for any slightest bungle. He figured he had him rushing and mistake-ready now all right; and as hard and aggressively as it was possible, while he flew, he watched for every conceivable split-second opportunity. He'd turn three. God dammit he'd go *home* if there was a misplay at that fence. Let 'em talk about the crazy kid from Augusta. Let 'em talk. But the ball came off the fence clean; and though, as the boy knew, there'd have to be that full-second foot planting and body turn, the throw to second was *very* hard and clean. None of that rainbow material he would see most times in the Sally. So he let his body go fully loose, as always when he hit the dirt, trying to protect himself from injury; and, as he read the throw coming slightly right, he hooked left into the bag, pivot foot ready to spring him up again and eyes wide open for the minutest chance to keep going.

"*Yer saaaaaafe!*" The Silk, his head down, blue wings spread wide, had come nearly to second to make the call—which it sounded like he stretched out *just* to let New York know they'd have to swallow his truth, like it or not.

And the boy now loved that! He lay still toe to the bag and let the stretched-out word fill his ears. A perfect dream come true! Oh yes, sir, he'd gotten started now! Sure as hell he'd arrived!

He knew, too, from a familiar warmth spreading on the back of his thigh that he'd broken open his wound. But how damned sweet everything felt now! Hell, he'd dye his whole uniform blood-red for this feeling! He rose and dusted himself, feeling *light*, so damned *light* now on his feet! And right away, Armour he could hear. "Hell, yes, Georgia! Hell, *yes*, boy! Thataway, Cobb!" And everyone that he could see in the scattered crowd was standing and cheering. And he'd knocked in a run, which made it all even sweeter. But his own teammates, he saw, were maintaining the complete silence. McIntyre and Killian and Crawford and Mullin—none of that mob was even looking. So the hell with all of 'em. He dusted his knees again, feeling the warmth of the blood spreading on the back of his leg. And, as he took his lead, he just had now to whisper a glad word to Happy Jack. "Ya know, it's been nice meetin' you, *Happy*! And it's so nice to *know* you. Pleasure's yours? No. All mine, *Happy*! All mine. Yes, I'd rather be me, than *Happy*."

But that day, though Chesbro fell to Detroit 5-3, Tyrus Cobb got no more hits. He walked once, though, and so it was a solid damned debut—a double, a run batted in, and a base on balls, in three official trips.

But no multiple hits; and when he sat on the bench it had been nothing, except a little slap on the back from Armour and a half-smile and nod from Donovan, who, however, didn't break any silences in front of the gang. So the hell if he'd hop around like some eager little puppy dog for *any* of this mob. He'd leave the ingratiating business to the good rookie: the one who could smile and understand that a deep freeze was just the normal daily temperature for a September baby's beginning days. He preferred himself right now *not* to understand this. And when they walked back into the clubhouse at the end of the game, he kept himself back, walking alone, knowing damn well he was widening a ditch that, dug wide enough, could become uncrossable.

There was only one shower. But he wasn't in any hurry, wanting still not to reveal the depth of his gash. While he sat alone again, though, once more boning his bats, he thought of a time in Augusta, when he'd made "Rapper" Rapp get out of a tub he'd been soaking in after an early departure from the mound. "What the hell, Tyrus, cain't ya even let me finish?" "That's just it, Rapper," he told him, "I *can't*." "Well, why in hell cain't ya, if ya don't mind my askin'? I mean this here ain't been my best outin', as you p'raps may a guessed." "Because I *can't* not be first, that's why. I've got to be first—I can't explain why. I just have to be. And I don't want to have to fight you, Rap, so if you'll please just let me in first." "Well bless *me*, seein's you's such a gintleman of a loony bird crackpate sonofabitch, you just be my guest, ya hear." He almost smiled now, almost admitted that nothing could have been truer than the Rapper's character of him. But he wasn't in the mood to smile, or to admit the first thing about anything. And whose *fault* was it—his or this team's—that no words were passing between him and the rest of 'em?

"All you have to do to be one of 'em is show 'em you are one of 'em." Donovan's words, he knew, were true. He'd acknowledged that. But a thousand things are true. And where was Donovan right now? And where was any one of 'em? Was it his job, God dammit, to get things started? He was the new man. Why was it *his* job? Where was the basic decency? The hospitality? Jesus Christ—these damned Yankees. And he was supposed to be so worried about *their* places. What the sweet hell—why would he be worrying about *their* places one spit more than they worried about *his* place?

He continued to sit alone, boning an ash, rubbing down the bat as if he were repeating some dark conjuration with his hands. And the furies would dance their dance all right when he overheard that no-account rat McIntyre say—no doubt deliberately loud enough (though as the boy sat isolated, his hearing was as sharp as hell)—"*Christ*, if there ain't somethin' about that sourpussed busher that makes you wanna bust 'im. D'ya see the way he cuts me off out there in the first? Jesus, Mary, and Joseph. And look at the mug on 'im, will ya. It's like the whole world's rotten for that sorehead pill. And don't *that* just make ya wanna bust his jaw."

Wounded, dirty, and painfully cut off, feeling sure that all eyes were on him as he sat at the bone, he rubbed his bat harder. And he thought, I'll bust *your* jaw, you white-rat sonofabitch. I'll bust your goddamned *skull*. Right now, you just push me to it. You just push me on. Do me that one kindness, you Yankee rat. You and all your friends. The whole lot of ya! And how long do I have to *wait*, God dammit, for that shower. Isn't any *one* of ya going to come up and say, "Hey, kid, your turn now"? No? Not ever? Not capable of that basic decency? God damn *all* of you. And couldn't I just hear you now, if I were to speak up about it. "Not so fast, Georgia boy. There's a line for that water. And the line ends with you. The last shall be last, sonny boy." And if this wound were to damned fester? Would you care? Hell no. You'd love to see that!

More time passed and he didn't look up and no one spoke to him, not Donovan, not anyone. He heard laughter, though—and his name? He thought he heard his name spoken amid the laughter. Then it grew quieter. He heard good-nights now. And gibings and teasings at the door. And more good-nights. Lights were going off. And then no voices. No sound. He looked up finally and saw no one—and only the one dim-shaded lamp that hung over him at the bone still lit.

He rose, looking back just at his locker, and placed his bats in the cage with his shoes and glove, annoyed and angered that they hadn't provided him with a lock. It seemed everyone else had one. Was he supposed to *ask* for a god-damned lock? He slammed the cage, the sound exploding in the silence. Naked, then, he stepped over the cold concrete to the dark, empty shower room. He felt about for, then found, the light, and set on the sink-ledge some fresh wrap that he'd brought. He turned on the shower. But he could see no towel left for him, and this angered him still more. But he had to clean the wound. He entered the shower, the water cold now as Yankee ice—the same stuff God froze Satan in, and Judas. Christ, he'd had much better than this in the Sally. Much better. The pain in his wound when the water came over it made him nearly buckle in the knees. But he had to let the wrap soak till it loosened or he'd bleed a river. He stayed there a long time, waiting for the wrap to loosen in that ice water—and no one came to say he was sorry. Though everyone had gone, the boy had some strange pitiful hope that this might happen.

Back at his locker cage, his teeth gritted, he gathered his ashes and his things to take safely home. He wouldn't trust any of these Yankees a first inch. But now, as he lifted his bats up on his shoulder, he saw there was a light lit down the vaulted corridor, in the Office of the Management. He wouldn't go down, though, to say good-night. Something in him—a sudden ache in his heart—said to him he could go down maybe and express his gratitude to Mr. Armour for the start, for intervening for him in the warmup, for complimenting him out loud in front of all his damn silent bastard teammates when he started off his damn career with a double. Or just maybe say good-night to the man. But he wouldn't, he *couldn't,* listen to these good signals in his heart.

He knew that there was a street door at the back of the locker room. But he decided he'd retrace his steps. And the metal, center-field door, he found, was still open. Quietly, he walked out—and stood in center field alone, in the six-o'clock cool, his first day now completed. And as he walked alone toward the plate over the rock-hard grass, the silent Bennett like a vast empty canyon all around him, he imagined his future. There would be Crawford to his left, and McIntyre to his right, and then the whole lot of the rest of 'em, friends and Yankees all. He'd started hard today—and why should he ever go soft? He'd decided he'd live—and it would take as much life as he could possibly get, to make up for passing on the temptation to end things. Bang, *over.* Going soft wouldn't give him enough life to compensate—and that was that, he was deciding.

He imagined his twenty-some years of gambits, sacrificing softnesses to gain higher and higher levels of accomplishment, drawing lines past lines of no retreat. But then, in another sharp, sudden turning in his mind, or soul, he wondered if running hard as hell to keep ahead of all the hatreds he would engender meant he really *would* run past all cure and forgiveness? All of it forever? No health, or goodness, ever again? As he stood there alone in that empty canyon of a park, the grandstand pavilion now hovering high over him, he felt an instant warsick heartache of regret and sorrow.

And he did, yes, want to head back and just say *something* to Mr. Armour. Maybe just that—just that first word of friend-ship—could change everything.

But still there was the tortured, powerful pleasure of his furies in the idea of going it *all* hard. To make people want not just to break his jaw but to break his cursed neck: That's what would make him good enough to be glad he didn't just plain end himself. And he would *be* glad, and live. So, *no.* He'd head on straight to the Union House, over the steps he'd come by. And tonight he'd give his father's book of shame its funeral of fire!

When he'd made his way through the tunnel into the passages beneath the stands, he saw the old gnome porter about to lock the double wooden door before the turnstile. He quickened his pace and, not to frighten the old man, made noise and came wide around him. Then, when he'd placed himself in front of him, he said, "Maybe you'll remember me tomorrow, eh, old fella?" But the old gatekeeper only half frowned and sniffed while he waited for the new rookie to make his way out. Then he brought together on their creak-ing hinges the big wooden doors and shot closed the bolt.

But out on the street, as he began retracing his steps as best he could recall them, above a hollow clopping of horseshoes on the cedar blocks, he heard a voice. "Well now, it ain't Cyrus after all, is it? No, sir. It'd be *Tyrus.* Funny I missed that, studyin' the spreadsheet dope the way I do. But I seen ya today, sir. I *seen* ya today."

Tyrus, if he was glad maybe for any voice, still cringed. It was the cabby who'd delivered him here last night.

"And what'd I see?" the greasy hackster said, smiling his rotten-mouthed smile as he stopped his cab alongside the boy. "What'd I see if it weren't some strange kind a blisterin' around them bags, eh, and a nice, sweet hammer on Ches-bro's hot stuff. Word is, well, there ain't no word till we seen ya go left on left and faced the big-league southpaw hook. Been some swift departures after that little trial a fire. But word is, Tyrus, ya run like we ain't seen, and all around with yer head up—with yer head *up*—a merit we, at least, ain't blind to; and ya got the battin' eye might put some people back in the park here—which there's us who appreciate, havin' an innerest. So good fortune, sir, from Mr. Freddie West. And we ain't like now to ferget it's *Tyrus*, sir. We ain't like to ferget *that!*"

He smiled, tipped his cap, and clacked his reins along his nag's back, again heading out the street that he'd come in on the night before. And Tyrus thought—stay separate from *them* and stay separate from *him*. God will know. You will know. He spat now in the dirt, for a period to that sentence in his mind. And he felt his independence from his father, too, like a triumph.

When his distance was good, he turned and looked back at Bennett, the grandstand flags lifting in slow billows in the early stirrings of an evening breeze. He heard too the heavy rumbling and banging and harsh whines from the sawmill across the street. Smoke, he could see, still poured from the neighborhood stacks. And a mighty pungency of horse dung rose from the dock areas, where the dray horses still stood in cart traces, waiting to haul away whatever it was that got made around here. It was no Garden of Eden, this place. But he'd seen Keeler and Kid Elberfeld and Chesbro and Prince Hal Chase today. God's real men, no matter their stains. And he'd let himself admit that Crawford and McIntyre and Mullin and Donovan were God's men, too. He wasn't about to thank a single one of his team ever out loud, but he thanked them all in silence now for being the reasons Tyrus Cobb could truly find and make himself—and prove a certain prophet wrong.

Chapter Five

WORD HAS IT

On the "American Plan," he had a supper he could actually eat, which beat Cincinnati, that's for sure. He had some friendly conversation, too, with the Cave-a-Marpheus barkeep, Tim, who turned out to be not such a bad Yankee, really. And he got back up to his room before the dancing girls started lifting their skirts over their pink-ruffly backsides. He had a book to read—and it wouldn't be his father's, which he buried out of sight now in his grip. He sat up in bed, taking the weight from his wound with a pillow, and began Plutarch's *Caesar*, which he read with sharp interest for over an hour, searching for parallels with his own life. He was finding them every page.

But he noticed, eventually, that outside it had grown dark, good and dark. He could see the fires burning again in the iron forges. He put down the *Lives* and went to look out at the night scene. At the window he could hear the saloon spill, voices coming up again from the street; but what caught his eyes now, down to the right, past the sawmill, was a man burning trash in a red-fiery barrel. The man seemed then finished, was walking away, clapping dust from his hands; and the barrel was flaming red hot with burning debris. Tyrus didn't like that he'd have to walk through the no-doubt now packed saloon, where that tinny piano would be playing and maybe those sorry can-can girls dancing, including maybe that beautiful, pathetic, slutty young thing from last night, with maybe her loving half-nigger hanging somewhere around. But, knowing he had a look ready for those two, he went straight for his father's book, removed it from his grip, and tucked it under his shirt. He went to the door, unfastened the chain, turned the brass thumb turn, and went down. The bar was as crammed full as he knew it would be. But he shut his senses to the smoke and sounds and flashing sights and got out—unstopped— then walked quickly past all the tough-looking types in the street, men and women. He didn't know if the beautiful young girl had been dancing up on that lit-up box of a dance stage, or not.

He fixed his eyes hard on the fiery barrel, now just ahead of him on the street. He walked as fast as he could without breaking into a run, looking at nothing but the fire. He came up on it quickly. He looked around but didn't see the man. He read the sign: LOUIS CHEVROLET: CARRIAGE-MAKER. But he had no intention of introducing himself. He took the book out from under his shirt and stood before the fire, which burned with a blinding red heat now down in the barrel. Then a last thought—*would* there be, if he lifted to his face the page that said *BURN THIS*, the scent of his mother? A sign, maybe even meant for him, of her having read there before him, when the gun got put . . . ? He did not want to know, and he thought no more. He lifted, and dropped his father's book into the red-hot flame; and, though it was hard to look, he watched the book landing flat on the flame-bed, a black rectangular eclipse against the white and blue and red-gold of the blaze. A black eclipse now with a white blaze all around it. Then he saw the flames roll their tongues around the book shape and saw the leather cover begin to curl and buckle in the tremendous heat. And then the stark black shape suddenly burst into flame itself. Then the distortions. Then the red ash floating up. And finally the moment when nothing appeared but the flames.

He looked around, still seeing no one. And he felt a satisfaction—if he wanted also to break down and cry, for it seemed to him as if he'd just, somehow, ended his father's life again. The man's real life. The bookmark clipping, too, he hadn't taken it out. And the thought of its being gone touched him with a tender sorrow of good-bye. It shamed and pained him, too, though, whatever pleasure he might have taken in his little deceptions, to think that the only good word his father had ever read of him had been one he'd really written himself, concocted for a trick. So let it go, he thought, this one pathetic little bit of newspaper wording he *had* controlled. Let it go with all the other cheap and bitter ironies.

He watched the fire. Then considered that, even if he damn well knew there had been this book, there at least wouldn't have to be any self-effacing, pathetic admissions of guilt in his life, not after this little fire baptism. And he found himself right now in fact *happy* that he knew there had been this book. And, again, that he had suppressed evidence. And that maybe later he'd watch his mother tell dead cold lies on the stand, and that he'd never say the first word about it. It would be hell; but what would come of it would be Tyrus Cobb's new kind of paradise: for with everything covered up but burning white hot inside him, there wouldn't be a single thing he couldn't do. "And you can call this," he whispered low, staring into the fire, "the initiation rites of someone who will never apologize."

He heard a noise behind him. He was startled.

"Say there, whatd'ya know?"

He turned around and saw a man in a smith's leather apron—no doubt the same he'd seen—now walking toward him from the shop. The voice had been friendly.

"Nothing much," he said, hating it like hell if there'd been any sound of nerves in his voice. "Just sort of staring at your fire here."

The man came up, extending his hand. "Louis Chevrolet," he said, smiling, friendly.

"Tyrus Cobb." The boy shook his hand.

The smith, maybe forty, a real working man, tough-built, with short-cut, bristly hair, scratched his head. "Tyrus Cobb . . . Tyrus Cobb . . . Would you be the new outfielder, up from . . . where was it?"

"I would be. Georgia."

"Well, I'll be damned. Got a hit today, I heard. First time up. And against Chesbro. Run quicker'n a bat outa hell, I heard."

"Well . . . heck . . . I don't know . . ."

The smith pursed his mouth, his lips turning down. But it was a smile, a knowing smile. "Modest type, eh?"

Tyrus grinned. "No."

"Thank God," the smith said, laughing. "Me neither." He stepped closer now and stood with the boy at the barrel. "Haven't got time for that bull. I'm workin' nights as well as days. Competition's got me on the run, Tyrus." He looked into the fire. "Carriage business isn't going to be here too much longer, you can bet your life on that. Automobiles period. That'll be it."

Tyrus nodded, actually not disliking, at least immediately, yet another Yankee. "So," he asked, "are you trying to get in—to the automobile business, I mean?"

"Trying like *hell* to get in." Chevrolet rubbed his hands, squeezing them. "Night and day. Figurin'. Figurin'. Trying to get a damned engine that'll run better than Olds's or Ford's. Ford and that got-damn Nine-ninety-nine. And it's crazy in this town; take my word, son. Survival of the fittest. No place for the slackers. They'll get eaten alive. So I'm figurin' *this* and figurin' *that* all day and all night. I mean I'm on to the science of engines in my damned sleep. Seriously.

Never stoppin'. And here I am workin'—and my wife's wonderin' where the *hell* I am." He looked up and laughed, his face glowing red and his teeth shining in the firelight. "But I've gotta say, Tyrus, if it doesn't kill me, it sure as hell won't bore me. This town's *alive*. And I'll tell you what—a little advice, eh." He lowered his voice a bit. "You know what they're gonna pay ya as a ballplayer, I'm sure? And that word is—well—*not enough*." He put his hand now on Tyrus's arm. "So you find a way to get yourself invested." He squeezed the boy's arm. "It's goin' only one way, son, this automobile thing. And that way is *up*."

Tyrus had to admit, too, he really did admire this side of Yankees: the hard-working, frank, wealth-seeking side—the side the South lost to. He admitted it to the point now of thinking that, after all—and just the thought set off laughter in his soul!—he was maybe something of a got-damn Yankee himself! And he sure wished he had a dime or two, because he could smell the truth in everything this Chevrolet was saying. And because sweet, sweet *money*—what did it mean but an individual's tell-'em-all-to-go-to-hell *independence*. "Wish I *had* a dime or two, Louis. Truly wish I did."

"Well," the carriage-maker said, loosening his hand, now patting Tyrus's shoulder a friendly pat, "you're in a good game yourself. Truth is, as fine a game as it ever doggone gets, because as fierce a competition as it ever gets. Hell, baseball and automobiles: you're talkin' about things that's comin' to be the heart and soul of this damned country. Let somebody say me wrong, I'll bet 'm my bottom dollar. We're in the right places, Tyrus. We just gotta figure a way to force the dollars out. They're sure as hell there, believe you me. They are sure as hell there, and nobody stoppin' us but ourselves." Chevrolet smiled broadly but nodded as if to say he had to get back to work.

Tyrus smiled. He liked this fella; he downright did. And he thought suddenly that maybe *outside* the team: that that would be where he'd find his Detroit welcome, and where he'd meet Detroit with a warm greeting. "Hell yeah," he said. "I like the sound of *that*, Mr. Chevrolet." He shook the smith's hand and nodded good-night and headed back to the Union House, quickly passing through the saloon, not looking; though sometimes not looking has a way of bringing a picture before the eye, and maybe a speaking picture with a welcoming, soft voice, all the more compelling for its dangerous differentness.

Up in his room, seated in the ladder-back, he looked out again and saw the barrel, still glowing. And he smiled, picturing shining teeth in the firelight and a burr-haired, stocky, friendly man. Then, after a time, tilting back every now and again on the ladder-back, he imagined a conversation, one that had him working on a Yankee voice in his mind:

"Well, son, about that wish ya got. I mean for some starter money, referring I mean to that dime or two of working capital that . . ."

"I *haven't* got."

"Well, yep. But how's this for one damned good plan, Tyrus. You get yourself good and famous in your game, and I pull outa the who-knows-where-she's-hidin'-now-but-I'll-find-her *dark place* where my engine is currently good and ready to be born. Which I intend to christen *Chevrolet* when she is born, because who the hell's brain is it I've searched about a billion and a half miles through? And then, ya see, I get my automobiles rollin'. And then—because what kind of a very sorry fool just sells his cars north, when he can sell 'em north *and* south—we'll have you ridin' one across the Ohio bridge and all the way down to Georgia, saying, 'Yes, sir, Tyrus Cobb drives a Chevrolet. And if you think he'd be caught in a Ford or an Oldsmobile, you're outa your pea-pickin' *mind*! He wouldn't be caught dead in one of those crates, and you shouldn't be either!' And then with you pitchin' it like this, Tyrus, or maybe a little gentler, eh—ha! ha!—we'll have so many damned Chevrolets honking across the state of Georgia they'll be flat-out bangin' into each other!"

And so the boy, who for some reason wasn't just smiling broadly but had tears welling up now in his eyes, let himself be warmly humored, thinking how money (as, Lord knew, no preacher ever could) might bring people back together again. And he let himself dream about Yankee business, even as his father's story lay in ashes in its barrel.

Then, after a time, he picked up the *Caesar* again, read ten pages, every one of interest. Then for some time, as a matter of never-neglected routine, he reviewed his own day-work, watching now in memory the moves of Chesbro and Chase and Elberfeld and living out in imagination triumphant stratagems of bunt and slash and shot, enjoying, as he planned, the feeling that the moves of these men really would become moves at the ends of strings pulled by Tyrus Raymond Cobb. And if there'd been no multiple hits today, his first nine innings in The Show got at least some people talking. So he would sleep tonight.

Not, though, before he wrote his letter. In his grip he carried always a pencil and a small box of paper, envelopes, stamps. But he found now in the drawer of the table, which, with the lamp, was set still by the ladder-back, some Union House stationery, a pen, and a bottle of ink. He filled the pen, looked out for a moment at the moon hung over Bennett, the pennants now not half-stirring atop the grandstand pavilion, pulled the light chain, and then wrote.

> *My dearest Charlie,*
>
> > *Today, sweet girl, I actually broke in. Hard to believe it's true. But I'm sitting here right now looking out over Detroit city and sure enough, there it is, Bennett Park, where Tyrus Cobb played today for the Detroit Tigers. Got a hit, too, Charlie, my very first time up! And off a famous pitcher. Wish you could have seen, girl. Wish everyone down south could have have seen. Especially my father. But*

I don't want to grieve you with any more of my sorrows now—though as you know, there's no one I'd share them with before you, ever. And I can tell you, the three days riding up here had their hard hours. Very hard, Charlie. Let's think, though, of better days to come. And don't I just know you'll give it your best when it comes to making that New York trip—and our meeting!—come true just the way we hope. Because who would it be who can sweet-talk her mama and daddy better than Miss Charlotte Lombard? Well, nobody! So you've got my hopes up, girl, you know that! Heaven and earth? Why, you can move those two little items, can't ya? And you trust an "old pro"—nothing makes time go by in a finer dreamy way for yours truly, on those long, long train rides, than thinking about you. How I would love it, with that engine chugging into old Grand Central Station, thinking that when I stepped off the train, there you'd be, bringing the sweet beauty of home, and all that touches my heart, to the city of New York. You work on it, dear girl, if you haven't got it already taken care of, which I suspect you have. And (so I won't have anything but you to think about, mile after mile) I'll work on getting fast as I can through the so-called standard rookie "treatment" that I'm getting here right from the start (not made easier by their knowing where I'm from, which is the South, and my knowing where they're from, which is the North, every single one of them). Truth to tell, I have a hard time cooperating with the notion I'm just supposed to turn the other cheek, and then the first cheek again, and then the other cheek one more time, and so on and so forth. To me, it's about the same as saying that, somewhere down inside, you're all right with not really breaking in, and not being your own true self or ever being truly outstanding. And that, well, I've seen it, Charlie—it can become one of those self-fulfilling prophecies. I've seen it. And I fear it. I won't say more about this until there have been more days. But I'll write again very soon, I promise. And wish me luck. Today

*it was the New York Highlanders. Tomorrow the Chicago
White Sox. No kidding, I can't believe I'm saying these
words! But it's real. It really is. And I feel like this was the
day I started to become myself, no matter who has plans to
hold me back.*

*Yours with all my tenderest love,
Tyrus*

*P.S.
As for writing me, C (and can ya hear me* beggin', *girl?
though I know I don't have to), I'd say General Delivery,
Boston, would be best. We'll be there from the 7th of Sept.
till the 11th. Send a warm word of* yes I'm coming *to one
lonesome fella up north, who misses the South, and the
truest girl of his heart and dreams.*

He got a stamp from his grip, addressed a Union House
envelope to The Oaks, Augusta, Georgia, kissed the envelope
softly and set it in a basket on a table in the hall, where Tim
the barkeep told him he could leave mail for pickup. He felt
for a moment then actually *good*, and *healthy* in his heart, like
there was a first itch of healing come over his life, thinking
of his beautiful, beautiful girl, and of New York, not fourteen
days away.

But the good moment was only that, a moment. His
mind taking hard turn after hard turn these days, he had
suddenly that strange feeling again that there was some man,
some *target* out there for him; and, almost mechanically now,
he set the gun again beneath his pillow. And when finally he
slept, he dreamed about Caesar. He recalled that he'd done
so when in the morning he woke and saw he'd left a bloodstain again on his sheet. It came back to him that during the
night he'd felt the pain of his wound and that in a sort of
waking sleep he'd refused to move to relieve it, recalling how
Caesar, with his mind every second of his life on the goal of
absolute power, never let *any* pain break him. And how he

conquered every enemy he ever faced, and what world-changing miracles he got out of his men because of his own miraculous determination and fearlessness and endurance. And as he looked at the bloodstain, he recalled too that he'd dreamed of the beautiful Yankee dancing girl again and lost himself in her arms.

In the locker room the second day, after he'd gotten out the bat he'd had his first-day success with, and had seated himself again at the bone, Bill Donovan came up again and put a question to him: "Did you ever try, Tyrus, just standing at a social gathering, you know, a party or something—just standing there and not making any kind of move to mingle with the folks?"

The boy didn't like this question, or that ice was getting broken, again. But he wouldn't be the rude one. He stopped, looked up at Donovan's friendly face. "I'm not sure what you mean," he said.

"Well," Donovan said, now taking a seat beside him on the bench, "I'll admit, Tyrus, I tried one time just standing by myself at a gathering. Put myself right in the middle of the crowd, too. And they were all people I know and like and who know me and like me, at least I think they do. Anyhow, I just thought I'd try standing there doing nothing and see what happened. See who'd come up to me and be friendly, while I made no move. You know what?"

The boy was torn, wanting to answer, and wanting to pretend that Donovan didn't exist. He hadn't responded.

"Well," Donovan said, "I'll tell ya. You're right. Nothin' happened." The pitcher chuckled and smiled. "Nobody came up. Nobody talked to me. And hell, they were my folks and friends. *Old time* friends. Ya see, that's just the way it works. People have to read some willingness on your face. Or you can stand in the middle of *family*, and nothin'. Absolutely nothin'. Trust me. But I won't school ya, kid. I'm just droppin' a friendly tip, get me?"

Tyrus didn't say thanks. But he didn't pretend either

that he failed to understand, though he was tempted to. He nodded, and half smiled.

The veteran star smiled back and patted the boy warmly on the shoulder. "Say listen," he said, "after the game, some of the fellas and I are headin' over to Houlihan's for a beer or two's refreshment. Why don't ya join us."

Tyrus now saw an opportunity to get away and—though he felt suddenly sick because he was taking it—was glad for the chance. "I don't drink," he said, adding, "I'm sorry."

"That's all right. I mean, nothing wrong with that. Maybe you'd just want to come along for the talk."

"Maybe so," Tyrus said, still torn.

Donovan, as he stood, patted him on the shoulder again and smiled. "Hope so," he said.

And when the pitcher left—*with* himself, *against* himself, *both*, the boy acknowledged in his torn heart not only that there was worth and merit to the star pitcher's words, but that Donovan could have added a further truth, known to everybody but the very sorriest fool: If you don't show up when people do invite you, it won't be forever before they don't invite you again.

But after the game, he was in no mood to see or to talk to anyone. The White Sox had had their southpaw, hook-hurling specialist, Doc White, working the hill. And he'd murdered the teenage rookie, striking him out four times, each time not just making him look bad but making a complete damned fool out of him. The second he knew, in fact, how completely he *owned* this Cobb, White didn't even bother with the heat or the change. Tyrus knew exactly what was coming: breaking stuff, every damned time. But the result was every time the same.

"Hey, Doctor," the White Sox catcher, Schalkey, had shouted out, not even bothering with the signals, "what cure ya got for this little rookie sickness? Curveball? Ya got a curveball, ya say? Yeah, I think so too. That oughta take care a this little *disease* real good."

So it was war on his heart and guts, an offensive to break him right now for good. And when he was through shouting, Schalkey whispered in his ear. "I hear ya got a big yap, bush baby. I hear ya did a lot a soundin' off at Happy Chesbro, ya smart little fuck. But I ain't hearin' nothin' now. So what's the matter, Johnny *Rebel*, or whatever the fuck your name is—why ain't you shootin' off that mouth a yours now?" Then again, after the *"Steeeerike!"* call, "Yes, *sir*, Doctor! The miracle a medicine, one more time! Goin' after the sickness! And *curin'* it again!" Then another low whisper, "Yes, indeed, that's what I heard, all right, a smart-mouth bush baby with a swelled head. And a sore head, too. That's the rumor I heard. But ain't he goin' quiet now." *"Steeeeeerike two!"* *"Yes, sir, Doctor!"*

And Tyrus hated his teammates—to a man hated them to goddamned death—because who else could have ratted him out with the word about his first game but *them*? *Nobody* else. And wouldn't they be fraternizing with the enemy and be traitors for it, thinking it more important to maintain their great veterans' fraternity than to win games! But God damn this goddamn breaking ball. It didn't do a thing. Didn't do a thing. Didn't show itself. Nothing. No chance to see it, and plot the bend. Nothing. Until *snap*—just before he saw it go— it was gone. Nothing to see. Nothing to study. And Schalkey shouting out, "Let me see, Doctor, whatd'ya think we should try now? Well, how about a bender, Doc? Think that'd work? I don't know. But let's give *that* a go and see what happens!" And still it didn't matter that the boy knew exactly what was coming. And the whispers kept coming. "But ain't you just a *little* bit worried now, my smart-mouth bush baby who's-your-name? thinkin' what a pitiful little September it's gonna be after all—and then what a long fuckin' good-bye train ride you'll be takin' home?" *"Steeeeeeerike thur-eee!"*

And that Cobb, before he took his seat on the bench,

had to pick up his two extra bats from the on-deck area was, he damn well *knew,* as delightful to his teammates as it was agonizing to him, all four times.

"Will somebody tell me what it is about a sourpussed, sorehead *kid* that makes ya wanna rub out his kisser on a fuckin' brick wall. Christ Almighty goddamn *Jesus!* I hate that kinda shit. We ain't heard the first word outa the mouth or seen the first fuckin' close-to-friendly expression on the puss a that sorehead puppy since he showed. I don't know why I *hate* that kinda thing the way I do—but Jesus *Christ* I do."

It was all the boy could do after his day of utter failure at the plate not to take his bat and start hammering his locker. When he couldn't begin to get the science on something that mattered to him more than his life, it made him want to smash things to pieces. But he had to take all the pain of failure in silence, because he couldn't show these bastards the first weakness. And now he had to pretend he couldn't hear what that white rat McIntyre was saying about him; for it was McIntyre, all right, loud enough.

But now someone was talking low . . . whispering something. And whatever it was, it caught the attention of all of them. Tyrus, who would not look up or over, could hear nothing but the whisperer. Was it Donovan? It sounded like him. But now the boy came completely alive. He heard another voice, louder: "By his *mother*?" Then a whispered but intense, "Word has it." Then after a time, "True . . . Leidy . . . three weeks . . ." Tyrus couldn't tell. . . . Was it Donovan? He wouldn't look up, because it didn't matter which one it was. He hated them all.

Around the handle of one of his ashes, he made a hard, sweating fist. "Would anybody be willing to tell me where you get a *lock* around here?"

He shot out the question and then began whipping his bat up and down before him, on the brink possibly of some raging action.

But he had stopped their little talk. Then, after a moment of silence, someone said, "Armour keeps 'em in the office, ya gotta ask."

The boy responded not a word. Didn't even spit out a mock thanks. And when he stepped through the gang of them, he carried the bat.

In the office, the first thing Armour looked at was the ash. Tyrus saw the manager's eyes fall on it. But he wouldn't let these Yankees take him for any madman. He relaxed his hold on his weapon—made it seem as if he didn't even know he was carrying it—and asked very politely for the lock. As if, then, he'd just recalled that he had one with him, he said his bats were special, homemade by his best friend back in Royston. He held the ash up horizontally, one of his hands at each end, to show his manager Joe's mill work.

"Beautiful, isn't it?" he said.

Armour glanced at it, nodded, then looked Tyrus in the eye. "I noticed you carin' for your bats out there at the bone, Cobb, very special like. Do *not* want 'em broke, eh?"

Tyrus never, when he spoke to management, finding a fighting word he wasn't tempted by, said, "Can't afford right now to have them broken."

Armour, deliberately ignoring the retort, managerially redirected the subject. "Doc White, Cobb. Guess tomorrow you'll be glad not to see *him*, eh?" Not waiting for any response, the manager then bent over and pulled a metal basket out from under his desk, picked out a padlock from the basket, sat up, and handed the lock over to the boy. A single small brass key dangled from a string tied to the lock's horseshoe bolt.

Tyrus's jaw was rippling as he took the lock and key. He'd said nothing.

The manager looked him again in the eye. Said nothing a long moment, then spoke in a softer tone; was even kind. "Tomorrow's another day, son. You know this game—'Right now and right now only' is its name. The day has enough damn trouble unto itself. Relax your pride and watch that ball. Where it's goin' is the only place there is for a ballplayer, eh?"

Tyrus softened at the softer tone. But he said, "In my mind I'll find it, Mr. Armour. In my mind, I'll find White's breaker. I'll get the science on that thing, and then *he'll* be sorry, take my word for it."

Armour pursed his lips up slightly in a smile, folded his hands, and nodded, also just slightly shaking his head.

In his room that evening, the boy sat by his window and looked blankly out at Bennett, the park flags gone limp in a dead air. He couldn't get the science on Doc White's breaker, so he couldn't think about the thing at all. Not at all. He hated guesswork, Christ knew! But that slight head shake Armour had given him: That wouldn't leave him alone. He'd noticed that, all right, and he'd carried the image with him on his walk home, not along the same path he'd taken the day before.

He laid his watch under his pillow, so he wouldn't have to hear it—then took out his gun, which he'd returned to his grip, and set it next to the timepiece. He returned to the window and sat. His wound didn't bother him as much as it did last evening. "I'll heal up fast enough, God knows," he whispered with bitterest self-contempt, "if things keep going the way they did today." He contemplated this exact future. He became sure that it could happen, because he could not *see* that breaking ball. He shook his head fiercely. But tears started suddenly in his eyes. Tears that couldn't be just brushed away. They welled. He couldn't muster shame enough to stop them. He began then out of a sudden feeling of complete black emptiness to sob, his shoulders heaving. He thought of his anger as a joke. A pitiful empty joke. Emperor *Cobb*—what a joke! Tyrus Cobb, a *joke*. A September-baby laugh. He couldn't muster any rage because it would be a joke for him to feel rage. For who was the biggest, flash-in-the-pan, one-day-wonder *joke* in the game but a left-hand hitter who couldn't find a left-hand pitcher's breaking ball. Gone! That's what that joke was. In one big damned hurry.

And they knew! The sonsofbitchin' Yankees all knew, every last one of 'em. No denying it. Dead: He flat-out wished *dead* whoever it was who sent the word up from the South. Leidy. But the word was everywhere. All over Georgia. And now here. Christ. He cried more bitterly thinking of this. And hated his parents. The disgrace. How he resented this *disgrace!* for which he was *not* to blame! But then thought of taking a train ride home to his mother and holding her. And then wished Armour dead for leaking the goddamned word to Donovan. And Donovan he hated for leaking it to the whole mob of them. For what? For pity's sake? He didn't want pity from anybody on earth, or in heaven either. And he expected about as much compassion from the rest of the mob here as he would from the White Rat. But at least he'd overheard them! So he knew what they knew and he could *test* their compassion, every day. And he *didn't* go to that tavern. He wished only that he could do something about the leak, other than just deny. It killed him to think that once something was leaked, it was leaked. No stopping it anymore. He wouldn't think it. He wouldn't accept this. He would take every leak and channel it back into the black heart it came from. But who was *he*? A joke headed for a fast, permanent damned laugh of a departure.

He sat for he knew not how long by the window in the dark. Bennett was dead and dull under a cloud-covered moon. The flags still hung motionless. He felt an absolute absence of hope. What remedy was there? He was almost afraid now to think of Charlie, suspecting—was he crazy?—that he might get punished for thinking of somebody who saw worth in him, and loved him. He thought he needed to go so humble that he should cry out loud a thanks for being allowed to breathe. But he took the stationery out, pressed a cuff hard in one eye and then the other, and filled the pen.

"Dear Charlie," he began. Then, with a sudden rush of

feeling, he crossed this out and started again—"Oh my beautiful, beloved girl . . ." But he knew instantly he was writing words now that no one would ever see. In his complete privacy, however, he wrote on fast, not stopping, letting his heart tell its secrets to itself.

> . . . *Oh, my Charlie, how I miss you. You don't know how I miss the smell and softness of your hair. Of your cheek. Your skin. Sweet, beautiful soft mouth. I need you, Charlie. I am so alone here. Connected to* nobody. *I am* nobody *here. I feel dead here. They don't want me to join them. They care so much about their places. And I* can't *join them. Something in me won't let me. But, let me admit it to you, it's a pleasure* not *to join them. It's what keeps me alive,* not *joining them. But what's* MORE TRUE *is that I am so godforsaken alone here I'm dead. So afraid of failure. So* tired *of counting on fear and damned anger to get me going. I want to come home. Get out of here. Have you take me in your arms and hold me. Charlie, listen. Listen to me— about my mother and my father. I know you know. I know it. But I want to tell it all to you. I think my mind could break and crack. It makes me want just to have you hold me. I want to tell you every secret. Hold back nothing ever again in my entire life. Ever! I burn so hot I could die from keeping things in. And maybe this fire* could *be good. Maybe. But I am failing here. And I am afraid for my life. I swear it.*
>
> *Tyrus*

He couldn't see what he'd written, his eyes blinded with tears. And he reread nothing. He no sooner finished it than he began to tear the letter up. Letting pieces fall on the lamp table, he kept tearing the paper until he was certain that if the pieces were ever found, no one could read a word. He gathered up the torn bits and closed them up in a fist. He turned out the lamp and headed in the dark to his bed, beside which there was a wastepaper basket. He let the torn pieces fall into the basket till his palm was clean, then undressed in the dark, setting his clothes out on the floor. He took the watch from beneath the pillow and set it inside one of his leaded shoes, both of which he tucked beneath his pants. Then in the same manner in which he had for the last several nights, he stretched himself out on the bed, arms up like a man under arrest, leaving the gun untouched beneath the pillow.

The next several days against Chicago, things didn't much improve. He got a scratch hit off Ed Walsh, just a bleeder, nothing solid. And he bunted safely in the third game but was out a damned mile trying like a hotshot fool to steal third on Schalkey. And this with two outs; so, when in scoring position, he had run the team out of the inning. He got booed, and booed hard over this by the slim crowd, which didn't seem so slim when it was one united voice against him. And on another bonehead play, trying like a big deal to get a lead runner at home, he ignored O'Leary as cut-off man and came *nowhere near* getting the man, rather just allowed the trail runner to walk into second standing up. "Ya goddamned stupid *sonofabitch*, you'll cost the team games! Ya hear me! Pullin' that shit!" So he heard it from McIntyre, toward whom he actually took a step. And from some loud-mouthed, know-it-all bug behind him: "Ya care about your-*self*, Cobb! Mr. Number One! Mr. Big-time Hero!" And what could he say? He had to swallow it all. He knew he would have to swallow it even as he started the fool throw, which he went through with anyhow.

And when he got to the bench, from Armour: "I'll put it to you this way, Cobb. You pull that kind of thing again and you *won't* get your chance around here, no matter what I promised." The manager came up then and stood right in his face. "And now I'm gonna ask you if you hear me—and all I want, boy, is a polite, Southern 'Yes, sir.' You *hear* me?"

To which Tyrus, as he looked in the manager's eyes, wanted desperately again to respond with a shot that would finish things, right then and there. But he swallowed his pride—hard—again—and said, politely enough, "Yes, sir."

He received no more invites to the watering hole. And, yeah, if you say "no," sooner or later you won't get asked. But around here, what could be clearer: It was one chance and you're out. And the hazing seemed to him to intensify by the second. He felt it was last place or his life in the batting warm-ups and in the shower line. And Armour didn't look ready anymore to intervene; so he was sure he'd lost the manager for good as a protection, or wedge, against the team. And what else did he have? Nothing, really. Nothing. He continued to use the bat bone to give him a head-down concentration that worked as a fence between him and the others—which self-barricading he knew they every day resented, but which resentment made him seek the bone even more eagerly.

"I'm sorry, but it ain't *just* what you said. It ain't. That cracker prick is the least friendly *human* I've ever come across. Just look at the face on 'm. What's it do but set me *off*! And don't give me no *he's just a kid*. And don't give me no shy, neither. That ain't shy. And you'll rag me to the point I'll go bust that kisser if ya tell me it is. Look at 'm with his precious sticks there, which don't seem to be doin' him or us enough good, do they, for all the bonin' fuckin' mumbo."

This time it was Killian, he was sure, echoing his friend. But who wasn't an echo of friend McIntyre? And that night, entrenched in his private compartment as they rode the night train to Cleveland, his first road date, he tried to find comfort in pointing the finger at one, and then another, right down the line, till they were all taken care of. But he had to admit, this was no solace. And, as he failed to sleep, he couldn't escape a torturesome mental figuring—a sleepless estimating of how many plate appearances would likely remain to him, given the number of games left in the season—and a calculating of exactly what every *out* would mean—and of what the numerical *decline* would be each time, from a perfect hit every time up, if he made an *out*—and of what changes in this mathematical plotting there *would have been* if in appearances he'd already made, he'd gotten a hit rather than made a godforsaken damned *out*. And on and on, again and again.

But, Christ Jesus, he thought. I've got to stop this thinking about myself! I've got to stop doing this! I *will* go crazy if I don't. And I'll fail too. Because *truth*—it's *not* energy or strength you get out of this. It's craziness. And failure. And no sleep. And everything the opposite of what I'm damned trying to get. And this godforsaken sorry anger, I'm not *using* it, it's *using* me. Insane thought about me me me. That's the *worst* for a ballplayer. What could be more true than what Armour said about ballplayers. Who in the entire world knows more than a ballplayer about the way you don't make yourself, you damned kill yourself thinking about yesterday and tomorrow. Just the ball. The ball right now. Nothing else. Nothing. It's the key to a ballplayer's life. And to hell with records. Record keeping. If they'd stop that, every ballplayer in the game would be better off. What, are they afraid it would be too boring without records? Or without gambling? They need contraptions to get somebody to give a damn?

But he knew that still he wasn't getting away from what he was afraid of, or any closer to sleep. He felt chained down, like a damned slave to this bad, damned *evil* Royston thing that happened to him. He hated that this *thing* wouldn't let him be what he was before the world changed. What did he do to deserve it? Sure, he was always a driven soul. The first week Leidy took over for Roth in Augusta, what did he call him? "Left-sided Lucifer-eyed Pure-bred Crazy." But it was a compliment. And Leidy said, cocking his eye, "It's what I like about ya, Tyrus."

And Charlie, when she saw him play. When she came to every game to see him play (even when she got told by her friends it wasn't ladylike to watch baseball). And then finally she came up to him after a game and, after they'd said hello and talked a bit and had done some right-off-the bat serious blushing, said to him, "You know, I've never seen the like, Mr. Tyrus Cobb. I mean the way you play. It's a fire. Such an incredible fire in the way you play. Nobody else has it. No one, not that I've ever seen." But, also, afterward, when they met at Florel's for lemonade and ice cream (after he'd taken enough time in the shower to get everybody sore at him, because, oh brother, he would be respectful of *the* most beautiful girl he'd ever laid eyes on, and who'd said *yes* when he asked her to meet!) and Charlie rode up then on her Highlander with her cheeks all flushed, even more beautiful than at the game. What did she say, after they'd sat and had ice cream and lemonade and talked for an hour, or two, or three? "And off the field, when the game's over, so different a Tyrus Cobb, such a very true gentleman. I mean this. I mean it when I say, as much as the fire, there's this, too, the gentle regard, which I can see you have for others." And if girls had any earthly idea what they do to a fella when they touch his hand when they say things to him. Any earthly idea.

He whispered in his imagination thanks and thanks and thanks to his girl. The best girl in the world. Born for her as much as for baseball . . . The words *summum bonum*, he whispered them over and over, like a counting of sheep, for Charlie. He'd be her Galahad, which is . . . the War Between the States . . . the Cause. . . .

When finally he slept, he dreamed of Joe Cunningham, smiling when he told him how to mill those weapons—exactly to *this* specification, and *this*, and *this*. "I love you, sir," Joe had said that day, "for all the things you think of—and then the way you *use* 'em all!" God bless Joe, *his* friend, who was never once mean enough to close up his heart. Never once in his life. But in the dream his Tiger teammates, who for six days now had given him the silent treatment—not the first syllable from a single soul of 'em, Donovan included—

all gathered round Joe and him and broke out laughing. "A lot a good *that*'ll do!" they said, roaring. Then he dreamed of Cleveland's Napoleon Lajoie, the star so great they named a team after him! The Cleveland Naps! That was the *team's* name! He saw this Lajoie, massive and powerful in his frame. The Emperor Napoleon, greatest hitter in the American League. He'd been a cab driver once. A hackster. Did he have teeth? Tyrus in the dream saw this great Napoleon smile, as if to answer his question. The man had big, clean, shining teeth, all right, sparkling like cool, rippling water in the bright sun. Then the man's shining smile turned into a deep laugh. Napoleon Lajoie was roaring laughing, with the Tiger team, at the kid Cobb's expense. For who was this baby Cobb, with his special sticks? Who was Tyrus Cobb but a one-day laugh? Herschel and Amanda Cobb's boy! with his special private little shiny black sticks! Yet in the dream Tyrus wanted to say I'll pass you someday, Napoleon Lajoie. And all your records and plenty more will be goddamn *mine*! But no sounds would come out of his mouth. Joe had hushed him, and the hush was magic.

That morning, at batting practice (because, as the boy was seeing it, the team wouldn't stop now till they had him humbled down to bloody, crawling knees) no one even looked his way. But then there was a moment—there *was* a moment—which his honesty would be compelled to ac-knowledge. The buffoon Schaeffer came buffooning up to the plate, swinging three bats in imitation of everybody knew whom. But right away the boy could tell something: This joke wasn't malicious. Truth: It was not. Rather, he could easily enough see, it was an invitation to somebody just to laugh at himself. And right then to join in. Germany Schaeffer was in this moment the whole team's spokesman—the boy let himself understand this, even though it proved him dead wrong about them—and they were saying that enough had been enough. They were. All Tyrus Cobb had to do was laugh, maybe just smile, ease his stiffened jaw . . . a simple little crack.

He knew this was the offer. But, in the moment, he found himself immediately starting to decide against this offer, disappointed by it, as it seemed right away to threaten a very deep pleasure. It seemed too like some kind of deadly temptation, a lure into a nice little energy-ending, honor-staining *dose* of surrender. Or he found himself liking to think so. And after all, he'd come so close to breaking off with these goddamn Yankee bastards *forever* wouldn't it be a shame, at this point, not to keep on going? After the distance traveled?

But of course it meant pain. All through himself, a sharp, sickening misery, if he was really turning away from this chance. But *no*. God *dammit*. To *hell* with these Yankee bastards if they thought they could push this Georgia boy as far out as they pleased and that he'd come back whenever they whistled. He'd teach these sonsofbitches the meaning of too damn far and too damn *late*.

He ignored Schaeffer, pretended not to have seen him—and—though it continued to pain and tear him—began to, or tried to, concentrate on another thing: the smooth, easy swing that would take the ball right back up the middle. That was the one that got a hitter who wasn't hitting, back hitting again. Evening out his swing and taking the ball right over second: That's what brought back the solid hits, and the groove. Concentrate on that, and that only, he said to himself. Concentrate on that, and don't compromise yourself. Don't give in. Do *not*.

And—the hell with 'em all—that day the discipline worked, and in good measure: He collected two solid singles, which he wrote Charlie about, and Joe. And on the second day, he forced an error (and don't preach to him about happiness if you don't know this happiness!) as he blistered out of the box and took a wide turn after a shot to medium-right center. He'd seen clearly over his left shoulder, and then his right, that the center fielder, who was left-handed (and so he had to be careful with him, for a left-handed center fielder would need to make no full body turn or momentum shift going not that far to his left) had moved, however, in no great hurry for the ball, which he would have to backhand (and God Almighty knew it—had he not practiced for a solid thousand hours running while looking left, then right, focusing on one object then shifting his focus to another, lead-weighted but at top speed, eyes sharp over one shoulder and then the other—and then hitting the pit of sand he'd dug for himself at the family farm, with a right hook slide or a left hook slide, exposing as little of himself as *possible* to hypothetical tags he imagined coming from this side or that side—and yet always getting his pivot foot firm so he could spring away if there were any mistakes made in the throw). And when, head up and eyes sharp all the way, feet lead free, he saw the Cleveland center fielder panicking and then bungling the ball when he finally got to it—there was no hesitation. He broke like all flying hell into second, showing these Clevelanders a quickness that they might not ever have seen before and got goddamn *Lajoie* himself to fumble the ball as the late throw came in on a bounce. And he let the great Lajoie know he was watching his damn fumble mitts as he sprang up and led, dancing, the exact same twelve feet away from second as this Napoleon had stumbled after the loose ball, the shortstop not at the bag yet to take a toss. And he could have led out more, plenty more, he marked—because if this Nap of the Naps had a bat, he had no feet. The boy saw. But then he went back safely to the bag, figuring he'd made the impression. In Cleveland, at least, they'd be afraid now of his quickness. And *that* was what he wanted. He wanted it spreading everywhere, the red, bloody fear of him. And maybe up in The Show he'd have enough time after all to create some real sweet terror, which was by a long, long mile the most forceful weapon on a battlefield.

In the fourth game of the series, with the ball still alive—second inning—he saw a hanging curve come in big as a turned-up dinner plate. His whole heart smiled. He had all damn day to drop his left hand down to his right for full bat-power. And to get his arms out, and his legs and buttocks and back into rhythm for a big drive. No trouble finding *this* one! And he murdered it. *BANG!* The second it met his ash, he knew it was gone. There was some modest little lamb's voice in him that then said, "Don't taunt. For God's sake be modest. Be modest and quiet. Think of what an absolute nothing you've done so far. You'll curse yourself into doing nothing forever, if you taunt." But he decided he didn't need to listen to any timid little superstitions of some false little conscience. He gave his weapon a flip and went into a slow trot so provoking that he knew he would raise up a monster of detestation. He knew he'd be not just feared but damn well reviled in Cleveland. And he loved it. *This* was pleasure. The only thing better than being feared, in fact, was being feared and despised: That was the sweet combination, not for polite life, but the real thing.

And good: When he rounded second, he looked back into his own dugout and saw not the first teammate standing or clapping or looking like he'd care ever at any future time, let alone now. Armour stood clapping; and the boy, fully pleased with the way things were working out here, took satisfaction in the manager's standing there alone. Maybe he could get the man to take his part after all. He took a smart hop on the plate to put a nice period to his first four-bagger, then sauntered over to retrieve his weapon from the dirt. Coughlin, who followed him in the order, hadn't done the usual and picked the bat up to hand it to him. But good for that, too, he thought, as he ran his hand now down the shaft of the ash to clean the dust from its smooth, boned shine. And good when he went smiling to pick up his other two, which had made his home-run bat light. And good when he came in—and he didn't get the first word of congratulation, or so much as a look, from even one of 'em. And *best yet* that he would turn Donovan's friendly little hint now right on its noggin. He'd stand alone in the center of this little social gathering and keep up the experiment just to *enjoy* how long the isolation lasted; for if it lasted right through all his doing good things for the team, he wouldn't have to listen ever again to any sonofabitchin' McIntyres preaching to him about debts to the sacred mob.

Chapter Six

HIS ASHES

Just a quick note to Charlie before heading to the Cleveland Central Station and the train to Boston. And, for Charlie now, just the good news about that sweet round-tripper. Forget the hard thoughts about the Tigers. Not enough time for that sorry poison anyhow. But then, even when there was time, after the train had pulled free of Cleveland and was rolling fast across New York State, he found himself—in yet another of those strange pure turnarounds his mind was taking these days—actually not feeling anymore like mentally rounding up or marking out enemies. For all the ice-hard satisfaction he'd felt in the dugout, he'd lost the energy and the mood now for thinking about how long he could go it alone, with no friendly move made by him, or to him. Nor was he going to think now about how many damned outs in his short time left this season he might make per plate appearance, with what damage each one would do to his chance of making it. What he found himself wanting instead was to think about how many days like this last in Cleveland, that is, about how many *great days* it would take before he'd start thinking about Ti-

ger victories rather than Tyrus Cobb's glory-numbers, or survival (and how many university books would you have to
read, he thought, before you knew more than a ballplayer
did about the sorry effect of one self-centered cuss on a whole
team's effort? or about the irony, if you've got to have one,
of the number-one satisfaction for the individual's pride being the team's victory?).

From the home run and his day, he felt good enough
even so that he imagined having to *make up* enemies and
grievances to keep himself serious enough for greatness
when all his real grievances were gone and he'd found out
that his enemies weren't real enemies after all. And then
maybe, he thought, when his was only a made-up anger,
serious as could be but all just for sport, he could be like the
Giants' Christy Mathewson, one dead-cold winner, you better believe *that*, but a perfect gentleman, too, who'd give his
opponent hell come Monday but who wouldn't even suit up
on Sundays, not on the Lord's day. Wasn't there some way
he could himself be two different people like that, and yet
neither a crazy man nor a hypocrite nor a failure? That he
could be a ballplayer, and not just any ballplayer, but the
best who ever was, and still a gentleman when the game was
over, like the day of rest coming after a hard week?

The way Charlie said he was. And wasn't it good and
fine (at least sometimes) the way other people made you live
up to things that maybe you wouldn't live up to if you were
alone. And could it not get insane, all right, being alone, and
nothing but alone, all the time. Nobody else around to knock
your mind off itself. That's when you start thinking selfish-
as-hell thoughts, crazy, proud, conquer-the-world thoughts;
and when that *making-up*-of-enemies business, it isn't the
healthy kind anymore, because it gets too hot and crazy to
be sportsmanlike stuff. Man oh man, how he wanted to talk
to Charlie. And couldn't his mind just go back there, back to
Florel's, with Charlie and him sitting for hours and hours,
not caring about the passing time? Or ahead to Grand Central

Station, when he would smell again that flower smell in her hair and on her dress, and he would kiss her? Or any place where there'd be those unbelievable times when she touched his hand while they were talking, the way girls will do and make a fella never forget it? Couldn't he just take some thought of a place like that all the way to Boston now?

There came back to him a moment at his father's visitation. Reverend Minifield, from First Methodist, which was next door to the Cobbs, the other side from the Cunninghams, came up to him, and they sat for some time. The Cobbs were Baptist, so Reverend Minifield wasn't their minister. And he was a strange, quiet, ghosty-gray man who lived alone and who kind of scared Tyrus when he was a kid. But he had a way of making you listen, the boy found out, as they sat in chairs in the parlor while Royston filed its way through the library to pay last respects to their former school principal, their former mayor, their state senator.

"You know, son," the gray-faced preacher said, "how hard it is sometimes to forgive people?" The man then smiled just the slightest smile, and nodded, then looked serious and sad, turning down his lips. "I think maybe you do. I think maybe . . . you do . . . and that the hardest to forgive are those we love the most."

The boy had heard more adult wisdom in the day and a half since he'd gotten word of the accident than he could begin to take in. But this was different. The man made him listen, with a voice that, out of that gray face, seemed to come from another world. He recalled the preacher's taking time now, closing his eyes, searching for an expression, showing he cared deeply about the point he would make—and that it wasn't easy for him to find the words.

"Sometimes, son, you will get split apart, in yourself— and one part of you—a very hard and proud part—call it your shame—will refuse to forgive the rest of you. And it can be harder for this proud part of you to forgive the rest of yourself even than it is for you to forgive others, no matter what they might have done. It can get," he said, "more than hard for us to stop being ashamed. To stop hating ourselves, and feeling disappointment in ourselves. More than hard. It can become for us *impossible*. Humanly impossible." He shook his head, slowly, turning his mouth down in intensity of thought, and of feeling. "There comes a time, Tyrus—and this no matter what we did, or did *not* do—when against *ourselves* we shut the gates of paradise. And that's the point when we have—do or die—to put our lives in someone else's hands. You remember this for me. And that I've seen your face—the soul speaking in your eyes—and that that was why I sat with you and spoke to you these words."

As the train rolled on, the boy began putting this preacher's words in the category of words we don't understand when we hear them but that come clear with time— and that make time even start to seem like some kind of very powerful teacher, one who's got a plan and a goal and some kind of secret commitment to make clear the truest words that come through our ears. It loosened tight muscles, and it made him glad his thigh wound itched some rather than ached, to think he was understanding Reverend Minifield's words, which of course he knew were about the Lord. And he thought of Charlie and of Minifield, one and then the other, until he felt some kind of actual peace of heart come over him.

And in Boston, would there be a *letter*? If he knew Charlie Lombard one dime's worth, there'd be a letter, all right. And if there was a letter (which there would be), he'd bet that dime and his $1500 along with it that it would say they'd be meeting in New York. He didn't leave his curtained compartment. He never joined the team, some of whom he could hear laughing, playing cards, just a few compartments down. But he felt a happiness come over him like the warmth from a tender kiss, soft, not clumsy; or like the good feeling that can move all through us when we finally stop warring with the truth and let our minds just *change*.

Allowing himself then some true, honest happiness and hope, even though he'd begun so much lately to fear that happiness and hope led only to their deadly opposites, he slept, the gun, though, still set beneath his pillow. And he knew he dreamed because in the middle of the night a sound, some kind of sound, in his separate compartment, aroused him to a semiconsciousness, disturbing his sleep.

In the dream, McIntyre, who wore a face not his own but one the boy had somewhere seen before (the face of that target that made his gun fingers itch?), was in the locker room in Detroit, surrounded by the rest of the Tigers. And deliberately he was whispering loud enough to be overheard. "Oh yeah," he said. "She's a sweet one, all right. Sweet little Mandy Cobb. Christ yeah. Pure sugar, boys. I tell ya, I won't forget *her*. We were in Augusta, back some time, for an exhibition, which she come out t' see, bein' a lover of the game, umm hmmmm. Got a tip on her from Cicotte, while she's sittin' there watchin'. And ooh la la, let me tell ya, fellas, she's a lover of the *game*, all right." And there he was, her son, right in that same locker room, not fifteen feet away—which they all knew! But what did they care, every one of 'em laughing, echoing, "Oooh la la. Oooooh *laa laa*."

It was in the midst of this nightmare that he heard the sound. He half woke up, and was thinking the dream was all true. That his mother *had* known McIntyre and that McIntyre *had* known her in Augusta somehow, when her son hadn't been on the lookout. He came more fully awake, but he was believing still that what he'd dreamed was all cold hard fact. And if he believed it by preference rather than because it was finally convincing, it didn't matter—not with his furies making turnaround *turn around* again—and his sweet little moment of heaven run, in no time, just like that, to its opposite extreme. He reached under his pillow and felt for the gun, then took the pistol in his hand and looked about in the dark, more fully conscious still. What had made that sound? Who'd been in his compartment? He swung his legs over the side of his berth and stood down now, shaking his head hard as he set his feet on the floor, to get balance, and to let his mind roll fully back to hard grievance and the burning awakenness of rage. Gun in hand, then, he stepped out from his curtains into the rocking corridor. Was that a figure ahead of him, scurrying, now ducking behind a curtain? Was it McIntyre! He set his pistol behind his thigh and put his hand on one of the panels between the curtains. Maybe it was Crawford. God dammit, it sure as hell was *one* of 'em.

"And I'll figure out who. I'll figure out which one of you bastards thinks he can come into my compartment when I'm sleeping. One of ya comes sneaking up on me, and I'll goddamn blow his head off. I swear I will."

Between his teeth, he'd whispered these words, audible, he would have thought, to no one but himself. And the gun was down behind his thigh. But when he turned to step back inside his curtain, he was caught by surprise. Billy Armour stood there in his nightshirt, not smiling, saying nothing, looking curious and worried. Tyrus kept the gun down and back behind his thigh.

Finally Armour, whose eyes had dropped from Tyrus's face to where the boy now concealed his weapon, said, still not looking up, "What the hell, Cobb. You all right?"

"I'm fine," Tyrus said, with all the powers that moved him in his life maneuvering to reveal *nothing*. He tried hard as hell to show no nerves, and draw no more attention to his keeping his hand behind him. He kept his voice as calm and polite as he could, in an effort to get Armour to look up, which the manager now did.

"I thought maybe I heard some angry words," Armour said. The manager now took his forefinger and thumb, touched them together in the center of his mustache, then spread them out, each to one end of the mustache and then round each corner of his mouth, finally touching them together again under his chin. "And frankly, son," he said,

"I've been worried as hell about ya. If you want honesty . . . Do you want honesty?"

"Yes, sir. Of course I do, sir," Tyrus said, again trying as hard as a Southern boy could to be polite, so as to reveal nothing.

"Well," Armour said, dropping his eyes a second again to the boy's thigh, then looking up. "In all honesty I'll tell ya, Cobb, I been seein' signs. I mean, I'm worried about ya. Maybe more worried than about any rookie I've ever been around. And that's a *lot* of 'em. I don't wanna pry. Please understand that, son. I do not wanna pry. But I'll tell ya this, all right? I seen signs, and I figure ya got some things weighin' heavy on your mind. It ain't my business to go pryin' into private matters. But I'll just tell ya. You ever wanna come and talk to me, I'm open for that. Anytime night or day. I mean it. Bein' a manager, ya see . . . Well, it involves knowin' that you're workin' with human bein's. Real live ones, with minds and souls. And it's been my experience, Cobb, that the difference between talkin' to somebody besides yourself and not talkin' to somebody besides yourself is—well—as big as it gets sometimes. So—count on me not to pry—but also to be here for ya if you need an ear to bend. And it don't matter much, I find, that I've got any fancy answers for ya. What matters is that you let things out rather than keep 'em in."

"Well," Tyrus said, still politely, still trying to reveal nothing, though he thought for a split second, as his mind said, 'The man is *right*,' that he might fail and break down crying and beg for help—from this Yankee! ". . . if there's ever any need . . . I'll be sure to let you know, Mr. Armour. And as far as my being a cause of worry is concerned, I mean, I can see that. It's the way I am, I'm afraid. But don't let it concern you. I'm just trying to work things out." He smiled now politely, searching for the look and sound of some truly agreeable modesty. "Trying to get Doc White figured in my mind—things like that."

He almost forgot his gun when he said this, smiling, attempting to coax a smile out of Armour. And thinking now that he'd nearly revealed himself, he gripped the pistol tighter behind him and, as he smiled, stiffened it against his leg. "I end up putting it all to account, ya see," he said, politely. "I mean the taking things hard, caring about 'em the way I do, until I get 'em figured out. It's just my way. It's always been my way, I'm afraid. Yeah, that would be me: the one people always figure they better take aside and talk to. But don't think about it, Mr. Armour, sir. I'll be putting it all to account; you wait and see."

Armour nodded, slightly, and let his mouth turn in a half-smile. He nodded again, more fully. "All right, Cobb," he said, "I guess I'll have to take your word for it. But let's see if we can get some shut-eye, eh? A long train run can be harder on ya than extra innings." Then he turned back toward his own compartment. And Tyrus, satisfied that, if he gave the man maybe a few suspicions, he gave him nothing else, drew his curtain open to step back into his private quarters.

But immediately, as the light from the corridor broke into his compartment, he saw on the floor that his bats were no longer arranged the way they had been, with the three handles set one atop the other and the three heads fanned out; for after his big day he'd come back to the old superstition. And he knew that his weapons weren't disturbed by the vibrations of the train. Not a chance, the way he'd set them. So someone had been there, all right. And it damn well satisfied him that he knew this. He felt a comforting, returning warmth of hatred, and of gladness that he'd set things just so, and that the arrangement had worked like a booby trap. He enjoyed, too, thinking of them as jealous, because of the run he'd had in Cleveland (and weren't they proven hypocrites the very second they preferred hating Cobb to feeling grateful that Cobb had won games for their team). And of certain of them as afraid for real now of losing their pitiful little places. And of how he would in some way signal to McIntyre—though he hated thinking of making the first signal to any one of them—that he knew *he'd* been in his compartment: so that he'd be afraid Cobb had one of his blue hawks open even when he slept. That'd spook hell out of him. Eyes in the back of his head. Eyes everywhere, all day and night. Never shut. That's what he wanted them all to think, especially the White Rat.

He closed his curtain behind him and would sleep. In the dark, though, he knelt first to set back his bats, just so, and as a trap. But the thought that any one of them had ever even touched his ashes suddenly made him rage again in his heart. That they'd gotten close to him while he slept. Good Christ how he hated that. But now, placing his father's pistol next to him on the floor, he ringed his palm and fingers round the head of one of the ashes and ran his hand slowly down its shaft, as if to clean away whatever stain it might have taken from an enemy touch. How he loved the boned, glossed surface. So smooth and clean.

But what was *this*! What the *hell*—a *seam*! An unevenness! He could feel a seam about six inches above the nub! He stood up quick and ripped open his curtain, and then knelt back down frantically in the light to inspect. Oh Jesus Christ in heaven, a crack! Not a crack, a seam! His bat had been sawed and glued! Jesus Christ Almighty they'd taken his bat and sawed and glued it! He looked at the second, and the third. He didn't need to run his hands over them! Even in the dim light, he could see that they'd been sawed, too! They'd all been sawed! His bats! His beautiful black ashes! So much care! Oh Christ in heaven. Those goddamned Yankee scum bastards had come in while he slept and taken his beautiful, beautiful weapons—and *ruined* them. Took them and goddamned sawed them. How could they hate *that* much! How in hell could they hate *that much*! What had he done? He hadn't done *anything*! And they had watched him, so often. They'd seen him caring for these bats. How could they be so goddamned Yankee cold and uncaring and hate *that much*! And they knew his situation! They knew what had happened back home!

He was moaning. On his knees rocking and moaning, running his hands over his broken weapons. Tears had begun flowing. "I'll kill them." He started to chant. "I'll kill those Yankee bastards. McIntyre. Goddamn McIntyre. I swear I'll kill them. I'll kill people who want to kill me."

"Cobb, for Chrissake, son, are you all right?" It was Armour again, standing at the open curtain, slowly shaking his head as he looked at the boy kneeling on the floor.

Tyrus ripped a sleeve across his eyes and moved quickly to block the manager's vision of the gun. "It's nothing," he said. "Nothing."

"It didn't sound like nothing, son." Armour now squinting his eyes, held a questioning, open palm out toward the boy, as if to say, "Look at you on the floor. And can I not see plain as day that you've been crying." He said, "Are you *sure* you don't wanna let me in on anything? It helps to let go, son. Nothing to be ashamed of in that."

"I don't feel *ashamed* of anything, sir," Tyrus said, setting his broken bats quickly over the gun and turning more fully to the manager. "Honestly, I just thought I'd lost something. But it's nothing. Absolutely nothing. Please," he said as politely as he could, "please don't worry about me, Mr. Armour. I just thought I'd lost something. But I didn't. So it's nothing."

Armour signaled with a pursed mouth that, while he might not quarrel with the boy's claims, he wasn't buying them either. Then he crouched down. "I won't say anything more, son," he said, "except this—that I'm about ten feet down the hall here. And all you have to do is give me a call— let me know you're in the mood for a little conversation. That's all you have to do. All right? You understand me?"

"Yes, sir, I do understand," Tyrus said. "And I thank you sincerely for your concern. But do trust me, Mr. Armour, when I say it's *nothing*. And you wait and see if I don't turn things to account. It's the way I am, honest."

Armour, still crouching, looking Tyrus in the eye, nodded, as if to say, "I'm not at all convinced by what you say—indeed what you say itself worries hell out of me—but I'll leave you alone now." Then he rose, asking, "Want your curtain closed?"

Tyrus, finding the most gentle intonation he could, said, "Thank you very much, sir. Yes. Please." But in the dark then, after the curtain was closed, he uncovered his father's pistol and took it by the handle. He prayed on his knees with the gun in his hand that he'd find out *exactly* who did this and get his revenge. But also that he'd never let a single one of them know they'd gotten to him. That he'd walk to the on-deck area tomorrow with three new bats and swing them exactly as he'd swung his own. For what did it matter if the whole world knew his home situation—that he'd suffered such losses—what did it matter if Armour saw him on his knees, heard him moan, saw tears in his damned eyes—if he himself refused forever to acknowledge any of it? He pointed the gun at the curtain and sneered, his teeth gritted hard enough to break. He found himself thinking again of touching the wool pate of some nigger child but also then spitting in his mind at every pitiful superstition he'd ever fallen sucker to. Touch this, it causes that. Follow this ritual, step by step, and that result will follow. The hell with it all. He rose, put under the pillow the gun, loaded as his father had loaded it, and thought that the only magic in the end was what the Lord's gift of anger did for his will power.

Before he climbed to his berth, he checked his pants, hooked on the wall. He wouldn't put thievery past the sneaking bastards—the kind who'd come at him while he was sleeping! But his money was there. The bats, though—and he was *glad*—proved him dead right about the bastards. They'd all been tested and proved now. So forget all the soft stuff. Save it for Charlie, *period*. And the cheap, stinking vandalism gave him that much more cause to fight. *Casus belli,* all right. And the war would be twenty years long. But as he lay on his back now, the train speeding, rattling on in the dark toward the so-called Cradle of Liberty (next step on this all-Yankeeland tour), he had again to rip tears from his eyes.

And all those damned hours. All those hours of care he'd spent at the bone, since he'd come to Detroit and before, so his bats wouldn't break. They *knew* that. And they knew . . . his situation . . . down south. They *knew* about it. God damn them with their break-your-spine initiations— he'd break *them*! He'd break *their* spines! He'd crack their arms, and legs, and necks. The worthless, sneaking sonsof- bitches. No compassion. None! Them and their organization. And not enough guts to give up a lousy inch for the new man—so scared to death of losing their pitiful little spots. But no—he'd admit he was wrong on this. They might let him in if he showed enough gratitude, or good, which is to say good-boy, humor. He'd admit this. All he had to do was laugh that his bats were sawed. Christ. And how much the moguls must love that: seeing *ballplayers* demand of *other ball- players,* as part of their rites of passage, that they act like grateful damned *creatures* for getting in. Oh God, how the moguls must love *that*! But it would be a damned trillion years before he gave in the way they all did, the smiley little agreeable suckers. Joe Cunningham would be great before any of these sorry birds would. And you could include Craw- ford and Donovan too.

He imagined miles, yards, feet, goddamned inches, and half-inches, and quarter-inches of decreasing space—dis- tances in which there was anybody or anything in this world in even the slightest way well-disposed toward him—all shrinking. Shrinking till there was an absolute nothing of friendliness of any kind anywhere. He imagined then too a raging wildfire bursting out away from him, carrying rumor after rumor in a tremendous roaring blaze—all of it, every word of it a word against him and his father and mother and family, spreading out to the four corners of the earth—in newspapers. Newspapers letting every last soul in the world know everything there was to know about the Cobbs. "And that's when I'll really start," he thought. "When there's no friendliness or kindness anywhere. There—with no magic bats or superstitions, talismans. Nothing. Just victories—period. And I'll watch my successes create total silence in them all. Watch all the people to whom I never apologized or said I was grateful, start apologizing to *me* and saying thanks. All of them. Because the new sacred man would be *me*. Because I made them. That has to be the faith: that not needing a single inch of comfort or a single friendly face or a single kindness in the entire world is what leads to the world's becoming yours."

He ripped his forearm once more over his eyes. He listened to the wheels rattling and clacking over the rails and ties. He thought of his championship watch. And of his journey: all the miles and the trains since he'd said good-bye to his mother at the whistle-stop in Royston. And then to Charlie in Augusta. He thought of his father's gun beneath his pillow. He wouldn't kill himself, and give these Yankees the satisfaction. It's what they wanted, after all—for him to put a bullet in his brain. He listened to the train and let it dull him, finally, to sleep.

"People are sheep. Learn that. Learn that people are sheep. So few learn this; maybe one a generation, or a century. It's the thing you learn when you don't go meek and soft for them at all—or accommodate them at all—or worry about offending them at all—but are mighty and powerful before their eyes. They're sheep and you can make them love you, even more than they would if you were soft and kind. And no more reputation is needed for winning them over to you than a reputation for power. Power that gives them life and greatness they can't give to themselves. Make them think they need you for their highest excitement and their real life. And then watch the gratitude come all your way."

These words, or words like them, were spoken to him in a second dream that night, by an imperial figure on a white warhorse, the horse standing atop a hill, with a black sky behind. The figure was Caesar—and then Jesus. And in the dream Tyrus went up to this Jesus, who, with his back turned to the boy, said, "I was once at a gathering, Tyrus Cobb. And I stood in the middle of the crowd and did nothing, sought no one's favor or conversation. Nothing. But they still flocked round me, because they are sheep, and their shepherd is the *Lord*." And then the figure turned round to him on its horse and was Caesar, helmeted, with short sword and breastplate and shield and buckler. "Peace," it said, and laughed, and turned its horse and rode away.

He found himself half-smiling as he began to come out of his sleep, the train rolling and clacking on toward Boston in the first pink-gray haze of dawn light. The dream made him warm, and he was comfortable in his berth, lying on one cheek and looking out his window with one eye. But then he recalled what had happened the night before. Or thought had happened. Was that a dream?

He jerked his head around hard, dragging his face across the pillow. Rubbing, blinking both eyes hard, he looked then and saw on the floor his bats, all three in no order, two rolled up against the wall and the third now rolling slowly in the middle of the floor, through an arc, and then not—just the flat roll of a rolling pin. It seemed then it was true. He rubbed his eyes again and blinked harder, trying to see if he could spot crack lines above the nubs. He thought . . . He wasn't sure. He ripped his sheet off and, coming fully awake, lowered himself in a jump from the berth. He got down quickly on his knees and, frantically, gathered all three bats together. His heart was praying. Pounding hard and praying. Was it true? He looked. He saw the lines. Oh, God. Was it *true*? He ran a ring of his forefinger and thumb gently, lovingly down the shaft and handles of one. Oh, Joe,

Joe! Do you believe what they did! Oh, Joe, do you believe this! It was the truth. Jesus, it was.

And the truth through Albany and through Worcester—through all those early and later morning hours to Boston—and on the streets of Boston, another Yankee town in which he walked by himself alone. The Common and Faneuil Hall and the North Church and the home of Paul Revere. He would have liked to take these things and haul them out of this Mammon's kingdom to Atlanta. All the old things, still standing, unburned, giving these hypocrites here the feeling they were God's righteous.

And isn't it just about as polite as hell around here, he thought, seeing nothing but white faces anywhere he went. Damn my eyes if a nigger wouldn't have a better chance of real kindness in Georgia any day of the year. These fraud, finger-pointing people. Do you see a nigger making it anywhere here? Do you see a nigger *at all*?

What a lie they live. But God knows about it. And may God damn them in their mogul, iron-gated, barricaded, red-brick and stone castles, thinking they're the noble guardians and kings of liberty, just because they had the luck not to lose a war and *their* city didn't get burned to the ground. I wouldn't be a nigger walking these streets for my life, not with one of those Irish or whatever-they-are thug coppers with their twirling billies. Look at 'em strolling along grinning away, ready to clobber the first nigger skull they see. The lying hypocrites. And who let a million of 'em into this country, after all? Just substitute niggers, that's all *they* are. Come over on substitute slave ships to slave away in some worse-than-cotton-field smoke factory for some mogul Yankee bastards. The mere cash connection. It is not God's way. And aren't the silk-hats who live in these damned red castles glad they've got white faces slaving away for 'em (and even being *cops* for 'em!) so they can point a fraud, hypocrite finger at the South and say we don't mistreat *niggers*!

But, then, it was one of these officers of the law whom

he would ask, politely, where the Post Office was. And then, right before him, he saw the flag, the red, white, and blue that meant U.S. Post Office, flying exactly where that billy-twirling whatever-ya-callum (who might have been, after all, just one more friendly-enough version of Timmy the bar-keep) said it would be. And out of a superstition that he couldn't stop, he whispered a mental thanks to the decent-enough fella for telling no lies—because if he didn't offer the man a thank-you, there might not be any letter from Charlie waiting at General Delivery, and so no word about any meet-ing in New York. And if there was no word—how could the meeting happen?

Then, as he began his way, leaded, up the high stone steps of the Boston Central Post Office, he thought of one more thing that maybe everybody knows but nobody knows better than a ballplayer. And that's how if you hope too much for a thing, you'll dead-cold jinx it, but if you don't hope enough, it'll just as fast go dead on ya rather than come true. So there you are. And there he was, keeping his fingers crossed, but not too tight, sort of like he was praying hard to get out of a slump but then making the prayer as quiet as could be so he wouldn't strike out.

"Cawb . . . Cawb . . . Let me just see if we've got anythin' for . . ."

"Tyrus Cobb. It'd be a Georgia postmark."

"Ya don't say." The banded-sleeved clerk looked up from under his visor and over his wire-rimmed spectacles, smiling.

Tyrus smiled back, polite enough, but not so friendly as to draw the man away from his task.

And the fella did then keep trotting his fingers over en-velope after envelope. Until, "Well, yep, heah we ah. Cawb, Tyrus. And let's see heah, Augusta, would Augusta, Jawja, be a desiahed point of origin, eh? And a Miss . . . Let me see heah . . . Shah-let Lombahd be someone we know, eh?" The man winked under his visor and over his spectacles as, smiling, he handed the boy his mail. Then a still broader smile, and a last, broad wink. "You have a fine day, son, heah."

And the boy, smiling, now even laughing, "Thank you, sir. And you bet I will, sir. You bet I will!"

Out the door, in the broad, shining sunlight, the boy took the letter to his face, smelled it, oh God, yes, and he kissed it; but he'd wait till he got to his room to read it. For now, flying down the stairs streetward, he put it away in his pocket and let it itch warm as love itself against his leg. Let his blood flow hot with happiness through his whole body as he carried, and felt, his letter in his pocket. And let himself now suddenly see this Boston—Spin me another *turn-around!*—as a city of old grace and of heroes and great men. So praise to those Yankee history books. They can't be all lies. And he thought, with his leaded feet still wearing wings, that if ballplayers more than any souls alive knew you couldn't let yesterdays and tomorrows foul up your damned mind, it was ballplayers too who knew how you need good past things and good hopes for the future to get the *confidence* to swing smooth in the right-here-and-now. And—no matter that his bats were all sabotaged—the fact that he'd kissed Charlie Lombard and would kiss her again let him see this city he walked through for the beautiful, beautiful old place it was.

In his room, he took the envelope to his face again and kissed it softly. He worked his finger carefully under the seal, wanting to be gentle as he could even with the envelope, if it was Charlie's envelope. But, oh, was he eager to see, too ... was he *dying* to see what the word was about their meeting, only a few days' count from now if it was going to happen.

Then, no surprise, but, still, just *finding* a letter really there inside the envelope made his heart beat even harder still with happiness. And then to see, when—with a whole blessed drum corps of expectation beating wild in his chest— he unfolded the paper—that the first words were—"Yes! Tyrus! Yes!"—it made this lonely, shut-out, anger-haunted boy so crazy happy he felt almost that he held his sweet Georgia girl right now in his arms. That he had there right before his eyes now her beautiful brown, brown eyes, and that pale, cream, rose-blushed skin of her face, and, for his fingers to run through, her dark, silky hair, soft, thick, slow-falling. Sweet home. Sweet Charlie. He kissed the letter one more time and read.

Dearest Tyrus,

Yes! Tyrus! Yes! We will be meeting soon! Mama and I will be in New York the day before you arrive. So, yes! I will be there waiting for you at Grand Central Station. Did you get that sad letter I sent to Detroit? Well, if you did, disregard! For I will be there in New York! And I can not wait! And please always know that no matter where we are, or if years passed (Lord forbid) and we were apart, that I would think of you the same way as you think of me. Each day we'd grow closer, even though we were apart. Truer to each other. Day after day. But we won't be apart long, will we!

And I am so truly, truly proud of you. Stepping up that first time in the major leagues and getting a hit off Mr. Chesbro. Oh, yes, I know his name, even though you didn't tell me. For the word made it down here, all right, fast as can be. I saw it the next day in the Atlanta Journal. *And I do believe Mr. Grantland Rice will follow your progress, Tyrus, as he has avowed a very close interest in Georgia's native son.*

But let me tell you something, too, that I did the other day, a little secret thing, with no one around at the Tourists' park. I was on Highlander. And the park, which somehow, hmmm, I just drifted to, was so empty and silent, not what it was when you were there, making my heart leap! But in the quiet, not a soul around, I found a passage through the gateway. I thought I'd hear someone shout me off. But no. Luckily, no scolds about. So onto the field I went and off I flew. I let High go and ran him round the outfield, fast as the wind, so I could feel what you must feel, flying over such green pastures. And how I miss already seeing you play, so fierce and beautiful. And all our times together here in Augusta. All our horseback walks through the trees here at The Oaks. And our times in town. But do let's make our first project in New York, Tyrus, a trip of discovery, to see if they make good ice cream up north, and good lemonade! I told Mama that she is to mind her fussy old self and to understand that I will be well chaperoned on the streets of New York and that she is to learn to love baseball and that she is to be as careful as if it were Derby Day to find the right hat. For we must be noticeable at the games, for you to see us! But listen to me speaking in this way. I'm sure it's you who have so emboldened me, sir, that I've become absurd. Fortunately, I'm even now laughing at myself. But it's in part, too, the giddiness of pure excitement, for I cannot wait to be with you.

And perhaps I could move heaven and earth if there were things really in our way. Nor can I wait to sit with you and talk—forever. Forgive me, Tyrus, but I think now of your letter to me. Of your not wanting, in your so thoughtful way, to lay upon me any weight of your burden now. But you know my heart is your secret chamber. I have thought so often of your train ride north. In my soul I have felt, or tried to, hour after hour, what that long ride must have been for you, leaving for such a dream, at such a time. I'll say no more except that there is nothing, Tyrus Cobb, that you cannot share with me, nothing, that you cannot tell me. I have a heart that loves all of you. And someone has said that love is the key to understanding. I promise you, too, that it is a key that will lock in safely all your privacies. And do they make it hard for you, your Yankee teammates? To be expected, I would guess, you being young, and new, and foreign (and they being Yankees!). Perhaps,

*though, your own recent sorrows, so hard to bear, have
given an extra weight to their fooleries—a weight greater
than they really have. I trust your judgment will lead you
always to see what's true. After all, you have come to love
me, and can see how much I love you.*

*Just days, my love. Just days till I see you in the
major leagues. And till we take our first stroll down the
avenue. Fifth Avenue, that is! Can you believe that such a
sweet dream is coming true. And may many, many more.*

I love you more than words could ever say,

Charlie

He was glad he was alone, so he could let his tears come
and not care. And he knew that the tears of the incredible
love he felt and of all his sweet happiness came and kept
coming because there was so much sorrow in him, too. He
could feel the two things together, his happiness and his sorrow. He couldn't help it. All of these things were just over-
whelming him now, coming at him all at once. And he
couldn't think it out straight—but he thought that his tears
were the things that more than anything else contained them
both, his happiness and sorrow. And—he couldn't say it to
himself or think it straight—but the way we just start crying
sometimes, like out of nowhere, when things just hit us, it
was like the way his mind turned so quick from one feeling
to another these days. And all this—whatever it was he was
trying to say to himself—was because the hell feelings and
heaven feelings he had these days were always there, that
they're in us all the time and forever, and that that's why
they can turn up so quick, like the things that just, out of
nowhere, or in no time, make us start crying. But that you
have to be for a long time on some damned and crazy verge
of tears (which that reference to a sad letter, which he was
deeply glad and grateful he never got, brought him to, also)
to understand all this. Which he didn't. He didn't under-

stand, even though his whole damned life seemed lived on the verge of tears, what it was he was he was trying to say to himself. But, oh my God, he was in love with his girl. And that he was lucky enough, sweet Lord Jesus, ever in this world to meet Charlie Lombard, his true girl, just as deeply true as his true calling. How did it happen in his life, his finding these things?

He had no answers for this, either. And now time had passed. A good bit of time. He had then quick to get ready. He tore his sleeve over his eyes. Then held it pressed against them, while he calmed himself with deep breaths. He got up and washed his face, then, to scrub off any trace of feelings that were completely *private*. Then he got his things, and went down to join the team, though he offered no waves to Boston as the Tigers' bannered wagon, rolling down the city's streets, ran its little game-day parade.

About the bats, he didn't let on the first thing; but with the new, low-grade commodity he took that day from the club's spares, he didn't hit the first thing, either. As he'd sworn he would, he grabbed three from the pile and swung them all together as he waited on deck, exactly the way he would have with his own three. They would never break him of a good thing: using weight to lighten weight. Never—the thick-headed jackasses. But, though he wouldn't give them satisfaction by looking, he could hear them sniggering behind his back as he swung the strange weapons. And he knew damn well that when he didn't hit that day—not the first, second, third, fourth, or *fifth* time—nothing—the full hangman's collar—they loved it, no matter what it might mean for their team. And, Christ, it ripped him hard, hard as hell on earth—that he wasn't able to prove them all powerless over him as well as worthless in themselves and *wrong*. He'd looked bad, real bad—all five times up. So he began to hear it, too—and hear it echoing—more and more—from the Boston bug chorus. And in the series against the Sox the sick pain of it all would linger—the second day and the third day turning out no better than the first—so bad he was afraid again even to think of Charlie now and New York because happy thoughts *would* lift him up just to drop him ten thousand feet into killing pain.

"Whatsa motta, ya rookie suckah. Got yuhself all nuh-vuhs, wondrin' if yuh gettin' invited bahck! Is thaht it, Cawb! Well just keep it up, bustah. Just a few moah days like today and the question's ahnsuhd. But don't you be nuhvuhs, eh!" "Yah, don't be nuhvuhs, ha! 'Cause if it's one moah day a bein' the bum you was today, mistah, it's *poof! Y'gon!*" "Yah, *poof! Y'gon!* Cawb! Ha ha ha! And ya won't be bahck no moah!"

By the second day, he'd wanted to climb the barrier for a throat. The rule of restraint. He couldn't accept it: that the ballplayer (a gentleman, all right, by *force*) had to stand there, inside the wall, inning after inning. Just stand there and ignore all the noise, swallow bug sewage, game after game, because these maggots had their fifty-cent "right" to hurl insults unpunished. And he imagined some future moment when he would turn to them and fire a challenge at them all to leap that wall—and then to any of the mob who had enough spine, to take the first step forward and *show it*. He felt a deep confidence that there'd be no such individual and that Tyrus Cobb could face down any yellow damned mob. But if all hell broke loose and it took riot police to restore order, so be it.

For all his raging anger, however, he couldn't now, in truth, see himself making *anything* happen. In his room at night he found himself thinking, not only not of Charlie but not of strategies, either. And it was right damned back, as if he were a whipped slave in chains, zero freedom of mind, pathetic, pitiful—right back to how many plate appearances he would likely have before the season ended and to how many he'd already had and again to exactly what effect varying combinations of hits and outs would have on his damned plummeting average till he had the number for every possibility worked out again clean as hell in his sick mind. He couldn't read about Caesar, not a word. But he couldn't keep the tears out of his eyes, either. For three nights he wept, as he sat alone in his hotel window, but now with no turna-rounds to any happiness. So much, then, for his theory, or whatever that was, about when out of nowhere you just start crying. His wound could be called full healed, too, shrunken to virtually nothing. And he found himself actually wanting to cut himself, he was so discouraged and ashamed.

Then on the fourth night, as he sat alone looking out over old Boston with a pure blank eye, he was startled by a sound. A knock. But just one. Then by passing footsteps something was slipped beneath his door. His imagination ran from hope to rage. The knock had made him wish instantly that some friend . . . *Some* friendly soul . . . Then whatever it was that was slipped in by those departing footsteps made him sure that someone with some vicious intention . . . But as he came to it, he saw it was a string-bound packet of letters. More mail. Three letters. All, he saw, as he tore away the string, had been sent to Detroit and then forwarded, one from Augusta and two from Royston. Augusta—of course Charlie. But he saw the date, and knew this had to be the sad letter, which he didn't want to open because he might believe it more true than the one that came *after* it in time. That's how crazy his mind was getting. And then one from Joe Cun-ningham, 211 Church Street, Royston. Bless Joe, his best friend. Or at least best friend so far. Then the third. 205 Church Street, Royston. And the light blue stationery he knew every bit as well as the street address, which was his own street address. For his mother would write him often when he was away from home. But when he went to his bed now and turned on the lamp beside it, he put this third letter off on the bed table, facedown.

He opened Joe's, hoping as he so often would, that his own soul might catch something good from the most unaf-fected soul he'd ever known.

Hello there, TRC!

Naturally, Tyrus, I'm gonna follow your progress every day. But I just this hour got word of your first at-bat. A two-bagger off Happy Jack! What a start! But I knew it would happen. Why, I've known you since we were still waitin' on front teeth. And what have I seen? The doggonedest cuss there is, that's what. What a critter you are, sir! I mean the world over I don't know if there would be the like. And did it not come to me as NO surprise that Tyrus Cobb made it to The Big Show. And NO surprise that he could handle their smartest stuff. And quick enough, this is what I know—they'll be the ones who's scared stiff. When this letter gets to you, I'm sure you will have done a great measure more of good for those Detroit Tigers. But already I'm so doggone proud of you. Always have been, old friend a mine. Always have been laughin' in my heart watchin' you. What a pleasure that is. Comes a point when you say, "Boy, I could never do that." And you'd think maybe jealousy or some mean ol' sort a poison would set in. But it doesn't. Truth'll set you free. And what it ends up is, it's just fun watchin' and takin' pride that that's your friend.

But what about those Yankees, eh? Are they treatin' ya right? I expect so. Clear enough they didn't care where you were from when they called you up. That's respect, sir. And I know you'll keep opening doors, makin' 'em all happy the way you play. Yankees are no different, I expect, when it comes to great ballplayers. They love 'em same as we do, 'cause a the way they put the hammer on the horsehide.

No news outa this ol' town, except, wait, ol' Carrie Breier. Ha! Didn't she up and marry right, right, right. Some banker boy from Savannah, who'd come over from the University to court her. All I can say is, if you're not happier to be a major-league ballplayer than to be that poor starch collar hitched to that . . . Well, all I can say is, I'd rather have to hand-saw down a county-full a bodoks than

spend a honeymoon with that one. But listen to me,
gossipin' like an old lady. I was out fishin' for cat on the
Trencher's levee, thinkin' about ya. Can't wait for doves,
when you'll be back. And together, sir, we shall hunt the
wild deer.

Your friend,
Joe

God bless Joe Cunningham. And Carrie Breier!—at least
there was some humor. The best unanswered prayer he ever
had, if he ever prayed it, which Joe knew he didn't, which
was why the funnin' with him. Caroline B and her stuff-shirt
daddy, who wouldn't let his little angel take a step of a walk
with a ballplayer, or anyone who, as she parrot-mouthed it,
"sought a station so low." Well, well, she might be a sort of
sidesaddle and parasol pretty, Carrie Breier, but what a true
deep laugh he could have when he compared such a little
sugary-precious figurine to Charlie. Talk about a truth that
sets you free.

But the boy found himself now wishing, after his little
laugh, that he'd just upped and gone *home* after his one appearance against Chesbro and that he'd had something like
Joe Cunningham's Royston life forever and that he was fish-
ing for cat with his friend and laughing about that poor university swell who got stuck with Miss Caroline B. He knew
Joe read every newspaper account he could get his hands on.
And it pained him to death thinking Joe was all let down by
those sorry appearances against Doc White, and now Boston.
And maybe wondering now if his hero friend, who was his
idea of something really great, and right out of their own
Georgia, was going to survive at all among the fittest. But at
the same time, the thought of any actual final end to his life-
dream woke him up in about his hardest self. He wanted to
say to Joe—Joe Cunningham, if you think these Yankees understand *respect*, let me just tell you what they did to that

beautiful, custom millwork of yours. Let me just show you the factory-line thing of a stick they left me with.

He didn't, though, want to argue, even in his mind, with his beloved friend. Rather, with that craziness that preferred to make a disturbed, sick nightmare into a hard fact, and something *first in time* into one *second in time*, he went to Charlie's letter, which he knew was the sad one.

> *My dearest Tyrus,*
>
> *I will write soon again, I promise. And we both will write letters that keep us close as we can keep ourselves with letters. But I fear to say, I think my mama's and my trip to New York may be canceled. After all my promises. It breaks my heart to say it. I've been so miserable for two days now that I'm glad you can't see me! But I can say that Mama has agreed that if we do go, we certainly will go when you are there. Bless her heart, she knows what it means to me and would never stand in the way. But she has commitments, Tyrus. To Mt. Olive Baptist. To the Hospital Guild. To the Home for Orphans. And she's had all these unforeseen problems with members of her little charitable organization. I won't embarrass myself mentioning for what reasons her uncooperative, squabbling and childish "friends" are letting her down. I'll only say that Mama, though she fears she's up against it, is working hard as we could hope to get the cooperation she needs. And believe me she asks very little. But I'll say no more because I've written to keep your hopes from getting up, not wanting more than anything in the world to disappoint you, or to embarrass myself with more promising and no keeping. I'll only whisper that I'm as impatient to see you as you could ever, ever wish me. That I love you with all my heart. And that all here are doing everything we can to make things happen as we all so wish.*
>
> *With my truest, truest love, always*
> *Charlie*

He shut his eyes tight and held the letter tight to his chest, almost preferring to imagine the letter had no successor, just as he'd thought he'd like even to cut himself. He reached back then and took his father's gun out from under his pillow. He wanted to hurl the deep-cursed thing across the room—to rid himself of it as he had rid himself of that godforsaken book. But he set the gun instead on top of his mother's letter where it lay turned down on the bed table, under the lamp. And then after a while he took Charlie's letter and Joe's and dropped them by the side of the bed. He looked at his father's gun atop his mother's letter and felt a rage of resentment. Signs all along. He knew. He'd denied them. The two of them never showed him they loved each other. Let him say it now. Never! Let him *say* it! There were signs forever. No other kinds of signs. And then its all ending in disgrace. Family *disgrace*! That he'd have to spend the rest of his life with snarling watchdogs in his brain, to protect him against *death by disgrace*! What a hell of death they sent him to! God damn them!

But before he slept, he took his father's gun and set it back beneath his pillow. And he left his mother's letter on the bed table. Then he thought not of Charlie but, why the hell not, of the beautiful dancing girl at the Union House and of how with her he would like very, very much to lose his precious virginity. A warm fantasy, with which he let his life flow away, just before he slept.

In game four in Boston it was more of the same. He kept taking it from the bugs. But he didn't scowl now because he didn't want to give them any easy chance to call him sorehead and sourpuss. He was sick as hell of hearing these names, everywhere he went. And he kept ignoring what he knew was going on behind his back as he would step up once more into the on-deck area and then to the plate. He kept saying to himself, in fact, that whether he could ignore this or that was a test of whether he could make it in his life.

But when he tried again, and again, just to take the ball

back up the middle, the way he always would when trying
to fight out of a slump, working to get his batting stroke
smoothed and his mind stilled by pure simplicity, he couldn't
do it. He'd pop up or hit an easy comebacker to the mound
or get all wound up and strike out. One time he got sawed
off and broke the cheap spare he was using—and he heard
one of them laugh hard out loud. And then there was whispering. And chuckling. He tried to ignore it. But he was getting dizzy, actually physically dizzy. And all the time it
pained him to breathe. His chest was so tight that the tension
would crack out loud along his breastplate.

"But don't you worry, Jawja boy, yah gon—right bahck
to Mama soon enough. Pain's gonna be ovah soon enough,
ya sorry bastad!"

The train ride to New York was a day trip, no curtained
compartment to retreat to. And so much work to do that he
didn't know how to do—and with only four and a half hours
to do it in. For that was when he'd see Charlie at Grand
Central! And in four and a half hours, in other words in *no
time* at all, how was he to get himself free of all this hell inside
him, so he could give her the Tyrus she expected—and so
truly and forever deserved? Give her the person she loved,
and the same one she last saw? What kind of prayers for
what kind of sudden conversion? He knew only that it had
to be sudden. And was there some kind of breathing? Some
kind of no thinking? He'd do anything, perform any kind of
rite. Go full meek. But he didn't know what to do. He knew
only that he was in a hell of misery and that he didn't deserve
to be seeing his girl.

It had been eighteen days now of the pure silent treatment, and it had come to where he didn't damn *want* the
hazing to end—ever. But there was something in him that
hoped, too, as he sat off from the crowd yet out in the open,
that it would end right now, because maybe that would make
it so he could give Charlie the person she expected, and the
kiss, and the warm and tender smile, and the days she was

so afraid she might miss. And how sorry and really shameful that he'd get off the train and see her and be able to introduce her to not one soul. But he couldn't help it. He looked hard away from them, out the window at the New England countryside and the towns, old, beautiful, never burned to the ground. And he found himself again thinking about cutting himself so he'd have a decent war wound to pain him, instead of the ache of his shame. Then, pitiful, even as Charlie was maybe laying out clothes to meet him, it was back again into his now nearly unceasing preoccupation with his past, and future, numbers. And his past being what it was, he didn't think he could get in his future, brief as it might be, to .300 or .290 or .280 or even .270. And in Chicago, there would be Doc White.

The at-bats against White were the appearances they'd really be looking at. What could be more deadly certain. And he had no science for these at-bats at all. Not a single real idea of how to prepare for them, though he'd given already maybe fifty hours of thought to them. And right now—with apologies to Charlie in his deepest heart—though he couldn't think of her for long—he wanted just to listen to the train's clacking and to make that clacking his mother's heartbeat and make it so he'd never have to come out of her and be born. No appearances ever in this world. But there was no such withdrawing.

"Tyrus?"

When he heard the word, he honestly didn't know if it came in a dream or in the real world, he was so strangely isolated.

"Hey, Tyrus."

There the sound was again, but he was almost afraid to look up, thinking the call also might be leading up to some bitter McIntyre joke. In his imagination, he could hear a chorus of laughs. But he turned and looked up.

It was Wild Bill Donovan. "Mind if I sit next to you a minute?"

Instantly, the words *Mind plenty* came to him again. But he would *not* not be polite. He said, "Please."

Donovan sat with the invitation and extended his arm along the top of the seat back, suggesting a warm gesture. And Tyrus found himself quickly ready to think that the hazing was about to end—and indeed almost ready to *beg* that it end. The hell with his sorry pride. He half-smiled.

Donovan smiled warmly back and tapped his hand gently on the seat back. "Tyrus," he said, "you remember when I slipped you a little advice your first day in Detroit?"

The boy found himself now, though, instantly turning hard. What? Was he being charged with a failure, when things were *not* his fault? He half-frowned, but nodded, just enough not to appear stupid, or rude.

Donovan looked at him now, a moment, with maybe the beginning of disappointment. But again he smiled. "That advice, you recall it?"

Tyrus again did not like at all the suggestion that he'd neglected some duty. Or that he was too stupid to have understood the counsel. So he still said nothing, frowned again, and nodded, once more as if against a hard grain.

Donovan didn't smile this time. He seemed frustrated. But he spoke in a friendly tone. "Did you think it was good advice?"

"I think," Tyrus answered now quickly, "that if you were in my situation and we were down where I come from instead of up here where you come from, we wouldn't be having this conversation. And not because you're different from me, more friendly or something, but because in the South what's happened to me wouldn't have happened to you."

"Good Southern hospitality, eh?" Donovan smiled. He seemed not to want to resharpen any old hostilities; but there were perhaps signs again of frustration in the way he would push forward his response now as quickly as Tyrus had pushed forward his. "You know, though," he said, "there are good people and bad people wherever you go, Tyrus. And it's always going to be a good man's job, I'd say, to find the good people and open up contact. It probably won't happen by accident."

"That's the point, right there," Tyrus answered again right back. "Whose responsibility is it to start things? You seem sure that it's mine. But have you talked to all your friends? Maybe it's theirs. And is it their *right* to do and say whatever they damn well please and my *duty* to keep still and shut my mouth?"

"Tyrus," Donovan said, now smiling as if things had come happily to a clinching truth, "You're a *rookie*. You're getting what everybody else got. No different. They all had to swallow the same dirt. It's all part of the game."

"That, too, is the point." The boy barely waited for the man to finish his sentence. "There it is. What does an individual give up when he says I won't be different? When he says I'll give myself up, go soft, and dumb, so I can be part of things, the same as everybody else? Should he? Should he do that? And did you ever stop and think what kind of an organization it is that demands that of an individual? Is it right to ask or get that? Is it good? Is it healthy? Is it best? I know. I know you think I'm just some disaffected rebel boy, still fighting the War Between the States. And maybe I am. But you make an individual into something other than an individual and, well, you figure the cost of that. What's the cost of *that*, to the *soul*, sir? Can you tell me? Can you?"

Tyrus was convinced, as he looked at him, that he'd put the veteran star back on his heels now—that he'd made Donovan realize that the little fish he thought he'd caught was strong enough to snap his line and in wisdom old enough to spit out his hook. There were things about this particular rookie (Tyrus was sure this was the conviction he'd instilled) that the man had never seen before.

But now the veteran, shaking his head, showing signs that he'd had enough and that these would be his last words on the subject, said, "It goes one direction, kid. And it keeps on going in that one direction when ya don't give in *some* and join up: and that's that the boys'll keep turnin' harder away. Fact is, ya bring on hell by not givin' in. But—you don't wanna go through the christening, I suppose that's your business. But if you're around to see the next rookie coming along, I'll bet you wouldn't think we were much of a club if we let him have it his way from the start. Never met an individual who didn't need something bigger than his own lonesome. And I'm not meeting him now either."

With that, Donovan rose and, leaving Tyrus to himself, headed back to join a group about to play a hand of cards (and there, Tyrus saw, would be McIntyre right among them).

But he had to admit that this Donovan was no fool. The man had a mind. And he'd made the move. Made it three times, even, as there'd been that first gesture in the locker, then the invite to the bar in Detroit the day he'd faced Doc White—whom he'd be facing again after the Tigers left Washington, which was right after Philly, which was next after New York. And still he hadn't plotted that curveball out in his mind. He had a vision of everything but the break, but none of what he saw was any good for even guessing what he didn't see.

He gave his mind again now to the breaker—his obsession—and let time pass. Then he was glad to think how it had grown too late for him to join the crowd. And that if Donovan had really given a damn about him, he'd have done something about the sabotaging of his bats. He allowed himself even to work up a righteous indignation against Donovan for not stopping the bat episode before it started. He *could* have, the boy was convinced, but he *didn't*. And what's the difference between not stopping something you could have stopped and just plain being the one who did it? No real difference, when you get down to it. Hell, who's to say Donovan wasn't in on it? Maybe the rest of 'em gave him the cold silence, but Donovan *said* it was a rookie's job to swallow whatever was served up. He said a team wouldn't be much of a team if it let a rookie off. How was someone supposed to read that? And hanging everything on Tyrus Cobb, as if these people were really good until Tyrus Cobb made them bad. Something about Tyrus Cobb—that seems to be the explanation for all the trouble. Something about a rookie who doesn't swallow what's served up. Something about a sorehead, bush-baby *kid*. It's *his* fault! Every damned bit of it—*his* fault! If that's what Donovan thinks making a first move is all about—then he doesn't understand as much as he thinks he does. Mr. Wiseman. Hell.

So he kept thinking from Hartford to New Haven to Greenwich to White Plains and right on toward Grand Central, only capable, even as the train pulled into the station's docks, of praying now for a small miracle—asking just to be able to smile.

Chapter Seven
MEETING AND PARTING

If he got off quick before them all, there they'd all still be, right behind him. He foresaw the uneasiness for him and the embarrassment of not introducing even a single one of his team-mates to Charlie, and of ignoring each one of them as they passed, and of their gawking at Charlie and him together. But if he waited, kept back in the car till they were all completely gone, she might wonder what held him up; and he'd have to answer questions about where they all were. He decided, as he looked out his window into the huge, dark cavern of Grand Central's docks, into which the train now slowed—screeching, jerking, to a final stop— upon the latter. He'd wait till they were all out and gone. And damn*nation* if he didn't resent, on top of all the other miseries of his life, the threat of embarrassment in front of his girl. This *waiting back*, too, he resented—though, resent it or not, he did find himself now waiting back as they all grabbed their things, and stood to go, and then filed out, and down, and away.

And *whose* fault *was* it that, as minutes passed, he found himself still ridiculously sitting there alone, acting like some pitiful little kid trying to avoid attention, or to get it? Or like some sorry crook ducking to hide? His fault? Or the ones who knew everything he was going through, north and south, and who, outside a scolding, annoying sermon or two, didn't send a word his way in eighteen godforsaken days of hell?

But now, he feared, was Charlie even there? He had a sudden fear, as well, that if she *was*, she would somehow, magically, see that right there inside his grip he kept his mother's unopened letter beside his father's loaded gun. But was she even there? Or might she have been, and then left, confused? As he moved along it, the now empty and weirdly silent car, its lights now blinking on and off and then going all dark, gave him a feeling of solitude as strange as any he'd yet had. He shook himself to get free of a dizziness. And he quick-stepped now because he feared that if he didn't get out fast from the empty, black-dark box, he'd get locked in for good. Then when he quick-stepped down to the dock plat-form, it was nothing but the tremendous cavern all around. But then, ahead, through a great arched, glass double door, he saw a chandelier-lighted lobby, wide, grand-looking. He walked faster. Faster. And then, under a four-sided clock, his hawks spotted—yes?—through the glass double door—a girl, looking this way and that, dressed in what he thought of instantly as New York finery—a light-pink dress and a white jacket and a white, feathered hat—*yes!* It was his girl! It *was* Charlie! Looking so beautiful, Lord save us!

And damn his leaded feet and all his pathetic, pitiful embarrassments and all the weight of that sorry, pitiful Cobb story in his grip. How could he keep a girl like this waiting? Or make her worry?

His limbs pained him. His heart pained him. It was so miserable and damned out of tune, and embarrassing, all this over-thinking and game-playing. This wasn't the way it was, ever, when he came home to Charlie from trips in the Sally. But he walked on fast. And now, yes, she saw him, too, as he came through the door! Bless her, she was clapping and pressing her hands together, as if she were praying some prayer of thanks. And he prayed his own instant prayer that it would be all of his sorry self now, every hardness of shame and pain and anger that her beauty melted when he touched and held her.

"Oh, Tyrus! You're *here*! I feared I'd come to the wrong place! But here you *are*! Thank goodness! Oh, I'm so happy!"

He smiled. His heart beat with every dangerous hope of happiness, his whole body lightening, as he now ran up to her. "No. No. No. No. You're in the right place, Charlie Lombard! And, oh my Lord, girl, you look so beautiful!"

She opened her arms to him. He dropped his grip, then took her and held her, lifting and twirling her. He smelled the flower smell in her hair, on her skin. He set her down, and she started to speak. But then he touched her lips, and, gently as he possibly could, raised her face up and kissed her. He felt the softness of her mouth, tasted her lips. And with the warmth now of their kiss, he felt all through him that *signs*, clear, clear signs, were being given to him for his life. Signs to change it. To change something.

"Grand Central Station, Tyrus!" she said, laughing, as they stood now before each other under that four-sided clock. "Can you believe we're here! And I give you my *word*, Mr. Cobb, New York is an absolutely amazing city! So many, *many* wonderful things! I promise you, we will have such a time!"

He smiled, acted almost as if he hadn't heard a word she said. But sincerely his words now just came. "I mean it, Charlie," he told her. "I don't think you've ever looked more beautiful. Your dress is the prettiest I ever saw, I swear. I swear it is the prettiest dress I ever saw."

She blushed, and laughed. "And I swear you know the right words to say to a girl, if ever a boy did." But it was no tease on him. She could tell his words were not just words.

Then out from under the four-faced clock they strolled, arm in arm, though with his free hand he hefted, too, the weight of his grip. And though the very first second in the street made it clear that this was no Detroit or Cleveland or Boston, but New York City—and the center of something, all right, and something hugely exciting—it just couldn't be now that they would explore it. Game time was game time, as they knew. And though there *was* time certainly for him to take her back now to join her mother at the St. Peter, which she told him was "such a beautiful place, right on Central Park, Tyrus, and right down from the Metropolitan!" he would have to get to the Webster before too long, to join the team, it being "the rule" that they went "as one to the game."

She slowed then, and stopped, right there in the bustle of the Grand Central outflow. No doubt she'd heard something in the way he spoke of his team obligations. She looked up at him. "Have things not changed," she said, "I mean between you and the team?"

He had had some kind of silent superstitious faith, he recognized now, that with his girl there watching, he would end his batting slump. Or if not he himself, some baseball god who watched over him would help him put Boston behind him and keep Doc White, for the time being, off his mind, because Charlie was there. But now what he believed was that if he didn't tell her the truth, he would get no hits today and fail at everything else on the field as well. So he said, "They haven't, Charlie. Things haven't changed. I'm afraid it's been a hard time so far, darn hard, to be honest. No signs of any real peace yet."

"I thought," she said, "when I saw this group of athletic-looking men . . . And then I didn't know . . ." She stopped, looked up at him, and smiled, fully beautiful, her brown eyes warm and a rose in her lips that, with the soft touch of a kiss, he thought, might cure what ailed a dying man. She touched his hand, the one that didn't hold his grip, and in that way of touching his hand she had that was like a magic knock on the closed door of him. "If I'm certain of anything, Tyrus," she said, ". . . if I am certain of *anything* in this entire world . . . it's that they simply do not know the Tyrus Cobb I know. . . . From the moment they know *him*, hard times can't last long. They simply cannot. Nothing could be more the truth, no matter what parts anyone might be from, nor whatever may have happened in the past."

He wouldn't be embarrassed in front of the world of New York faces here, but he could right now for love and comfort have put his head on her shoulder as he did after his father's death, when he broke down and cried. And, truth—it was an unexpected, confusing truth—but he felt a rush of even more special love for her now because her words made him think that it was *Tyrus Cobb*, and nobody else, who would have to introduce the real Tyrus Cobb to the world. Instantly, confessing this, knowing it, opened his heart—he felt it strong—right down to that place where sudden tears come from. But no breaking down now. He squeezed back the hand she'd touched him with and smiled, not just to send to her warm signs of gratitude, but to let her know (he wanted her to know it forever) that he felt a deep, real happiness in being grateful to her; that, in truth, he felt it like an honor to owe her thanks.

But then it was what hat *would* her mother wear? And would it be this beautiful white one that *she* would wear? And she would try to sit *where*? He made sure of everything as their cab—a snappy, canary-colored *automobile* with a black, foldable hood drawn up to shade passengers from the sun—turned up Fifth Avenue toward Central Park. It was the first automobile ride for both of them, ever. And in the fun and excitement, with her telling him about the many, *many* wonders of New York City (where she'd been now a whole day) and him now telling her about Louis Chevrolet and Olds and Ford and survival of the fittest and how if he had a dime he knew where he'd place it, all right, they both just started laughing, the horn of the cab croaking in tune and making them laugh even harder as they rode along, still laughing when they pulled up at last to the St. Peter, which surely was a fine place, right there across from Central Park and down from the Metropolitan. And he let her know, as he showed her every courtesy in parting, that the same true pleasure he took in being thankful to her, he took in being her gentleman.

In the locker room, three hours later, he would check with Armour, to see if he was right. And he was. The New York rotation was such that he would not face Chesbro again; and he had to admit in a secret place in his heart he was glad, for if he didn't hit the Happy One, he would feel he'd lost one of the few things he'd gained. Which could do *what* to Charlie's being out there watching? But at least he'd sniffed out now three bats that he didn't altogether despise from the team's pathetic store of runs-of-the-mill. Nor had anyone challenged his property claim. At least there was that.

With his own bone, in the locker room now beginning to stir, he finished work on the third stick, then took the chamois to his shoes. The minute was close. It was the voices of game time that could be heard now. And he knew, no matter what fancies he might entertain about a magic in his girl's being out there, watching him, and about his playing before her eyes like a knight of old trying to win his lady's favor, that what it is that gets a hitter out of a slump is just plain impossible to say. With what god, after all, does he have to get himself right? What prayer, what shutting down of mind, what deep promise to wait with patience gets it done? Brings back the swing that went *where*? In Boston, through that full agony of soft flies and pops and comebackers and getting fisted and getting fanned, he'd still kept up his discipline. Just trying to take the ball back up the middle. Just to meet the thing and take it straight back up the middle. Again and again and again. And today, would it finally come? that murderous bullet right over second: the one that *nobody* could get to?

But now no more questions. No more thinking. It was time. Armour called 'em up, read out the lineup. And just that fast, spikes began clacking over concrete. The boy rose and moved with the herd, and if he'd given no sign yet that there was some other Cobb, some Tyrus that none of them knew—still, in the first instant that the Tigers came into the light, he had the eyes of that secret boy out looking for a pair of Southern ladies far, far from home. One in a yellow hat with a white band. And one in a white hat with a feather.

He looked first to the third-base side and close to the field, where Charlie always sat in Augusta, and where she said she'd try to be today. Was she there? Was she? He didn't see. He looked and didn't see. The crowd was a big one. And wouldn't ya know it but ladies with hats were out in fair numbers (so civilized a recreation had this national game become, blast it!). But wait a minute, there they were! He could see, yes! And the two of them, Mizz Lombard *Ma'am* included, waving handkerchiefs like a pair of silly girls, all right, and didn't he love 'em. But he couldn't wave back. He just looked right their way, smiled, and tipped his cap, which he knew they saw, because there was Charlie grabbing her mother's arm and pointing and showing her, and then the two of them just flapping those hankies all the harder, right his way, as he stepped down into the dugout, trying hard not to laugh, especially in front of the Tigers, and in front of the gods, who might not like these little moments of happiness.

But now, still, could it be the time? Could now be the time for that sweet reward for a hitter's long suffering? He'd waited one hell of a long while. That's all he would think. No more. He wouldn't be such a fool as to think hot streak, or anything . . . not hot streak, not that weird beautiful opposite of slump, when the ball just comes in bigger and slower and, because slower, even still bigger till ya just kept tearing the thing apart!

No . . . No thinking. Especially not, when after McIntyre and Schaeffer and Lindsay, it was, just like that, Tigers by one, and only one out and nobody on, which meant he'd be making an appearance any moment now, in front of Charlie. As he stepped into the on-deck circle, with his three sticks, he wouldn't think anything, not even that Charlie was out there. He wouldn't think a thing. But there was Crawford, and damn the bastard if he couldn't hit, all right, slamming the second pitch to the gap for two bases, which meant it was, one more time, *"Cobb! Tyrus Cobb! Now batting for Detroit! Cobb, batting for Detroit!"*

And of course in no time it was that yap McGuire with some of his tired yapping about Cottonball County and such like, well, well, well, and what have we here? But the boy wasn't listening. Not a bit. Because, by God, he *was* feeling something. Like an aura, which was familiar to him. Down deep, like the smell of meat to a dog. But still he didn't think. He just tapped his steel and stepped in and bent to his crouch and fastened his split grip round the bat handle and sent his blue hawks out to claw on to the Highlander pitcher, Louis LeRoy.

And what the aura told him was that it *was* time, no matter if the whole world's eyes were on him. But he wouldn't think. Just level that swing and take it right back up the pipe—for which, nothing *better* than a belt-high, flattened-out fastball like the one Mr. Louis LeRoy did *now* provide, first pitch! And the great, big fatness of the thing, with so little on it, just splitting the plate! So *whack*! right bang up the middle! and so bullet-hard you—truth—could barely see that little white pill! And did he not tear out of that box to put serious tight knots in their guts. Hell yes he did. And in would trot Crawford, like nothin'. So hello, Charlie, girl! My good-luck charm! Wave me that hanky, Georgia girl!

They had cut the throw, to keep him from advancing. So just a single. And when he led off first, though he knew that hanky was there all right, he didn't go tipping his cap or anything (which he wouldn't do anyway, because this was business, that was pleasure). Nor did he open his mouth. But he sure wasn't shy and retiring, either. No time whatsoever did he waste before starting gleefully to torture LeRoy and the great first-sacker, Chase, with long, insulting leads and then lightning jumps back to first, worrying and forcing no fewer than *nine* throws out of the sorry LeRoy! Then after all this ineffectual watching of him, he *went*! breaking so hard that his jump, which was as good as it would be after he'd studied the man's move nine times and gotten the complete science on it, made their jaws drop. The breaking speed was the kind that turned jealous minds downright crazy hateful (*so* sorry, but how he did love this!). And hell if he wasn't down to second a solid hour before that smartmouth Mc-Guire's useless peg. But then Elberfeld gave him the hard "teach," nearly snapping his neck with the late tag. The boy spat out half a fistful of dust and was glad it wasn't his teeth, especially with his girl there. . . . But it was all right. Hell, he'd have done the same: tried to intimidate the guts right out of anybody who did to him what Tyrus Cobb just did to them, making a laugh out of their nine throws.

The New York crowd had been flat-out electrified by his speed, and was still full charged, he knew—from the buzz. And he knew how Charlie got the whole picture, because that girl knew the game. But business was business still, right here and now. He didn't say a word as he brushed off the dust. Wouldn't give Elberfeld the satisfaction. And immediately he took a long, torturing lead off second, keeping one hard eye on LeRoy and another hard eye on the second baseman, Williams, and the eyes in the back of his head on Elberfeld. Still no words now, the way there'd been back in Detroit (so maybe he *could* be the gentleman ballplayer, and good sport, after all). But words spoken or not, he'd have them all know exactly what this Cobb was saying, which was that he not only wasn't intimidated, he'd go *home* if they tried to pick him off and that ball leaked out to center just a little too far. No words, but his body's language and his maddening quickness and speed were a boast and a goading insult, a fact he couldn't help but enjoy.

He didn't score, Chase spearing Coughlin's grounder on the right-side hole and flipping to LeRoy in time. Beautiful play. Tyrus saw it over his shoulder. But he played a little hell with these Highlanders when he took off with the grounder and showed that speed. He was around third flying and, when that toss from Chase arrived at first, stomping right on the plate. Which would make imprints. And definite imprints, definite fear-inducing imprints: If you couldn't see the value of these, and that every moment has its future value, then where were you? Oh God, it was hell's own heaven of insane joy when you capitalized on earlier psychological intimidation. And every intimidating imprint made on others was a contract you made with yourself, either to make good on your threats, or feel the shame. But what places these contracts put one in! So exciting that . . . who *cared* if it involved risk of oneself (for to rattle 'em *good*, one had to do what a cautious soul would never do). The hell with the risks, and the embarrassing mistakes, too, because the immediate brain race over the wildly increased possibilities when earlier-planted intimidations, come their time, just cracked things wide open—was—well—one had to have felt such an exhilaration and freedom! But who ever feels this kind of joy except someone who never compromised himself in the first place!

These, though, for his girl, he put them in slightly different words, a bit gentler, a bit more modest, simple, were things that Charlie made him feel he could go right on about. No missing it, even, that there was a very warm excitement for her in hearing these kinds of things, as after what proved to be one turnaround day indeed, three hits and a walk in four trips (and the Tigers winning, 5-4, Cobb scoring the tying run in the ninth!), as after this wonderful, exciting day, hankies having flapped and waved over and again like happy pennants in the wind, they took that first real stroll along Fifth Avenue and then into Central Park, where they sat now on a bench beside a pond with swans. The mid-

September evening was as mild as the day had been electric. A bright crescent moon was up early in the blue-pink sky, over the lighted buildings. And it was New York.

"But it isn't, Tyrus, that we're here," Charlie said, "in Central Park! and that you've ordered up the moon the way you have, sir. . . . And by the way, no matter where we are, I will not be satisfied one bit until we find ice cream and lemonade. . . ." She laughed as she touched his arm. "But I mean this so truly. . . . It isn't any thing of this moment, that makes me say that when I'm with you, that the reason I'm here, the reason I came out every day in Augusta to see you play, is . . . well, there's something in a girl that wants a man to be, shall I say, mighty, courageous, and bold." She laughed again. "I'm sorry if I embarrass you, Tyrus, with such stupidities. You know I'm no fainting flower. I know you know that. And it just *is*—it's the champion in you. I knew it was real the first second I saw you. I think the most real I ever saw in any person in my life, or ever will see, *in my life*, and, well, it has made this girl's heart flutter right proper for her fella, sir. Can't be helped. I mean even the New York following spoke in, shall I say, warmest terms about *that Cobb*. And I don't know, is there anything that beats a much-begrudged compliment?" She laughed. "I was so proud. So proud. And Mama, call her an instant convert, will be there again tomorrow, I promise!" She smiled, looked at him, then lowered her eyes. "And then there's *you* . . . the boy who's with me here now, the one who makes me feel so beautiful."

He smiled, and took her hand. He closed his eyes a moment, nodded his head in a quiet yes. He paused—some time. Then, "Charlie," he said, "I've been thinking." And still he wondered should he just *not* say what had come to him, for what he would say would change this conversation and the feeling of the moment. But something in Charlie's loving words to him seemed, word by word, even to have brought it out—the feeling, so long with him now, that he had, even *more*, to open up his life to her. He knew too that it was in keeping with the person Charlie said he *was*—to tell her— "In this last month, Charlie . . . some days . . . I've been thinking that I might be, maybe. . . ." Still, though, it was hard . . . to *impossible*, to get out the words.

"Go on," she said, with an immediate soft encouragement, letting him know that whatever he needed to say, she understood, and was already there for him.

He looked at her, then lowered his eyes. "I mean, even good days, I've thought I might be just about all of the time completely on my own, *alone*. It's got so bad, I mean, let me admit it to you, Charlie, it's got so bad and . . . so crazy . . . there are times when I just sort of say forget it all and I *enjoy* running out the list of people who are not on my side, all the way up to the whole world, except . . . one." He held her hand more tightly. "But now, truly, I'm here with you, and I'm thinking that if there really is that *one girl* out there who loves a fella like me, then he goes from something like always and everywhere alone to never and nowhere. Just like that. And I think a change . . ." He looked at her, still so earnestly. "I mean, you've heard me go on now, about all that intimidating and stuff and putting fear in people's minds, on the field, and Lord knows I can get wound up, when it comes to the game. But, for life, what you do to me is the opposite. You say words that make my soul or my mind relax and, not go hard; and sometimes, these days, my mind gets so . . . I don't know . . . almost crazy, Charlie, and angry that I . . . I don't know. But, with you, I mean I can feel my whole self relax, and it's like a wall comes down between me and everything from right in this Central Park here to I don't know where all."

A pair of swans was gliding close toward them. She touched his cheek. Smiled, with all the quiet, wonderful power of a girl's tenderness. "Walk me down," she said. Then, as they stood by the pond's edge, and the pair of beautiful white birds floated past, "You've been through things, Tyrus, in the past month, things more exciting as well as things more heartbreaking, than most people will go through in their whole lives. I'm sure that's true. I know it is. And the heartbreak, it's why you're feeling so alone. But I promise, I am with you. Every minute, every second, I am with you." She touched his arm, and looked into his eyes. "I know there's a burden on your heart that I could never credit myself with having the strength to lift. But I am here for you. Not just the girl who loves you, but your . . . confidante, always. And as far as that helps any good beginning, ever in your life, as far as I can make you happy, and help you know your own goodness, that's how far I am happy."

He took her hand, and kissed it, holding it then against his cheek. He smelled the flower smell on her skin and kissed her hand again softly. They walked back up the slope then, and on to the paved path that led back to the street. On the full-lighted Fifth Avenue, buildings aglow, gaslamps running up and down in beautiful spectacle, people everywhere, they walked. He held her hand now tightly, to let her know how her words had touched him, heart and soul.

But suddenly, with the back of his other hand, he pressed each of his eyes hard. He couldn't help tears, even in the crowd, though he tried, with a jerking sigh, to stop himself. He breathed. Gritted his teeth. Breathed again, sharply. Then, "In March," he said, "she will stand trial. . . ." He couldn't say more. He took the back of his hand to his two eyes again, hard enough to pain himself.

Instantly, she pressed herself warm against him. She put both arms around him, as they walked, and set her head against his chest. "I will love you forever, Tyrus Cobb," she said. Then no more. She just held him as they walked, and, after a time, as they walked more easily, just warmly held his hand.

He breathed more fully. He laughed a short laugh that could any second have gone to tears. But he breathed more easily. And they walked more easily, down the gas-lit, beautiful, famed street. And then not a block farther down, and

just a half-block off to the left, with an organ-grinder's play-
ful sounds drawing their eyes, what would there be but a
crowd of happy-looking, still summer-dressed ladies and
men in boaters and children all gathered under an eye-
grabbing, everybody-come-on-in electric sign that said ICE
CREAM!

"Fate," she said, and looked up grinning, as she held
him again and squeezed him, keeping both her arms around
him as they walked up into the happy crowd. And when, a
tall glass of pink lemonade before her as well, she took off
slowly a first cold spoonful of ice cream, just a smear left on
the spoon, she said, "I have got to admit..." Then she
hushed a bit. "...these Yankees..." She laughed, but then
looked at the smear on the spoon, smiling. "They can indeed
make a fine ice cream."

They spoke no more that night of the boy's griefs. But
over the next days, as *that Cobb* continued to generate talk
among the New York bugs about his hitting and his blistering speed, playing well every game, and he and Charlie had
a time, all right, taking in not less than a multitude of
sights—things came out. About the bats, about the silent
treatment, about the warm-up batting line, about the shower
line, about the whole crowd of them, and about McIntyre,
but about Billy Armour and Bill Donovan, too, and about the
arrest, and about the coming trial.

In Cleveland already he had in his lone wanderings begun to take in the arts a bit, a museum and a concert hall. In
Boston, too. He found himself, in fact, liking such things very
much (nor did he fail in this regard to congratulate himself
on having chosen the life of a ballplayer—or, in this regard,
on being a loner—for how else would he have discovered his
interest in art and symphony music? Could he have found
such things out about himself in Atlanta? or with the frater-
nizers?). But in New York the culture, too, was altogether
another matter, with the Metropolitan and Carnegie Hall and
the bohemian element (which he let himself be very curious

about), with all their easels out in Central Park. And the power of the place, too—it about knocked the breath out of him when he and Charlie saw and walked the Brooklyn Bridge. And all the automobiles! You'd have to be a natural-born, plain fool, he thought, not to want to make yourself a part of this.

But when it all was with Charlie, the excitement, and the music, and art, it helped words come out. Some here. Some there. Until by the end, the two of them having talked often about what they meant to each other, and so what a girl means to a fella and a fella means to a girl, they came to talk about what a mother and father together mean to a child. And if no word got spoken of any rumors, even if they were front-page rumors, about any lover or any gun, there was an unspoken understanding that the best thing maybe about Charlie Lombard's taking the train to New York to meet Tyrus Cobb was that her being there helped him hold himself together when there'd been a tragic accident involving the two people, besides her, who made up the very center of who he was.

"My father," he said to her, as on what would be Charlie and her mother's last day, they sat together on that same bench in Central Park, near the pond. "I always said about him to Joe, Charlie, not just that he was the only man I ever loved, but that he was the only man who ever made me do his bidding. I guess I never mentioned that to you because it made me sound too darned stiff-necked proud and all, which I know it does, and which I am. But don't you think the two things go together? I mean that we love somebody who makes us understand we aren't going just to have it all our way, because our way might not be the right way, which right way he's going to hold us to, like it or not? Don't you think that that's not what we *don't* love but what we *do* love—about fathers?"

"Sometimes it's mothers for girls, and for boys, too, I think," she said. "But mostly fathers, for boys, I'm sure of that. And I'm sure we do love it, and need it—so much in fact that we'd make it up if we didn't have it. I mean a powerful, you know, *legend* of a person, who shows us the path, and puts us on it. And with girls . . ." She'd begun now to grin. ". . . Or most girls, anyhow, it's a gentle, but then strong-when-it's-time-for-it kind of fella that they like so very much to kiss." She laughed and smiled. She spoke easily and freely now, as the conversations they'd had over these last days had accomplished a good measure of emancipation. "But, you know, too, Tyrus, the way you've said, we need somebody also who just plain loves us no matter what we do, and someone who, the way you've told me about your mama, I mean somebody who feels that if we're *happy* that's a pretty sure sign we're going the right way. And that would be mothers just about all the time for boys, and pretty much mothers, too, I guess, for girls; though those *daddies*, they love just to keep on smilin' forever at their girls and see them happy, happy, happy, which is a thing we *do* adore. Not to say we'd ever take even the slightest advantage of it." She smiled, and winked. "But, seriously," she now said, "when you're growing up, if you have the two things, I mean a firm guide of a person and a forgiving heart of a person, I'm sure it doesn't matter what names the things go with, your mother or your father, just so long as you have the *things*."

He smiled. Took a breath. But now suddenly he bowed his head. And breathed fast. Again he was agitated, pained. He couldn't sit. He rose from the bench, found a good-sized stone, and whipped it hard into the pond, not to skip it but sink it. The swans, wings ruffling, turned away sharp when the stone broke heavily through the water's surface and plunged.

Immediately she came up to him. "Forgive me, Tyrus. I'm afraid I find out that it's not the time yet for some things, when I've already begun them. Forgive me."

"It's not you, Charlie. It's not you. It's me. With me, you can't tell what the right time is for things now, because I can go in no time, right out of nowhere, into some whole new feeling. If there's a good feeling, I swear, it's like the bad feeling is sitting there waiting and then just says, 'Not one more instant for that good feeling' and breaks the door down, just like that, and takes over. I mean, with me, it's like some sorry war veteran walking down the street and suddenly, out of nowhere, he remembers something he saw in some insane battle."

"It will take time, Tyrus. But there will come a time when that won't happen. And between now and then, it will happen less and less."

With his entire heart, he loved her. But he had to say, "Charlie, it's just so hard. It's this thing I've seen." He wouldn't name people, wouldn't say man or woman, even though he knew she would know whom he meant. "I mean when it turns. When someone of principle doesn't let principle keep selfishness out of the way anymore, just lets so-called principle turn into hard, selfish vengeance. Or someone who says follow your happiness follows happiness right into a selfishness just as hard as any. And then they meet, Charlie. Like a head-on train crash. It's tragedy. *That* is tragedy. God bless me. That train crash. That exact meeting."

She held his arm, touched his hand—then slowing, softening her voice, taking sincerest care with her words, "I think, Tyrus, that people get afraid," she said. She paused once more. ". . . so very afraid . . . that maybe the only thing there *is*, is themselves. Maybe like those ballplayers who can't take risks, and stay stuck in ruts, and go dead." She held his arm more tightly. Smiling, she still tensed her face, and spoke even more earnestly. "But that's what love's for. So you aren't ever afraid, thinking there's nothing but your dead self, stuck in a rut. When you love, you go out of yourself every generous moment, every loving moment, until you know what I know, and that's that love is true and fear's a lie. The only thing that hardens for people who love each other is their determination *never* not to love each other."

He nodded, and closed his eyes, as if to place and secure her words forever in his mind. But now once more, as if in accord with some mysterious, gentle tact, they went no further with a conversation that they both sensed had reached the point where silence is best. Healing, as they understood now, unforceable, could come only in gradual steps, over lengths of time.

Sweet sorrow of parting, then, it must be. The next morning he would see his girl and her mother off at Grand Central. They passed once more under the four-sided clock and then stood by the double glass door. "Funny how ya love trains, and then ya don't," he said. "Angels, they bring your girl to meet you, and then big, black devils, they take her on back home. Sort of like words. 'Hello' we love, and 'good-bye' we don't love."

"No," she said, " 'good-bye' we don't love." She paid no mind then to her mama's being there. She put her arms around the boy and held him, resting her head against his chest. "But *you'll be on a train home soon*—those words I love."

There was a low blast of whistle. It was time. They had to let each other go. But as the whistle sounded again, they still stood with each other. Then Charlie's mother, gruff, smiling, "Oh, for heaven's sake, kiss her, boy, it's time to go."

The two lovers smiled at each other, embarrassed, Charlie with a tear now in her eye. And he did, he kissed her, if about as clumsily as that first time. But the sweet taste was always the same. And in the window as he stood on the platform waving good-bye, he watched a handkerchief bobbing till he could see it no more.

His last game against the Highlanders turned out to be a bad one. Hitless in three trips, he singled his fourth but was out by a mile trying to stretch it to two. Nor was he satisfied that with this move he put the idea of threat in Highlander minds more than the idea of fool. Then back out in center, right at the wall, just come now to sit there, was a man wearing a marker the boy was soon positive he'd never forget, an alpaca jacket. A self-appointed umpire, right out of some dark corner of hell, this jacket was yawping, "Yerrr OUT! Yerrrr OUT! HOTSHOT!"—and with a kind of sick fury that the boy, who'd heard a lot, hadn't heard yet. "Yeah, Cobb. I know you! I know who you are, hotshot! I know your mama, too, hotshot! Though I can't know your daddy anymore, can I! Can I, hotshot! But maybe you don't know your daddy either. That's what I hear, hotshot! That's the word from home, Cobb! That's the word from home!"

It happened late, with two outs in the bottom of the eighth with the very next pitch an inning-ending strikeout. And the Tigers would go down after failing in the top of the ninth. And it came so fast, out of nowhere, that the boy wondered if he was really hearing what he was hearing. But, as *always* with such things, it was real, all right. And he knew, the first second he looked back and saw the red-lipped mouth that went with it, that with a vengeance he would remember that alpaca jacket all his born days.

Just one in a crowd, that's all it took, he thought, to run a stain through something as fine and beautiful and good as what Charlie had made of his last several days. And the jacket's words against Charlie's: it was so hell-miserable that it would be the jacket's, not hers that he thought about all that evening's train ride to Philadelphia. So slow and careful you had to be, building back your mind's health. But the furies eager to tear it down needed no time whatsoever. They had the echo of that cripple-minded troll's words taking over his whole world while they put beyond the short little space of the next horizon Charlie's waving handkerchief.

And that night, as he lay back on his bed in the Hotel Belhaven in Philadelphia, sleepless for hours, he thought, after four nights without it in New York, that he'd place his father's gun once more under his pillow. God damn that alpaca troll. But taking the pistol out again, slipping it apart from his mother's letter, brought on a hot, sick arousal in his loins. And that voice. "That's the word from home, Cobb!" But he thought then in his arousal of the target, that face from somewhere. Not the troll's. The one his father's gun made him hot to find, and put a bullet in. Kill that face, or he'd have trouble maybe from his father's ghost. Or maybe the target was just Tyrus Cobb, and he kept that gun close in case he needed to finish himself.

That night in his dreams, Charlie turned to him, but she was the dancing girl from the Union House, who laughed and then walked up to him, slowly, and put her warm lips to his ear and whispered, "Poor little Charlie drowned in a river." She laughed again, but then softly closed her eyes and held her mouth half open to be kissed. And with wild arousal he kissed her. But then he broke away and said he hated damned women like her because they made him feel ashamed. His mother, that's who his father's gun was for; and she made him feel ashamed of himself. Then it was Reverend Minifield, telling him that without Jesus Christ our Lord it was impossible for the proud, hard part of ourselves, the part that threw stones, ever to forgive and stop hating the part of ourselves of which it was ashamed. Humanly impossible. But he said to Reverend Minifield, "Render unto Caesar what is Caesar's. You can't give me, preacher man, what I need to become a record-breaking major-league ballplayer."

Chapter Eight

A DISGRACE TO THE GAME

That morning, in the City of Brotherly Love, while Charlie's train neared home in Augusta, he was thinking that for now, for his own mind's safety, he would have to keep on splitting himself in two. As he put the pistol back in its place in his grip, he was relieved, even, that he hadn't shown the Tigers anything yet of that Tyrus Cobb Charlie knew. First off, there'd be the risk of offering his friendship to their confirmed damned hostility, a move that the Tigers, outside a feeble word or two from Donovan and Armour, had given him no sign he could place much hope in. And then, sure enough, wouldn't there be some still, little, conscientious voice in him saying, "You've started things in the right direction; you can't turn back once you've started." Which would mean then the pain of ignoring such a voice, because ignore it he would. And wouldn't he be even worse off with the team than he was before he made his friendly move, if he took a few steps forward only to retreat right back? It was just for a while, anyhow, this continuing to divide himself. As Charlie said, he'd be on a train home soon, and with her he could put himself back together again in no time.

But what did it say that he was in fact relieved, too, that Charlie's train was a full day gone? *Rationalization*, it was a word that by the hour now he was coming better to know the meaning of. No true conversation with his conscience, or with Charlie, just an easy yes-saying to himself, which made things easy in the same way that separating himself off from others made things easy, sick easy. No outside challenges. Nobody's words but his own. And so no healthy changes. But for right now he *needed* things to be easy. And if that was a rationalization of a rationalization, so be it. The fact remained. He had too many other things, things like Doc White, and his survival, to worry about to be working on cooperativeness, which, as he damn well knew, could kill him by making him soft.

But as a ballplayer, where would he be if he took things the easy way like this? He knew where he'd be. Was it not his deepest secret pride, in fact, that no ballplayer who ever lived knew better than Tyrus Cobb where he'd be. And what if gradual healing lost all it had gained if you stopped it, even "just for a while"? What if there was an actual moment when a point of no return *was* reached and "just for a while" became forever? A point when you became a complete sorry slave to the easiness of your deadly rationalizations, split off from your good side for the rest of your life? That he could become a whipped slave to a sickness, he knew once again now from his uninterrupted hours of wound-licking after the jacket spat out "the word from home."

But not an hour later, he let himself take what he knew to be a sweet, unhealthy satisfaction as, unbeknownst to the man, standing the other side of a column from him in the Belhaven lobby, he caught a few choice words of the White Rat. He could have moved, or let McIntyre know he was there. But he didn't. And after all, why would he, when these were the words he was catching? "Yeah, well, life goes on, or it don't go on—dependin' on how you decide. Ya come up to a crossroad and you can rejoin the human race or you can take it out on the human race. And that'd be up to the individual himself and what he's got in him. As for me, I ain't gonna make reclaimin' that johnny-reb sonofabitch my business. Don't expect it." So yes, and damned *right*—if he knew it was unhealthy, was it not still a sweet-sick joy to have suspicions dead cold confirmed again and to *know* he could expect nothing from this Yankee bastard through all the world to come? *This* made things easy, all right. He found himself liking very much, too, that he didn't know who it was McIntyre was speaking to, because then he could make it any one of them, which (though he knew that this sort of putting a mark on all of 'em was just moving in an old mind-groove of his) he was sure was fair enough. Whoever it was, though, may have noticed him because the conversation ended abruptly and the men moved off.

He took to the Philly streets when they were gone, feeling good to be alone again. And he was just about completely satisfied, too, that he'd done no cheap spying on that rat's privacy. What it was, was coming into possession of some hard evidence to which he had a perfect self-defensive right. So he insisted (enlisting in his mind even Charlie's approving word), as he continued tight-jawed through Independence Square and into the yard of Independence Hall and saw the cracked Liberty Bell. He read on plaques about The Society of Friends and refuges for men of conscience who wished to be guided by the Inner Light. And where did Tyrus Cobb's inner light lead? That there were signs to read in this life and that conscience was a guide, who knew better? But he knew just as well that conscience could trick you into self-submissions and false reverences and pieties so that you had to watch out for it. It could be as violent and rotten as the White Rat himself, who'd drag you to his little "crossroad" and rip off half your life so you could be granted the great happiness of joining *his* society of friends. Well, not so simple, my White Rat friend. For Tyrus Cobb intends, maybe just as you say, to take it out on the human race—but *then* to rejoin the human race. First hard, then soft. And he doesn't want to hear just now about irreversible first directions, though with pleasure he'd take one to avoid you and your kind.

Against the great Mack Men—Bender, and Waddell, and Plank and company—he had a respectable run, one for four the first four games and two for four the fifth, with one screaming double off the Chief; and another screaming double (after much conversation and taunting and prophecy) off the Rube, a very notorious southpaw; and a sweet bunt single off the A's other big-name lefty, "Gettysburg Eddie." And he scored every game, and he knocked in three, and he stole two bases—one of them third, under a very hard late tag, for which he made a silent vow of revenge against the City of Brotherly Love and all its third basemen, present and to come.

He let the time pass on without opening his mother's letter. He kept it tucked inside the *Lives*, every day resetting his father's gun beside that book, which he left buried in the grip. And on the train to Washington, while he wrote Joe (telling him now about the black ashes) and Charlie, he composed no letter of response to his mother, rather calculated how much time would have to pass before she'd begin feeling some pain, worrying whether he knew what he knew. For this is what he wanted to happen. He wanted, too, to signal difference. And this was a good way, not writing. For hadn't he written back every single time, and right away, when he was in the Alabama-Tennessee and the Sally?

Against the Senators, he raised his average to .260. But in the last game of the series he made a complete and perfect jackass of himself, coming in on a line drive that sailed on him. He tried to stop it with a desperate stumblebum leap but felt the sailing ball rip a hole in his glove as he tripped backpedaling and fell flat on his backside. Nothing worse. *Nothing*—than having fast work to do, getting up and chasing an error you made in front of a world of staring eyes. He felt puke-sick in his gut, his legs trembling, as he ran to the fence and picked the ball off it and dutifully, but with a strengthless arm, made the relay to O'Leary.

"Nice catch, Cobb!" "Yeah, nice catch! You really had that one figured out!" "Nice catch, Cobb! Nice catch!" "Yeah, nice *catch,* Cobb!" "Yeah, nice *catch!*" Over and over he heard it from the Washington chorus, and he wanted now truly to stand down the mob. It got so bad that, with no beautiful pink dress there, no white hat, or handkerchief, the thought of the girl he loved made him suddenly crazy even to throw away everything, cut every last attachment, so he could stand hard against the entire goddamned world. Heart and mind shut hard, he was an inch, right now, from turning and inviting the full two thousand onto the field and then inviting the first one who wasn't too yellow, to step forward. He would laugh when not *one* of 'em did. But now he'd lost the right to say a word. He *had* now to be the gentleman and stand quiet and take it. The only thing that could cross the wall, after Cobb's bungle, was that jabber of the apes.

But McIntyre was enjoying himself, too, he saw. And there was supposed to be respect and support among players, no turning on each other like this! And who *didn't* make errors? The reaction shouldn't be different for Cobb, God dammit! But with every "Nice catch!"—and they kept coming in a nonstop song—McIntyre shook his head laughing. And wasn't it funny, all right! So specially funny when it was Cobb! Tyrus glared at his fellow outfielder, who kept laughing, as the chorus kept hooting. "Oooh, look at his puss, will ya!" "Hey, sorehead, nice *catch!*" "Nice *catch,* ha! ha! ha!" They saw his face as he glared at McIntyre, who kept laughing. "Hey, *sorehead,* nice *catch!*" The hoots kept coming, now louder; and McIntyre kept cackling.

Tyrus turned and, out from his position, took a step toward his teammate. He was near exploding, though the game was beginning again, the pitcher winding. He didn't care! He didn't care a damn, even if he'd make world news, let alone the *Atlanta Journal*! He let it out! "You call that team spirit, McIntyre! Eh!" He shouted out, and caught his teammate's ear, all right. "You call that playing for the *team*, you sonofabitch! You expect me to do everything humble and quiet. But no rules for you, eh! Everything's *funny* for you! Well you can drop dead where you stand for all I care! You *hear that*! You can drop dead right where you goddamn stand!"

The boy knew he was bringing on a strange crisis now, further and further with every word. Here it was right in the middle of the game! But he didn't care. In fact, all the goddamned better. Kill that little voice of yellow conscience. Hell yes, he'd be disappointed now if this game didn't break wide open and he and McIntyre didn't have it out right then and there!

He didn't look at the play. He kept his face to his teammate-enemy. "You think it's so goddamned *funny*, you Yankee sonofabitch, I say you can rot in hell!"

It was Donovan on the mound, and the pitcher was beginning to catch wind of the disturbance in his outfield—and rather than come to the plate, he turned, awkwardly in the middle of his delivery, stopped, broke his rhythm, to look back at his teammates.

McIntyre was turned now, also, to Cobb. "Ya cracker piece a garbage, the only time ya open yer trap in three and a half weeks is t' let everybody know how much yer worried about number goddamned one! Stuff it up yer cracker backside, ya hear me!"

Things like this just didn't happen on the field. Never. There was a feeling of real strangeness. But the hoot chorus, caught up in the mad novelty, stepped up its chanting to insane. "Nice catch nice *catch* nice *catch* nice *catch* nice *catch* nice *catch*." And that did it. Tyrus threw down his glove. He broke completely out of his position and started striding hard toward his teammate-enemy. He could feel himself at the center of a real chaos now, and he felt a new pain and puke-sickness and trembling. But he didn't care if this was the end of everything, the game included, or even if he made it *impossible* his girl wouldn't get the word, he wasn't going *yella*. He was going *straight on*, each step a goddamned contract to take the next. And McIntyre himself, for all his previous team preachments wasn't showing the first bit of restraint. He couldn't now either. And the game was past shambles. So the hell with it all. He came. And Tyrus came. Step after step after step, they kept coming. Time had to be called. Teammates, led by Donovan, began making their way fast to the outfield. But something was going to happen, no matter what.

"Come on, ya miserable piece-a-shit-goddamned-insane-cracker! Just keep comin' and see what it gets ya!"

"Is that what ya have to say to me, McIntyre! After all this time, is that what you have to *say*, you second-rate son-ofabitch. I'll tell you what I think of you! I'll tell you exactly what I think!"

The boy now exploded into a full run right at the left fielder as the chanting crowd grew still more frenzied. And McIntyre, seeing the boy now break into full speed, came on full speed to meet him. Neither could stop. It was too late for anything now but total head-on attack.

The boy, though, watched things. He watched McIntyre's right fist cocking for a punch as the left fielder tore over. He slowed his own speed, to fool the Rat, and then changed his pace to full speed ahead again and exploded head first into McIntyre's chest with a vicious tackle, wrapping his arms around the left fielder and grappling him to the ground before he could throw that punch. But now the two of them wrestled in full clumsy violence on the grass, striking each other where they could with awkward short punches and ugly hammer blows.

The crowd was roaring, hooting, chanting its chant. If there was disbelief that this was actually happening, there still was insane delight. And laughter at the sheer ridiculousness—for no matter how seriously these combatants might have detested each other, they fought about as grace-fully as hair-yanking washer women.

Yet the two grotesques looked sure ready enough to kill each other, rolling over the ground and striking wildly to tear one another apart. Now McIntyre tried to butt Tyrus's face with his forehead, but the boy stopped the man by catching his chin in the palm of his hand and was now pressing McIntyre's head back by driving up the heel of his palm. The man strained back with all the muscles in his neck, his chin digging into the boy's hand. "You miserable cracker shit, I'll kill you! I'll goddamn *kill* you!" The veteran spat through his teeth, the veins in his neck seeming ripe to explode. And on his part, Tyrus did his best not just to shut McIntyre's mouth but to make the man's teeth break against each other as he rammed up the veteran's jaw. And then he pulled the trigger, firing off his real mind. "You second-rate bastard, you'll never drive me out! You'll NEVER drive me out, you second-rate bastard! I'm better than you and you know it!! I'm better than all of you Yankee bastards EVER were!!"

"Break it up boys! Break it up! We're a TEAM, for Chris-sake!" It was Donovan, now come running in to restore peace, or at least separate his center and left fielders. Mc-Intyre at that juncture had rolled on top of the boy, and the pitcher grabbed the veteran by the waist and was dragging him off. "Let me at the miserable piece of garbage! The smartmouth-sourpussed-bastard-sonofabitch! Let me at him! Ya shoulda heard what he just said! I'll kill the cocky bas-tard!" McIntyre was screaming. And Donovan, as he lifted him off by the waist began repeating "Easy, Matty. Easy, for Chrissake. Easy. Easy now. Easy. This is crazy."

"What the hell's goin' on here! Who in hell started this?" Armour had now arrived. "I spend all my time tryin' to make you bastards into a team and LOOK at this! What in HELL is this? I've never seen anything like it in all my time! It's a disgrace! It's a goddamned DISGRACE!"

The two combatants—now separated—Donovan and

Armour between them—began shouting over shoulders: "That sorehead bastard started it! You shoulda heard him spoutin' off! I tell ya, he started the whole thing!" "That's a lie and you know it! That's a *lie*! And what are you doin' talking my way now. You haven't talked to me in weeks, and not a damn *civil* word yet! NOT ONE! Ya wanna know what's to blame. THAT'S to blame! YOU'RE to blame!"

"All right, I've heard ENOUGH! I'd throw ya both outa here, but we got a game to play, for Chrissake, and I ain't got no subs. So SHUT UP, both a ya! And anything like this comes up again, I'll see ya run outa The Show! I swear I'll do everything I can to get ya OUT, 'cause ya don't *deserve* bein' in, not respecting the game, for God Almighty's sake! Now play ball, ya hear me—or ELSE! We gotta GAME here! Remember that! And, god*dammit*, after this is over, I'll see you two in my quarters at the hotel—IMMEDIATELY."

The Washington bugs kept up their "Nice-Catch!" chant through the rest of the nine innings, punctuating the steady bass with a melody of laughing insults and goads calculated to set the Detroit outfielders further against each other. All as it was their free-speech right to do, from their side of the wall. And Tyrus, his whole body and mind on fire, had to stand and take it, as it was his gentleman-ballplayer's duty to do. And he got no hits. And the Tigers lost (But so *what*? Maybe this was the only *good* thing!). And after the game, at the hotel, he had to go, head down like a whipped dog, and wag his tail and bow his head even further for his manager. And, hell enough that he had to share the space of an outfield with him, he had to be then, too, in the same room with the Rat.

"Ya know, I don't care who did start it," Armour said, as he had his outfielders with him in his suite at the Washington Winston. He had stood glaring, and was now pacing before them, having seated them in armchairs some six feet apart from each other. "I'm so sick a both a ya I can't even damned speak. In all my time I ain't seen it. Two players on the same team attackin' each other in the middle of a game! Any time's bad enough. But in the middle of a *game*! That's what I call a manager's truest *hell*. And I don't wanna hear your damned self-serving jabber about whose fault it was and who started it! Believe me, I DON'T! You, Cobb, you don't think a rookie's gotta swallow nothin'. And you, Matty, you think 'cause this kid don't wanna swallow *whatever* it is you think he's supposed to swallow, then you have the holy-God's obligation to shove every piece a shit there is right down his throat! The last shall be last—period. Well, I'm gonna offer one managerial word and one only—to both a ya. And that's *stop*! Ya just *stop*! ya hear me. Ya *stop* right now—or else you're both gone. Because you're both equally damned crazy. I ain't sayin' no more. Not a word more." He scowled at the two of them, back and forth, his teeth set in deepest anger and frustration. He breathed a last snort of contempt, looking as if he wanted to spit at them. "Now *get outa here*!" he said, and turned his back on them.

Tyrus wasted no time. He rose and beat the veteran to the door, then walked straight down into and across the hotel lobby and out the door into the streets of the capital, which, when he'd ridden them in the team's carriage after the game, sitting as far apart from the rest of 'em as he could, he had imagined on fire, the sacred buildings going up in flames as Confederate grays roamed with torches and naphtha from one to another.

And he wouldn't be suckered now. He would not be suckered. There was the capitol dome, rising up over Capitol Hill; and, down Pennsylvania Avenue, there would be the White House. Impressive. Impressive. Impressive. And beautiful. Oh so beautiful. But he wouldn't be suckered. He walked half crazy down the streets, his shoes pounding the sidewalks. He didn't look at people. He rushed by them. He imagined himself a Confederate raider with a flaming torch. Could he set the White House on fire? Could he set the Capitol on fire? He sure as hell could. He wouldn't be suckered by the beauty and the impressiveness, or by anything that stood in his way.

He walked for hours, thinking about what happened that day, about that filth McIntyre, about the chanting Washington mob (spewing out whatever fighting words they wanted, with their privilege), about what Armour had said about his not respecting the game (And to *hell* with the game, if it came to that! He'd rip up the whole rotten world rather than be a sucker for anybody or anything! But who knew more about what the game meant than Tyrus Cobb, after all? Who had more real respect?). Goddamn them; he'd burn this town down in a damn minute! Capital of *what* nation?!

And he'd be bitterly disappointed if he thought that his instant, springing departure from that room at the Winston hadn't struck Armour as a sharp-as-hell comment, indeed an unyielding statement of legitimate grievances. A sign clear as hell that he wouldn't be suckered or stopped by the first word, or the last, coming from any Armour. And that he wouldn't stay in the same room with any McIntyre even a second longer than he had to. He thought this in an implacable bitterness as later that evening, his anger not even slightly abated, the team's train rolled west out of Washington toward Chicago—and Doc White.

How the hell could Armour compare him evenly to McIntyre? Anybody with legitimate brains could see where the trouble started. Cobb's *wrong* because he refuses to swallow the treatment he gets? He's *wrong*?! And McIntyre's just the same, no different, for trying to cram things down Cobb's throat! It's all equal! If that's the world, the truth, the law, the rule, the whatever the hell have you, then let it burn! For a while, an hour, maybe two hours (he couldn't have guessed), he let himself enjoy the thought that his dream about McIntyre and his mother was true, Cicotte the pimp. He let himself feel the sweet-Satan's pleasure of a perfectly unalloyed hatred. And he let his overhearing of McIntyre's response to the word about the Royston accident, as it spread from goddamn Armour probably through goddamn Donovan to the goddamn world, with that *Jacket* in it, serve as evidence that his hatred was justified.

He had a door to his compartment this time. A metal door, the lock and latch of which he looked at now for the sixth or seventh time in an hour. He'd sealed himself safely in, he saw again. He went back to his hell-hatred, to whip it up once more. To whip it up . . .

But Oh God *Jesus*! he thought (as extremes in his mind once more stepped smack into each other: his determination to be damned, if that's what it took to win, evoking now his need to be reclaimed) how could he ever get all this puke-sick hell cleared out of his life? How? Somebody tell him! The pain. How could he get rid of it? The sick pleasures? "You tell me, Lord," he prayed. "And get me out of here. Bring me to Charlie Lombard before it's too damned godforsaken late . . . forgive my curse words, Lord.

"But You're gonna have to forgive me, too, for the fact I don't believe that goodness is enough. When I think of McIntyre's face, those veins in his neck, his Yankee threats against my *life*, I can't turn the other cheek. Goodness isn't enough. Its own reward, *not* enough. And Armour trying to force me to my knees with his threats and coercions, saying I'd be gone if I didn't play by the rules; trying to instill some kind of phony-intimidating guilt in me, saying we were a baseball 'first,' fighting each other in a *game!* I can't not resent that kind of manipulation. A manager's 'hell.' A 'disgrace'! And you *stop, right now*, he says. And you *come, immediately*, he says, to my quarters. I want to clean and clear my head, Lord, but I can't.

"I *can't*, even though I know that against Doc White it might be my one and only hope. I know it—making my head pure clean. I don't have the science on that breaker. I don't have it. And now, *of all times*, we're heading for Chicago. I didn't lie. I told that McIntyre my mind. And I don't give a damn—forgive me, Lord, this cursing—but I don't care if they all did hear. I *do* believe I'm better than they are—and that they're jealous as hell of me. They can't move the way I do. They don't see the way I do. They can't put the ball where they want to, the way I know I can. They can't tell when opportunities are coming. I know they can't. I've seen them miss chance after chance, and never mark down anything in their dead minds, after either a success or a failure. They learn nothing. They make no advances. They don't know how to make things happen on the field, to *make* the enemy do what they want. They don't know the long-term value of taking chances, of making a fool out of yourself now (and who cares! who cares if you get called crazy!) for the sake of the new ballplayer you'll become. The way I told Charlie. And I know You know her. If there's anything true in the world, You know her, Lord. Love is true and fear is a lie. If she didn't get that from You, where'd she get it.

"But this Doc White, I could get killed by that man. I wrote a blood-oath with my soul when I let it out that they would *never* drive me off and that I was better than they *ever* were. I know this blasting away, this running at the mouth, could turn into the last cheap, bitter irony against Tyrus Cobb, who might not be back after what Chicago does to him. And I feel it deep now, *deep* as my life, that I should pray. Like a *beggar* I should pray. Who on earth knows this need more than damned Cobb? Minifield as much as said. But I can't. I can't! *Not now.* Because it's war here, Lord; it's war, and I can't turn the other cheek, or clear my mind of the hell on earth that's in it. Forgive me. I'm not in Your Kingdom, where it would be different."

He was so near waking by the time he finally fell asleep that he was remembering his dreams even as he dreamed them. He could hear and feel the train rolling while at the same time he was Caesar with the face of Robert E. Lee, a map of the North spread before him in his tent, the Yankee cities he'd played in all marked in black—Detroit, Cleveland, Boston, New York, Philadelphia, Washington—and now a red circle set around Chicago, toward which an arrow pointed from the east, an arrow that moved, inching closer and closer to the red circle, indicating the continuing westward movement of the train.

"One might make peace with the whole world," this dream-Caesar said, running his forefinger like a ferule in a sweep around the marked cities, "and perhaps that way have it all. Or one can *conquer* the whole world, and *that* way have it all." He clenched his sweeping hand now into a fist, pressing it down hard on top of the red circle. "Let me be the madman who takes the second route rather than the fool who takes the first. And let me remember," he said, now standing, thoughtful, making both hands into fists and tapping them together before his chest, "that the ruler who would rule everything *must fear* becoming absolutely nothing: that every day he *must fear* the closer approach of total loss and shame: that for the accomplishment of absolute power what is demanded is absolute fear of failure."

Chapter Nine
MOVED FROM CENTER

With every breath he breathed, as the team's train clanked in over Chicago's far-spread steel delta of docking rails, he took in the stink of the city's hog and beef slaughter. This whole place was *gone* thirty-five years ago, he thought, as he looked out, running his eyes over the city's smokestacks, seeing buildings taller than he'd ever seen anywhere else, breathing in that stockyard stench. All of it, burned to the ground. Ashes to ashes. But their fire was not like Atlanta's. No one to blame for the conflagration here except God. Makes things a helluva lot easier (the mind being naturally too loyal and pious to complain long against the Lord); and he was certain that these Yankees here, in their sweet ignorance of real devastation, got past their losses the day they got new roofs over their heads. And again he confessed an envy, at the very least for their freedom from the weight of resentment. He could smell some big money too in that shambles-reek. And see the energy of these nothing-very-dark-to-recall ignoramuses in those buildings taller than New York's and these endless docking rails, which the train now moved through even more slowly. A huge bloody sledgehammer and reeking butcher knife. That's how he thought of this place. But he had to admit he liked the muscle, and even the stench in the air.

He had some fine Chicago adventures, too, in the first game with the Sox. They'd seen him bunt before and were afraid as hell of his bunting skill (so thank you, Papa Leidy) and of his speed (thank only God and the Chitwood half of his blood). So they played him in very close. And he set up for a bunt, all right, and went into his bunt action, to draw them even farther in—but then stepped back and took his bat fully back and slashed a murderous shot right past third and into the corner for an easy two, which turned into three after a speed-forced bungle in left!

And in the sixth, after singling, he danced off first well beyond the normal tether—but always sprang back too fast for them to get him, for all their furious efforts (which, as the world's number-one believer in the significance of small measures, he attempted to frustrate just that much more by foot-tapping first base toward second every time he returned to the bag: the base posts allowed just an inch, but if one cared and knew, he took it). And he wouldn't fall for Schalkey's snap throws from the plate, of which there were three (expressive indeed of the man's violent, frustrated animosity; and a very sweet stimulus to the base runner, who remembered this catcher's mouth and who prayed hard for an overthrow). And he got a very sizeable jump on a 2-0 pitch to O'Leary (not fearing with that count any sneaky little pitchouts, which he'd noticed previously that Schalkey telegraphed with a slightly farther spread-out right foot, one he'd named the quarter-duck). And so he *went*! And that fine little devil O'Leary played it like a perfect, nerve-shattering hit-and-run, ripping the ball right into the hole vacated by the second baseman, who'd gone to cover second. Tyrus didn't hesitate then. He took off for third at a speed this city full of butchers hadn't seen before.

Nor did he hesitate at third! He had looked over his

right shoulder as he tore around second and saw that the ball, while it wouldn't get through the gap, would take the center fielder, a righthander this time, enough to his left so that he'd have to stop and turn and change his momentum when he threw. And he'd seen the shortstop make himself a target for the cut-off, which all would come, Cobb being too far on his way to third and O'Leary holdable at first. They'd be looking to stop O'Leary from taking second, conceding third to Cobb. So he now did the insane thing and kept on going, not slowing down at third an instant, indeed turning his speed *up* and heading straight for home!

The White Sox in disbelief saw what was happening, and, if confused by the surprise attack, were enraged and determined as hell to nail this upstart madman! So there stood Schalkey ready to block the plate with his life. And here came this cocky-insane teenager (who had the look, however, of someone who'd read with a very keen understanding those ordinances of the game that gave him as runner a right to the basepath). And here came the throw, rushed, a bit up the line, and late enough so that Schalkey had still to be looking for it as Tyrus came in.

The boy had the throw beaten and knew it. But, by-God tasting now every bitter damn syllable he'd had to swallow from this smartmouth Schalkey when he'd faced the Sox (and Doc White) in Detroit, he let the vulnerable, stretched-up catcher have it full-speed with his left shoulder and then drove him right over the plate and down into the batter's-box dust.

"*Saaaaafe!*" was the call from old Jimmy Conlon. But there'd be no chance now for Tyrus to stand up proud and self-congratulatingly to brush the dust from himself, triumphing that he'd made it home from *first* on a godblessed *single*! For an insanely enraged Schalkey had faster than the sound of Conlon's call gathered himself out of the dust and jumped the boy and begun slugging to kill. And all the White Sox squad were gathering faster round the fracas than sharks to blood. They'd all love a piece of this hot-shot bush baby, who sure as hell could bring it out in people. First to home on a single. It would be the goddamned *last time* this cracker with the sour puss pulled that maneuver. And the cheap, easy taking out of their man, which could've been for life!

"Ya dirty-playin' sonofabitch, ya think it's just fine to end a man's career! Well we'll end you, ya hot-shot prick!" "We'll goddamn stuff ya with dirt and feed ya to the dogs, ya murderin' sonofabitch!" "Take him, Ray! Take the dirty-playin' sonofabitch by the throat and rattle the fuckin' life out of him!"

So the song from the White Sox. But where were the Tigers? *Nowhere:* that's where. So the boy said over and over and *over* to himself in his room after the game as he thought back on the fight. It didn't last long. Conlon broke it up in no time. And he had no injuries, other than a five-inch cut on the back of his shoulder, which wouldn't stop him a minute. No let-up, then. Just a goddamned delicious sense of bitterest resentment. Where were the Tigers? *Nowhere!* Not a single one of 'em got up off the bench! They sat there and watched, no doubt cheering Schalkey on! After he'd scored on a *single*! So why should he *ever* be *anywhere* for them?

And goddamn Chicago, calling him a dirty player! As he'd stood, fists iron-clenched, pressing hard against the outstretched, separating arm of Conlon, who was holding Schalkey back with his other, he'd had his words for them! "The path belongs to the runner! Go read the rules, if ya can read! And if you don't like 'em, take it up with Gentleman Ban. In the meantime, you stay the *hell* out of my way! I promise you, I'll take what belongs to me every single time! You mark that down: *Every single time!*" He was pressing harder and harder against Conlon's separating arm as he blared his message, and vow, right in their faces. But there was no more battle. Just the pleasure of an impression made and of a wildly energizing heap of hatred piled up against him, now in Chicago. And of his sweet-savage indignation regarding their lies about his playing dirty (and what did they think the game *was*, after all, a church social? not even God could stomach those things). And of his satisfying response, invoking the rules, which were on *his* side. And of his resentment against his teammates, who'd about permanently now forfeited any claim to know the person Charlie knew.

The next day, about the fight they said not a word to him. So more proof positive, if any was needed. And, *therefore*, he said not a word to them. He would let his bat and his speed do his talking; and he'd see that they talked so loud that they would force this team (not one of whom could take home from first on a single in six lifetimes) to admit their absolute need for Tyrus Cobb, to confess it on their knees. He'd get his revenge that way—until Detroit's payment was exacted.

His mind was so full of this thought that in the sixth inning, he didn't have to think much anymore when something happened. A decent but catchable shot by the Sox's Allison was coming . . . his way? McIntyre's way? It was dead in the middle. He looked and saw in the instant that McIntyre, with his white-rat face, was looking at him. Whose was it? McIntyre wasn't moving for it, not a step, either to catch it or to back up Cobb. Even if it weren't the left fielder's, which Tyrus was right now determining it damn well was, McIntyre should be moving fast to back up Cobb. But the sonofabitch wasn't taking a step. So, by *damn,* Cobb wouldn't be taking any steps either. He stood every bit as still as his enemy-teammate. Each of them, standing like wooden posts as the ball came sailing out, would rather starve now than help the other. And there went the ball, an easily catchable thing as it turned out, sailing right past the two staring enemies and on toward the wall. And still neither of them moved.

The hitter, Allison, had to be piqued by a "Get your ass movin'!" from his teammates. He'd thought, apparently, that he was dead as soon as he hit his can of corn and had begun his flaccid trot of defeat. But now, a slow, slow man, he jerked himself back as best he could into full lumbering motion and was making his way toward second. But still neither Tyrus nor McIntyre moved. They continued just to stare at each other as the ball rolled up to and settled in at the foot of the wall.

The crowd had gotten the picture. And they knew the McIntyre-Cobb story, and now were crazy with delight getting their own chapter. All the maybe eight thousand of them stood now and cheered wildly for Allison, who in his slow-chugging carrying of that weight around the bags was now slogging, windedly, toward third. It was clear that Freddie Allison, the least likely candidate on the Sox and one of the least likely in the history of the league, would be able to boast of a stand-up, inside-the-park round tripper! And the longer it took him and the longer Cobb and McIntyre stood without taking a single step after the ball, which now just rested spectacularly and absurdly plopped in the grass at the wall, the more the crowd loved it! The ludicrousness of it all, as the ball just sat there and Allison took one of man's eternities to get around the bags and Cobb and McIntyre still just stood there, staring each other down: It was too damn crazy and good! There was something, too, in that the game was close. It wasn't a joke. So it was serious things here *becoming* a joke that made it somehow crazy funnier.

And now as Allison finally scored, taking a triumphant, if not-too-high leap, and stomping down two-footed on the plate, the roar was deafening, and prolonged. The question arose then, too, as to who finally would go get the ball so the game could go on! It wouldn't be Cobb. And it wouldn't be McIntyre. That was clear! And it wouldn't and shouldn't be Crawford come over from right, or Coughlin come out from third, or O'Leary come out from short. Why should *they* have to humiliate themselves? It wouldn't be Conlon. Why should *he* have to humiliate himself? It wouldn't be Armour.

Why should *he*? Why should *anybody*? No answer to that, apparently. So *nobody* was coming. And the chorus was going crazier by the moment, while Cobb and McIntyre still just stared hard at each other and the ball just sat there, in an unforgettable absurdity.

At last, a grounds keeper, scurrying along the wall, trying not to be noticed—but for that reason all the more noticeable—retrieved the ball, bringing the house down when he finally got to it and picked it up. And the roar of the crowd again did not let up, the man having to run the ball, first along the left-field wall, all the way back into the mound, no one on the field looking at all as if he'd submit to catching it or throwing it. And then when Siever, the pitcher, finally did take it, the crowd went crazier still. And when he actually began his delivery and the game began again.

Nor did the resumption of the game distract one bit the center-field mob's delighted concentration on the boy. "Congratulations, *Cobb*! You're not too much trouble, are ya?" "That was a beautiful effort, *Cobb*! Just beeeeee*yoo*tiful! I tell ya, a sight to remember!" "You don't think about number one, do ya, *Cobb*? I mean, I'm just askin'. It's a little hard to tell." "That's it, *Cobb*, oh yeah, just keep on smilin' the way you do. Keep on smilin', Mr. Happy-go-lucky! We *love* that face!" "Say, ya know, *Cobb*, I wish my kids was here today, to see some real team spirit. And ain't you just the example— for the kids. Ain't you just perfect! A real American Hero!"

As they kept on, and on, and on, it was some comfort, at least, that he could hear McIntyre was getting the same over in left—the two of them "teammates" at last. But then, when finally the Sox were retired, Siever striking out the eighth hitter and then the pitcher in a rage of angry fastballs (he'd hit the seventh hitter on the elbow and thrown four straight balls to the sixth, none of them close) it was time to go in—and face Armour.

The boy had thought since the deed was done, and even while he was in the middle of this latest insane *non serviam*—

just standing there and refusing to move—that Armour now might really make good on his threat to have him canned forever from The Show. Not that he'd have let this stop him. *Hell no*. It was one of the things that made him do it. And if all this fracas made Charlie start to look at him funny, whose fault would *that* be? But he'd begun to imagine a timepiece ticking as the chorus mocked on and Siever was raging away. And with each tick of the watch, the further untwining of a binding cord. Then it was time. And the thought that this might really now be it, suddenly made him weak-kneed and nauseated as he began his trot in. Not that he'd reveal the first thing. And if McIntyre didn't admit it was *his* ball! God dammit! *Let* Armour can me! he thought. *Let him!*

"Fuckin' Christ, Cobb, that was *your* ball! Don't you deny it! Don't you go denyin' what you damn well know to be the *truth*!"

So he heard it immediately from McIntyre, who did not face him as he spoke, just stared out of the dugout. But Tyrus wouldn't take this. Not one second. He went straight over to the veteran and yanked his shoulder hard to get him to face him. "I'll go to my *grave* denying that, you *liar*!"

And McIntyre had his fist raised now ready to strike him, and was screaming "I'll bet you will! Wouldn't that be *you*!" But a handful of Tigers on his side grabbed him—and a handful on Tyrus's side grabbed *him*. The two were being pulled apart when Armour, who hadn't yet said a word, stepped in between them.

"I don't know what page in the book a hell you two are tryin' to write. I honest t' God ain't smart enough to figure you two pieces a shit out. The kind that threats on their life don't stop is a special kind, that's for goddamn sure."

He stopped. His head sank. Then, looking up, his face concentrated in deeper frustration and anger, he began again. "It's like ya take what the game's all about and ya do the goddamn *opposite*! *Deliberately*! I ain't seen nothin' like it! And I been around a long fuckin' time! One day we can't pull ya apart, the next day ya won't come together; the only thing consistent bein' that it is *not* fuckin' pretty t' watch and *not* the game a baseball! But I'm tellin' you," he snarled, pointing his finger at one and then the other, "I ain't lettin' two cock-fightin' pieces a shit tear this whole team apart, much as they'd clearly fuckin' love to! I am *not* gonna let that happen, not 'less it's over my dead body! And all I can say is if you two care about this game—for Christ Almighty's sake!—you'll make peace." He scowled now in contempt and swung his clenched left fist vaguely back and forth before his chest. "But since ya both seem bent on playin' hard as ya can some upside-down, goddamn opposite disgraceful *game a hell*! I don't know if ya *can* do it. I honest t' God *don't*. I don't know if ya got the *guts* for bein' decent. But I ain't lettin' ya tear this team apart! That's for damn sure. Wahoo!"

"Yeah, Billy?"

"You're in center. 'Cause there's two bastard idiots who can't count past the number *one* that I gotta keep apart."

"Good enough."

"Thank you. And you, Cobb, you get your too-damn-good-to-be-decent rookie ass into right. *Without a word!* Or in your case, a *look*! Ya hear me!"

Tyrus felt that strange disappointment again that he wasn't being expelled forever. And he didn't like it that Armour started with Cobb's being moved and not with McIntyre's having to stay put: it suggested some kind of order of disapproval (nor did he like it that McIntyre would *get* to stay put). And he didn't like right field, not one goddamned bit of it. It wasn't *center*, which was prestige and *his* and which Crawford was miles and hours too slow to play. But he nodded to his manager three times silently, liking it still less that they'd have discovered some way to get rid of him after all. And then he found himself, as he nodded, taking pleasure, a suddenly growing, deepening pleasure in this: they *hadn't* canned him! They were backing off! So he must have gotten them to need him! And forced maybe a command from Navin. And he wouldn't have figured this out so fast if he hadn't called their bluff and tested their resolve, being a "bad boy."

"And you, Matty, you keep your miserable damn self in left. You, who oughta know better. You call yourself a pro. Ya act like a goddamned idiot child. And I don't wanna hear your answer to that. Not a fuckin' word of it. And you just *stay the hell clear* a the kid if you can't do better 'cause ya ain't got the guts to."

By now, those holding Cobb and McIntyre back from each other had let go, not without expressions of disgust at Cobb, frustration with McIntyre (because the Tigers were *not* out of this game, just two, now *three*, behind—not that it would have made any difference if they were out of it completely). But Armour had some last words for both. "You know, you two," he continued, "God dammit! It's *not makin' a laugh out of it*: that's what holds things together! And you and scum gamblers and such-like traitors would destroy the heart a things. Get people all around ya, kids even, not believin'. Ya ain't got the right!! Ya hear me! 'Cause nothin's worth that, least of all *your* goddamned fool pride."

"*Attention, Cobb now playing right field! Crawford in center! Attention, Cobb in right, Crawford in center!*"

The bugle would go around the outfield blasting his meg at the much-amused crowd, the right field portion of which got on Tyrus the second he assumed his new spot. "Attention, Cobb in right!" "Yeah, did ya hear that everybody? Cobb in right!" "Wonder why!" "Yeah, wonder why they put a slow, old tortoise in center! Ha ha ha ha! *That'll* help 'em!" "Hey, Cobb, why ya out here? Do you know? Awww, I guess he don't know! Leastwise, he ain't sayin'!" "Why ain't ya sayin', Cobb, eh?" "What's with the tight lip? Been a bad little boy, hmmm?" "But that's all right, Cobb. *We* love ya! Hell, you're doin' more for us than our own boys! Thanks!"

Chapter Ten

MANNA FOR THE CHOSEN

That evening, walking the streets of this stinking town—a place that made its sweet peace with the animal kingdom by about a million times a day slamming its sledgehammer on a cow's brains, and an equal number of times sticking a pig—he swore he'd never be suckered. Oh the game! Oh America! Oh the children! Oh the cock and the bull! And who's making a laugh out of things? Cobb? or the ones who put lead-foot Crawford in center, to the team's clear-as-hell detriment? What's a real laugh, after all? (But he must admit, he liked it that they'd hurt themselves now to hurt him: It would prove him right, one more time). And all of 'em out boozing and taking up with dosed damned trulls. McIntyre. He'd kill that bastard after one more incident. *One more.* And which one of 'em was thinking now? planning ways? inventing? Which one? Only one—Tyrus Cobb.

But he wasn't. He was only going over and over what Armour had said about the game. Fighting against it. Pleading his case sometimes before a Charlie he'd now turned into an easy, agreeable applauder of his rationalizings, which was something she never was, and something he could never love, if she had been. And then going over and over the incident. Again and again, he saw that ball coming out and saw it moving into the dead middle between him and McIntyre. He had to try hard in his mind to get the ball to go farther toward left. And if he managed it, the intense effort would soon collapse. And the ball would become his. In a perversion of admission, of self-inflicted pain of damned false-confession, he'd see it this way! But once more hard as hell he'd fight back, and make maybe his concocted Charlie smile his way.

He'd gotten a shoulder holster, and as he'd walked, he'd felt sometimes the weight of his father's gun swinging against his chest. He became conscious of the beat of it now as he walked on hard, finding himself stepping under the shadow of the tower of Polk Street Station, where the team's Union Central had arrived the evening before last. The words "Don't come home a failure" came to him—out of who knew where. He thought of all his journeying, trains and trains. Of how many miles and worlds he'd traveled in the last two months. Of Charlie at Grand Central, both when she met him and when he saw her off. Of the black of her train heading south, horizon after horizon. And of Reverend Minifield, who, like Charlie, told him he'd gone further than most would ever go into the human soul, and who said that because he had, he might find his salvation after all.

But now with the gun beating against his chest and his father's forbidding of any failure still haunting him, he admitted with his heart sinking what it was that was going on all along, these last hours and days, through all the incidents, repressed hard beneath them. He was afraid. Afraid that he'd be finished—and not because he *chose* to be a hard item and not cooperate. But because the breaker of Doc White would break him. That he'd be out of the league, gone, because he was a left-hand hitter who couldn't hit a left-hand pitcher with a sharp curve. That he'd be dead because, after all, he just wasn't good enough.

And no hiding now. No keeping his fear down out of sight. For this was Chicago, and tomorrow was Doc White, sure as game time was two o'clock. And wouldn't they be happy, all the brainless ones, with their four-letter filth and their alcohol and their whores. But would God reward him for keeping apart from such night-filth? He couldn't think. What kind of mind did God want him to bring to the game after all? He worked a theme of his last letter to Charlie, which he wrote before the last Washington game. Merit sometimes is just a falsehood, who knew better than a ball-player? When does a slump end? When God decides it's time, that's when. The Lord is the cause that makes the bat come to the ball.

He tried these words again, figuring God might listen, recognizing honest changes of heart, especially in someone as damn near crazy as Tyrus Cobb. But as he walked along Printers' Row and heard the repeating roll and clang of the presses, what came was another spasm of calculation. What would the difference be if he went four for four, as opposed to three for four, or two for four, or one for four? Or zero for four. He had the zero already worked out. He'd had it worked out all along. And as he worked the numbers for the other, positive possibilities, those calculations seemed like sins against the piety of zero. And he felt a sick remorse that he'd chosen to be himself rather than be "good" and join the team.

If there had been for him a pleasure in figuring they needed him and a pleasure in seeing them back off because he called their bluff—in his room that night, any such satis-factions had all gone dead. Any sweet vengeful gratification he'd felt in thinking that to hurt him, they would end up hurting themselves—that *they*, the hypocrites, were the ones who really injured the team—all of these sweet little vindi-catory reflections seemed now to be setups for a fall not just into a fear of failure but a *conviction* that he would fail. And he didn't even try in his mind to get the science on White's pitch. All he could think was that he must have committed some terrible crime in God's eyes. And he thought this ending, this before-it-started finish of his career, for all his flirting with causing it, his crazy-suicidal courting of it, would be worse than his coming to the end of his father's book.

And in his terror of being denied his calling, he felt that he *had* a calling, all right: that the sign of that calling's truth was the terror—the terror of losing Tyrus Raymond Cobb. He foresaw a life of meaningless work, doing things he was never cut out for. He saw himself giving up a never-ending, spooky, who-knew-where-it-came-from invention and the passion that produced it, for the nothing of some mere role he would play.

It would be hell, doing for the rest of his life something he was never cut out for. *That* is slavery. And it's wrong, even for niggers. He admitted to himself, even for niggers. A nigger is a man. No denying. And no man should have to spend his life at something he wasn't cut out for. No sense trying to hide this. Damned hypocrisy and burying of the truth. Denial upon denial. The damned never-ending *weight* of the lie and hypocrisy. And hell, he felt like a nigger himself. A nigger soon-to-be, after Doc White was through with him. "White" supremacy! Ha! There's a joke on Tyrus Cobb! Who would *not* be someone Charlie Lombard loved oh so much to kiss.

When at last, fitfully, he slept, his loaded gun under his pillow, his watch buried away so he couldn't hear its ticking, he dreamed of his father, saw him rising to the podium in the Georgia senate, and heard him speaking in a self different from himself. "How, my fellow Georgians," the Senator asked, his eyes sweeping over face after face, "can we have real harmony unless we let men be free? There are those who say we'll have nothing but chaos if we let men be free. But I say we'll have nothing but chaos if we *don't*! Think first off of the anger. Think of the *anger*! You can't deny men their freedom without arousing *rage*! And then that rage must be quartered off, set apart, imprisoned, denied—by laws. Laws which work as walls. This is *not* harmony, or unity. This is *tyranny*. But let men be free—*all men*—and what do you have? You have each and every man discovering how much of himself there really is. You have each and every man finding his soul, not just his terrified pitiful body, which dies, and which he fears he must protect with laws that are walls, or which, if he is the slave, he inhabits in a state more abject and depressed even than the master's terrified despair, till at last, inevitably, his rage comes. Let a man, however, in freedom find his soul and he will break down walls in his spiritual fearlessness. Or he'll just let those walls fall, too busy in his creativeness to bother with them. And joy will replace anger. And joy will run free over the barriers that fear erected, until those barriers are no longer even remembered. The soul will triumph over the body and create a true union of free, living souls. And, my fellow Georgians, we must confess that all men—*all*—white and black—have God-given, living souls! This is the thing that in the end we *must* admit."

He saw now walking into his dream, right down into the Georgia senate, his mother, accompanied on one side by Reverend Minifield, and on the other by their nigger, Uncle Ezra. And now, from the seats, Charlie rose, and came before them. She came dressed in white, like a bride. And then the senate rose to cheer them all, while up into the capitol dome and out its top flew the face, that face from somewhere, that target from somewhere in his past, screeching hideously and awkwardly flapping away like a terrified caught bird, getting out. And with that face gone, the feeling at last was innocence. And peace. Even as he woke into his real life, no longer tossing and turning, he felt as if he'd been baptized and freed, every demon exorcized. The bed felt as good now, in fact, as any he'd ever slept in, the sheets over him and beneath him cool and yet warm, and clean.

But after a while he began to smell what? What was it? Those slaughterhouses. Christ. He looked out his window and saw big-buildinged Chicago, alien as Detroit and Cleveland and Boston and New York and Philadelphia and Washington—with this added sickening reek. And in just a few hours now, it would be Doc White.

Rising to dress, he felt again as if he'd committed a crime. And not just his private battles with McIntyre, but everything he'd done in The Show—every hit he'd gotten, every lead he'd stretched off a base, every base he'd stolen, every extra base he'd taken, every forceful proclamation of his rights on the path, every hotshot throw or good throw he'd made, every time he'd opened his mouth on the field, every boast, every insult, every silence, every attempt to rattle another man into an error, every attempt to form a fearsome impression, every show of speed, every opportunity seen and seized, every opportunity made, every run scored, every attitude he'd taken toward the crowd, every look he'd worn on his face—all seemed to him now like crimes that today he was going to pay for. He found himself wishing he'd done everything the veterans asked. Like a gentleman, he found himself understanding their every request. And who was *he* not to submit himself and go through the normal rites of passage? Who was *he* to think that joining a team didn't mean joining a team? Who in hell was Tyrus Cobb, *right fielder*? Who in hell was *he*?

And what now? What was this? Under his door, he saw, had been slipped at some time in the early morning, another packet. Two envelopes, this time both blue, one marked September 13, the other September 27, just one week ago. He knew he should open them. There would be time to read them, even respond if he rode the team carriage to the park and didn't walk by himself as he had yesterday (Armour making the exception with a "Suit yourself"). But he didn't open either letter, wanting (as maybe he wanted Doc White to end his damned career today) that permanent change for the worse in his relationship with his mother. And so he'd punish her; though as he buried this second and third letter away with the still-unopened first, he had a thought—that the sweet smell of her dress, her skin, would be the last thing he would recall in this world.

Again he walked by himself to the park; and in the locker room—beyond now, possibly, being able to stop himself—he remained apart and alone. Even more than on the first day, he found himself despising the irritation of his uniform and ashamed of the bright polish on his shoes. He was badly sick-nervous, sure if he just touched his gullet he would heave up his guts. On the two miles over, he'd looked one more time for a nigger child, to rub a pate, but no luck. Race riots. Hadn't he read of race riots in Chicago? And deaths? And they talk! But shouldn't he be humble now? Wouldn't the Lord demand that? No magic without it. It wasn't the man who moved a bat through a swing. It was the Lord God Almighty in his most secret magic. But what grace now for a criminal fool? If he hadn't demanded so much to be a pure individual, maybe he would have gotten to be himself after all. But it was too late now.

He was spared an appearance in the first inning as the Tigers went down to White one, two, three (which the boy felt good about, not wanting to die here by himself). But in the second, when his time came and the bugle took his megaphone stroll from third, around home, to first, announcing "*Cobb, Tyrus Cobb.* Batting fifth for Detroit, *Cobb!*" he was pained to bitter damned misery. And though it would have been impossible not to at this point, he wished he had never in his life taken up his three bats at once. God damn me, he thought, as he dropped the extra two. And losing the weight of them made the one he carried feel now not one fraction of an ounce lighter. Maybe even heavier.

He stepped in, and Schalkey wasted no time. "Well, look-ee-here, Doctor. If it ain't the one and only Tyrus Cobb, dirtiest little Southern gentleman on the paths. Wonder if he'll watch your stuff go by, Doc, the way he watches balls in the outfield go by. But wait now—as I recall, it ain't gonna matter a whole hell of a lot if he watches or he don't watch. Seems t' me he had a little trouble with your medicine up in Detroit, Doctor. As I recall, he did indeed."

The boy said nothing. He figured he had no real magic but believed silence would please God better than shooting off his mouth. He felt heavy as a wet sack of sand and, even though he'd done nothing so far, energyless, exhausted. And science: He could feel his mind's quitting on it coming over him like a chicken's going dead limp in the jaws of a fox. Yet out of mere habit, or maybe morbid fascination, he studied White. He watched the tobacco spit, the wiping of the chin with the back of the hand, the look in, the smile, the nod, the gripping of the ball behind the screen of the glove, the no-doubt telling forearm twisted sharply (with the elbow out away from the body), the dip of the glove, the rock forward, the swing of the hands, the rock back, the rock forward again, the right leg rising, the push off the left leg, the hand coming out and up—for a curve—and *over. Now!*

"*Steeeeerrrrrike one!*"

"Oh *yeah*, Doctor, it's all comin' back t' me now! Oh yeah, the cure for this disease—I believe it was a curve. Yeah, I think that was it. Wipes it out in no time. Just three little doses."

The boy wanted violence. Real violence. At the pitch, he never lifted his bat, but he'd like to lift it now! And, Christ, if he really could *kill* Schalkey! But he felt so weak and heavy and brainless and guilty-afraid that he couldn't even utter a word. He hadn't seen the thing. It had come—and gone. Off the table and out of sight. He felt like tearing at his own blue hawks, gouging them out and throwing them on the ground, then groping around like a goddamned blind man. But he stood back in—far up in the box as he always had—and felt the pure hell of his chances being about as good as they would be if truly he had no eyes.

Sick-worried, he watched mechanically again for indicators. But what the hell did it matter? It was the breaker that was coming, every time. He knew that. And what did it mean to know, and not know? What did *that* do to your confidence? To know and *not* know. That was his situation. Again! Again his situation! And here it came—and there it *went* . . . with the exact same result. Only this time he swung and missed about as badly as he ever had in his life, nearly falling on his face as he took after one that started out over the plate but then dipped low and away, a good foot off the plate and only inches out of the dirt.

"Steeeeeerrrrrrrrrike two!"

"Oh no doubt, Doctor. No *doubt.* Just three little doses oughta do it for this dirty-playin', big-mouth, gentleman bush baby. Three little doses of the what *was* it? Oh yeah, the *curveball!*"

And sure as hell the breaker came, one more time. And the boy didn't know where it would be. He couldn't follow the goddamn thing at all. So he guessed. And guessed wrong, coming over the top of the pitch by about half a foot. He couldn't believe it wasn't where he guessed it would be, for all his previous failures. But it wasn't. It was not.

And so he had to listen to it pronounced again by the judge in blue. *"Steeeeeerrrrrrike threeee!"* And swallow down the finality.

And, naturally, the parting salvo from Schalkey: "So long for now, cracker pie! Till next time, when we'll be feedin' ya a nice steady diet of . . . What'd you say this kid should *eat*, Doctor? Oh yeah, nothin' but *curveballs."*

He couldn't think of the game. As the innings passed, all he could think of was his death and damned disappearance from The Show. He scrambled over possibilities. Should he try this? that? But no scheme had for him any credibility. And he felt guilty for even thinking, ashamed of every slightest self-protective mental foray. He was on fire with his shame. And truly, maybe for the first time in his life, he didn't know the score, or even who was winning. He didn't know the inning. Or the number of outs, of balls, of strikes.

But he knew the Tiger batting order, and when he'd be coming up again.

Yet the more he anticipated his appearances, the less magic he would bring to the plate. He became more and more sure of this. And indeed the second time, he again struck out and felt he'd been made even more a fool of than the first time. And the third time, thinking that if he'd move still farther forward in the box he could hit the ball before it broke, he was called out by umpire Frankie Cornish for stepping outside the front line! Never had this happened to him! Never! Not one time in his life! He'd never imagined it, or anything like it! And who the hell *did* it happen to?

"Aww *criminee*, Cobb," Schalkey then mercilessly ragged him, laughing hard, "if you wanna run, ya shoulda gone out the back door, or maybe the side door!" The catcher rose out of his crouch and, before making his toss back to the mound, shook his head, mockingly. "Or maybe, Doctor, he was comin' out to thank you for savin' him the trouble a wastin' his time in the wrong business. Expressin' his gratitude for your helpin' him get started in another career. I'll bet that's what it was. The Southern gentleman doin' the grateful thing." He tossed the ball to White and turned to fire a last insult to the departing rookie. "Forgive me, Cobb, I didn't know you was so polite. I thought you was just too stupid, or too *yella* t'play the game inside the lines."

Tyrus kept silent, just swallowed it all. And more—for every bit as painful as Schalkey's mouthing away was his certainty that, to a man, the Tiger team was goddamned joyful watching Cobb going down. They hadn't said a word, not even McIntyre; but there'd been no need. The boy could read it in their faces (especially the White Rat's snout and eyes), as he'd been able to read their malice from the first second he arrived. And forget consolation or encouragement (it would be a cold day in hell before he'd expect things like this), what little hint even or tip did he get from these veterans? Christ, if they cared about their team, they wouldn't make him beg for such things, the way they clearly were making him beg! And didn't they know he'd die or have to change himself entirely before he begged, or even acknowledged that they *could* help him. Of course they knew. So they wanted to see him die, right now, before their eyes.

And the chorus never let up. The miserable *right-field* chorus. "Hey, what's it mean when a left-hand hitter goes O fer a million against a left-hand curve?" "Did he strike out every time?" "Nah, one time he jumped out." "Jumped out?" "Yeah, jumped right outa the box." "Well, I gotta say that's a strange one, all right. But the case is, that when he ain't jumpin', he's strikin' out?" "Yep, that'd be the case." "All million times?" "Yep." "Well, I think that means he ain't worth nothin'!"

Even as he remained unconscious of innings and nearly everything else, except Tyrus Raymond Cobb, he could hear them clearly, make out their words. And in intense flashes of anger, he thought again of how the price of unrestraint for a lousy bug was two damn bits and for a ballplayer his whole life.

But before his last appearance, as the poison chorus sang on and on, something came to him. Something came. Like manna, when God remembered the Chosen, it came. And it was as simple as could be. Not *up* in the box, not *forward*, where he'd always placed himself—but *back*. He would change himself by setting up *back* in the box. As far as the lines would permit, that is. He wouldn't give any bastard on earth another chance to say a word about where he set up. He'd go back just to the edge, plant his back foot *there*. And what would happen—he hoped—and prayed—would be that he'd see the thing. After it broke—be able to follow it— and *find* it. Just that extra fraction of a fraction of a second. But it might be all the time he'd need to get the science on this mysterious sonofabitch White and make him his. He would know—and he would *know*. Or he hoped he'd know. . . .

He'd been aware only that he'd get but one more appearance. Now, however, feeling this new, growing hope, he checked the scoreboard. The Tigers were down three to one in the bottom of the seventh. He'd have to wait till the ninth, most likely, the way White was mowing them *all* down; but he'd get his chance. He shook himself into an awareness of the count and situation. He put the crowd farther back in his mind. He felt an urge, even, to shout in an encouraging word to Killian—say "Thata boy, Eddie! Thata boy, Twilight!"

But he imagined the whole sweet thing getting started if he did that. And his mind ran right to its groove of denying that it had been his responsibility all along to start up the good thing. And to his fear that if he came out and tried to get things started, they'd just give him the cold shoulder, for which discouraging of him he'd give them zero opportunity. But he let himself enjoy the thought that, after all, he might win one for the team by nailing this White to the cross.

And, sweet Jesus, yes, the opportunity came just about exactly the way he hoped and prayed it would. The Tigers did nothing in the top of the eighth, which he wanted (McIntyre's making the last out on a called third pleasing him especially). Nor did Chicago do anything in the bottom, which was good, too. He had to admit, Horse-face Eddie was doing one helluva smart job. And then in the ninth, the Tigers got it going, just enough. Schaeffer led off with a bunt single and then Crawford followed with a cheap bleeder. So the table was set, just so, with White still snapping that breaker, and only because of a little bad luck, in any trouble here at all. But trouble it was, nonetheless.

The boy heard a groan, though, coming from his own dugout as he lifted his two extra bats from his shoulder. And then this bitter murmuring, just loud enough to be heard: "Christ, Billy, couldn't ya get somebody else in there? I mean *anybody* but Cobb. He can't hit White for his life. Ain't that been well enough proved? Game's on the line here, after all."

He felt a temptation to turn to the dugout and give his

extra bats a brash flip to the ground in a clear signal of contempt and hatred, but then felt the familiar pious superstition: If he was going to get back the magic, he had to be
modest. But then in a sudden flash he became powerfully
convinced that that was what modesty always was: a pitiful
superstitious little begging prayer that through our meekness
we would win favor and be *permitted* to do well. Oh please
let me do well—I'll be good—I'll be good. He looked back,
and flipped the bats. And he liked hearing Armour spit out
an angry *"Shut up*, will ya."

And when he stepped into the box, he was glad as all
bloody hell he'd flipped those bats and hadn't gone modest
on himself; for that sonofabitch Schalkey, who was the one
with the team in trouble here, wasn't about to get meek all
of a sudden.

"Well, ain't this timely, Doctor. Just when ya'd like a
little turn of the luck your way, doesn't it come on through
like the Illinois Central? Ain't we just got the Southern gentleman bush baby here, most convenient like. And *woop!* . . .
woop! . . . what's this! Oh my precious word, Doctor, he ain't
gonna get caught leapin' right out to the mound this time.
No sir, he's makin' darn sure a that! But criminee cripes if
he don't look like he's gonna leap *my way*! Help me, Doctor,
and get rid of him fast! Throw the nut a curve, won't ya!"

Tyrus still said nothing to this Schalkey, just spat over
his shoulder and dug his left foot in hard at the back of the
box. They were giving him the left field line, which was another hope come true; for that's exactly where he planned on
taking the ball when that breaker came in low and away. But
the first pitch he would let go by, to look it over. And he
hoped he'd see the thing this time all right, all the way in.
He even hoped it would be a strike, so that White would stay
cocky with his curve.

He watched White's gestures, watched his motion, studied every stage of his delivery, with the sharpened, excited
mind now of a detective on the verge of what he hopes will

be a breakthrough discovery. And here the thing came. Would he see it all the way in? He watched. He saw it. . . . He saw it. . . . He saw it. . . . And? And sure as hell he *did* see it all the way in! Oh hell *yes* he did! And so when the judge in blue called it *"Steeeeeeerrrrike one!"*—and when Schalkey began again his familiar ape-jabbering, the boy still more confidently prepared his retort. And he found himself hoping there was somebody in the Tiger dugout moaning even louder and that Armour was telling that particular somebody once more to shut his mouth.

Then he felt an irresistible urge—and pushed—and broke still harder out of his egg. "Schalkey," he said, without looking back at the catcher, rather just standing in with his left foot planted hard against the back line, "tell your *doctor friend* to send up that breaker again. Tell him if he's got the goddamn spine, he'll send that piece of garbage up again."

"Oh *my*, Doctor, we've gotten a *request* from the Southern gentleman! And guess what Jack Cracker wants to see? The *curveball*! Can't get enough of it, I guess. Just can't *wait* till he's completely finished off. Well, I say we help the little dirty one get on home as fast as he can get. Not that we don't like him, a course."

The boy took a poker-face scan of all fields—but, not letting on—was looking diamond-hard at left. He dug in his left foot still more firmly. And, in no way now despairing of his science, he watched White. He watched, hoping hard that he'd see the breaker even better this time than last, which gave him a very clean look. He studied the enemy southpaw through every stage of that now-familiar delivery, and saw everything coming out essentially the same way it had in the past. And sure enough, here came that breaker. But look at it—it was starting too far out over the plate. The boy wouldn't fall sucker for this. He'd make this bastard throw him a sweet strike. And what was this offering? Not a strike. No. Rather—there it was—he was seeing it again all the way in: a ball, low and outside. Outside by six inches and low by four, a sucker pitch, not only clear completely in the boy's eyes, but right where he expected it to be, having seen the thing all the way in now *twice*.

"*Ball* one!" So, after it arrived, the man in blue saw it, too.

But what Schalkey saw was the same boy he'd seen every time before, despite the fact that, this time, the kid had not been suckered. "Well, well . . . Hopin' now for a free pass he is, Doctor. Knowin' he can't see ya, he's closin' his eyes and hopin' for a free pass."

"If you can get that thing in the strike zone, White," the boy broke in sharply, "I'll let you know exactly what's just happened to its value."

"Oh, *Jesus*! we got big, big plans now, wouldn't ya say, Doctor. Damn big plans for somebody who ain't had a single experience a *touchin'* ya. Christ, let the baby have it, Doc. Send the bush-league gentleman right on back where he belongs."

"You'll see where I belong, Schalkey," the boy now said through gritted teeth. "You'll see exactly where I belong."

And now he watched again every phase of the delivery, which . . . still . . . showed . . . no-o-o-o-o-o *changes*. And here came that pitch . . . this time . . . yes . . . starting inside enough so that . . . yes . . . it would . . . but wait . . . wait on it . . . wait . . . yes . . . there it was . . . now breaking off . . . and right on the outside corner just at the . . . *knees!*

Having waited and looked and waited and *looked* and now brought his left hand down to his right for full power, the boy at last unleashed himself. He went with the pitch exactly as he saw it, right there on the outside corner, and he got it *all*, firing down the wide-open left-field line a true poison bullet. The third baseman didn't have a chance even to tell it good-bye; and the left fielder had no chance to get to it before it would run into the deep corner. Schaefer trotted home in a breeze; and Crawford, never faster than he needed to be, by the time the left fielder was able to smother the caroming thing and scoop it up, was already coming into third. He had his steam built up, too, and didn't hesitate now a second, scoring easily and tying the game. And for his part, the boy had just about caught Crawford and would have headed home for his own inside-the-park four-bagger! But not even he could run over his own man, and he had to settle for a stand-up triple.

But he didn't *settle*, not a bit of it. "Ohhhh, Doctor," he began, as, not even winded, he was already dancing off third, provoking, biting, "isn't it just one helluva lot worse, Doctor, to have had something and *lost* it, than never to have had it in the first place? Oh yeah, Doctor, you thought you *owned* somebody, and now it turns out that he owns you. Isn't that painful, after all?"

He turned now to the catcher. "And you, *Schalkey*, how's your rib cage? Feelin' a little bit tender, *Schalkey*? Whatdaya say if I come on in and pay ya another visit, eh? Or maybe this time you'll move outa the line and won't be standing where the runner's *entitled* to be."

He knew this Ray Schalkey. He knew he couldn't scare the sonofabitch. But he could make him try *too* hard: get *too* determined to finish off Cobb. And for his own part, he was swiftly now determining, right now, no outs yet or not, to goddamn steal home! Hell yes! They'd never expect it, especially with no outs. Surprise would do them in. In the meantime he'd just make them tight and brittle by his dancing, and his biting, maybe even make White throw a wild pitch or a wild throw to third or get Schalkey to give up a passed ball, which would be, oh Lord, a sweet as hell pleasure.

He took a crazy lead—and then faked that he was leaning. But White (no doubt thinking that no one in his right mind would steal home in this situation) didn't throw, didn't even really look him back, just gave him a glance and went into his motion. And his motion was as slow as a mouthful of old molasses. Yawwm. Yawwm. Yawwm. And—something was coming to the boy—something was coming . . . something out of his having studied White against Coughlin, the hitter now . . . in the game in Detroit. He'd hit Coughlin with fast balls, and then the change. After a couple of fast-balls, the straight change, low and away. The perfect as hell pitch to steal home on.

He watched. And from what he saw, he figured fastball, because there hadn't been that twist of the forearm, with the elbow stuck out away from the body; and it wouldn't be the change yet, most likely. And yes, sure enough, it *was* the fast-ball. So he'd figured right. A victory for eyes and brains (or at least for guessing that was educated). But look now at that bastard Schalkey, ready to snap down a throw. As Tyrus knew, however, having seen with the eyes in the back of his head, the third baseman, Clintock, wasn't near enough to the bag to take any throw.

The boy trotted back to third, then began to take his lead again. The heater had been a called strike. So what would it be this time? Fastball again? Or would they mix it up with the curve? Or try that change now? The boy watched. No forearm twist. No elbow out. And no observable difference from the last motion. So fastball again. Yes? Yes indeed, and another strike, this time on a swing.

So now too, he thought, there was true justification. In-disputable. Why in hell would it be wrong to take home now, when it was clear as day that White was in total command over Coughlin and next up was the even weaker-hitting O'Leary, proven more than once incapable of a sacrifice? And why not now, when surprise was on his side? And, given the history, wouldn't it be now that White would try that change, low and away, which meant Schalkey would have now not just a slow-moving pitch to deal with but a much more difficult, across-the-plate tag, especially hard to manage if the runner hooked in now from the third-base side and offered nothing more than the tip of his outstretched toe?

And the boy would admit now, readily, White's control

was fine enough so that, even with the lead run on third, he wouldn't hesitate to waste one low and away. And this was especially the case, the boy was willing also now to concede, with one Ray Schalkey behind the plate. And wouldn't a runner like Tyrus Cobb have another huge advantage if, knowing what indicators signaled curve and having seen the fastball delivery, he determined by process of elimination that the change was coming? And wasn't this pitcher's damned molasses delivery slow enough, anyhow, for such a runner?

And now there it *was*—Christ—something different: an exaggerated scowl and tensing of the face, which seemed a bad poker put-on, very bad, no doubt meant to suggest that the heat was on its way, but readable enough as a lie. It would be the change. So extend the lead now. Yes! Extend the lead again—farther—as far as you can now—yes, yes—another step—another now! And White wasn't even looking, the damn fool. But what about Schalkey? The boy glanced in quick. Oh Christ! Schalkey wasn't looking! *Schalkey* wasn't looking! And the catcher was set up now low and away—bent out that way now! Just as predicted! So take another step! And now another! And now it was that old molasses motion again . . . yawwm . . . yawwm . . . *So go! Christ hell Jesus yes!*

The boy was gone. Before White realized at all what was happening, he'd come all the way through his motion and released what turned out, however, *not* to be the straight change but another fastball: and it had a real good blaze to it. But Schalkey *was* pulled far to the outside of the plate by the pitch, well out of the strike zone. And lo and behold Coughlin, who obviously couldn't *not* catch on, actually had enough sense to throw his bat at the ball and make a sacrifice of himself to create a distraction for the catcher, who—well . . . did he hate Cobb just enough (having received in the past an impression in his rib cage) so that he bobbled the ball a little, a fraction of a second? He bobbled it: That was for sure.

And it was enough. The boy, who had thought about everything that he was going to do, now did it all without thinking—though, out of the corner of his eye, he sure as hell noticed he was wrong about the change-up. He came in hard as he could, maybe *harder* than he could, even, because he was wrong about the change. And he hooked hard to the right, too, and *did* give Schalkey no more to find than the tip of his toe. And Schalkey, with the bobble, didn't get there in time anyhow, despite a quickness which the boy now acknowledged as supreme. Acknowledged it in the instant, that is, that he heard the call *"Yerr saaaaafe!"* and saw the blue wings of Frankie Cornish spreading wide. And there would be Cornish, bent over close, his eyes peering in, repeating the gesture. And rapid-fire repeating it a third, fourth, fifth time. The wings of the safe call, here flapping repeatedly in the faces of Ray Schalkey and Doc White! The boy, as he stood up now and carefully, triumphantly, brushed off the dust from his uniform, could not have felt a more complete pleasure (but for that small bit of guilty shame in the back of his head that he'd been wrong about the pitch). But now he'd discovered he could beat the fastball, too! And how would he have found this out otherwise? Answer: He wouldn't have otherwise.

So as he walked off toward the dugout, he had a sharp parting word all right for this Ray Schalkey. "Too bad we didn't really *meet*, Ray," he said, "but maybe next time. And maybe then we'll let the steel decide who has a right to the path." So another impression left.

And what pleasure he did feel. But mixed? Half of it the daredevil pleasure of a fool? A rash damn fool? The hell with that. But what now was this? Nothing on that bench, even *now*? Not a single one of 'em standing up to say a single word? Not even Armour? Not after all *that*: the triple that drove in the two tying runs, and then the run scored that put the damn *team* in the lead?

As he came in, no one even looked. But they were talking, loud enough to be heard. "Who's he in it for? It's clear enough now, ain't it. Nobody out and he's standin' on third, with the game on the line. And all we need with his friggin' speed is a halfway decent can a corn. But what's he care? All's he cares about is his sourpussed, can't-stand-nobody-else-but-sure-as-hell-loves-hisself *self*!"

It wasn't McIntyre this time, but it was his echo, Killian. Killian—who stood to notch a win because of what Cobb had just done. And *he* was moaning. How crazy much do you hate somebody if he just bailed *you* out and the first thing you have to say is that he cares about nobody but *himself*. The boy determined in a burning anger now that it was a fool notion, selling yourself out to the sweetness-and-harmony crowd.

And feeling the power of his triumph over White, enough so that he couldn't have cared less how he misread that pitch's indicators, he fired off a loud shot—into a mob to whom he'd said almost nothing in over a month. So his words cracked the air. "Beautiful expression of gratitude *that*, Killian! I get *you* off the hook and that's all you have to say! That's all any of ya have to say! Hell!"

Killian turned immediately, his face already reddening, and walked over. "*Gratitude!* Christ, look who's talkin', Cobb. You oughta be grateful that nobody's fractured your friggin' jawbone, ya sourpussed sonofabitch. Come up here and act from the first minute on like you don't owe nobody nothin'. Play the game like you don't owe nobody nothin'. Not even a damn word, let alone a laugh, ya sonofabitch. And I'm thinkin' now that maybe you wanna showboat on home out there—and that's what it *was*, bub, *showboatin'*—'cause you don't even know that in this here game a baseball there's a thing called a damned *sacrifice*. That'd be like you all right, ya stupid little shit. And ain't you all over too dumb t' know what's good for ya, with yer damn sour friggin' puss. And you believe me: It's gonna cost ya, yer attitude is. It's gonna cost ya big, Cobb, before things is over, which it might be sooner'n you think, for all yer showboatin' bullshit."

"*Yer up*, Killian!" Armour shouted down from the other end of the dugout. "That is if yer not too busy to take any more part in this contest!"

The pitcher gave Tyrus a last hard look and spat on the dugout floor before he grabbed a bat and stepped out onto the field. But the boy didn't let him go without some sharp parting commentary. "Stupid. I'll tell you who's stupid. You don't know *what* was going through my mind out there, *what* I was reading, *how* I was figuring. And why? Because you don't see half the things you need to see, ya jackass. So you can't tell what's selfish and what's not. And wouldn't it be just like a jackass to call something showboating that brings in victories—for his team—and *him*."

Killian walked off toward the plate, pretending not even to hear. But now that he'd started, Tyrus wasn't going to finish up in any hurry. He turned now to the rest of them, looking especially at McIntyre. "And you're all not just stupid, but *hypocrites. Hypocrites!* You talk about team play, but what you really care about is seeing Cobb going down. And don't you prove this when Cobb scores the lead run but you don't like it. But no surprise. I could tell it all from the first second I got here, and have known it every second since. If *we* had to go through it, you all say. If *we* had to go through the ritual . . . If *we* had to go through the silent treatment and the vandalism and whatever else. Then why in hell shouldn't Cobb. Who does he think he is! *We* learned to laugh at ourselves. Why shouldn't Cobb. *We* learned to take it. *We* learned how to get along. *We* did. *We* did. And if Cobb won't, well by God then we'll make him feel the pain. And we'd love to see him gone. Because we lie when we say we care most about the game. We *lie*! What we care most about in the entire world is that *Tyrus Cobb* go through what *we* went through and that he keep a godblessed smile on his face and his goddamn mouth shut—just the way *we* did! Well he *won't*! I'm telling you right now—and forever! And I suppose you think

I'm crazy for that! I'm lookin' at ya and you look like you think I'm crazy. Do you think I'm crazy? Well, I'm not. And you won't make me crazy! You'll try like hell! I know you! But you'll fail!"

They all, including Armour, stood staring, speechless. Tyrus took it to mean he'd convinced them of something, or half of him thought he had. But if he hadn't, he didn't give a damn. Let them think whatever they wanted to think. Care what people think and you're dead. *Dead!*

Right then, Killian struck out to end the Tiger half. And no more got said. The Tigers took the field for the bottom of the ninth. And they held on to win. Thanks to Cobb, as the boy saw it, Killian upped his victories.

But—and, oh, what a surprise—the pitcher never said a word to him beyond what he'd said in the dugout. The patent, damned proven hypocrite ingrate! God damn him. And the threat in that little speech of his: that for his "attitude," Cobb would pay. The murderous little threat because the man couldn't live with somebody different. Scared his little self to death, that's what a true, "uncooperative" individual did. Christ.

Chapter Eleven

STILL THE SADDEST, ANGRIEST BOY

They all, except one, were glad that night to get home—to Detroit. The whole ride the boy had kept well apart. But as the crowd began to scatter from the Michigan Central, he caught out of the corners of his eyes two or three greetings of team members by young wives. But then for him, too, there was a hand waving. It was the cabby West, not yet in an automobile.

Clear voices told him he shouldn't have been glad—but he was—or half. After all, Tyrus Cobb could be thankful as the next fella for something familiar. And the cabby was driving up. How could he not climb aboard, having no hard feelings anymore, really, about that gaslight assay of his five-cent piece, or about other things? The man's dirt wouldn't rub off on him, after all. And who put it more honestly than West? Cobb's trial would be settled with the answer to the question: Could he follow a major-league southpaw's breaker, and find it, and kill the thing? It would be a pleasure to share the verdict with the man.

"Hey, Mr. Tyrus—not Cyrus—how'ya be?"

The black-toothed smile, though seen close

it disgusted him, didn't repel the boy enough to make him turn away. But in a sudden instinctive impulse, he did pretend to have forgotten West's name (which he not only knew but remembered he need only whisper). "How are *you*, Mr . . . ?"

"West. Freddie West, sir." The cabby laughed. "Leastways ya didn't call me the wrong name or nothin', like I done to you at first, eh?"

Tyrus, though he sensed a parry and thrust here on West's part, smiled now at the man's continuing comfortable familiarity, and, glad also to be quickly away, threw his grip into the back bed of the cab and climbed up. "You just lacked information then, I believe, didn't you, Mr. West?"

"You are right, sir. No word at the time in the spreadsheet dope, which'd be a generly reliable organ. And which I read it most careful, havin' a perfessional innerest in the game. But let me tell you somethin', sir," he said, as he snapped the reins along his nag's back and clacked his tongue, "about what's bein' spread in the dope nowadays regardin' Tyrus—not Cyrus—Cobb."

"Oh?" Tyrus said, as he felt a sudden irritation of shame and remorse (if the cabby's hint sounded hopeful, did they dope Cobb still as a trouble to the team—A source of dissension? A crazy man? Some kind of rebel-sinful disgrace to the game? What?—he was sure if there'd been a good word, there'd been a bad one, too).

"Well . . . the word is," the cabby said, a bit teasingly, as they began to roll along past those eateries and taverns that the boy had come upon that first night, right before he found Mr. West—"the word is . . . that . . . Mr. Tyrus not Cyrus Cobb has got himself a *future*." He turned around now and smiled his rotten-mouthed smile. "Nice thing t'have, a future. Very nice thing, ain't it?"

"Depends, I guess, on its nature," the boy said, halfgrinning back.

"Well," Mr. Freddie West said, "would it bein' a *baseball*

future be the kinda thing you was perticular for? 'Cause the word is, Mr. Tyrus, that a certain Doctor White outa Chicago, for all the bite in his leftways hook, ain't gonna be noisin' off about how he's got the number of a certain you-would-know-who. Somebody, that is, who waited on him and took him the opposite way, *ve-ry* hard."

Tyrus smiled and felt a warm pleasure. "The word spreads that fast, eh?"

"Oh you betchya it does, sir. You betchya." The cabby turned around again and smiled, and winked.

But Tyrus couldn't like this damned overfamiliar wink— from the man whose name he need only whisper. And suddenly, in anger, he imagined himself dogged down some endless night-dark roadway by sounds of his father's prophecies about wagerers: "thieves who'd sell the entire reality of the soul for the cheap price of a sure thing." Yet he considered the dirt of the hackster still innocuous enough, and, dam*nation*, he did like to hear what this West, with his "innerest" in and clearly sharp brains for the game, had to say about Tyrus Cobb and one Doctor White, outa Chicago. But he would make the conversation stop now—and give the man zero encouragement. He said, "Hmmm," in a way that said he didn't like that wink.

They entered then the deeper dark of the warehouse and factory district. A forge-fire's red glow lit spectacularly the back of an alley, and, along the empty canyon of stone and brick buildings, the clopping of the horse's shoes echoed loud on the blocks of cedar.

The moon was full, as on the night the boy arrived; and he thought of how his imagination had been affected then. He knew now, though, that The Show was no place of moon glow at all and that the parks were not paradises and that there was a word to be said, all right, for the South's scorn for smoke-filled, foreign-babbling Yankee towns with their no connections but the cash nexus. But he knew too, for certain, how the mind's power could make a heaven or hell of every instant in the Bigs, the conditions in The Show being indeed that intense. And he knew that if a particular individual wasn't likely to find any heaven's joy in team spirit, then a hellfire of discontented private determination was, for him, just as good. Arguably even better in God's eyes.

He thought of how he had pages still to read in his father's life the last time he rode this street with Mr. West. It seemed a half-dozen lifetimes ago. But now a thought came to him, one he first had when they laid his father to rest, and that had numerous times recurred to him. He would build a tomb, a mausoleum. And when his mother died, he would have his father disinterred; and he would bury the two of them together in one wall of the tomb. And when he died, he would have them bury him alone in the wall facing his mother and father's. And he'd have placed in the back wall between, a beautiful stained-glass window with a white lily, for peace, in its center. And in the gray stone above the entry he'd have them carve the silencing word, "Cobb."

"Mr. Tyrus," West, the cabby, now said, disturbing the boy's mind from this present groove, "you may recall. . . . Well, let me pipe in outa nowhere that it'd be a true shame, sir, the way them Brahmins gets away with not appreciatin' a ballplayer's value 'n merit. I mean you can be sure a one thing, sir, and that's that Frankie J. has heard the word on ya 'bout as fast as even me. . . ."

Jolted now out of his musings and forced back into this conversation, the boy thrust an inquiry between him and his interlocutor. "And how *do* you get the word so fast, Mr. West, if you don't mind my asking?"

"That'd be the modern miracle a the telephone, sir. Spreads the word speed-a-light among us students a the game." Mr. West, whose preference appeared to be indirectness and evasion, was irritated some himself, it seemed, by a direct question's interrupting his conversational point, to which he now returned. "Now take that maneuver a comin' home like ya did, sir. I ask ya, is Mr. Frankie J. gonna appreciate the value a that? The calculatin's and such behind it, I mean? Or's he gonna scold ya out, or some such, fer goin' on yer own, which I heard some has, who don't know what all you was thinkin' when ya done it, which I'd measure by the success a the thing, and trustin' that ya had the odds calculated—*very* fine, sir."

Again there was the turn and smile. And again Tyrus had the feeling that he was being hounded down some dark road (and how in hell did this sonofabitch know as much as he knew?). But for the moment, still, he let his mind turn toward West's. He couldn't escape the cabby's flatteries, or the feeling that somebody really did appreciate his value and was willing to understand him and *did* understand him. This even though he had the feeling, the conviction, even, that he was being manipulated (for the effect of this conviction was a kind of sick pleasure of complicity and mutual-secret understanding!). He said, feeling the silent delight of a shared dishonesty, "You're right as the rain, Mr. West. Anything they can find to devalue a man, they will find, and use. Never a real conversation with ownership. Never a Christian moment. Just sweet self-interest on the owner's part. And an owner never chooses to understand a ballplayer. Never trusts him. And never admits a thing. Just plays the cat and the mouse."

"Frustratin', too, ain't it, sir, when ya know they got them contracts on their side. Doggone cussed un-American is what *they* are. I mean a man can't just up and quit the bastards—excuse me, sir—and go off elsewheres! Got t' stay where he's *put*! Don't take much t' see what they'll do with that lil' ol' gun in their hands, likes a Navin, likes a Comiskey, and all the rest of 'em. There ain't no differnce between 'em, far's I can see. Gods all, in their minds."

They had made their way far enough down the street toward Bennett so they could see the outside projection of those wildcat bleachers extending beyond the corner of that last factory building before them. So the boy knew that soon, when they passed enough of that building's street front, they would see Bennett's grandstand rising in the moonlight— what had he thought?—like some great ship coming in at night to Charleston harbor? But Mr. West's talk here had about driven off any suckering fancies and emotions. *All I care about is getting the chance to play in the major leagues:* the harmonious song of the sweet and noble ballplayer, the all-American hero, who never complains. He's *just grateful to be here.* Well, the hell with that. If Navin, that damned Chinaman—that damned Shadow of Mystery with his smoked-glass wall—used Cobb's "attitude" as a way to avoid admissions regarding his merits, then, hell, he'd hold out! and let 'em black-list him!

They passed on in the midnight moon, and the grandstand eventually appeared: a huge spread wing of dark in the silver glow. But stubbornly the boy did not look up, until Mr. West got his attention by pointing, not to the grandstand, but to the turnstiles at the front gate.

"Ya see them objects right there, sir?" he asked, as he stretched out his arm and hand and extended his forefinger.

Tyrus grunted that he understood. But an unshaded light was on in a room he hadn't even known existed, not far off the gate—and he was distracted by it—and didn't really answer. And such is the effect for a passerby of a night light in an unshaded room that he saw very clearly what was in the room, and who. It was that old crusty gatekeeper. Pagliotta, or some such, his name (another Yankee foreigner, anyhow): the venerable one. This must be where he lived. And what was he doing in there now? Saying his prayers? Tyrus saw the old man take, apparently, something off the wall, and then get down on his knees. And yes he did have some object in his hands. . . .

"What spins them turnstiles," Mr. West was saying, "is the likes a *you*, Mr. Tyrus Cobb. Where would Frankie J. be without the likes a *you*? He'd be *nothin'*, sir. And if he flips that around and says where would the likes of a Tyrus Cobb be without him, then you figure this: How many folks'd put out good money and spin through them turns if the attraction was Frankie J.? How many'd come out t' see *that*? It's what comes first, as should get the credit. Ballplayers is the cause a all the commotion. And folks around here is gettin' real excited, I'll tell *you*, sir, 'bout the ballplayer name a Tyrus Cobb."

Tyrus was catching the words now of his driver and was eager to offer him something more friendly and polite than some conversation-ending mumble. But he'd kept looking in the window of the old gatekeeper's quarters and had seen indeed that the old man had gotten down on his knees to pray and that the object that he'd taken from the wall, and then kissed before he began to pray, was a cross. All the gestures of prayer the boy had seen through the lighted window—the going down to the knees, the folding of the hands, the bowing of the head, the shutting of the eyes.

He shut his own eyes, but he said to Mr. West: "The question is, Mr. West, will a ballplayer ever fully, *can he* ever fully, and I'm talking about with the *utmost* possible energy, be what he was damn well born to be, if he is nothing but a good little boy for the organization? Will he have the courage?"

"And the answer t' that question'd be *no. No, sir.* I say *no*, he can *not*. Won't have, if you'll excuse my way a puttin' it, sir, the stones. That's what I say."

The cabby, as happily he brought things to this period, now slowed and pulled up his nag. They had crossed past the sawmill and arrived in front of the Union House, where the usual spillover, including women with smokes and bottles of beer, were out on the street, cackling and drunk-flirting. The door opened—and Tyrus could hear the tinny piano getting raucously slammed; so he figured the frilly-frills were dancing . . . and maybe tonight that beautiful young thing . . . a possibility that made his blood beat faster.

"I say *absolutely no* to that, Mr. Tyrus. And . . ." Mr. West now jumped down, tied his nag to the Union's hitching post and scrambled back to the bed of the cab, where he snatched up Tyrus's grip, an action that the boy took as intrusive but would have minded a hell of a lot more had there been a bat bag containing still his Royston ashes, or if his father's gun weren't now in his shoulder holster. "*And,* sir," the cabby said, familiarly smiling his rotten-mouthed smile, handing the boy his grip, "I want you t' remember—and don't you forget it this time, all right—that if there'd be any kinda service ya might need, any *whatsoever,* at *any future time,* I'd be at it."

This was followed, once again, by a broad, familiar wink.

Tyrus, considering suddenly the life-silencing power of his pistol, stuffed two bits in the man's paw and nodded to those smiling black teeth in such an unsmiling way as to suggest that no such occasion would be likely to come up, ever. And—he thought to himself—if he were going to offer a word now to this man, which he was not, it would have been that the only cause for Cobb's having seen West more than once was pure accident. Not giving the man a chance, then, even to say thanks, or put those black-scum teeth of his on his goddamned piece of silver, the boy walked quickly off through a huddle of Mickey-sounding and Mickey-looking patrons gathered round the Union House door, then through the green, latticed swing-panels and into the saloon.

The crowd in the bar, even at midnight, was nearly wall to wall, and the smoke hung like a thick cloud stuck against a Carolina mountain. But through the bobbing heads, the boy could see the can-can girlies lifting their black-stockinged legs, and he stopped to look. By some chance . . . maybe . . . He moved his head back and forth to see, standing on his tiptoes, peering. He caught, as he could, the painted faces of the dancers under the glaring lights inside the little red-curtained box of a stage. There were five—but no—all of them were older, road-worn "girls," whose looks made you wonder just how lonely were the sorry sonsofbitches packing this dive.

He gave up his little eye-quest and began to wedge his way out through the throng and toward that narrow stairway up. He admitted to himself he would have been excited to see the girl—that lost, beautiful face—very much excited—very much. But only because it could come to nothing—no more chance of anything happening than of his not killing himself before he'd carry the stain of such a girl Charlie's way. Just fool looking, the kind of stupid thing any boy does when he's alone, his true girl not around. But not finding her there, or her "beau" either, he was glad enough to take his cooling blood out of this sorry, smoking booze-sewer.

He looked for and got a wave and a nod from Timmy the bartender, a good Yankee, really, who'd told him to hang on to his key and that his room up top would be waiting; and he nodded back, as he sidestepped and continued to shoulder-wedge his way out of the crowd. He was getting free. Things were breaking up as he got farther from the stage and the noise of the piano's tin. The smoke was clearing, and he turned and walked straight, no longer needing to sidestep.

But then—exactly as thoughts would sometimes come suddenly to him from who knew where—she was there before him, bare-shouldered, except for the thin black straps of her dancing gown, her lips touched up red, but nothing gross, the touch of color making them even more warmly beautiful. Her hair was pulled up behind, but also here and there fallen in wisps. She was leaning with her beautiful, pale, bare shoulders touched against the wall, one of her black-stockinged legs crossed over the other. Now she took a glass up in two hands to her lips. Over its rim, she saw him.

She didn't bring down her drink, rather sipped it slowly and looked at him from under lowered lids, over the rim of the glass. He halted—stood still a moment as their eyes met—but tried to betray no sign of *anything*. Yet, as she showed no fear of him, indeed revealed not the slightest trace of anxiety, calling for no one, looking for no one, just looking steadily at him, he had now a powerful, strange feeling that she had been waiting there for him: that she knew somehow he had been looking for her. And now he couldn't get to his room without passing her, for she stood right next to the base of the narrow stairway up.

He tightened his hold on his grip and walked toward the stairs, trying to avoid her look. And she had lowered her eyes now into her glass. But then as he came up beside her (pretending she wasn't there), she took down her glass and held it in both hands before her. Still she didn't raise her eyes, or turn his way as he was passing to the staircase. But she spoke, looking straight ahead of her.

"You still the saddest, angriest boy in the world?"

He stopped again, and found himself hating (but also loving) that such a person pretended to such a wise understanding of who he was. Who was she, after all, to think she knew him? He wanted to get past her, but he couldn't help liking it that she hadn't let him, and that she was so unafraid, and so beautiful, so . . . incredibly . . . beautiful. He felt immediately some tremors of the thrill of losing himself and of losing his *soul* that falling to a temptation here would mean. In a quick, warm rush of imagination, he saw himself letting walls fall for this Yankee girl and granting her a right of admission into his privacy, no matter how far she might want to probe. For had he not held a gun at her, Jesus Lord in heaven. He wanted to say he was sorry. . . . Or that self-justifying, self-*excusing* rationalizing voice in him made the warm suggestion that he owed this girl an apology. But he wouldn't be weak. Not in *any* case would he be weak (since he knew, too, she would despise that).

"Do you often," he said, as he stood halted at the bottom of the stairs, "try to make people into things with words?"

He turned to her now, but found her still turned away, looking straight ahead. "I thought that night," she said, "that

I might get made into worm-food by a certain someone's gun." She turned to him now, still leaning her smooth, pale shoulders against the wall. "Do you often make people feel they're not going to see the morning sun?"

Her beauty was so real and powerful—God in heaven—her rose mouth so tender; and her eyes, velvety dark under dark brows; and her skin, a now beautifully blushed, golden cream, unblemished no matter what her life might have been. And her soft Yankee voice, maybe the only one in the whole North not one bit harsh . . . warmed him still more. This moment seemed to have been waiting for him, with all its moment's worth of warm, and deadly deceitful happiness, which a voice in him might whisper he owed himself. Yet he said, with a careful reserve, "If you thought you were going to die, Miss, why would you be speaking to me? Why be polite? Why not call the police?"

She didn't answer. She took a sip of her drink, slowly, now lifting, and emptying it. Then she lowered her glass and laughed. "Do I look like the kind who calls the police?"

He didn't answer. He looked at her and kept looking, so that she would feel the warm concentration of his gaze and then look back at him, which finally, after a silence, she did. "Did you really think I would use the gun?" he asked her, a moment after their eyes had met again.

With a deadly electricity now, she canceled any sign of mirth from her face. "Do you think I would stop you now, if I didn't?"

Immediately, he didn't like her thinking she'd stopped him; but she *had* stopped him. And who was she? Who *was* this girl who was sounding for him now crazier even than he had been that night? Talking like she liked it that he would have gone far enough to use a gun on her . . . the gun he felt now against his chest. He couldn't think this through, not while he looked at her. He found himself, though, wanting to play along with her. Or become her kind. He didn't know where his own voice was coming from. But he said, smiling in a way that he thought she would have herself, carefully keeping his mouth and eyes from coming really to life, "Like to play with trouble, eh?"

She looked away again. "Would have been more than trouble," she said, then, turning, slowly, "unless you're a bluffer."

He knew he was wearing a mask, playing a game, the way he went on with her now. But he was warming to the point of fire. "You like to gamble?" he said.

She ran a finger around the rim of her glass. "Only for the highest stakes," she said. Then, touching her finger to her tongue, "All or nothing."

He waited. Peered at her. "You like to think that way," he said, "all or nothing?"

Just slightly she curled her rose-touched lips in a smile. "Same as you, sad and angry boy," she said, "same as you." Then, after a pause, looking in his eyes, "Have a drink with me."

But he didn't drink. Never. Never had he touched liquor in his life. Not once. And with her suggestion to him, or her telling him what to do, he began now to recall himself. To stop himself from a move for which he knew he'd hate himself more than he ever had yet. And after which he could never again face Charlie honestly. Never. He knew. And there were only so many dishonesties he could keep covered up in his mind before it broke. Still he felt a burning fire of pleasure when she pretended so deeply to know him. He *wanted* the drink with her, his first. He *wanted* to pour out to her crazy words, to say to her, "You understand me better than anyone in the world." To fold her in his arms and whisper these kinds of crazy things against her cheek. And he *liked* her telling him what to do, because where she'd lead him, he knew, would be to an easy place of no recovery, where there was happiness because there was no more point in trying to be decent and good. There wouldn't even be a woman in it, in the end. Because this place would in the end *be* the hatred of women. He could sense the whole field of such craziness in a wild, wild brain race. See it all. But there was Charlie. And so *no!* He wouldn't give himself away for this kind of beauty here. She wouldn't order him. No matter how beautiful, and tender. Nor how intense that moment's happiness with her would be. He said, "I don't drink, I'm afraid."

She looked into her empty glass. "You know, sad and angry," she said, "there's a start to everything."

But something in him thought, "Wouldn't she know *that*." And she wanted him. He felt she'd revealed herself, confessed that weakness: that she wanted him to stay. And instantly this gave to his resistance enough power. He wouldn't follow any orders from her. There's a start to everything. "But," he said, "with me, not everything starts." He began then to go up, taking a first step up the stairs, hoping he hadn't sounded triumphant to her. And wondering . . . would she . . . ?

But she wouldn't beg. She didn't look up. She didn't say another word. And he crazy-loved her for that. Loved her. But he wouldn't begin any drinking life. Or hang with whores, for she was one . . . not to hang with. He walked on—up the narrow and sharp-turning staircase. His eyes, rather than looking back, ran stupidly, for safety, over the false gold leaf of the close staircase wall, all browned by smoke and only dimly lit. He touched it, ran his finger along. But then turned the first corner, taking with him a trailing hand. Then the second corner. And, as he reached the corridor leading to his room, it relieved and it killed him, knowing she wasn't the kind who would follow.

He locked his door, but let the chain latch hang. He set his forehead against the door panel. He closed his eyes and pictured her face, her soft, moist mouth, saw her moist lips glistening in the bar light. He wanted to touch his lips to that beautiful mouth. To kiss her and hold the pale cream warmth of her in his arms. He wanted to run back down and find her. Right now. He would beg her. Anything. He'd never seen a girl more beautiful. Never. He shouted those crazy, untrue words in his heart. Said he wanted the moment more than he'd ever wanted anything. Asked himself, because sometimes the rationalizer did his work with challenges: Was he just too much of a sweet little virgin coward to go back? He kept his eyes closed and waited. He waited, hoping he would hear her, that she would come up the stairs and come down the corridor to his room and knock on his door. And in an insane way he hated himself for a coward.

But time passed. And, while he knew he would never forget her, a point of desire for her having been reached irrevocably, he was relieved down to the center of his soul. He had saved himself, for Charlie. He was not what his father predicted he would be. Or what his father himself was . . . when he threw away his principles.

He set his things down by the bed and walked to the window. Flushed hot, beating still with the hot pleasure of her image, which was there before him in his mind (just as she was still right below him), he sought more soul's relief in other things. He was much too disturbed to write Charlie. There'd be so many things crossing his mind that he feared, if he even picked up a pen, he might drop it and head back downstairs. And there *was* something he'd wanted to know— yes—since he'd seen that red glow of a fire down that dark alley on his cab ride home. Was the carriage-maker Chevrolet still keeping a midnight flame, postponing his seventh-day rest while he forged a competitive engine, one he could run against the Nine-ninety-nine?

But he saw first in the full silver moonlight the pennants billowing over Bennett, curling slowly, floating up and spreading out in the silvery light, falling and rising again. And he thought, they won't take it from me, after all. The chance to be a no-lies-at-all baseball hero. Papa Leidy's prophecy. For how was it possible that anyone who didn't play the game as hard as he did—and he was deeply in his heart convinced that that was everyone who ever had played it, or who ever would play it—could be more pleasing in God's eyes, and in the eyes of true lovers of the game? Who possibly could more electrify and stir the American heart? What would America be, after all, if it didn't most value excellence and victory? But it did, he knew, most value excellence and victory: one country under God in this respect. And rather dead, than second-place. Let a Southern boy teach you *that*.

He looked down the street, toward where he'd incinerated his father's book. And he was pleased. He saw the same trash barrel aflame. And out from the shop of Louis Chevrolet, another fire was glowing red hot in the dark. If a man like Chevrolet, he thought, could see all the fires at once like this, all the engineers, and wheelwrights and other wagonmakers no more asleep than he is, he'd only burn harder and hotter. Survival of the fittest. Put *that* on the American dollar. And let God be the first to tell you there's absolutely nothing of real beauty that'll get accomplished in a more compromised spirit.

He thought of her very real beauty downstairs. He wanted suddenly again the softness and moistness of her lips, so much that he thought he could fly downstairs and beg her on his knees for a kiss, a touch. Her lips. Her unharsh voice, soft, mysterious. Oh Christ. But he wouldn't hang with a whore. He would *not*.

Time passed, and he cooled some. He thought of his mother's letters, which all three remained unopened under the cover of the *Lives*, buried in his grip. Was it time now to open them? She wanted to open her heart to him, he was sure, and communicate with him, her son. But her son didn't want now to be touched. He wanted more time to pass, in order to punish. He wanted her to *know* and for things to be *changed*, forever.

But hadn't that been the story of his childhood? Punishment. The true story of his—let him admit this—unhappy

264 | PATRICK CREEVY

childhood? And who was the one who tried to keep him from being the saddest, angriest boy? He thought, with his heart again pounding, of the beauty downstairs. A start to everything. He wanted to go and beg her and thank her for letting him buy her a drink. But no. God damn the disgrace of it. He wouldn't go down there. And he wouldn't open the letters, though who on earth knew better than Tyrus Cobb how a hard unwillingness to communicate could become harder and harder, taking on a life of its own?

But he didn't go down, or open the letters. Did not—though he was sure that with his not sending yet a first word of response to his mother he was indeed heading toward some point after which, like his father (expert on points of no return), he could never reverse the damage done. She'd know he knew something. And after that, how could they ever truly speak again? She would know for certain he took the diary. And the gun. And that he would have pieced together the entire story, from what he'd read, and known. So how, after that, could he cross back, with all the bridges torched? And why did he take the pleasure in good, good things being so fully ended? His relationship with his mother. Why?

And wasn't he curious? Did he not want right now to know what she'd said? He was curious as all hell, as he'd been all along. And he would read these letters, but not now. Rather on the train home, the way he'd read his father's version of the story on the train here, his detective's eye growing sharper in fact the more he let his curiosity build up. He'd be ready for any lie. And by the time he saw his mother in Royston, he would have an explanation for why he'd not returned a word to her.

Before he slept, he whispered a prayer for Charlie. And against the still-beating arousal that he felt for the beautiful attraction downstairs, he whispered for his true girl, "You're more beautiful, Charlie Lombard, far more beautiful." She'd kept him safe, too, with the strength of her loving heart and beauty, from God knew what brain-addling disease or death. But the one who came to him in his dreams, still, was the Yankee girl, who whispered to him, as he held her in his arms and made love to her, "I want you to be happy, sad, angry boy."

And in his dreams something else came, too. From somewhere—that face, that target he would shoot dead center if he hadn't already, maybe, so much pistol-whipped it into obscurity in his memory. But in the dream this face, a man's, came clear. Above the stairwell in the Royston house, in the hall between his room and his parents', it came clear, and it asked, "Do you remember now where we met?"

When he woke, it was the sun shooting in his east window, the heat and light catching him in an eye. He knew he'd find himself soiled, though the truth of it disappointed him. But he let it go in the confusion and trouble coming from his dream of that face . . . he'd somewhere seen? He threw his forearm over his eyes to stop the light of the sun. But for another reason, maybe, too? He didn't know if he was remembering or imagining, still maybe half asleep. But he pressed his forearm harder against his eyes, thinking it might bring on more of a memory, or an imagination of himself when he was what? He didn't know. Fourteen? Thirteen? Or no age, because it never happened? "Do you remember now where we met?" He pressed his forearm harder still over his eyes. And he recalled or imagined that when he was some age, or in some *dream*, he had done this—pressed his forearm over his eyes so hard that his arm trembled—because he thought he'd seen someone and wanted to make the vision go away. He was in his room at home. Was he dreaming? Just making his sick imagination glad as he contrived things? Or could it be true, that he'd seen someone?

He'd come home one night when he wasn't supposed to have come home? He didn't trust his imagination or any of its sick pleasures, the soul's true disease. Had he not had enough of it! But in the dream, or memory, which on his

Detroit bed he gave life to now by pressing his forearm still harder over his eyes, he'd come home . . . like his father. *Just like his father*, he was supposed to be at the farm. And his mother didn't know he'd come home. He'd slipped quietly into his room to sleep. And his father, not at the farm, was at the University. But someone was there with his mother? He thought he heard through the wall a man's voice, saying, "Useless. Pointless." Then the laughter of two. And the sounds of the bed. And then, "Absolutely nothing!" Then more laughter. Then, "Care now about nothing. Nothing. Except this happiness. Oh, thank you for this! Thank you!" His mother? Then, after some time, footsteps on the floor, moving toward the door? Then his own going to see? Opening his own door—to see. . . . "Do you remember now?"

He ripped his forearm away from his eyes and let the sunlight fall hard on his face. He would stop this imagining as he would stop thinking of that Yankee whore. He hadn't lost his mind *yet*. Or his soul either. His only further thought on his dream of the face from somewhere was that the parallels and coincidences in it, the resemblances in it between his situation and his father's situation on the night he was killed, *proved* it a false dream. False from the beginning. Or a false imposition of his present upon his memory of his past. Blame him for that, but no more. Too much pain, God damn all, in any more guilt.

Chapter Twelve
FURIOUS CONFRONTATION

He pulled himself out of bed and, walking back and forth in the familiar room, turned his mind to a combat. He considered his calendar. This was it. The last week, and only seven games to play. To his own satisfaction, he'd survived his great trial. They couldn't say no to him now for next year. He'd made that impossible. And as he paced the floor, he imagined a conversation with Armour and Navin in which they confessed this, listening to him and taking care to understand him and admitting he was right: right about his speed, for which there was no substitute; right about his hitting, which had been proven now incontrovertibly major-league; right about his fielding; right about his daring on the paths, which would never seem any daredevil rashness or stupidity to those who cared to understand. In his imaginations they agreed with everything he said, and not because he'd worked their minds with some subtle persuasion but because by his actions on the field he'd made it impossible for them not to agree with him.

But now he slowed, and stopped. He sat in the ladder-back and looked out at Bennett, his mind turning, as it would, in an opposite direction. With his several slumps deadening his numbers, he wouldn't, most likely, rise above .260 for the forty-one games. If they wanted to, they could ignore what he'd really shown and just concentrate on that. If they wanted to, they could ignore everything he'd imagined them agreeing to. If they *wanted to*, he admitted to himself with a sick feeling, they could do whatever they damn well *wanted to*. And one thing was dead cold certain, he thought, as he looked down the long length of the cedar-block street: They wouldn't be telling him the same things that Mr. Fred West was telling him.

He could wait timidly to find out. Just play his game quietly and then wait till they told him whatever they were going to tell him. He might precipitate a negative response, in fact, if—before they'd made the first move—he were to go up to them and try an inquiry on them, let alone a demand. Wouldn't they say to themselves, naturally, "Who the hell does this kid think he *is*?" And they might not even bother then with remarks on the mere .260 average, or the attitude problem (which maybe all boiled down in the end to a particular war with the White Rat, McIntyre); they would just say good-bye.

But, God dammit, he thought, as he rose from the chair and began pacing again, who in hell ever got anywhere without being aggressive? without having the guts to fight for his position? He wouldn't sit around like a good little boy and wait for the word. He'd get the first word in—and the last. Or so he convinced himself that morning in his room, as he tried to shake off his dreams. When later he started making his way to the park, however, he thought it might be suicide to raise now the question of his future. Best for him just to play his game and keep quiet. And wait and see. So he was thinking as he found himself failing to recall which steps he'd taken the last time he played at Bennett—not that he wanted to retrace them—those being the steps he took to his first meeting with Doctor White, which didn't seem so long ago.

And there now would be the old pious keeper of the gate, Pagliotta, his age-worn cap askew, bent low with his broom before the turnstiles, sweeping away dust and scraps of paper. When he saw the old man, the boy felt instantly a sharp conflict of emotions: on the one hand, he wanted to go up to the gatekeeper as politely as possible, with no look on his face and no tone in his voice, and pay the venerable old figure his respects, ask him how his day went, and then just wait patiently for the gate to get opened; on the other hand, he found himself hating everything the pious old bastard crab represented and wanted to give him a look that would let him know this as clearly as would spit in his face.

And dammit if there weren't Donovan and Crawford jumping off a cab now and heading toward the gate from the other direction. He couldn't dodge off without them seeing him. Hell. And look at that: Pagliotta tipping his cap to those two, rolling out the red carpet. That old crab wouldn't have said the first word to Cobb. Instead of the royal welcome, it would've been the royal dirty look.

Expecting, of course, from neither Donovan nor Crawford, any hale that would prevent him, he turned away down the street that skirted the grandstand and would head around and enter at the clubhouse street door. And who cared if they saw him dodging off, especially when it was just one more pure certainty that if this situation were repeated, truly, a *million* times, they'd never be the ones to act first?

It had always to be Cobb. *Always* Cobb. And if that was the last damned word on it, well, he thought to himself, as in the clubhouse he took his gear to his locker and hung it, then Cobb'd start things all right. He'd start them right the hell now!

He shut his locker hard and headed out of the locker room and down the vaulted corridor to the office. In the hall, he didn't look right or left, but, at the door, he stopped, and set his hawks on the gothic inscription on the smoked glass. THE DETROIT TIGERS BASEBALL CLUB. Then right on the letters, he rapped with his knuckles three times, hard and loud.

"It's *open!*" Armour, in his office voice, gave the boy the same salutation he'd given him the first day he got there. And Tyrus ran his mind over all his past experiences, determining with absolute certainty that never one time in his life down south had he been greeted in this manner.

Armour sat there in his office attitude, leaning back in his chair with that fancy boater of his tipped back on his head. He held his cigar in his teeth, and, bobbing his smoke up and down as he puffed on it, he blew up a good-sized cloud of blue gray as the boy entered. Then the manager took the cigar between his first two fingers, and, after a last drag on it, as he lowered it to his ash tray, blew a thin stream in the boy's direction. "Cobb," he said, nodding to the chair before him, "what might I do for you?"

And though immediately he damned himself for being *again* a sorry superstitious fool, the boy wanted now to say, "Nothing, sir. I'm sorry, Mr. Armour, sir; I'm not sure why I came in. I'm sorry to have taken your time." Because if he didn't say some such thing, and say it quick, and then shuffle back on out, he'd ruin his chances for a future completely! If *he* didn't wait to hear from *them*, he'd give himself no chance for survival at all!

But he didn't wait for them. "I've come," he said, as he took the seat in front of the manager's desk, "to talk about my future."

"Is that so," the manager said, not indicating in any way whatsoever that this was a subject he found interesting.

"Yes, Mr. Armour, it is so," the boy said, feeling now that old excitement of passing a line, the kind you can't cross back over. "I figure now," he said, "that I've got a right to know some things about what ownership thinks of me and my chances."

"Do you?" Armour said, now smiling in a way that said he found this an amusing display of innocence on the rookie's part.

And the boy could see now the Shadow of Mystery, Navin, moving in the Inner Sanctum. "Yes, Mr. Armour, I do. After how things went in Chicago against Doc White, I think I've won some rights of inquiry for myself, at least. And what I want to know, because of course I've got to make plans for myself, is what exactly my future is here."

"Cobb, you're a pistol, all right," Armour said, curling his lip in a half-smile, flicking his ash in his ash tray. "I've got to give you credit for *that*, at least. You *are* beautiful."

The boy decided against any smiling back. And God damn how he hated it that it was all right for Armour to dig trenches between himself and his player but that it was not all right for his player to do the first thing for himself. That that would be "beautiful" and the kind of action a "pistol" would take. And speaking of trenches, did not this whole damned opposite of a good relationship start with that owner in there, who never even welcomed the presence of his ball-player here, let alone acknowledged his worth?

The boy was growing angrier by the second, though for pride he wouldn't show it. He could dance his part, too, in this dance without music. But hell, Fred West knew what his effort was worth and said so, out loud. These close-to-the-vest sons of bitches—why—they were so afraid that a word slipped out between their filthy lips might sound like a verbal promise that they wouldn't whisper a syllable. But it's Tyrus Cobb who's a sinner for not cooperating! It's Cobb who's the damned sinner! Always Cobb! How in God's name the world got built into this particular *necessarily so*, who knew? And he thought: a free country my damned *eye*! "I was hoping," he said, "that you would give me credit for other things, like my hitting and running the paths."

"Wehhhll, you see, those would be subjects we'll introduce at a later time, Cobb, when the season's over. You're just gonna have to wait, I'm afraid, for any word on your future. The ownership will take its own time with that. So you just keep *your* mind on the here and now. Remember—

that's a ballplayer's job." He smiled, looked down at his smoke, and flicked his ash before looking up.

But the boy was not to be put off. When anybody made him wait for anything, it drove him about half-crazy. But this sort of managerial game got to him way down deep. And God damn them: If living in the here and now was good for some things, for others it sure as hell wasn't. "I think," he said, "I've established my value clearly enough by now so that you brass have enough to go on."

Armour acted amused. "Have enough to go on, eh?" he said, smiling, then turning his smile into a tight little grin. "Well, Cobb," he said, "maybe we have enough to go on— and maybe we don't." He made his smile now more seeming-benevolent. "But in any event, you see, we've got to take into consideration *all* our needs, not just the situation of one particular ballplayer." He looked down at his cigar and spoke while flicking his ash. "I can understand your worry about your future"—this again with that seeming benevolence (although the boy could read the real, manipulative point of the remark). "I can *understand* your worry there. But we've got a whole team here, Cobb, that we've got to put together. And if we decide to fill a need *here* . . ." He touched with his cigar a spot in the air above his desk—then—sweeping his hand before him and touching another spot, on the other side of his body—". . . we've got to take into consideration what we might have to give up over *here*."

"So, what? you might put me on the block?" the boy said quickly, emphatically *not* disguising his bitterness at such a notion. Every player despised the feeling of being owned, and tradeable. But the boy knew too that it was management's oldest game, just letting players know that they were owned, and tradeable. He asked, "Is that what you mean?"

"Well . . ." Armour said.

The two of them now could hear Navin moving in the office. Armour didn't show any signs of noticing, but this said to the boy only that the man had known all along that Navin would be listening in on every word he uttered. The movement also said to the boy that Navin was probably thinking now Armour was going too far, a little past his pitiful little tether. The boy noticed a nervousness in the manager, who said again, shaking his head, "Well . . . Cobb, you are beau. . . ."

And sure as hell now, at the threshold of the *Sanctum sanctorum*, there would be a click and a creaking. Armour didn't look back; he just stopped in midsentence, and waited. The door, as if it had been only touched and left to swing on the hinge by its weight alone, now opened, slowly. The boy looked up, beyond the manager, to watch as heavily the door came full wide. And there, for the first time become real substance for the boy, would be the Shadow, Navin—bloated, bald as an egg, his small, round, black-rimmed spectacles seeming even smaller on his huge head. In an undertaker's-black suit, the owner was as pale as a man who'd never seen the sun (though there was a gripe word the boy had overheard in Cleveland that Navin, whose own brother had done time, had spent maybe a thousand afternoons at the track, laying down Tiger dollars that should have been spread).

At last he spoke, his first words ever to the boy: "Disruption, Mr. Cobb," he said, then moved his white, expressionless face as if by a lock-step into a scowl. "Disruption of the team, sir, is a factor we will be considering in your particular case, and that you'll have to be considering as well, won't you?"

With everything in him, Tyrus despised this playing it for awe—hated especially the mysterious sudden entry, because it goddamn worked for a second, setting him back a step. But he recovered himself and acted as if it were nothing much that he'd finally heard his owner speak. "There's always the question, Mr. Navin . . . I take it I am addressing Mr. Navin. . . ."

Armour ran his eyes up skyward, and Navin offered the

slightest nod he possibly could and have it still register as an acknowledgment.

"... Always the question of who *starts* a disruption. I hope we'll consider that, because I'm sure there are some factors here...."

The white bulk under the lintel didn't wait for the boy to finish his sentence. "I noticed no particular problems, Cobb, with *esprit de corps* before your arrival. *Post hoc ergo propter hoc.* I don't suppose you're familiar..."

The boy (thanking his father in his mind) fired back his own combative intrusion. "I'm familiar with *post hoc* as a classic fallacy in logic, sir. And aptly referred to here, I'd say, in my particular case, given the fact that my arrival must be an insufficient explanation of cause...."

"A student of logic are you, Cobb?" The owner couldn't help but break into a slight smile as he interrupted, though he repressed his smile as best he could, moving his face back quickly that one step to expressionlessness.

"Put it this way," Tyrus said, determined now never to back off with this man: "I know speed and hitting are absolute necessary conditions for victory and that I can bring that combination in a way that no one here can and that *therefore...*"

"Christ, Cobb," Armour now fired in, "ya hit two bits. Ya'd think we was talkin' here to Nap Lajoie."

"Thank you, Billy," Navin said, but in a tone that ever so slightly suggested impatience with the manager. And in this little exchange between the two brass, the boy discovered a volume, of which his reading was: God damn—they might not admit it even at gunpoint—but they need me. And it'll all work out, all their humbling and demeaning tricks aside, according to a nice, simple logic that I've *forced* on 'em. And Lajoie—why did "Mr. Name-a-team-for-him" come up if comparisons hadn't suggested themselves to Armour's mind?

The boy sent out a probe. "Mr. Armour," he said, ignoring the manager's point regarding someone's .250 average, "made some remarks earlier that suggested the block. Have I been discussed as trade material?"

"I am sure," Navin said—and the boy watched every slightest muscular action in the owner's face, noticing an increased blinking of the eyes and a tightening of the lip, "Mr. Armour would agree that it's best to wait before discussing trades or any such thing. Best to wait on everything. . . ."

The boy sensed victory now. There'd be no block for him. No possibility. He could read this Navin the way he could a pitcher. Nor did he mind seeing others sniping at themselves now instead of sniping at him. He liked that, in fact. And he thought, rash my eye, and was glad as hell he'd come in here now. And, though he wanted to disguise every trace of emotion that he felt, he wore a not-dissatisfied look when Navin finished things off with a mere curt nod and an "I think that'll be all for now," quietly closing behind him the door to the Holy of Holies.

And that day and on through that last week he would go right ahead and hit respectably, run respectably, play respectably. Not to say that he wouldn't go right ahead, too, and make his mind into its own hard-working factory of Tyrus Cobb trade rumors, putting himself on the block enough times so that he began picturing himself even in pure shackled mortification. Or that there was holiday either for his old fear that the end of his journey would be that he'd make himself crazy. From the series in Philly through the one in Washington, and on to the end, as days had passed and he'd gotten further away from his time with Charlie in New York but closer and closer to his seeing her again, he had let the angry side of him more and more just have its temporary way. But what morphine madness didn't start up the same way?

He'd given Charlie the Union House address and he'd gotten letters from her there now, warm, loving, written to the boy she believed in. And he'd written her faithfully, mak-

ing it his regular practice to eat early with Timmy the barkeep and then head up to his room for thinking about his
game, for reading, and for writing his girl. He avoided any
unsafe encounters, too, with any other girl, taking good care
of his soul, and putting it hard in his mind that carelessness
and suicide were the same word when it came to failure
there. But still he'd left his mother's three letters unopened.
And in that room at night, after he'd sealed his latest letter
to Charlie and could hear his watch tick and sometimes the
bass rumble of that beer-cheered piano downstairs and could
see the flags rippling or not over Bennett and he thought of
his father's life story and his loaded pistol and the face from
somewhere, which he *would* pistol whip into oblivion if ever
he found it real, and that damned alpaca jacket safe on the
other side of the wall, he'd feel his mind sometimes trapped
in so hard and tight that he was sure that if he had that letter
for Charlie written, he still was sending it from a prison on
a lifeless island rock that he'd never, in the time he had on
earth, get home from. Never.

But still he wouldn't open his mother's letters, and when
he thought of them in the room there with him, and of his
mother, and then of that seductress slut beauty downstairs
promising him happiness and death, the rock-prison for a
moment did become a hatred of women, or all but one, because couldn't they just kill a man with sickness and disgrace
forever. But to hell with Minifield, too, if he thought that
Tyrus Cobb, when it came to any agonies of shame, was going to seek any help beyond the gift of his anger and his
obligation to finish off a revenge. For the time of his wars on
the diamond, at least, he thought now he would never surrender.

He would pace to the window and look down the street
to see if a fire still burned at Louis Chevrolet's—but then pace
away—for he couldn't go see Louis with that Scylla below
him and the Charybdis of all his shameful behavior in Washington and Chicago (for he was sure that if Louis Chevrolet

understood fiery competition, he was sure, too, that the man would not understand fighting a teammate on the field during a game, or letting a ball fall and then sit there on the grass while a run scored against the team, or getting yourself moved from center to right when *center* was where the team needed you to be).

As he paced, though, he imagined conversations in which he got Louis to agree, easily, that he sure as shootin' showed ownership that they could not do without Cobb and that he'd by-God *forced* 'em clear as could be to admit this necessary fact—or at least admit it in so many words. But then he'd think, with the word out everywhere on his unsportsmanlike behavior, that Chevrolet would look at him now in the curious way someone looks at an insane man. And that he'd no more buy Cobb's logic on Cobb's importance than ownership would, which was not a spit more than we will wait and we will *see*.

With the Tigers and him, the last week of the season turned out exactly as he expected. The veterans didn't break the silence, and neither did he. But he'd goddamn starve before he'd blame himself for this now. And though still he never outright accused McIntyre of vandalizing his ashes— not wanting to hear the sonofabitch's lying denials—he let him know he knew. He'd improved his bat trove with some fairly decent H&B hickories, and purposely, whenever McIntyre came into the back territory of the locker room, to shower, or take his own bat to the bone, the boy would take out one of the hickories and either look it over and rub his circled hand down its shaft, as if to see if there was any seam cut in it by some sneaking vandal. And it was very strongly Tyrus's preference to let the man know he knew in this way, without saying to him a single word. He liked the suggestion it made of an unknowable and gathering vengeance.

But he overheard things that raised wild shouts among his brain-furies, not that he was one bit surprised by what he overheard. "Crazy. I tell ya I really, honestly think so, the way he looks at ya sometimes. I swear he's *off*, never sayin' a word, just lookin' at ya like ya was from the friggin' moon. What the hell does *that* say?" This from one among the McIntyre huddle, offered, the boy supposed, as a final summation of his rookie season. For wouldn't it be exactly in the White Rat's interests to let that stand as the summary word: the redneck rookie was insane, a crazy man. And also, from the same source, this: "You can blame yourselves if ya like. But don't even start lookin' at us. Does he look like he wants a friendly word? Hell, he looks like he'd *shoot ya* if ya said hello."

"Shhhhh. Christ. He'll hear ya."

"Ahh shush yourself. The way I see it, he figures he's got some kinda special right to everybody's understandin'. Well, he ain't got *mine*. He's a damned spook if ya ask me. A damned born crazy spook. Cracked from the damned start. So don't go talkin' to us about it."

And letting such overheard words, proof-words, work him up, he in silent distance would begin working another groove in his mind, repeating over and over Navin's "Disruption. Disruption, Cobb, is a factor in your particular case." And a raging desire would grow in him then to give them all, before this season officially ended, some disruption all right: to show 'em what the word really meant. And if it became a dispute between "factors"—the disruption "factor" or the "factor" that he'd made himself a logical necessity for the Tiger lineup—then let the chips fall where they may.

Indeed it excited him to think that if he in fact had made Navin need him—that if he in fact had established this necessity—he'd still maybe set a storm going that could blow away everything he'd found out he'd won. After all, Tyrus Cobb never liked a sure thing for long! He had too many hankerings for explosions! He was thinking this as on the final day of the season, he sat alone, turned away from the team to the last.

In his final appearance, exactly as in his first, he'd

gapped a blistering shot for two bags, which spooky little symmetry, he thought, should have said things to them about him, making it clear he was no ordinary item, no mere flash without a destiny. And so he was thinking, too, as he was about to take himself for the last time out of that hair-shirt discomfort of a Tiger's uniform, that after he'd waited like a good little boy for them to make their decisions regarding him, the first thing he'd do would be to ask for more money than they offered. Not a moment's delay: That's how fast he'd put in his claim.

But out of the corner of his eye now he caught his enemy, and he thought again *disruption*. With now truly just moments of this season remaining, did he or did he not have the spine for it? He thought of his dream of McIntyre, of those words about "sweet little Mandy Cobb," which came for him not unconnected to another of his dreams. "Do you remember now where we met?" And did not the kind of callousness his enemy-teammate had showed prove the dreams all about the same man? Same kind of man in essence. Same man, after all. Same thing. And the dreams true enough, in *essence*. So *what*—was he too yellow to make something happen before the clock just ticked away his last opportunity?

Out of the corner of his eye, he'd seen his enemy moving his way, coming over to take his privileged little spot in the shower line: that damned step-ladder that as it hadn't been reconfigured one bit in the five weeks the boy was up, continued to show just how happy these suckers were to use privilege on others in the same way privilege got used on them. It made the boy think the brass must indeed have some secret one-shower plan, to use as just one more ploy to make little ape-moguls out of ballplayers and so get the system deep down into their systems. He shot up quick and put himself in the line before his hated rival.

"What the *hell* would this be, hot shot?" McIntyre responded with a ferocity that made it clear a very large investment was at stake for him here.

"Are you talking to me?" Provokingly feigning surprise, the boy threw down the gauntlet putting this question.

"And who the hell might you *think* I was talkin' to, somebody who's smart enough to understand he's gotta wait his turn? Excuse me, but I don't see nobody that smart where you're standin'."

"Well, you'll have to forgive me for being surprised, sir, seeing how you don't send many words my way."

"And whose fault would *that* be? That's what I'd like t'know." McIntyre acted as if he'd asked the question of questions.

And the boy felt pleasure. The team were all gathering round; and this had all the promise of a moment big enough to satisfy him for his long, long ride home. "You know, mister," he said, "if you think it's *my* fault, I don't give a damn what you think. Not the first damn."

"And there would be the problem all right, ya supposed-to-be-gentleman Southern hypocrite sonofabitch. You don't give a shit what nobody thinks ever any time. And don't go congratulatin' yourself on bein' some proud *rebel* fuckin' hero. That'd be the dead center a your phony fuckin' life, Cobb. Southern horseshit. Yer no *rebel*, yer just a miserable piece a shit who wouldn't smile for his own goddamned mother."

"You keep your rat's mouth shut, you hear me. Or so help me, McIntyre, I'll blast a hole right through you!" This remark, once started, would move the boy to complete it in the clearest terms: "I've got a loaded gun in my locker, I swear I do. And don't think I won't use it!"

"Say, do ya hear him, everybody! The crazy sonofabitch says he's got a fuckin' loaded gun in his locker and that he'd by God use it! Blow a hole right through me! Everybody—do ya hear the fuckin' madman! And wouldn't he be just about crazy enough, though he'd call it courage, or some such self-satisfyin' lie, I'll bet. Wouldn't ya, ya crazy loon. You'd call it courage, wouldn't ya."

The crowd had closed in a ring around the two, and voices now started. "Come on, Matty. Stuff his big words right down his throat! Johnny fuckin' rebel!" And "Hell yeah. Let's see 'em settle this thing once and for all. Christ, I'd love to see *that*." The closing ring moved the rivals toward each other, closer and closer, bringing them face-to-face under the green, tin-shaded locker-room lamp. "Yeah, let 'em settle this thing. Show Mr. Exception to the Rule who's got the real goods, once and for all!" "Yeah! Bring it on, Matt!"

Smack! Like lightning, before the boy had raised his fists in defense, a blow came across his upper jawbone. McIntyre had shot his fist hard from the hip, and now Tyrus felt blood warming, dripping on his face.

"Come on, ya sorehead lunatic, put yer dukes up! And don't say *you* didn't bring this on!"

Tyrus took pleasure in the blood warming on his cheek. He wiped it with the back of his fist and said, "All along it's been *you*, ya sonofabitch. And *none* of you is going to hang the first thing on me!" With that he shot his own quick fist into the face of his rival. Then he danced back, raised his two fists like a fighter, and began to move. "And all of ya on his side! Ya dumb *suckers*! All of ya! *All of ya!*"

"*Kill* the sonofabitch, Matt! The crazy peckerhead. Thinks the whole world's against him. Stuff his sore head right up his ass!"

McIntyre was bleeding from the corner of his mouth. And now the two of them, bloodied, began circling under the green-shaded lamp and bobbing, eyes over their raised clenched fists, looking for chances.

"Make him sorry, Matt! Make the sonofabitch *sorry*! Thinks he don't have to pay no dues. Don't owe nobody nothin'."

"Ya hear that, peckerhead," McIntyre said, as he took a quick swipe with the back of his right hand to wipe the blood off his mouth. "Whole gang thinks yer a friggin' ingrate and a sourpussed fuck!"

"Yeah. Askin' for it since day one. Put him in his goddamned place, Matty!"

McIntyre now came with an uppercut that missed the boy's jaw but grazed his mouth and caught his nose, bringing on a new run of blood that the boy could taste.

The veteran said with his hit, "There ya are, hotshot. A little punishment for ya, which I leave it to you if you think you fuckin' deserve it!"

The boy spat the blood from his mouth and, forgetting the distances of sporting boxing, dipped quickly low and took a full lunge at his enemy and threw himself into the man's body. "You yella goddamn sucker sonofabitch, I'll kill you!" he yelled as he tackled the left fielder, hitting him at the waist and lifting him as he grabbed him behind both thighs, then driving him back and down. He then screamed out a wild animal howl as he leapt up to put his hands on the man's throat! "Yaaaaaaah!!"

"Oh Christ, he's got that rebel yell goin' now, Matt! Roll the sonofabitch over and give him a lesson in Shut The Fuck Up!"

McIntyre did take quick advantage of the wildness in Tyrus's tackling leap and had rolled away to a side. Now he spun back and on top of the boy, where instantly he took hold of the boy's two hands, which still Tyrus was reaching to strangle him with, and pinned them back out straight over the boy's head.

And with his hands so pinned, Tyrus became still more crazily angered. He didn't care what anybody heard or thought or how far or fast the word would spread, about how he *was* insane. He screamed, foam gathering on his bleeding lips, "I'll kill you, you sonofabitch! I'll blow a hole right through you! I swear to God, I'll kill you! Don't think I won't!"

McIntyre, older and heavier and stronger, held the boy

still pinned hard, and looked down now into his face. "Yer brain's crackin', Cobb. Yer crazier'n a fuckin' loon." He brought his face closer still to the boy's, to inflict more humiliation and punishment. "Comes a not givin' a shit, Cobb, about nobody but number one, or about how the boys feel about yer not doin' what every last *one* of 'em had to do!" He was inches away, and the blood from his cut mouth dripped on the boy's face. "Comes a stickin' by nobody but goddamn *you*, Cobb, ya stupid sonofabitch, and not talkin' t'nobody but yer own fuckin' shadow, who'd be hell for company, all right." He shouted now at the top of his lungs. *"So see what ya brought on! See what ya brought on, ya crazy fuck!"*

The boy felt more rage maybe than ever in his life, at being pinned fast the way he was and over the White Rat's face sticking in his face, and his words. He couldn't move. The man's weight on his abdomen and chest was too much for his strength. And his arms were pinned back so straight he could get no leverage. He felt crucified and was truly near insane with anger. "My family!" he shouted, with his eyes rolling back. "My family taught me what you don't have the goddamned souls for! You damned, ignorant animals! My father and mother . . . !"

McIntyre still held his face right in the boy's face. He was maybe a useful straightjacket now for a madman—but he loved too his cruelties—deeply. "Your father and your mother, sonny boy . . . ? Hoh hoh . . . Don't make me say it. Don't you make me say the words, sonny boy!" He held his face now close enough to rip his teeth into the boy's skin.

And this godforsaken nightmare. This hell nightmare. The boy could not believe it, that he could not buck this weight from off his chest. And *right there* was that face, the white skin, the black shadow-stain of whisker, sickening, revolting. And the teeth. The gold in the teeth. The boy couldn't move. He had no power to lift his arms or hands out of the pin. His muscles were rippling, trembling, but he couldn't move. So he spat, shooting blood and foam from his mouth into the man's face. And spat again. And again, to get that face back away from his. He raged in his crucifixion, his arms still pinned. He'd get that face *away* from him!

"Get off me, you scum Yankee filth! Get off me or I'll kill you!"

"Not till you say yer sorry, sonny boy *reb*! Not till you say yer sorry for bein' a sourpussed piece a shit! Not till you say you're sorry! Not till you *say the words!*" He kept his face right in the boy's face, even as the spit ran over his cheek.

The boy concentrated his face in pure hate. He spat words now from his mouth. *"Never! never!* And you sawed my bats, you Yankee *bastard*! You sawed my bats! You sneaking rat sonofabitch I saw you! I've known all along it was you, you sneaking rat filth."

"Listen to this, boys! Listen to *this*! I never touched your crazy-man goddamned bats! You never saw *nothin'*, ya crazy piece a shit!"

The boy now began swinging and butting his head in fury, backing the man's face away. "You liar!" he began to shout. "You liar! You goddamned *liar!*" Then again, "My family! My father and mother! You ignorant, soulless scum . . . !"

The man thrust back his face, dodging the boy's head swings. "You keep wantin' to make me say it, Cobb. You keep askin' me to say it. . . ." He let these words out between his teeth, and now to stop the boy's wild swinging of his head, caught and met him and set his own forehead with trembling force against the boy's forehead, the pressure of the two heads against each other seeming ready to explode in someone's death. "And I *will* say it! Your goddamned *family . . .* I'll *tell* you . . . !"

"Christ, Matty, that's enough! God dammit, that'd be *enough!*" Donovan had stepped now out of the crowd and, stronger even than McIntyre, was pulling the man off the boy.

"All *right*! But *that* ain't the explanation anyhow!" Mc-Intyre began yelling. "It ain't the explanation, I tell ya, a this sonofabitch! Goddamn excuse. It ain't gettin' my pity! It ain't gettin' my pity! And what's he mean about them fuckin' bats! What the hell's he *mean*! God dammit! Ya hear how he keeps a fuckin' grudge in his cracked brain! Sayin' nothin' and bein' fuckin' crazy all along! I didn't have nothin' t' do with his fuckin' crazy-man bats! And his goddamn shit fuckin' crazy *family*! I *will* say a word or two . . . !"

"Enough, Matty! So help me!" Donovan had the man pulled off and then pulled him away and was facing him, as the mob broke up. *"Not one more word! Ya hear me! Not a word! Or so help me I'll shut you up!"*

The boy stood. His eyes were red and wet with tears of rage and sorrow. "I *spit* at your pity," he said, furiously ripping his forearm over his eyes, directing his remark nowhere and everywhere. *"I spit at you!"* Then he turned to his locker, tore off his uniform and left it on the floor. He dressed in a pure rage, as if his clothes were a child he was shaking in a fury of punishment and hate. He stuffed his spikes, his empty bat bag, and his gun and holster in his grip, and he left.

Chapter Thirteen
UNCOMPROMISED DEPARTURE

As he pounded his feet on the street outside the park, an imagination came suddenly and violently to him that he would see old Pagliotta now ready to show him *out*—out to the cab of Mr. Fred West, who would be dressed now in black and have the face of that target, the devil of his dreams, only still with West's rotted, sickening teeth, like a skull's after a hundred years of burial. But no one was there. "An accident!" he said out loud to himself as he walked the streets in pounding fury, the cut on his mouth bleeding so he had to wipe the blood away with an angry fist. "Now *there's* an accident!" He shouted this to no one as he walked on in a way so furious that, had he been seen, might have gotten him put on the train to the madhouse, all right. *"An accident, ya hear me!"*

Another imagination came violently to him that he'd see the girl waiting for him at the base of the steps in the tavern in the Union and that he'd strike the witch to the floor—Miss Beautiful. That he'd raise his fist and lower it on the side of her head and neck and fell her and leave her senseless, witch-slut body where it lay. But no one was there, not even Timmy.

There was a smell of supper. But repulsed by the stale reek of last night's drunken boozing, he'd get the hell out of this hole. And he wouldn't eat Yankee poison now at gunpoint.

He locked his room with the dead-bolt and the chain. His chair was by his window and he dropped his things by the bed and went and sat. He looked at nothing. He felt the weight of McIntyre on his chest and abdomen and the pinning down of his arms to motionlessness and powerlessness as the crucifying defeat of his life. The muscles in his arms still trembled from their failure and defeat. He wanted to kill. To break things apart and kill. To roam these Yankee streets with his gun drawn. He wanted to go back to the Tigers' brass and point his pistol in their faces and force them right now to take him and put that White Rat on the block or goddamned *else*! He saw himself pistol whipping McIntyre and his twin, too, that face from somewhere, at the back of some blind alley and leaving them both dead in their blood.

He had been glad as hell he'd gone right into the office of ownership and made a noise for himself and declared his rights and gotten concessions—revelations and admissions that he'd *forced* out of them.

But what a bitter joke that all was now. And if he even *did* force anything—why? What was the pleasure? As he took the back of his hand again to his mouth and cheek, he felt another sharp turning in his soul. He felt again that need for *some* kind of better life. The cry for some change. It hadn't been silenced. Not any time. There's no time in the soul. Just the truth. Waiting till called on.

And as much as he raged against the idea—he knew he'd caused it all. Admitted it now with a rush and wave of confession, tears gathering in his eyes. Putting himself up in the shower line like that. He brought on the fight. It was Cobb's fault. Everything. They'd have a team if it weren't for Cobb. They'd have a team. A *good team.* If it weren't for him. Who knew better what all there was to admit than the one who had never admitted a thing!

He despised himself. Everything. All of it was his fault. All along everything had been his fault. And this is where it ends—in damned pain and agony. And pain is a sign! He felt a crazy need to beg forgiveness for everything. Every evil thing in the world. To beg. And then say out loud he was guilty. Shout it in the streets, so there'd be no hiding, and then start his life over again, pure and clean.

His eyes closed on the burning salt of his tears, the salt stinging his cheek and his torn mouth. If he lifted his arms, they still trembled from his defeat. He sat in his chair, feeling the pain throb for some time—in his arms and face and mouth, until he reached a sort of trance. He bowed his head in the dark, not looking out. He could at some point hear the ticking of his watch, but he let the sound drift away. It came and went. And he could only guess the time. Some long time passed.

But now he was surprised. There was a knocking at his door. He couldn't imagine. That face from somewhere come to meet him? It must ... Or was it the girl? The knock sounded again. If it was the Yankee witch ... Oh God. He'd do it. He'd throw himself away on her. He'd take her in and take her to his bed and throw himself away on her, all his honor and pride. He'd throw his soul away for those soft, beautiful lips. His life. For the beauty of her face. All night long, he'd make himself nothing for her. His first.

"Tyrus?"

Who was that? A man's voice. Not the girl. A man.

"Tyrus, are you in there?"

Another voice, different, but also a man's. Who were they? Who knew he was here? Who knew where to find him? Who in all Detroit knew where Tyrus Cobb kept himself? He hadn't told a single soul. But West knew. Was it West, and some gambler? Gamblers. Emperors. Owners. Half-niggers, and niggers like Ezra. His grandfather, whom he hated to death. Matty McIntyre, whom he hated to death. Gatekeepers. Cutty Hayward. They all came to him now, no logic. No.

Or yes? Accidents in his brain? The knock sounded again.

"Hey, Tyrus, open up, all right? We'd like to talk to ya."

"Go away!" He let them hear that, but then regretted letting them know he was there at all. And who *were* they?

"Come on, kid, we just want to share a few words with ya, let ya know we're on your side, eh? It's me, Billy Armour; and I got Wild Bill here. Just a friendly visit, kid, honest."

"Yeah, Tyrus. It's me, Bill Donovan. Just a few words, maybe?"

Something in him wanted to get his gun back out of his grip and blow holes in the door. He ripped his sleeve across his eyes. He was ashamed that there would be signs of his suffering written on his face. But still in a part of himself that would use no gun, he was sick of not blaming himself. And he went now to the door, turned the thumb turn, and unfastened the chain.

"How'd you find me?" he asked, as he saw the manager and the veteran pitcher, their hats in their hands, now standing in the doorway.

Donovan wanted to speak, but he let the manager start. "We saw old Sam Pagliotta," Armour said, "at McCarthy's, where we was havin' a little end-a-the-year thing—a lament—I guess you could say. Anyhow, Sam said he'd seen ya come to this place after games." Armour was using that voice other than his office voice. And now Donovan said, in a warm voice too, "We'd have found you anyhow, Tyrus. We just would have, that's all."

Donovan, Tyrus thought, Donovan—he'd pulled off McIntyre—and he'd pulled him off once before, too, in that war in the outfield. A number of moves. Other ones, too. And he'd stopped McIntyre's voice. But the boy hadn't expected any of this. Pagliotta! Through what crack in his wall had that old crab squinted Cobb's way? And what, after all, were the manager and pitcher doing here? Come to tell him just to stay home once he got there? Hell, yes, that would be it.

He'd bet that would be it, all right, a bit of friendly advice: forget The Show.

"Can we come in?" Donovan asked, in that same warm voice.

The boy wanted to shut them out, hard, but he would not not be polite, or hospitable. "Please do," he said, and held the door open wide for them. "Sorry," he said, "I have no chairs other than the one. Let me go ask."

"No need," Donovan said, "comfortable right here." And he sat on a corner-end of the bed, inviting Armour to take the other, which he did. The boy then pulled his chair in from the window and sat with them.

"Today . . ." Armour said.

"It's about McIntyre, isn't it?" Tyrus said, thinking suddenly now that what it was, was that these team leaders didn't want to leave for the year without trying to patch things together, and in his heart he felt suddenly glad that his triggering an explosion *had* had a large disruptive effect.

"Well," Armour said, "yes, yes it is, along with some other things." The manager bowed his head a moment, swinging his boater between his knees, then looked up, seeming now to the boy just an earnest man, not some dude, for all the fancy grooming. "I mean, well, Tyrus, you know how I was with ya in the office the other day." He tapped the boater against his fist. "Look, son, I'm a ballplayer myself. I don't like to play games with ballplayers. But I find myself in the middle now, ya know? Havin' to speak for management—and pass *their* word on—and somehow keep both sides together." He frowned, bowed his head, then looked up. "But we ain't in the office now. So I'm gonna tell ya in my own words what I didn't tell ya the other day."

The boy thought instantly again that this would be a farewell—and not because of some mere trade but because his career was *over*, just like that. He knew it as well as a man standing for the verdict in a trial for his life when he hears the word *guilty*.

But the manager smiled. "Son," he said, "you're gonna be a great, *great* ballplayer. It gives me pleasure to say it. Leidy. And Byron. They had the dope, no chance of a doubt about it. I mean sure there's been some talk a trade—and yeah, 'cause a the trouble—but Navin knows value, Tyrus, and he'll swallow a little trouble or he'll fetch one *big* damn bundle a happiness for it. But he don't think there's enough out there, I mean of what other people's got. And no matter what I'm supposed to hold back on sayin', from management's side, I ain't got trouble admittin' this kind a thing about ya right to your face."

"Me neither," Donovan said, offering, along with a smile, an earnest, nodding look.

The boy knew that no one, from any side, had ever said anything like this to Matty McIntyre and so felt the nightmare weight of that man, and of defeat, lifting from off his chest. He could breathe, as he hadn't been able to breathe. And the pain of his cuts was for the moment now gone. But he knew that these men hadn't come here just to tell him he was, as a ballplayer, what somewhere he *always, always, always* knew he was. *Always.* No. This had to be for some other thing.

"But ya see," Armour said, "there's questions about what price ya pay, Tyrus. About what's worth what. I mean who am I to say. After all, all's I produced was another losin' season. And I ain't got too many more before I'm gone." He smiled, and then his face tensed up, as he felt the true pressure of his professional life. His look went into a meditative blank, and he said nothing for a moment. But then, "Still and the same, Cobb, though I admit there's gotta be a change of attitude before winnin' comes to my teams—it's how *much* do we change.

"I mean I always figured the Good Lord wants us to win and that winnin's a sign that the Good Lord is with us. It's like the ultimate test a the value a the thing you're workin' on. Is it workin'? or isn't it? And the Good Lord lets ya know."

The manager tensed his face and bowed his head again. He let out a deep breath and sighed. He looked up, with care in his eyes. "And, well, ya see . . . Ya see . . . I'm *sure*, Cobb, that if everybody on our team played the way you did, nobody'd touch us. I mean I have no doubt about that. Nine Cobbs and *nobody* touches us. Christ yes. Maybe five. Maybe three. But I have to believe in a decent way a doing things, Cobb. A good way. One you can win in, and yet not . . . Not hurt yourself. And the Good Lord, he doesn't cut it so simple. Win—and He's *with ya*. Nah—it ain't that simple. 'Cause ya can hurt yourself, too. And ya gotta ask how much, or where's the line, between winnin' and hurtin' yourself. See, it's always two things true at once, you know, like win—but it ain't worth it when you hurt yourself bad. There's a point it comes to with the misery and things. And people who think it's only one thing true at once, they ain't with the Lord, as I see it. They're with themselves. Win win win. Or lazy and sweet, lazy and sweet, lazy and sweet and don't hurt nobody. Nah. Ya can't be stupid and one-sided. Yuv always gotta be on the ball, watchin' the winnin' and watchin' your . . . well, your heart and soul. You know? The Good Lord puts signs in the way your *mind* is, too."

The boy after a while had a feeling that this is where his manager might take things in the end: to some point where he'd call him insane. But now that the words were out, instantly he resented this first and only visit he'd received. "You mean to say, Mr. Armour, that you think I'm crazy."

"*Those* weren't my words, Cobb. You know that. But I told ya before, I was worried about ya. And I'll tell ya again. Yes. I am worried. Seein' the look in yer eye. And the way ya cut yerself off completely from the whole world. And here ya are, a potential like I ain't seen. And I think, Christ, I gotta help this kid. What if he gets lost. It's real business here, I say to myself. This kid could get *lost*. And the thing with Matty. I mean I can write it up to jealousy, though I think it's bad as hell to say that to ya. And I ain't talkin' about cagey salary or negotiatin' horseshit, neither, not lettin' on I think yer good. I mean I don't wanna talk about the jealousy a other players for *your own good*. It's for your own good, keepin' ya from a big head, that we don't tell ya stuff sometimes. Cat's outa the bag, though, now. But I gotta ask ya, Cobb, could you accept the idea a *both a ya* bein' at fault? I mean I think that'd be a real start for ya, son."

"Right now? Right today accept that? After what he did, and the words he said?" The boy indicated in the clearest manner that right now he was *not* ready to accept the notion that the fault was half his, for all the manager's earnest pleading and despite his own passionate thinking of just moments past. For truly the habit of turning away at the approach of any Tiger any time had become now like a blind instinct with him (though he could see it working, clear as day).

Armour bowed his head again, now taking his forefinger and thumb and pinching them over the bridge of his nose, pressing the tip of his forefinger into the corner of one eye and the tip of his thumb into the corner of the other.

"I was hoping," he said, still with his finger and thumb pinching at the corners of his eyes, "yeah, that you'd make a start with that. Begin some healin' with that, yeah. Although I can understand. . . ." The manager now wiped his fingers hard across his forehead, and said no more.

"Words Matty said, Tyrus. . . ." Donovan now began. "I mean we've known for some time. . . ." The pitcher lowered his eyes and spoke more softly. "Forgive me, Tyrus, but . . . about your father's death. And the circumstances . . ."

"It was an accident." The boy interposed these words in a tone of absolute finality—and yet he felt instantly a mixture in his mind of a thousand different things. Resentment that an opening of this subject had been so long in coming, when they had to know the pain he suffered. But now gratitude that it had been opened. A gratitude so deep that feeling it made him fear he'd cry out his thanks in tears, right now. But at the same time that hard, hard instinctive refusal to show the first thing of any kind, let alone gratitude.

"I understand," the veteran star said. "And I'm sure it will be so proven. But we haven't brought it up, Tyrus, because we respected your privacy. I wanted you, and Billy, too, to understand that. It wasn't that we didn't care." The pitcher stopped a moment now, pursing his lips, looking thoughtful, careful. "But sometimes privacy, well, it needs, sometimes, to get broken into a little maybe. Things go on when you're just talkin' to yourself, you know, up here in a room like this, alone so long. They can start spinning. Suspicions. Anger. Hard feelings. Such like. And so we came over, you know, to let you know it wasn't that we didn't care. It was because we thought it was your business, very private business, that we didn't say anything. I guess you'd wonder why we'd wait so long. And that was it, you see. But now it's the season's end. And we wanted to get the word to you, so we came by. We figured it was important to get you that word. And to be honest, Tyrus, I was worried about you, too. About what your imagination and your mind might start working up if we didn't get you the word, before we lost the chance."

The boy—habits, grooves of his mind be damned forever—wanted to say thanks. From deep down inside himself, he wanted to say it. He knew, and who *better*, that gratitude, real, true gratitude came out of the center deeps of a human being's soul. But he couldn't. He couldn't say the word *thanks*. It was too hard, things with him having gone now as far as they had. He almost nodded a grateful acknowledgment. He hoped he looked as if he'd almost nodded. But he didn't nod, or say the word. And then he was glad he hadn't as his mind ran over the strong signs that the team were given far more to McIntyre's cruel compassionlessness than to Donovan's sympathy, their words about his craziness, just loud enough to be overheard, drowning out Donovan's one or two of sympathy for his life and dreams.

"So," Donovan said at last, breaking a lengthening silence. "That's why we came, to give you the word—that we didn't not care, Tyrus. We just respect you."

"That's right," Armour said.

"It was an accident," the boy said. "That would be something I want you to know."

"Good, Tyrus," Donovan said, nodding, lowering his eyes. "We were sure. But we're glad to hear that, from you. Thank you."

"Yeah," Armour said, smiling a tense smile, tapping his hat on his shin. "And listen, you take care of yourself, all right? I mean if you ever need any help from anybody, don't be ashamed to ask for it. That's a key thing, kid, that asking for help. The Good Lord wants ya to ask. I'm sure a that. Makes ya need help on purpose, I figure, so ya will ask, and not always go it alone."

Armour smiled, gave a last firm tap of his hat to his shin and rose. Donovan smiled, nodded, and rose, too. The pitcher then said, "I think one time we talked about responsibility, Tyrus." He squeezed his two hands now together, concentrating, serious. "When you have greatness, or the potential for it, you have a job. And that's to take care of yourself. So you do that, all right? You take care of Tyrus Cobb, for all of us."

The boy said, "I'll take care of Tyrus Cobb."

The veteran gave him a thoughtful look that wouldn't quite soften into a smile. Then he nodded, as did Armour. The two men bid the boy good-night then and headed off. And Tyrus, as he relocked and rebolted his door, listened against the panel to their steps in the corridor, and on the stairs, going down. He thought suddenly, as the sounds grew faint, that he might run after them and pour out his thanks for their showing sympathy the way they did, for caring, for coming to lighten the weight of his defeat. And they'd admitted to him, frankly like that, that the word "greatness" would be associated in time with the name Cobb. But he never moved, or opened his mouth. Nor did he go to the window, even though there was still time to call to them. He waited by his locked door; and, in the ensuing silence, he felt freed, relieved that he'd kept himself unsoft and resolute to the end, not opening up *once* in the entire forty-one-game trial. It was satisfying.

But painful. *Sick* painful. He wanted still to go to the window and shout. But he didn't, just as he hadn't answered, or even looked at, his mother's letters. And now the year was truly over, and he would be heading home first thing in the morning. Armour and Donovan had made a move, a very large move. No denying it. And his mother had written, and written again, and written again. So why no response? Why did he wait as he did now still by his door, until it was too damned late? Why was it such a relief to him when it was too late? Didn't he have the guts to move?

Later, when he packed his things, he sought to comfort himself with assurances not only that he would read his mother's letters but that it was not too late, that it was never, ever too late. And that he'd be able to redeem himself with her in Royston.

There would be those sweet days first with Charlie, too, in Augusta. But now it struck him that in the upcoming great reversal of things—in his packing his bag and grip in Detroit and his leaving from the Michigan Central and his going backward to Toledo and Cincinnati and back across the Ohio into the South, back through Kentucky and Tennessee and then across the last line into Georgia, till he'd be standing on that platform at the Augusta station, waiting for the Southern Line spur to the whistle-stop back home in Royston (where his mother, not knowing when he was coming, *wouldn't be*)— that, every inch of the way, something would be growing, intensifying. That everything would be coming back to him more and more powerfully as he went backward over his journey here. And that never in his damned life would he get free from anything he wanted to get free from.

He didn't pack his gun, rather placed it beneath his pillow, as always now when he slept. And in the morning, waking when the sun shot through his window, he found himself facedown with his two hands raised up as they had been those nights of his coming, as if he were being arrested. And now, from his cut mouth and cheek, there was blood on his pillow. But he didn't brood, wanting as he did to get out of the Union quick before anyone saw him. He rose, washed, and dressed and strapped on his holster and leaded his shoes and, noting the time at 6:10, clicked his watch closed and put it in his pocket next to his wallet, which was fatter now than when he came, though not as fat as it would be before his twenty-year career was through, not by a long shot.

He looked out his window at Bennett, the flags already down for the year (saying what to a man's ambition for lasting fame?), and then at the wagons already rolling and at the mill already steaming up its great saws for a day of whining and grinding. And down the street to Louis Chevrolet's, where by God he saw that fire going already. That damned Yankee never slept. Praise him. But it was time to go, unless he wanted to say some words of good-bye to mustachioed Timmy, which he did not, or be caught by any beautiful slutty nightcrawler scurrying from her shames to her daytime hiding hole. God be praised, he was still pure and had his honor and honesty. Nor had he given in to any softnesses of any Armour or Donovan. He'd take care of Tyrus Cobb, all right. No Yankees, no matter how beautiful, need worry about that.

And with a quick click of the door, he was gone, though he thought there might be eyes on him. And, freed of the Union without a word of farewell, he moved fast and silently past Pagliotta's den, praying an angry prayer that he would not be seen by that venerable crab, and damn well liking it that he was getting out of Detroit without any sweet good-byes or feelings for a single soul.

He walked like a thief, quick, peeking down streets and alleys, angrily praying, as he stepped along the cedar blocks, that he wouldn't be seen, though still figuring superstitiously that he would be by somebody: that there'd be some goddamned spook meeting with Mr. Fred West. At last, though—while he would step through the early-morning cab line with a final superstitious certainty that his back was watched—he arrived safely in the station.

He was relieved, too, that none of the team was there in the Michigan Central concourse, or on the train. But he had a sudden nightmarish imagination in the station docks as the southbound locomotive—before he blinked it smaller with repeated hard blinkings of his eyes—seemed to be the biggest he'd ever laid eyes on or dreamed of, huge as a Chicago building, only black, and with its blackness made still more black by the gigantic, silver-steel rods along its steaming sides.

Book Three

THE VERDICT

Chapter Fourteen

WORDS UNSPOKEN

Augusta—he closed his eyes and thought it with the first chug of the train. *You'll be on a train home soon.* Charlie. But not out of sight yet of Detroit, he thought, his mind fast-spinning as the engine still chugged slow, how it was harvest time on the Cobb hundred and so he'd be able to tell his girl that with the cotton to get in, he couldn't stay now more than a day in Augusta. He'd be back, of course, but right now he'd have to get on home. What, though, could be more strange than wanting to hurry his Royston arrival? If there was a place on earth more alien to him than the home city of the Tigers, now growing small behind his shoulder, it was his home town in Georgia, where his bedroom window, not a dozen feet from his parents', looked out over the porch roof on which his father lost his life.

On such a journey, time would move through every degree of slow and fast, as his mind moved through rapidly alternating seasons of eagerness and revulsion. And the fresh cuts on his face and mouth made it certain no one would want much to do with him, so he wouldn't have to take down from the seat beside him the separating wall of his grip.

As the Michigan Central made its way south toward Toledo, he found time now and again to review his quarter-season in The Show, which sometimes, though it was distant only by a day, seemed very far away now. Far enough even so that he could smile at some of his absurdities—such as his erecting Matty McIntyre into a figure of mythic proportions. The man was an enemy deep dyed and true, hard as envy and fierce in the way that one man's anger over another's refusal to cooperate could be as fierce as that other's need never to give in. And the boy could feel pulsing in his face now the ache of those wounds that proved every bit of this. But he could allow easily enough even that, about the black ashes, the "White Rat" may have been as innocent as he claimed. And contemplating how over this winter he would gain strength and pounds and not only not lose but gain speed as well, the boy knew his war with the left fielder was no real war at all. Matty McIntyre was not a name America would remember. And as for the name Cobb, the boy had a strong, true confidence that he really could make it one this country would never forget.

If he showed, too, that he could hit southpaws like Gettysburg Eddie Plank and Rube Waddell, what was he doing turning Doc White into the trial by fire of all his value and righteousness, making Doc White the key enemy position in his battle for survival? White was one hard customer, all right. And he'd scared him true. But there was also the mind's needing a good, hot story to fire its energy. And its inclination to dream a story up if it needed to. And as the itch in his hunting finger (an itch he'd known since the very first time his father took him out to the woods) needed a target, so a good story needed a center of attention. A *target*. But that face from somewhere? Was the story of that face just another thing he made up, thinking crazily as his father had about that schoolboy Hayward (whom himself he'd have whipped good and hard)? Or was the beard-shadowed white of Matty McIntyre's Irish face a reminder of someone he'd seen, in a single but real moment of real time? A moment that would last as long as truth at the dead center of his mind?

Miles and miles, down through Ohio, toward the river, he thought past Charlie to Royston. But not until he'd left Augusta and was riding the Southern Line spur would he open his mother's letters. His unresponsiveness, he was sure now, *had* put him beyond a point of no return. For his mother surely would know why he hadn't written, as as she would know who took the book and the gun. And he wondered for the hundredth time why he ever would be happy about such a painful, final end of something that had been as good as what he'd always had with his mama? How many times had she saved him, from, God knows, maybe wanting to kill the man himself?

But not expected, he might enter Royston the way his father did that night, when, the *Record* said, the man was seen "by several," lurking about back ways, trying to hide his identity, some two hours before he was gunned down at the window of his own bedroom. Would his son, as he came up in a few days now to the door, or window, at 205 Church, see things that would bring down and kill *him*, too? Catch his mother there *with* somebody, the way his father wanted to? Spying like this in the dark: It was an act that would make him not only like his father but exactly like himself, for wasn't spying, peering in a window, like thinking about things in the solitude he so damn much preferred, where no one had an honest chance to answer or confront him? But would he find her, his own mother, in her spied-on privacy, turned into that sweet little "Mandy Cobb" who loved the game all right? Christ Almighty. That the mind could *want* such things.

As the locomotive chugged slow back over the Ohio rail bridge, in this exact backward journey, he was saddened thinking he hadn't gone back for a friendly word or two with the carriage-maker Chevrolet. But in his wallet now there were those dollars that hadn't been there before; and he thought: cotton futures. He could make that startup money with cotton futures, for he knew the cotton business—just as well as his father had taught him. So he'd make his startup capital there. But then he damned himself for thinking he might even watch his spending a bit in Augusta, start saving right away every red cent he could for investment in cotton futures, when he should let himself go, and his wallet go, for Charlie, on the one day he'd set aside for her now!

Slow and fast his train moved, heading south from the river. And he thought again and again, and each time differently, about the time it took to walk "back and forth across a room." "Ten seconds": the *Record* said that, too. "Perhaps some ten seconds." And he thought of Joe, who must have been the witness who talked about that interval between the blasts, as he must have been the one who saw the handgun sticking out from his father's pocket. Ten seconds—time enough to walk right up and see exactly whose face was in the window, before you made that face into an unrecognizable *worst thing* anyone ever saw on this earth. But why would he make Joe into the only one who could have spoken of the time between the blasts? He knew in fact it wasn't true that Joe would be the only one. But then why, too, would he be jealous that Joe was the one who came upon that two-times-shotgunned body, ripped completely apart, as the charge had it, by *voluntary manslaughter*?

There was a small, cheap billboard outside Royston with a sorry painting of Jesus and the words REPENT NOW, FOR THE TIME IS AT HAND (and speaking of strange things people love to think of—why trash like *that*?); but he changed this sign to a sign that said Royston, Home of Tyrus Raymond Cobb, and that had a picture of him in his Tigers' *D* sliding hard into the plate. And he made a groove in his mind repeating a fantasy about a brass-band homecoming parade that Royston would have for the return of its conquering hero. But he did this, he knew, just to add fire to his fear that if his mind was destined to go, his home in Royston would be the place where it would finally do it—or maybe as well to add some nice mocking ironies to a story in which the real target was himself.

Across southern Kentucky and then Tennessee, as his train moved closer and closer to Chattanooga, he began more and more to see the white of cotton until he saw it everywhere, puffs lining every road, with the great bales rocking on the flat beds of mule-team wagons. Then over the Georgia line, even more still of that soft white snow, now fringing the red-dirt gravel, everywhere. His mind kept returning, of course, to his hundred-acre responsibility, but also to a long-, long-repressed question. How many times? How many times were the children sent to the farm when his father was away? Ten? Twenty? Thirty? Forty? He one moment would fight hard against pain and shame, bringing the number down to insignificance, then the next, with an insane eagerness, raise the number till it broke his heart.

He wondered if Uncle Ezra would be back at the farm, tending to things now. It wouldn't surprise him, not now, not at all now, if his mama had brought Ez back—which would be one more thing that she and her son would never in their remaining lives talk honestly about, both of them forever playing the same game, saying there was nothing to it, that it was only natural, seeing how Ez knew the farm so well. And of course when he came out to supervise, there would be Ez and Aunt Mary talking sweet nigger talk to their "baibih Tahrus, who done gone up nawth, whey they ain't no point in niggahs goin', nawsuh, 'cause them Yankizz ain't no good to niggahs." And such like sweet talk, with all the big, white-toothed smiles and laughter about to break their spines. Because—truth—all the hard work the South had done of terrorizing these "aunts" and "uncles" of the one

Southern family, and policing their every move, had produced just that, pasted smiles and phony laughter. And
sweet-talk words. But odd as it was, as his train rolled on
past Kennesaw Mountain and then moved into Atlanta's
Central and then he transferred for Augusta and watched the
nigger car get hitched onto the back of the new train, he kept
thinking that what he would do *at least*, with every record
he set on the diamond, would be to get the whole country's
words so damned well under control that all anyone could
do would be to sweet talk Tyrus Cobb, the way the South
made niggers sweet talk white folks.

Strange and painful though, too, the way he kept up his
thinking about this hard labor of his future all the way over
to Augusta. Kept himself locked up in it, tight as that tomb
with its two side walls and lily of peace between—even as
the train pulled into that station where such key turnings in
his life had taken place ... where there was that telephone
office. . . . It was as if he'd been caught up in a bad dream,
until he came at last now to the point where he was about
to die. God *damn* me, wake up! he said to himself. And get
your sorry self *rid* of that damned yellow selfishness of yours!
And God bless Charlie Lombard, there she was. Right there,
waiting, his beautiful girl. Look at her, so fine and beautiful.
And true. All anyone ever needs is one person like that in
the world to love him—and she loves you.

Trains and words, he thought, as the whistle blew his
arrival. Weren't he and Charlie right about how these remarkable two little inventions could set the whole human
world wide apart or bring it right together. *You'll be on a train
home soon.* And now here he was, and she was. So let everything pasted or phony or even a single, one-inch measure
short of a beautiful honesty move along the fast track to the
hell that it deserved.

But—first thing he did—was explain the cuts and
bruises on his face with a lie. She was worried, and she wondered. . . . But he told her it was "nothing." Just a rough-and-

tumble slide with a fine old head-on collision in the last game against the St. Louis Browns. Yet had he sounded truthful enough to make her believe him? And was it at all well-timed—changing the subject right away then to the harvest and his need to get on home, even if he promised he'd be back to visit once the crop was in? She knew, of course, that he made up no story when he told her about his home re-sponsibilities. A Georgia girl understood that perfectly. But had there been something in the way he said it? She still looked questioningly, worried. And his mind went every-where—from fearing she could tell he'd put off showing *any-thing* thus far but his hard side to the Tigers; to a superstition that she'd been able to see him in a certain moment by the stairs in the Union House or even to see into the deepest privacies of his dreams; or to fearing, again, that magically she could see, in his grip now, his father's loaded gun lying next to his mother's unread words. Nor was a word said all that day about what Mr. Grantland Rice might have written recently in the *Atlanta Journal* about Georgia's native son.

He didn't hold back, though, not a penny. He took her to Benning's for their famous elegant lunch, and it was noth-ing but the best: so much so that they both had a good laugh at the boy whose pockets his first bit of money burned a very healthy hole in. And then—and no he would *not* be dis-suaded—to top it off, it was twelve red October roses at Miss Courthope's All-Season Floral. Then, that evening, beautiful Georgia October evening, with the hay fields having gone now green to gold after the mowing and the mounded stacks set out at distances, they rode those beautiful yellow pas-tures, all closed in by great, deep-green Georgia pine and studded too with the incredible, rich green of shadow-casting cedars, the ones that rise out of the lucky places that no hay cut ever gets to and that every pasture needs for the coun-tryside to be beautiful.

So they talked. And he realized again, as they rode slowly back toward The Oaks, the full danger of dividing himself for too long, ever, from the Tyrus Cobb who rode then next to Charlie Lombard. What is more, he confessed his lie—about the cuts and bruises. He even told Charlie things that Matty McIntyre had said about his family. And if this revelation, truth to tell, came by way of his *justifying* why he sought the fight with the man—he nonetheless admitted that McIntyre's words came *after* his own actions had begun things.

As they came back home into the barn, two sweet hours gone, the level beams of sunset were breaking into bright shafts where the wood slats of the barn had breaks. The smells were beautiful, the motes in the light shafts, the sounds of the horses' thuds and their snorts and their swishing in the dry hay, the dark, rich wood color in the stalls, the horsey smell of blankets, the leather smell of the saddles as they hung them, the jingling and gleaming of bridle gear, and the clicking closed of the stall gates.

But in the peace, as they stood now together and Charlie looked as beautiful as he'd ever seen her, she touched and held his hands, and asked him, "Will there, Tyrus—between you and your mother—be a strangeness now?"

Had it not seemed to him suddenly like some moment of truth for their love, he wouldn't have suffered as he did when he lied to her. The lie would have been just another that at some later time he could have confessed to. But all he could do was pray she couldn't in that dimming light see his sudden misery and sick fear, as he said to her, "No. No, sweet girl. Things will be fine—as soon as I get there, and from then on."

Next day, on the Southern Line spur to Royston, he would pick a black-haired man six seats in front of him and let his mind turn that particular choice of his into the *face from somewhere* and let himself take pleasure in the time, and in the warm weight of the pistol that after his farewell embrace with Charlie, in the men's stall aboard train, he'd holstered again beneath his coat—till his choice would turn his head and disappoint him.

That run—the Southern Line's Augusta-to-Royston—was one he knew so well that he could remember the tilt of mailboxes, the exact repairs that houses and barns needed or had gotten, the rockers and swings and chairs on porches, the moss on shingle roofs and the rust stains on tin—and the exact distances these things represented, and the time left till home. So when the chaw-mouthed conductor, who'd licked his stub pencil and written down the boy's destination when he took his ticket, said, " 'Bout an ahhr more nah, Royston," the boy didn't need any such unasked-for help. But it was time. And when that damned cracker oaf was gone off far enough, listing his clumsy way right and left, seat back to seat back, the boy ran his hand between the loosened opening of his grip and then finger-searched till he found, under the cover of the *Lives*, his mother's three letters, the dates of which he knew without looking, and took up the earliest, setting the other two on the seat beside him. He glanced at his name and at the return address, that of his own home, and felt as he ran his finger under the seal and tore the envelope, about as estranged from himself as perhaps was possible without his mind just breaking, right then and there. But, slowly, taking out now and unfolding the familiar light-blue paper, he read.

Royston, August 31, 1905

My dearest son,

What happiness to see in the newspaper today that in your first chance, against a famous pitcher, you made a hit! Such a beginning, Tyrus, and such a sweet prophecy of things to come! And how your mother rejoices for you! But hasn't she long known that it was a ballplayer you were meant to be. The right place, the wrong place to put one's life—we've discussed them, haven't we. And the difference between the two—how that's as large a difference as there is, for one's happiness. And I know you are in the right place now. And you know how much my heart is with you.

He stopped. Already he felt hard suspicion, even anger—despite all the tenderness he could read in her words, and feel in his own heart for her. The right place. The wrong place. Knowing what meaning she wanted to convey, he wondered still *why*, why at this point she would take a side on the disputed issue of his becoming a ballplayer. It almost made him wish he were never a ballplayer. And the need to be in the right place as as large a need as there is, for one's happiness? Of whose situation was she speaking? Was she enlisting support for hers? But *what*—now? Could he not listen simply to even these words? Where in *hell* did it put him, having to *interpret* his own mother, the way he was doing? But he couldn't help himself.

Oh, my sweet boy, how I have thought about you since we last said good-bye. About the pain you must be going through with your father's passing, and all the horror of that night. We couldn't speak our thoughts when we were last together, could we? But maybe now, in this letter, I can find the words and you will be able to listen. If you have had dark thoughts, I understand—and I forgive you, Tyrus. With all my heart. How could you not have had dark thoughts, with all this unbearable horror? It is impossible. What have I left you with but that impossibility. Please forgive me. I beg you to find it in your heart. But I beg you, too, to believe, my beloved, there is no cause. I have thought of your train ride—all those hours—all you must have been thinking. My heart worries, and bleeds. And now you are up there in Detroit for your dream, to make it come true. How much I want it to come true! But you must have such deeply painful, troubling doubts, about your family, your mother. Yet please believe there is no cause. You know I loved him, dearest boy. You know that what they suggest in the newspaper is untrue. Rumors and lies. They would have it that your father and I were mortal enemies. Need we say more? And in their mercilessness, they say worse things, *things about my trueness to him that I cannot even write— and that a mother in a hundred lifetimes should never be pressed to talk about with her child. But these things are public now. And God help us all, how the most malicious words have the swiftest wings. And you know what it is that I refer to. I don't have to say things for you to know what I mean. But again believe me: There is no cause for what they say. Absolutely none, Tyrus,* nothing.

I understand that after a point the more one denies, the more one is disbelieved. So I will say now only quietly that the truth will come out, and your family, and your mother, will be vindicated. God is and will remain forever on your family's side. I want you to believe this. And that while it is no doubt impossible for you now to escape dark thoughts, it will be possible *in time—for though rumor might have all the strength of the devil himself, there is no cause for what is said. You will see this, and it will sink into your heart. Be as sure of this as you are certain there is no evidence for anything that any of the voices in Royston might say.*

And please, please think of me in my loneliness, I beg you. They don't speak to me, Tyrus. They punish and torture me with their silence, worse almost than their words. Old friends torture me. They don't look my way on the street. I have thought of following you to Detroit, to get away. For home has become the farthest thing from home. But, until my trial is over, I am not permitted to leave the state of Georgia.

I can only write, and hope you will write me back and tell me you believe me and that you have found a deeply deserved happiness in the life we both know is right for you.

Please give me word of yourself, my beloved. In my Royston loneliness, I need your words.

Bless your heart and life,
Mama

He was torn through his heart. He hated himself to death for not answering her, not giving her the first word of comfort when she was bleeding. His mother, who stood up for him and comforted him. How many times? How many years? She *saved his life.* And God damn worthless Royston for giving her the silence! God damn Joe. And all of 'em. The *Royston Record.* All of 'em eager as hell on earth to leap to conclusions. Innocent until proven guilty. But not in Royston. And don't they all just love it, seeing the Cobbs in trouble. People hate a Cobb. They *hate* a Cobb. While the cat's away. And watch your home. God damn them—no need, when every last one of 'em will watch it for you, with their sickening little curiosity and envy and lust for vengeance. He'd bring his gun into that courtroom, that's what he'd do, for all those sorry little curiosity seekers, so eager to call the Cobb home a house of ill fame!

But wasn't he glad, too, he had not written. He hadn't known what was in this letter; but still he'd gotten the thing going that, had he known, he would have wanted to get going: that sweet punishment of her, which had indeed a swift-growing life of its own. For she was lying. No one on this earth except her son would ever know she was *lying.* No one except Tyrus Cobb—and one other, who might have heard that the evidence whose existence she denied, was missing.

He folded the letter back up and put it again in its envelope, which he set back now in the grip, beneath the cover of the *Lives.* Then from his seat, he took the second, opened it, and read.

Royston, September 12, 1905

My dearest Tyrus,

I get word of you still through the papers, but it comes
irregularly and uncertainly. Not knowing how you are
doing, I pray that you suffer no terrible distractions. I think
of you and worry about you every hour, please believe it, my
dear one. But I feel that I send these words out to nowhere.
I have no way of knowing if this will reach you, or if my
first did. Forgive me a thousand times, but I fear that you
do not wish to hear from me or to reach me. Oh, you don't
know how I fear this. If you have been reluctant to send
word to me, I understand. I forgive you. But I beg you,
please, do send me word. I cannot tell you what it would
mean—that first word of comfort from my son, and his
father's son.

I confess I have terrible dreams, Tyrus. I see your
father. I see him at the window, as I did not see him that
night. Please, please believe me. If you don't, I will die. It
will kill me, if you don't. It will, truly it will. But now I see
him, and in my dreams, night after night, he cries out to
me. But I don't listen. I turn hard. God help me! I take the
gun and I shoot, knowing it is your father. Seeing him and
knowing, but pretending not to know, not to hear him say
my name. Then I shoot again, exactly the way they say I did:
after time for reflection, deliberately, against a helpless man.
It is so horrible that they have put into my head a night
that never happened and then that that night becomes the
night that was. The lines in the mind begin to blur. You
don't know what is real and what is not. You begin to
believe what you know is not true of you but what
nonetheless has been said of you. Believing what you don't
believe: this illogical black miracle of a thing can happen.
And there you are, knowing something is not true, but
feeling all the horror and pain you would feel if it were.
There must be some terrible desire in us to concede to
charges against us. Maybe this is the cause. Some deep,

mysterious need to welcome blame. I don't know. I don't know.

And I don't mean to place a burden on you, Tyrus. I pace and I pace at night fearing to place a burden on you, thinking that if I throw out words at you they might do the same thing to you that Royston's words have done to me. But I have to say something. I have to say that if I knew you were with me, I would be all right. I would live. I wouldn't die, as I fear now I might. So please send. I loved your father in the same way you loved him. The same way. *And I sit here now in tears at his desk and think, in this emptiness, of what he was to the two of us. Our own love: I think of it as the clearest evidence of what he was to us. The evidence we will keep fast in our hearts?*

Mr. Karchner, and Mr. Rawlings, and Mr. Fenton have been a deep comfort to me. They know what I go through, having defended so many charged with grievous crimes. They understand what other people's words and my own imagination do to me. They help me reconstruct things truly. And I need help, because my mind is ready to go anywhere and everywhere. I would confess to anything. I swear I would. But they assure me my mind is just what they expect it to be in my situation—that is—charged in the death of someone I loved.

There was a time, Tyrus, when I enjoyed a perfect reputation, though I am sure I did not think about it. No doubt, however, that, without thinking about it, I still worked hard to win it and keep it. For what is our reputation but a kind of existence, before death, in the world of the spirit, of ideals, and goodness. The eyes of our fellow men do do this to us: They make us better than we would ever be alone. But who would know this better than you, who play before thousands and thousands of spectators—the whole country. And spectators, Tyrus. We must care what they think. But there is another side to this, as maybe you know. For just as much as the eyes of others make us better,

so they see us as worse than we are. There is a spirit-
breaking cruelty in people. And the ruining of a reputation
can spread fast as wildfire because in the dark of their souls
all people love to see it happen. My name is caught in this
endless wildfire, my beloved son. And my reputation cannot
be my care now. It is out of my hands. I cannot care what
people think. I can look only to God, who knows the truth.
And to you. Without you, the loneliness would be too much
for me. Only you have the strength to fend the world off
from me, in my loneliness. Please send me word. Let me
know by a kind word that you believe me.

With all my love and tenderness,
Mama

He pressed the pages of the letter tight between his forefinger and thumb, and now, tighter, in an effort to keep back
tears. He fired to the idea of his being her champion against
a world of *spectators* (who worshiped power, after all; and he
would show them power!). She'd made his heart proud to be
her champion. Made it burn with compassion. For had he
not suffered from the silence and torture of others. So how
could he do the same to someone else? To *anyone* else, let
alone his mother?

But as he heard her cry for help, he felt again that cruel,
savage delight that he'd given her none. He understood how
we are eager to accept blame: that some mysterious force
drives us to welcome it. But at the same time he *resented* her
dragging him into the snake pit of *her* trouble and shame.
She would die unless he believed her. He liked, when he
heard this, thinking he would let her know he did *not* believe
her. And he was the only one who could help her. But he
wouldn't help her.

What time now? The train was beginning to move
through a coming darkness. He put away this second letter
as he had the first, then took up the third. He held it tight

between his forefinger and thumb in the corner with the return address. He pressed hard on the name, and on the town, until the sweat began to smear the ink and blur the words, which in the crush of his thumb and finger were dirtied. He began to rub and smear the writing with dirt and sweat until the name and the town were fraying and crumbling and disappearing. But at last he finger-tore the seal where he'd frayed it apart and took out the light-blue paper. What he found this time, when he turned open the fold, was no more than a note.

> *Royston, September 26, 1905*
>
> *Dear Tyrus*
> *This is my third time writing. My heart must assume you have not received my other letters. If you have, I can say only that I know you would not want me to beg you any more for a word. If you have not, please forgive all misunderstandings. Also if you have not, most likely you will not receive this either. But should it reach you, please write me right back, or wire, or telephone (of course I will take the charges), and tell me when you are coming home. I will want to make things ready and to meet you at the train.*
>
> *Always, Mama*

He closed the single fold and placed the light-blue sheet back in the torn envelope, then set the envelope in behind the other two, closing the *Lives*. She hadn't given him anything more. He was disappointed by the chill, the brevity. He wanted to hear her say again that she looked to him to be her champion (and for a brief moment he'd seen himself as a lover opening love letters, feeling an excitement at the sight of that familiar light-blue paper).

He felt the return of his vengeance. He would give her the perfect chill response to match this note. When he walked in and—surprise—was just *there* at her door, she would know in the first *second* that it was no accident she'd received no word. He'd give her such a look. Then nothing ever would be the same between them.

But now it was *no time*, not time enough even for him to hate himself for every feeling of vengeance he'd had, when the door at the end of the car opened, letting in the roar; and the conductor, in the quiet once the door swung back shut, shouted, "Jes a mahl er so now, Royston. You jes listen fer the whistle and then when we's slowin', come ohn up t' th'doah."

He set away the third letter quickly and then fastened closed the grip, which he held now tight in his hand. Then, no time and the whistle roared. He was shaken by the enormity of the blast. But before he rose he looked out the window—the locomotive in the same moment relaxing its power—and the train's speed dropping. He looked, and in the deepening dusk light, saw on the outskirts of town, the first crosses and stones of the graveyard where his father lay buried. And his eyes instantly were lashed to the cemetery, though he could make little out. Then, suddenly, his mind sought reasons not to have to take any action. Not to have to go into that town, not to have to walk down those streets, to see people, to take the turn toward his home, to go home to his family. His mother. Every reluctance he'd ever felt seemed summed up in his reluctance now, as his eyes remained fixed on the graveyard, his head turning, rotating with his gaze, as the train pulled past like a rope running out to its *snap*.

The whistle blew again a tremendous blast. The train rocked less and less, slowing into its own great, iron weight. He turned. And, like a clock, would come the conductor, and his voice, saying, "Here ya be, Royston!" And there he was, before he knew it moving down the plate-metal steps, nearly stumbling, then click-crunching over the white-brown cover stones of the embankment to the level below. The conductor waited till he was safely away. Then shouted to him, "So long, *Royston!*" looking not at him but straight ahead as he leaned out by the hand bar and waved his all-clear to the engineer, who blasted the whistle in near-deafening response and set the great wheels creaking, and grinding, back into motion.

Like the man his father, the boy would wait till the town was off the streets before he came in. And he headed slowly back away now, out along the tracks, near a mile to the town's far edge, and the graveyard, taking at last across a pasture and through a grove of white oak, to the cemetery side gate, a path he knew from boyhood and could follow even in the dark. For it was now near full dark.

At the path's end, as he tried the gate's rusted iron and found it loose, he thought of rose trellises, the one his father climbed, armed, exactly as he was now, and the one about which his mother had lied; and he found himself once more absurdly putting them together. What? In the way his mind in its depths had refused to but still did, in a secret silence, since he was fourteen, *put things together*? He heard those words he'd heard in the dream that he found himself now calling no dream: the words "Nothing," "Absolutely nothing," and "Thank you . . . *Thank you* for this *happiness*": the words he heard before he met the *face* in that real location he remembered now, between the door to his room and the door to his mother and father's.

There had been no stone, the day they buried the man. But now there was a stone. The boy, making his way in moonrise light over Royston's graves, having seen a tablet marker at the head of his father's still-fresh, grassless mound, walked up fast to the gravestone now. He dropped to his knees. And he set his eyes on the moonlit inscription.

William Herschel Cobb
Born, July 15, 1860
At rest, August 10, 1905

He pressed his cuff hard into each eye, and again, but no good. The tears came. He couldn't speak or think, some long time. At last, then, he managed to whisper, "I've come home, Father." But his throat pained him and tightened so, he could hardly sound out, "Come home no failure." Then again nothing, as more time passed, till—tears falling from his eyes— "And I'll silence *all of them*. I'll silence every last one of them, Father. Because that's what it *does* . . . greatness. It keeps mouths shut. And it forces forgiveness, with the praise. All the sorry damned hero-worshipers, they *need* to be around it, to be part of it, and not to ruin it, the hero's greatness. Which is coming to me. I can say it, Father. . . . I can say it." He swallowed hard, pressed his sleeve into his eyes, and was again crying. "And . . ." he whispered, "they *never* violate a hero's private life. Never do. They'll just keep outside my life and silent, except to tell stories about how one day, maybe, they saw the great Tyrus Cobb play the game."

He bowed his head and closed his eyes, for what length of time he couldn't say—till suddenly he began sobbing, hard, full. Then more silence, some time. Till again suddenly, "Oh Christ Jesus in heaven, Father, I wish I'd never seen your words! And that you'd never written your words! Though you know I read those words harder than I ever read any other book, or ever will. You know it. And what else you *know* is that you wrote those words out for the same reason I read them. You know it! You know you wrote out your book because you had some crazy wish to bring an ending to your life! That every time you took a word out of hiding, you thought of it as putting a further nail in your coffin! And that you longed to write the final one! Did you hear a voice say, 'Go ahead and write that final word'? I confess that I heard one say, 'Go ahead and read it.' "

He was breathing fast. He started to break into a sob, but he stopped himself hard and ripped his arm over his face. "But I *promise* you," he hissed then through his teeth, "that no matter, Father, what I've read, I'll deny everything! Under oath. At gunpoint! If I could still say a word with a bullet ripping into my brain, it would be a word of denial! I have your gun. You know this. . . . But . . . I will hush now. I will hush. Christ, don't you come before me! I couldn't live *seeing* you. The obscenity. I know I would die—of anger, and hatred."

He blinked his squeezed-down lids, then closed them more softly. He took a deep breath. Then whispered, softly, almost smiling, "And you could see all along, couldn't you, Father. You secretly admired me, didn't you. Yes, you did. I read your words. And you know I have secretly hated you."

He tightened down his lids again, squeezing hard and harder, till there was aching, pounding pain in his eyes. "You know it full well, but I'll confess it—*I will confess* I had a great weight lifted from me when she killed you! One hundred million tons! Off me! But you know also that it was a two-hundred-million-ton weight placed *on me* when she killed you! Two hundred million billion tons all crushing me! But tell me, Father, would it all be gone if I killed her? Is that what you want me to do? The way you were going to kill her! Don't deny it! I've read your *words*!

"Or maybe you think it was a lie, Father! Watch your home! The mouse will play! That someone *lied* to you about this! That maybe she was innocent after all! That it was all an accident except for what was your fault! Do you think she was innocent, *maybe*!" He let his tears fall. "*Maybe!* Do you think! *Maybe you dreamed things! Maybe!*"

Crazy superstition then became belief—that he might hear some word out of the grave if he stayed. Might truly hear a word. He rose, took his grip—and would have run, if he weren't so weighted from exhaustion, with his damned soul spreading like a thick weight all through his pained, hard-breathing body.

On the road, crazy, exhausted, he laughed hard at himself as, sure as joking hell, he passed into town under that sign with that sorry Jesus, and all its dead-sorry trash. Brass band! What a perfect laugh! The conquering hero comes home instead like a damned criminal returning to the scene of the crime, hoping he won't be identified. And as he let his mind think every rash, self-killing, exciting thought about finding his mother *with* someone right now, as he let himself picture things that could be happening *right now*, he felt a further dead weight of incredible reluctance. A leaden unwillingness to move, to say or do anything or meet anyone ever again, a lead weight that multiplied, beyond all logic, the weight still in his shoes. And yet he moved—down the emptied streets of his home town, the only lights now house lights. House lights. Every single one of them he knew. Every house. Every street. Every family. He was sick-glad now, though, to see not one single soul, and to be seen by not one, even though he took the most roundabout and long way, so he could rid his face of any traces of tears. But then it had to come—Church Street had at last to come.

And of all his destinations—his godforsaken little *destinies*, every one of which he wanted to vomit out of himself so he could get clean again, and modest—there was none more dangerous to his life than the orange-bricked, two-story house that rose in moonlight before him now, set clear against the large shadow of the First Methodist church. The two-story brick. The white-painted porch columns. The rose trellis climbing to the flat porch roof, with a gutter that had held more than rain. And the two front upstairs windows looking out on that roof, one dark but black-glistening. And the other, which was new, now lighted.

Lighted—and—*true* (as lovers were sometimes lucky enough actually to catch their ladies in bedroom light)—with a figure moving in it. A woman, not old. Not at all. Graceful. Not wearing mourning, rather some light-colored dress. She was moving in and out of the window. Was she there alone?

Those words of her letter: Home was the farthest thing from home. Who knew that better, he thought, than her son. And who was it that that boy could *thank* for feeling so divided right now from himself that as he stood beneath the windows of the home where he grew up he felt himself cut apart ten billion miles from anything he ever knew or ever was? And who put in him this deadly weight of reluctance to go and ring his own bell and come home to his own house, and mother?

He thought crazy things like she might shoot him when he came to the door with a face like his father's! And what *made* him, as he spied on her, for God sake, so sick disappointed that no one could be seen in the window with her. He waited some long time, *spying*. He wanted to punish her, to get something on her, so that *right now* he could come down hard. But he *had* punished her—by not responding a first syllable to her, which spoke a million very clear words to her, all right. He was paralyzed with shame thinking of it. What would he say to her now about his silence? But then in an explosion of anger that *he* should be the one feeling shame and embarrassment, he tore up all weights and chains of reluctance and moved himself to the walkway, and straight to the door. And he determined as he pressed his finger hard on the bell (which his father had not rung) that when he embraced her now he'd make her feel the gun beneath his jacket.

But how could he? How *could* he when through the front door's oval glass he saw her now coming down the stairs, looking curious, uncertain . . . *afraid*? and showing him back his own eyes, blue, Gramma Chitwood said, as bluebirds' wings, and looking so beautiful . . . and so *young*, young enough to be as beautiful as Charlie. Or as the white-slave Yankee dancer when she eyed him over her glass in the Union?

"Oh Tyrus, you're *here*! It's *you*! I didn't know! I was afraid. . . . But my word, what's happened to your face."

He thought rawness from tears. But no. The cuts. The bruises. Healing, but still there. He said, "It's nothing, Mama.

Nothing. Just a hard slide and collision in my last game. Nothing."

He set down his grip. But then (and never in his life, not a first time, ever, had he hugged her in any way but fully and warmly) his embrace of her was as awkward as would be expected when he carried a gun he'd wanted to *show* her but now wanted *not* to show her—and so, to hold her, he bent his shoulders forward, but kept the rest of himself cold away from her, as if truly he wanted not even to touch her. "I'm sorry," he said, "to come on you unannounced like this, Mama. And to have been so silent. Not letting you know . . ."

But she did *know*, it seemed, reacting to the strange, and cold-painful embrace by backing away herself and then stopping his apologies (and were they such?) with a raised hand of dismissal, which had, as did her words, the chill of that last brief note to him. "No. Forgive me, Tyrus. It's just that I would have had the house ready, you see, and met you at the train."

Perhaps, with an irrevocable action, he had begun it the last time he was in this house. But the change between them, if in this manner near enough to silent and invisible, was unmistakably now started; for the slightest gesture or altered tone in things, in such a case, at such a time, must be everything and forever. He had wanted *not* to show her he had the gun, but exactly that had started it. And now, with the difference in their lives set in motion by that merest fraction of a moment that was everlasting, he found himself wishing he'd made it clear as hell to her he did have the gun, and had it on him. He knew his anger again. His desire to punish. Both raging harder the more deadly quiet he kept them. He saw again all her pleas for a word from him as some soft but truly hard coercion. And though as they sat then and talked in his father's library not a word of accusation or confession got said, things were understood, instantly, and completely. For that was exactly it: The change would be that not a real word would ever again be spoken between them.

No mention was made of her letters, not that night, nor ever after, by either of them. She would ask, as she sat at his father's desk, her crooked hand set soft on the writing surface above the locked drawer, if he had found his "happiness" in his choice of life, a question he *interpreted*. Nor, though the sight of her hand tore him, would he give her even a first sign that he'd found happiness, for this would bring her satisfaction. Instead (and he found himself hating the entire idea of happiness as he'd hated even that he *was* a ballplayer), to make an unsaid point, he told her that it seemed more often than not he found himself, up north, re-fighting the War Between the States.

"Oh do forgive me," she said, "but I'm so unhappy to hear you say that." She was squeezing her hands together now on her lap, trying, it seemed to draw his eyes right into hers. "Tell me *why*."

He turned his eyes down. "I don't know," he said. "So many causes . . . You can imagine."

But again she said, "I do so hate to hear you say, Tyrus, that there has been that kind of unhappiness. . . . I want only some good word, I suppose, because I couldn't be more certain that you've followed your dream. That you've gone where you'll make your name. But I pray you'll find a way, too, so that it will make no difference where you come from."

His mind took her words and turned them from their apparent purpose to that of a bitter jest. He wanted to laugh. No difference where he *came from*! He felt a bitter, impulsive need to shoot some rash word back at her. To say "Father was warned he should watch this house. Did you ever hear about that?" But he said, "Well, Mama, my batting-championship watch, you know, it says, 'Let 'Em Know Where You're From, Tyrus Cobb, in the Big Show.' I guess I like *that* idea, too."

She bowed her head, closed her eyes a moment. This conversation would have connections. Piecings together, of a kind. And because of course the subject of her case would naturally sooner, not later, come out, she spoke, with reference to the boy's *watch*, about *her* life now in the town where they were from. Immediately she began repeating things (with no reference to the letters) that she'd said—*in* her letters. How people might be polite, but how one could tell they must be thinking something other than what they were saying. That she couldn't look at a face anymore without sending her mind in behind the skin and looking into the brain to find what was really there. Only she couldn't, really, so she imagined. All day long, she imagined and came always only to the worst conclusions. She spoke of rumors and lies and people's making up of things. She hoped the truth would come soon to stop them. Soon. And how their politeness sickened her. Because what they really wanted was to prove things they'd always suspected. Or they wanted to *find* suspicions they never really had: to make up old suspicions, so they could have old things that got *proved* by what they made up now. She said she could read this on their faces.

And he thought, I can hear you, Mother. I know what you mean. And what do you read on my face? He hoped, in his sick, despairing satisfaction over seeing things as beyond recall, it would be the story of a silent war that would never end. Of acknowledgments without spoken words, and with tacit battles in which he could punish her and at the same time never begin an admission of anything himself.

She began, now it seemed compulsively, repetitively, to fill the painful quietnesses with more words recalling her letters. No one, she said, really spoke to her. And among polite lies it was impossible to live. And what evidence, she asked him, do they have for anything?

There was a silence. She filled it, changing the subject— to that "great word on our lives": *reputation*. After a point, it's no longer in our own control, she said. Our reputation becomes "public property." And God help us if our minds don't love to become our own worst enemies and to take on the guilt people want us to take on. So we surely can be thankful for the protections in this nation and that we cannot be made to testify when we are the ones on trial because we might start up against ourselves in some crazy way—even when the facts are all on our side and there was no evidence against us. Nothing. And thank God for good lawyers who protect us from our own words as well as those of the world's rumormongers. And expose the nothing of their so-called evidence, when there *is* no evidence.

"Happiness, Mama," he said then out of nowhere, "did you ever want to strike back at someone who holds a gun to your happiness?"

She said nothing. He looked up to see a worried, quizzical look on her face. Did she think he was crazy, talking in disconnection like this? No. She was performing, he was sure, with her look of surprise.

"Did you ever, Mama, just want to thank the one who recognizes your right to happiness? Just say thank you, thank you, thank you—over and over to him, whoever he might be? For the happiness?"

She didn't answer. She just looked at him with what he saw as eyes turned dead cold steel. Ice blue. That's what he saw, though he knew she was trying to look only bewildered, as if she were listening to someone whose mind was disturbed.

"I don't know," she said, after a long, painful silence, "what you mean. I'm sorry, Tyrus. I don't follow."

She didn't follow. What? Because his words came disconnected? Well then he'd tell her directly about the time and place, about the face he'd seen with his own eyes, here in this paradise of a home of theirs. But no, he preferred an unending punishment of her damned, soft beauty, which would be possible only if he did *not* explain his words.

He said, "Forgive me, Mama. I haven't slept. Maybe not a good night for months. Exhaustion. It's been a long journey. And forgive me but—what I said—I was thinking of the suffering you must have found impossible to accept. So great.

And their giving you the silence. It's a pain I know of. But we'll talk about me some other time. As for your *case*—a word I can't believe they've made us say—it's nothing. Absolutely nothing. That's what you have to fear, Mama. The truth is going to come out; and when it does, there will be a complete vindication." He raised his eyes to hers. "And that will be the end of it. It may seem now like there's no stopping things. But the truth will come out and stop things. You'll see."

She looked now herself at her crippled hand, again on the surface of the desk. It was a long time, and, in this conversation, another new, awkward element, and sign. At last she spoke, but without lifting her eyes, which remained fixed on her hand. "They have nothing, Tyrus, but their imaginations." Then, after another long, strange silence, "And *yet*, you see, I am warned, innocence is never enough. So I have to turn to my comforters, the people who love me. . . ." She looked up now from her hand and met him eye to eye. ". . . and ask them—they have no evidence, *do* they?" She continued to look him in the eye, strangely, overlong, using the power of her beauty as she never had with him, to change the nature of this conversation. She said, her voice softening into a strange new kind of warmth and intimacy, "Tell me, Tyrus, that they have nothing but their imaginations. Tell me I have nothing to fear."

He felt now the thrill of a silent conspiracy, a union in a crime far beyond those prophesied by his father in this room—beyond whoring, beyond gambling his game into meaninglessness—and beyond even what the mind fantasizes when a gun is secretly strapped to the body. But he felt also a ferocious urge to say to her I *have* the gun. I know you've been here with a man. I know now I wasn't dreaming. I've read every last word of Father's book. He was ready to say the word *whore* and the word *murder*. But a tacit pact, following her soft, strange, leading words, was thrilling to him. He couldn't help this. He wanted to say the name

"Hayward." But that might just elicit from her again some disappointing, hypocritical mask of incomprehension, which he did not want. He preferred deeply the new strangeness of their silent understanding. He said, "Absolutely nothing, Mama. That's what you have to fear."

She smiled faintly, but with that strange warmth and power. "No one," she said, "knows, Tyrus, the truth of what your father and I had the way you do. No one. And when the times come for someone who knows that truth to protect me from this town, from their story-making and their lies, that someone will be you, I know it. You spoke of the person who understands one's claims to happiness, of the gratitude we feel—to that *someone*. And I believe I understand you now. And I am grateful to you. I say thank you. Thank *you*."

The blue of her eyes was now shocking. He looked at her pale and flushed skin, at her thick auburn hair, in the lamplight falling in waves of sheen. He felt the power of her beauty. So beautiful, a woman at thirty-three. And the warm pleasure of conspiracy, of melting into harmonious complicity. And the joy of lies, of honesty among thieves, of getting away with murder. If there was a murder, he felt the joy of being a part of it—an accessory after the fact. His eyes met her eyes. He saw she wore a soft, demanding look—a look, he thought, in determined search of ease and happiness. But did he not despise happiness as much as anyone ever had? Was it not happiness that gunned his father down? He waited. He said nothing. She had repeated her thank-you's, and still now he said nothing, letting more time pass, and more time, making things more and more awkward again, frustrating her gratitude. And it was again that pleasure he'd felt in not answering her letters—this torturing of their conversation. Only now, rather than staying silent from a thousand miles, he looked straight into her eyes. He saw the faint smile fading from her mouth. And he liked seeing it fade. And disappear.

"The truth," he finally said, feeling as if he pointed at

her a gun more powerful than the one he carried beneath his jacket, "Yes. I know the truth, Mama. The real truth." He waited again, as if taking still deader aim. And he waited. Waited, staring into her eyes. At last he said, "And *you* know something, Mama. I know you do. You know that I will do for you now and forever what Father would have done for you himself. You can count on that."

As long as he'd been silent, so now was she. She looked still into his eyes, but said nothing. And he knew that he had succeeded. He had ended their relationship. There would be a tacit understanding, forever, but not for another instant any conspiracy, or sharing. He both felt sick to death and believed he'd right now defined the place from where his energy would come for the rest of his life.

She looked at him with no pleading look, and spoke with the loss of a warmth that, he was certain, would never return. "I have for a long time, Tyrus," she said, "been thinking about what might be going through your mind. I don't need to think anymore. I'm not sure I'll ever be able to tell you what that really means to me. I'm not sure I ever will."

That night, in his room, he lay in his bed with the gun in his hand. He let himself imagine as the minutes moved past one o'clock toward 1:10, the time his father died, that he heard noises on the roof outside his window. The bed lamp beside him cast a glow on the glass. He let himself think he heard a tapping. Then he looked up and saw a figure, himself holding a pistol, grim-faced, with jaw set hard as his own. But neither of them fired. And when, now recognizing each other, he and the figure nodded to each other, each lowering his weapon, the boy turned in a new direction. He wouldn't fire at the window. He knew what he had to do. "You know what you have to do." He imagined the ghost confirming it, as if in a close whisper in his ear, the second he thought it. Then he turned toward where he heard his mother now turning on her bed, heard the squeaking of the springs, and her groaning, loud, clear, tossing, he was sure, in some bad, or . . .

sweet dream. He raised the gun toward the spot where she would be lying, right with him where he lay himself. And he counted ten, slow seconds, before he lowered the weapon.

Through all succeeding days, confirmations of suspicions would give him only more grim, despairing satisfactions as well as what he saw now as opportunities for silent signallings to his mother that he knew what he knew. So it pleased him all to hell to see that, exactly as he'd predicted, Uncle Ezra and Aunt Mary were back at the farm. Of course, though, the words in which he noticed this fact to his mother, as they sat at supper after his first harvest-day's labor, suggested it had no special meaning for him. Yet now he'd found a *tone*, too, for suggesting to her that such facts did have very special meaning for him. And she had found a tone. But Christ in hell! To live with your own mother in the house you grew up in, speaking only in a false voice while every second looking for deadly signals in a whole other language! Keening your hypocritical self with watching constantly for some real, unspoken truth about your own mother! Yet he could feel it once again replenishing itself, feel it coming with all this careful intense falseness and spying: the energy he'd need for greatness.

At the farm there was, too, the sand pit he'd dug for training. After his hours of fieldwork, that first day, he'd cleared the pit of weeds and raked it and took a light scythe from where it leaned against an equipment shed and cut down the approach path and checked for where there might be ankle-threatening holes and depressions. Then he began. He prefigured in his imagination a hundred different possibilities, and he thought of how best to play and exploit each one. He thought of this, and this, and this, and this, and this, and this, setting every problem down in his mind with a knife and superscribing the solution in blood. In blood and in sweat—as he tore right past sickness and pain in running, wings for feet, this way and that way, turning his head every way so he could see everything. And every time, the outfielder was McIntyre, who got moved as needed (and who the boy now preferred to think *had* lied about his part in the sabotage and would have said his full say of words about the Cobb family all right, if he hadn't been stopped dead silent). Left, right, and center: There, for the boy, was his enemy's ever-so-useful picture, as he went to each and every field and gap.

And with every slightest body twist, every slightest fraction of time gained, of vision improved, of safe space won, of momentum shifted exactly right, he made an act of faith in the smallest of small numbers. Just this—just one half of one half of a split second—and you triumph. Fix your mind in complete faith on these kinds of measures—do it a million times—until your mind's inner eye is so much more finely sharpened than anything anyone ever thought of, that you won't have to thank anyone, or God either.

And never submit to pain. Never. The boy said this to himself as he spat some last bits of vomit from his mouth, having after a hundred runs brought up puke onto his lip. He kicked over the vomitus with sand and wiped his sleeve ferociously over his mouth, dragging off the last foul, acidic spit. And then he went back to his mark and ran again. And again. And again. And again—till it was a dry heave and dry, bitter sputum. Dry except for an added taste of blood, which he immediately marked as a point to be reached when he conditioned himself: the point of the blood-taste in the mouth.

But, then, times he was free, he did go see Charlie, too. He would keep every promise to her. Nor was it ever anything but wonderful, being together with his girl. And yet he never confessed his lie to her. A lie that became more and more of a lie every day he spent with his mother. For with the trial every day coming one day nearer, there was (though, of course, not a first spoken word would signal it) a strangeness that kept on growing.

With Charlie, however, all he would ever say was that

he was sure she'd be found not guilty, a verdict he indeed hoped for every second. For though his imagination worked frequently on revenge gun fantasies, he liked better the idea of the Cobbs' never having to admit a thing. All or nothing, saddest, angriest boy. And to the nothing of *not being*, which silent, easy death he knew was the real end of his gun fantasies (killing his mother, then killing her son), he preferred the all of greatness, his quest for which he knew would be energized by, as his hard self would forever take its stand on, the words *not guilty*.

Doves with Joe in the cornfields—this never happened. He stayed clear of Joe Cunningham completely, and pointedly, since, before he saw his best friend in the world, he heard Joe's name included, along with Reverend Minifield's among the witnesses for the prosecution.

But alone, once harvest was done, he did hunt. Let it be squirrel or wild pig, or turkey, or duck, or deer, deer, deer—with his shotguns and rifles he worked for an all-out *Nimrod* triumph over the sharpest defenses of Georgia's game. He'd create names for their movements (movements no one else would ever notice), and for the types of weather and the times of day in which they would do this, or that. Names for the ways they'd nest or forage, or for the changes in the sounds of their calls to each other. Names for every roll of the hills in every last section of his private hunting grounds, which he had an ever-more-detailed map of in his mind. Names for countless marking trees; and for the little half-creeks that no one had ever named; and for the feeder rills, which no one would ever think of naming, but which the deer knew, and that he knew they knew, down to the exact places where that sweet-tasting water would pool beneath strange exposed roots of various types of trees.

As he covered the hills, he took pleasure again thinking of how all the McIntyres up north were day after day numbing their skulls with alcohol. And how while he tracked down deer, they would be tracking down floozies till they caught themselves a nice, sweet dose. They didn't know how to care for themselves, or for anything. But sure as hell he knew how to care. And his care would prove itself in the end. Meantime he made maps and charts of the American League in his mind, refining and refining his nomenclature, identifying and tagging everything he'd seen, every pitcher's motion, every pitch type, every tendency he'd noticed of every infielder and of every outfielder, all analyzed down, too, into nameable subparts—and as well gave names to every scheme and strategy of his own (which he sometimes summed up as the McIntyre plan, sometimes as the Hayward) for defeating them all to hell and gone. As he heard the cracking of fallen branches or the sounds of hooves pressing on fallen leaves and knew exactly what to expect and where and when, he thought, raising his firearm to the level of his eyes, how his hunting and his ball playing were synonymous.

He got his contract! Christ, yes he did! But when he returned it, signed, he included a letter (an apology, in fact) to Navin saying that certain family matters of an extreme importance would make it impossible for him to be present for the beginning of spring training, that he'd have to be, in fact, a week late. He assured Mr. Navin that he had gotten himself in "good, hard condition" and that he'd be ready as the next man, come the seventh of March, when, he promised, he would arrive. He said not word one about what the family matters were; and he tried to obviate any future necessity for revelation by being as polite as he possibly could, not only apologizing but expressing some concern that he "not be taken as presumptuous" making what he hoped "did not look like a demand but a simple request that a one-time family necessity be met as responsibly as it should." Anything to prevent the first word of discussion on the subject. Anything.

And his careful effort proved to a point successful. Navin wrote back saying that he was not only glad to have

Tyrus Cobb back in the "Tiger family" for the season of '06 but that the Tiger Organization had no objections whatsoever to a player's absence from team affairs when he had to stand by his family in a time of need. "About such a matter," he concluded, "no reason to say more. All of us here understand."

So not a word, really, about the subject. But what about that "All of us here understand"? It didn't take an expert in hieroglyphics to read that. And hearing it now everywhere, he wondered how much of this language of suggestion he'd be able to listen to in his life. But he concluded that he very much preferred suggestion to the open word. And he congratulated himself on having reduced things to this sort of whisper, and so accomplishing at least the beginning of a final silence. In the meantime there would be, too, the satisfaction of being able to read all their whispered little signals.

Some days before the trial, he came home early and heard sounds, not his little sister, Floie, but his mother and a man, a lawyer, with her in the library, with the door closed. The boy felt a heat of excitement. He stopped, then moved, with the quietest possible stealth . . . down the corridor . . . toward the base of the stairs, which landed not five feet from the library door. He stopped there to listen.

"Amanda, I assure you we've examined their evidence a hundred times over. They have nothing. Not a shred, though with the publicity, we won't get a dismissal. Such is the power of the press. But their witnesses have repeatedly contradicted not only each other but themselves as well. Not a single, blame one of 'em has got his or her story straight. There's the time, of course. Ten seconds from all of them. But the patent contrivance of such a tidy, rounded-out figure. Not only is there the obvious appearance of estimate, but the consistency suggests a group conformity of opinion rather than the truth. So the stricter it gets, the better. It's a poor job altogether, this prosecution. And there's no more about you and Senator Cobb than mere rumor, which will be thrown out faster than we can say the word *hearsay*.

"For instance, *what pistol*? And what indication ever that you and the Senator had anything but a successful and happy marriage? Any introduction of any counterelements will be objected to and silenced, as it should be. The jury will be forced absolutely to *ignore* everything that the prosecution and the newspaper have so loved to noise about. A courtroom is no newspaper, praise be. Words can't fly around there any which way. So let me repeat: While you have good, solid, indeed the very most solid answers for more questions than the County Attorney, or for that matter all of Royston's eager little imaginations put together, could ever contrive, there really isn't any need for you to take the stand, at least as we see it now."

The boy gripped a baluster with each hand. The voice paused, then continued. "As we've been saying, Amanda, an accidental catch in your throat (and don't underestimate the power of an enemy questioner to produce such), a trembling of your hand, a nervous response (and you want to know that in circumstances like those we face, the naked truth itself will tremble), or just a thoughtful response, Amanda, when to an eagerly condemning eye an honest and innocent *thought* can look like unforthcoming self-protection or suspicious reluctance or evasion. . . . You'll need to think about all these things. About *why* you'd give the minds that have produced all the vicious canards about you even the remotest opportunity to make their bloody little dreams come true."

The boy stepped closer. He wanted to catch every word, every syllable and breath, of his mother's response. He had a feeling she'd want to take the stand, for all her expressions of concern about being mind-trapped in a self-incrimination. Gripping balusters hard in each hand, through them he listened close.

"But I do not like, Tom, people being allowed forever to assume things about me because I've remained silent. I've had to remain silent too long, and it's killing me. I want my day in court. So I remain determined *not* to leave my story untold. I'll say my piece about my relationship with my husband, about the cruelty toward that relationship and my memories that people show when they so eagerly find meaning in a pure accident...."

"Perhaps best, Amanda ..."

"Please *now*, at least, don't interrupt me, Tom. Please. You don't know what silence on these matters is like, when you know all night and day that what is going on around you is noise, noise, noise, noise. When the only person at all obliged *not* to speak is you, and everyone else on earth is fully licensed. *Good*—that you'll not allow things to get admitted into court and that you'll raise silencing and disqualifying and dismissing objections. 'The jury will disregard....' But I beg you, don't silence me now, when I want to raise an objection even to the *notion* of a failed or unhappy marriage in this house! What evidence ever of such a thing! And of my husband with a gun! Good God in heaven! And of a third party! How dare they with their *rumors*! And don't think those prosecutors won't get their *words in*! You'll be quick, but they'll get their words in."

So many differing privacies. And hypocrisies. And lies. The boy had held the balusters tighter and tighter as his mother had gone on. He hadn't moved, rather watched the door so hard that, in his mind, he made *it* move, and open on a beautiful, blue-eyed woman standing there with a shotgun pointed at his life.

But now there was a healthy bang from the back screen door. Floie. Come in from the yard. And immediately in the study a silence. Then against the silence a sound. Someone in the study, rising, coming toward the closed door.

He made his move, stepping now quickly onto the staircase and beginning to climb, praying that the noise of his steps would be drowned by that of the steps within the room. And if he reached the top of the stairs before those steps reached the library door, he thought superstitiously—nearing the top—he would be protected. But now the library door opened. He took the last steps clumsily, nearly stumbling. But he didn't look back. Then he slowed, to go again quietly. Still he didn't look back or down, rather moved toward his room, back along the corridor and railing.

But he couldn't stop himself. Before he reached his room door, he looked down over the bannister—and saw his mother looking up, following him, the blue of her eyes as deadly in its beauty as the power of the gun that took his father's life. She had to know that he'd been close and eavesdropping when she'd said what she'd just said. And instantly he hated her for making *him* feel ashamed for this. How on this hell earth could she ever. But he vowed in fiercest resentment that she wouldn't make him feel ashamed like this again. And for his vow's seal, he stopped dead, looked back down over the railing, and stared as hard at her as she at him. Then the lawyer came, papers in hand; and mother and son moved off in their separate ways.

So then to hell with *everything*, including that morning in the dark when between the kitchen door and the screen he found a string-bound gunny sack—and he knew. No name. No note. But he knew the second he lifted it, what it was, and who had left it. He had tears in his eyes when he stepped back into the kitchen and turned on the light. He sat with the sack between his knees, crying, when he opened the sack and saw three black ash bats, milled to perfect beauty.

The trial was set for the Fourth of March. And the boy recalled, sometimes even in his fingers, his turning the pages of his father's diary, as now the days turned one into another. But then with these days there were a thousand different rates of time—slow, to lightning-fast—just as on trains there were a thousand kinds of motion—all, he knew, depending on the weather in his mind. He was in his room, awake, thinking, at the exact midnight when the end of February came and the first seconds of March. He recalled then his night-crossing of the Ohio—the long, lantern-lit, iron bridge, and the lights of Cincinnati on the other side of the black-glimmering river—and the midpoint, fixed by his eye.

March First. March Second. March Third. Though they came at different paces, and each of their hours was different from every other, they came. And the feeling of inevitability was as powerful as it had ever been when those wheels of locomotives rolled over miles northbound, and then east-west across Yankeeland, and then again southbound. March First happened. March Second happened. March Third happened. And now March Fourth. So close to impossible to believe these actualities. But—truth—it was here. March Fourth.

He again had been sleeping with his gun beneath his pillow (in the home he grew up in). And now he turned from his window and lay on his stomach, once more with his hands raised, as if he were being placed under arrest. But it was time to rise and go, the house already silent from his mother's departure with her lawyers.

He dressed himself. And armed himself, buttoning his jacket high over his holstered gun. But as he made sure the holster was tucked in tight toward his arm and inconspicuous, he noticed: there truly wasn't a sound. Floie had stayed at McCallums'. Of course, with the trial this morning. But he was troubled suddenly to think how alone he was in the house. He opened his door, slowly, and called, "Mother?" He got no answer. He called louder, "Mama?" And louder, "*Mama!*"

As his voice rang with the word through the empty rooms, he found himself having suddenly to fight back tears. Blinking hard, though, refusing to touch his stinging eyes, he came out of his room, hearing the floorboards voicing accusations as he stepped.

He shook his head in anger, and to bring himself back to his responsibilities. He didn't have much time before he should go. He read his watch, catching the inscription before clicking the gold case shut. Squeezing then the case hard in his palm, he shouted out, knowing that she wasn't there, *"Mama, are you here?"*

But he was surprised, couldn't fully believe it, when he received no answer. Nonetheless he stepped now not ahead toward the stairs, but left. Left, where he had to cross a space he'd avoided as if to enter it would be to feel a scaffold floor drop: The sinister space where he'd seen a man standing, not his father. But he closed his eyes, and stepped over, and stood, then opened his eyes before the door of his parents' bedroom.

He hadn't been in this room one time since he'd come home—another of his silent signals to her. But he opened the door now and let it swing inward on its hinges, slowly, full wide. He found himself looking for the shotgun, which would be set by the side of the bed, leaning against the wall. But it wasn't there. Of course not: It had been placed in evidence. It was in the courtroom at Lavonia, where not long from now his mother would have to look right at it and say, "Yes, this was the gun."

He looked at the window, which was actually there, as everything killing-painful was. Oh hell Jesus! Then, with his body gripping itself hard enough nearly to create injury, he stood where she would have first held the gun. He looked at the window. How close was it? What was the space between? What was it? How close? How far? He tried to imagine the darkness of that night. He pretended that he held the gun, and he raised his arms to aim. The distance passed back and forth from her story's distance to a distance that made her story a murderer's lie, back and forth as he held his aim, from the space of an accident to the space of a deadly intention, from the space his mother had not been able to see across clearly to the space a whore's eyes could cross as easily as she could sell her soul. He heard his watch ticking. He looked at the second hand. He gazed at it passing over the seconds to ten. One. Two. Three. Four. Five. Six. Seven. Eight. Nine. Ten.

It was an eternity. If there was any truth to what was said about the time, it was an eternity! The whole heart of the matter of his father's book could be known in that time. She could have gone over her whole life in that time! He looked again at the watch's face and stared at the second hand as it passed again through ten seconds. But this time, because he *wanted* it to take forever, it took no time.

But he panicked now, suddenly thinking he would be late! He shut the watch tight and made his way to the door. As, however, he crossed into that forbidden space, the figure of the man came back before him! Right there, standing! The boy shook his head, to expel the vision physically from his mind, and life—forever—to kill it. A pale, shadowed face. A black-haired man. The vision, which, that time he saw it, had disappeared down the stairs, out the back. And now he found himself following it down the stairs to the back of the house and out.

He shook himself again, walked quickly past the wood-shed to the barn, where he hitched his mother's mare fast to the buggy. Then with a snap of the reins and a sharp crack of the buggy whip, he took out from the barn.

Chapter Fifteen
TAKING THE STAND

The minutes of the quick trial, not three hours all told, would like buggy-wheel spokes blurring to sheeted disks, sometimes fuse in his mind into long single moments of impotence and bewilderment; for the trial wasn't a ball diamond—it was a field for a war of words in which he had no say. Just fifteen rows of seats in the entire courtroom, and still his hawks failed for the first hour to see even his brother, Paul, up from Tech, sitting only four rows before him—though he would put hard focus now and again on the back of a black-haired man, who in time would turn and show himself to be no one the boy had ever seen. Nor would his mother—though the boy watched for such things so hard he believed he might make them happen—turn once either to this black-haired man, *or* her son. She would turn as far as her lawyer's ear, whispering into it as a woman might into the ear of some lover (but not for a single one of her betrayals, or crimes, would her son have anyone but himself even think of punishing her).

The jury-room door's clicking open and the twelve's emerging one-by-one woke him with that one-after-another undeniableness. He found himself wishing immediately as they moved into the box, like a Mr. Fred West, that he could get inside those dozen unknown brains, rip out the wrong words and with the right words put the fix on, make this trial a sure thing (and let truth be damned for an enemy of the Cobbs and of anybody who wanted to keep on *living*). But then with the "All Rise!" he found himself just caught up with the wave of rising bodies, listening to the mass sound of shuffling, and the rumbling and knocking from the shiftings of weight. Then just listening to the quiet. Then expecting what would happen next, which did happen: the door of the judge's chambers clicked and creaked open. And then seeing the judge, watching the gray-haired, sixtyish, strong-built man come through that door, arrange his black robe, and rise to his bench, lighted now by some broken rays that fell from half-shaded windows above. Then once more just moving with the wave of people as the bailiff got it to shift its weight back, settle, and not move again, while he announced the day, and the place, and the fact that this court was "now in session . . . The Honorable Winston R. Sudduth, presiding."

In a brief, quiet hiatus the boy enjoyed some seconds then of bitter contempt for every miserable Royston curiosity seeker who'd come the sixteen miles over, he knew, and packed this courtroom, just to watch the Cobbs go down. He could smell 'em all around him, and he thought he might show these rats the gun, all right. But then it was the gavel cracking down for the start of something that, completely unreal as it still seemed, and must be, was actually now going to begin.

"Case 41427: The State of Georgia versus Amanda Chitwood Cobb on a charge of voluntary manslaughter in the death of William Herschel Cobb." The recording clerk nodded. She was ready. For another brief free second, the boy shut his eyes in a cocoon of thought, imagining now his acquiring some day in secret all records that ever would emerge from these proceedings. That's the kind of thing friends, and money, were for. But then a last hard, determinative gavel-crack and Sudduth's directive word that "The State will call its first witness." Tyrus Cobb. At some superstitious depth in his mind the boy felt a fast-panicky fear that the first witness would be Tyrus Raymond Cobb, to be questioned on matters of destruction and concealment of evidence: obstruction of justice. He had begun sweating under his gun; and he felt even some real surprise, when it was the coroner, Reginald Mickelson, who was called instead.

The attorney for the State, one William Whiteacre, with a cross-county reputation as a sharp-as-hell mind and hard warrior, and with a long record of victories, had a pure bald skull, all shining, that the boy found himself now contemplating. And as that starch-collared, plaster-haired scarecrow of a couldn't-do farmer Reggie Mickelson swore on the Book that he'd come there to tell the truth, the whole truth, and nothing but the truth so help him God, the boy thought about what a shotgun blast could do to that shining bald skull, as it nodded now the coroner's way—and then as it got from Mickelson the day, the time, and the cause of Senator William Herschel Cobb's death, "which again would be, August 10, 1905, 1:10, A.M., and two blasts from a shotgun."

Then what seemed no time and it was details—sickening, grotesque details of his father's wounds. The boy was caught up. But then startled, and pleased, by the "Ob-*jection!*" of his mother's lawyer Fenton. The boy loved the sound of *that* word and the way it stopped cold the filth spewing out of the trap of goddamned Reggie Mickelson, one more *former* friend. And what in hell was Whiteacre doing but exactly what Fenton *said* he was doing—"attempting, your Honor, obviously to stir up adverse sentiment with lurid detail"? The boy couldn't believe there'd be any answer to this except pure silent acquiescence. But the bald skull had his answer: establishing *sequence of events*: that's what he was doing. Making up *your* filthy story out of the accident, that's what you're doing, the boy thought, in silence.

But, though he bitterly despised himself, he found himself in fact greedy, too, for every sick detail. Sudduth, who could make any word here he pleased into the last one, had come down against Fenton (and so made the boy sure for the moment that the Cobbs were going down) with his damned binding spells and directives *"overruled"* and "The State may proceed" and "The witness will answer." So the coroner's spew could keep on coming until a full record was established of Mickelson's "findin's": that the first blast was to the "ubdumnal area" and the second "to the face" and that both blasts "come dead on" and that "the second'n come at a goodly closer range than the first'n." For wasn't there a far greater concentration of pellets in the face than in the stomach? And could it not well be inferred from "the way the Senator's layin' full straight back from the windah" that the blast he took *second* was that one he took *closer*, that is, the blast to his face? And did not the fact that the wounds were—not "whipt acrost like t' a flag in the wind"—but instead "full wide split apart, blown out from the center" indicate that both blasts "they was dead on"?

The boy had never gotten these particulars. And for some insane reason he did *want* them, every last one. But if for such sick, greedy curiosity he hated himself, he hated, too, that anyone other than a Cobb would ever know these things about a Cobb. Then he felt a frightened ignorance—a *conviction* that in fact Tyrus Cobb knew nothing about his own family and that everyone else in that courtroom knew everything—that if he'd read a book, they'd all read *the* book, and that it was one he'd never seen.

But when that pathetic fool Mickelson began at last really to work up effects, deliberately choking up in his expressions of horror, hoping he'd be forgiven, " 'cause'n it was hard" to say what he had to say about Herschel's—he meant Senator Cobb's—body, the way it was when he actually examined it, Fenton cried out, *"Your Honor!"* and Sudduth, who saw the coroner as indeed now having crossed a line, wasted not a second. *"Enough!* Mr. Mickelson. Not another whimpering syllable, sir. You'll just answer the questions, and *no more* of any such sorry theater work here!" So, *good.*

But the bald skull wasted not a second, just left his point and moved like lightning to possibles and hypotheticals, which he shot out like Gatling fire. Could the Senator after the first blast have still been conscious? Yes. Could the Senator still have spoken? Yes. If the Senator had, let us say, still a full ten seconds left of his life could he have said such words as "Amanda, it's Herschel!" Or "Amanda, for God's sake have mercy! Don't shoot! Have mercy! Have mercy! Help me! Please, Amanda!" And though Fenton shot to his feet now and screamed his objections and Sudduth was just that fast with his *"Sustained!"* and *"The State will refrain!"* and "The jury will *disregard!"*—the jury, the boy was dead positive, wouldn't disregard. Could not. Whiteacre had gotten in his words, and they would linger to the end in the air that jury breathed, with an infection, the boy feared, that might make the last difference for the Cobb family.

But he knew nothing really about courtrooms yet, with their direct, cross, redirect, recross, though he would hear these names now, and they'd stick in his mind like battle reports. And God help him, and God love this country, was it not a beautiful, beautiful thing the way Fenton came right back and worked that clodpole Mickelson and got him to unsay about every last word he'd said! Immediately the so-called coroner was forced to admit that the testimony of the witnesses as to the time of the shooting varied as much as ten minutes. And he'd kept that back, *hadn't he!* And, pellet holes or no, he couldn't say how many feet either the first shot or the second shot was fired from, *could he!* He couldn't say if Senator Cobb had said a single word before the first shot, *could he!* Or before the second shot, *could he!* He couldn't say if Senator Cobb *was* conscious, or even *alive,* after the first shot; or if, before either shot, Senator Cobb had been facing the window directly for more than three seconds, or two seconds, or one second, or *one half of one second—could he!*

No. And so from lawyer Fenton, who now closed his eyes, then opened them, and turned them again right at the man, "Just one last question for *you*, Mr. Mickelson. Just one—last—question. Is there anything, sir, in your *findings*, that makes it impossible for you to say that Senator Cobb's death was, after all, an *accident? Anything*, Mr. Mickelson, at all?"

"Im. . . . possible?"

"Your Honor . . ."

"Answer the question yes or no, Mr. Mickelson."

"Could you repeat it, sir."

"Gladly. Is there, Mr. Mickelson, anything in your findings that makes it *impossible* for you to say that Senator William Herschel Cobb's death was an *accident—yes or no?*"

"No. Nothin' that would make that impossible. But . . ."

"So it could have been an accident?"

"Well . . ."

"Yes or no!"

"Yes."

"That will be all, Mr. Mickelson. I have no further questions for you."

This was so fine and beautiful, it dried the sweat beneath the boy's gun. And maybe—to whatever this interchange of inquiry and cross-examination would turn out to be—Tyrus Cobb would not prefer now the shattering noise and permanent dead silence his gun could cause (sweet fantasy and now regular groove in his brain). He let the words *not guilty* take on a little life again in his mind. And, hell *yes*, just the way he'd wanted, he'd take his stand on those very words, no matter what he knew about his mother and father—for (he smiled an invisible smile to think) what better stimulus for keeping *sharp* than having for your whole life to keep—if you liked it in law words—*justice obstructed.*

He felt good. Dry. He breathed, not hard, relaxing. The packed room seemed to ease outward from what had been for him a closed-coffin tightness. And if still he couldn't scan the field, he could look at his mother and not want to walk up and whisper, or shout, a threat of exposure into her ear.

But he hadn't expected the word "pistol." Nor would lawyer Fenton's declarations about the nonexistence of any such item help him one damn. Whiteacre had called Raymond Crichter (and God Jesus how the boy wanted to tighten that Sunday necktie even tighter round the bulged neck of "Constable Ray") and he asked Crichter if in his on-the-scene examination of the body he had discovered in, or protruding from, the Senator's pocket a *pistol*. And—*no*—not one single miserable spit on earth did it matter that Fenton shouted, "What pistol! *There is no pistol!*" The boy would have loved to laugh like hell—and take some nice cynical pleasure in Fenton's hollow lawyer talk, even as all the while he *wore* the gun. But the laugh was on him, and the Cobbs. And what did it matter that Sudduth sustained Fenton and yanked up Whiteacre to the bench and warned him in whispers that got hissed so fierce you could have made them out if you stood in the road. What the boy believed—*believed* in a way as true as his sweat and his heart's pounding—was that the prosecutor had some god-honest gift, of mind, or of eyes; that the man could see beneath the coat of the Senator's boy; and that that boy would sure as hell now be called up and told to strip off his jacket and be arrested not one second after he'd done so. For there *was* a pistol, and the Cobb "case," and everything with the name, or the disgrace of the name Cobb on it, would fail its way from there to the hell and gone it deserved.

The boy sank back into a lead stupidity of anger and fear. He couldn't think. He hated—to the point of wanting to rip out his pistol, all right, and kill—that there'd ever been a start to this trial, a first out-loud word spoken against his family by this pack of rats. He felt his sheer, crippled inability to stop *anything.* And his complete ignorance in this goddamned box of a place. His having simply to wait here, mouth shut, powerless, crammed so he couldn't move.

Nor, still, some time after, did it matter that Fenton, so fast that Crichter couldn't even nod an answer, would get Sudduth to declare *"inadmissable* any reference *whatsoever"* to Mrs. Cobb's having taken on a lover (for exactly as there was no pistol, there *was no lover!*), for Whiteacre managed still to force in his question, which again would poison the air and every individual brain on that jury, like some lethal plague germ: *Were you aware, Constable Crichter, that Mrs. Cobb was said to have taken on a lover?*

That the last word belonged to the defense would provide the boy some measure of comfort. When Fenton put a hard-as-hell beating on Crichter for pretending he could *interpret* Mrs. Cobb's demeanor on the night in question, the boy felt good about every savage blow—the last so fierce that Whiteacre would make Fenton stop, objecting that counsel was berating the witness. Fenton, though, quick enough to prevent Sudduth, took back his last query-remark about the Constable's special gift for "reading things," with the "Withdrawn"; and it was like, the boy thought, the withdrawing of a blade, stuck up to the hilt.

And yet Crichter had been able to say, "Well, she didn't have no tears."

And to Whiteacre's damned *leading,* repetitive poison in damned redirect—"She made, Constable, no expression then of grief over having lost her husband of *twenty years?"*—Crichter was able to answer again, "No, sir. Leastways, not to me."

Fenton would go one more time then after the constable's credibility, wondering about Raymond Crichter's obvious love of rumor and his inclination to inflate, if not imagine things. "Things you *wanted* to be true, sir . . . So . . . what? So you wouldn't have to be dealing with something so unexciting as a *mere accident,* something with no more *cause* to it than *mistaken identity!* Because how important are *you,* Constable Crichter, if all we're talking about here is just pure, unexciting *accident!"*

"Don't make no difference to me, whether 'tis."

"I'm sure not. I'm sure that the single 'great event' in the history of the town of Royston—that that event's coming in truth to *nothing*—makes no difference to you, the town constable. I am sure not."

And the boy especially liked this exchange—for Raymond Crichter *was* Royston. Royston rumor. Royston gossip. Royston love of a story. And Royston jealousy and hatred of the Cobbs (for hadn't his father run candidates against him and his mother always spoken of him, and made it known that she thought of him, as a malicious, leering busybody). And destroying Crichter was destroying that damned town, call it rumor mill. Yet all over and through Fenton's recross, he kept hearing Whiteacre's *twenty years:* the time his parents were married (a marriage whose ending produced no expressions of grief that the constable could see), the time his mother could spend in prison, the time he asked for in The Show (and if in exchange for his soul, so be it). And he couldn't help a numb, stupid thought: The day his mother was released from prison would be the exact day he would end his career.

Witnesses who claimed to have seen the Senator, on the night in question, lurking about in the shadows some hours before the shooting were all shown to be blind, and stupid, enough. Easily discreditable. Dismissable. So much so that the boy took for a moment even the same scornful pleasure that Fenton took when one of them let out that the figure he saw in the shadows, ". . . was lookin' like some kinda burglar, or some such."

"It appeared to be a *burglar?"*

"Yessir, an' tha'd be how I put it to Ray Crichter."

"Indeed, sir," Fenton said, "and I thank you for that. I thank you very much for that."

And thank you, too, to Mr. Shipton and to Mrs. Shipton and to Joe Cunningham, Sr., for admitting that indeed when they determined that that time between blasts was ten seconds, they'd just been awakened by the first of the two and so indeed were sort of sleepy. *Sort of* sleepy? Well, all right, *sleepy.* And that yes, all right, yes, they *had* spoken to each other about it—and not just Mr. Shipton to Mrs., but the two of them to Joe, Sr., as well, and all three of them, *yes,* all three *together at the same time,* to Constable Crichter at a meeting in his office. Yes. And so thank you. And wouldn't Joe, Sr., agree that a space of time like *whatever* it in fact was, was something you could make just about anything out of that you wanted to? Well, he supposed . . . maybe. And that when we look back on things, once there's been a serious event, we can sort of start imagining things as having occurred, you know, side things, to sort of bolster up our theory about the main thing? Well, yes, Joe, Sr., guessed so. Yes he did. So, good, the boy thought. Good.

And he let himself think back now through the State's roll of witnesses so far—from Joe, Sr.—to Mr. Shipton—to Mrs. Shipton—to Kyle Forbus, Phil Treach and old Mr. Kenilworth (none of the three of whom saw any more than the old man's "burglar, or some such")—to Ray Crichter, with his ever-so-eager, hot *eagerness* to give to sorry no-event Royston its one big moment—and on to that damned fool clodpole Reg Mickelson. And he let his mind run over their words and think, for a breath or so now, that they were the ones who had nothing. The State had no *case.* Was there anything they had that would make it impossible to say that his father's death was not an accident? Nothing. He let himself think—they had nothing.

"The State calls Joseph Cunningham, Jr."

Christ. *Joe. Joe!* And what a sorry damned laugh *this* was! The boy truly almost laughed at himself out loud—and wanted (so maybe people *would* look at him like some crazy man) to mutter out a thought that came to him: that there's a God all right and He hates every little Cobb moment of joy. Every second of it. And that he'd not yet spotted Joe, who was sitting there right next to Joe, Sr.! His eyes and mind must have gone completely useless!

And—truth to God—somebody tell him how it could be that there Joe Cunningham *was*, with those same kid freckles and that same sandy hair, cut the same way it was when he was nine? And that same lanky body, only grown ten years? And now that, like all the rest of them, *Joe Cunningham* was up swearing his oath on the Book, to tell nothing but the truth? The boy wanted to let his hate build for the one who'd first seen his father lying in pools of blood, and who'd tried to bribe his heart with those new bats. He wanted to suck on the pleasure of losing for good now his best and last friend, who'd be a true Judas here, exactly as expected. But he was in a way honestly stunned. It made it hard for him to move his own thinking—that he hadn't by not seeing him these last months made Joe Cunningham not exist.

He would shake himself harder into attention. There'd been something. Whiteacre was reminding Joe. Some previous taking of statements from Joe. And now the bald skull, not difficult to imagine as pure skull, not with dark eyes but dark eye holes and not lips but mere teeth in sockets of bone—was asking questions, about how long, and how well Joe knew the Cobbs. And now the boy woke harder, all right, listening. "Tyrus and I were best friends right from the start. So I've been over there pretty regularly these past ten years ... though not lately. Tyrus and I lately ... well ... We haven't seen each other." The boy felt, with this, immediately that all eyes were turning on *him* now, and that the whole mob was prepared to blame *him* for everything. He jutted his jaw and pulled tight against him his high-buttoned coat, and focused hard on the witness.

"I see. Ummhmm. But at any time during those ten years, Joe, have you known there to be any trouble in the

family? And by that I mean, particularly, between Mrs. Cobb
and Mr. Cobb?"

"I don't know. . . . I mean . . . I'm not the one. . . ."

"Did you ever at any time come up on Mr. and Mrs.
Cobb when they were quarreling, and overhear things?"

"Well . . . I don't."

"Joe, I ask you to recall statements you have made in
deposition. I ask you to recall those sworn statements. Or
would you care to have me read them?"

"I just don't. . . ."

"Would there be any reason, Joe, for your not recalling
clearly now those things you said?"

Joe looked up into the crowd. Tyrus knew that he was
looking to see if his best friend, who'd been right next door
but hadn't one time said a word to him or even shown himself to him in his five months home, was looking back. And
oh hell yes he was. Tyrus kept his jaw jutted, and his eyes
fixed hard in Joe's direction. When Joe saw, he lowered his
head.

"Would there, Joe, be any *reason*?"

"No, sir. No. I recall what I said."

"And could you now tell the court?"

"Well, I . . . I did one time come up to the kitchen
door. . . ." Joe lowered his head still more and became almost
inaudible.

"Joe?"

"I'd come up to the door. . . ."

"Yes. Tell us."

He cleared his throat, looked up, but away from his
friend, now and again even to the windows above. "It was
when Tyrus went off to make his first try, as a ballplayer,
with Augusta. It'd be two years this month. I didn't know if
he'd left or not, or left with his father's blessing or not. He
was fixin' to cut, I think, if he didn't get his father's blessing.
But that's not the here nor there. I came up to the back door,
the kitchen door. And it was warm that day. So it was just

the screen that was closed. And I was about to knock when I heard some shouting coming from the kitchen. It was the Senator and Mizz Amanda. And they were arguing about Tyrus. So I couldn't help myself. God knows I just shoulda cut. But it was about my friend. So curiosity got me. And I listened. They were going at it . . . pretty hard."

"Can you recall for us, Joe, the gist of the argument."

"The Senator, he was angry because he thought Mizz Amanda was the cause a Tyrus goin' off to be a ballplayer rather than headed to Athens to be a medical doctor, or off to West Point, the way he'd always planned and dreamed for Tyrus."

"Do you recall, Joe, the Senator's saying anything about the character of Mrs. Cobb?"

"I can't rightly . . ."

"Joe, I'll ask you again. . . . Should I read. . . ."

"He said, from the start she was no good for him. From when she was a girl, she was no good."

"And did the argument end there, Joe. Or did it become more heated?"

"I shoulda left. . . . It was private."

"That's not what I'm asking, Joe. What I'm asking is did the argument end, or did it become more heated?"

"It got hotter still, and Mizz Amanda told Senator Herschel he'd be sorry some day if he kept up not caring about her and paying mind only to his own things."

Yes. Yes. He'd be sorry some day, for not caring, paying mind only to his own things. Thank you, Joe. And on the *night in question*, Joe, did you hear anything, coming from next door, at the Cobbs'? The blast of a shotgun, yes, and when you heard it, were you sleeping? You were *not*. And did you have a clock in your room? You did. And it said? One-ten, yes. Thank you, Joe. And then? Then you made quick to get dressed. I see. And as you dressed, did you look out your window toward the Cobbs'? You did, and you saw? You saw the flash from a gun barrel. Thank you. And when you saw through the side window of Senator and Mrs. Cobb's bedroom the bright flash of a gun and heard a second blast—you?

"I said to myself, 'I'll be damned.' "

Ummhmm. Interesting. Yes. *Very*. And did you, ever, Joe, *afterward* I mean, take care to measure the time needed to get yourself as far dressed as you had gotten that night when out your window you saw, in the bedroom of the Cobbs, the light flash from a gun and heard a second blast come from that gun? Yes? You did? Well, no need to apologize, Joe, we're all curious by nature. And that time it took, to get as far dressed as when you heard the second blast?

"It came to eleven seconds, by my clock."

Eleven seconds, by your clock. And your profession, Joe, is *carpenter*? And you can read an angle? Yes. I'd guess you can read an angle, all right. And given the relation between the side window of your bedroom and the side window of Senator and Mrs. Cobbs' bedroom, you would say that a gun would have to be *how far forward* in that room for you to see, from your room, the light flash from its barrel when it was fired? Halfway forward in the room. You say *halfway*. Thank you, Joe, very much. And now this gun here, this shotgun that I hold before you. Do you recognize it? Yes, of course. And let the record show that this is the gun Joe Cunningham saw in that bedroom when he ran up there on the night in question.

The boy, by now, had been some time bound in a hard spell. The glare he'd given Joe had gone soft into a stupid, limp gaze, maybe the look of a man about to be hanged. But he was jolted by the gun, as Whiteacre now held it up. The Cobb family gun. But it couldn't possibly be the one. It didn't look at all like the one that had stood from back in furthest memory beside his parents' bed. But it was. The boy knew it was. And with the Cobb family gun in his hands, held across his chest, Whiteacre now walked over to the railing of the jury box, standing right against it. He began then stepping heel-to-toe, foot after foot, in a measuring way, counting out audibly twelve steps, which brought him back before the witness stand. "Now, Joe," he said, but as he did he turned from the witness stand and faced himself again to the jury box, "I have stepped out from the jury box what amounts to the distance from the Cobbs' back bedroom wall to their bedroom window. What I'm going to do next is walk back two full paces, which will take me across half that distance; and I'm going to do it in the time you have said it took you to do all those things you did that night, before you heard the second blast."

He now raised the shotgun, slowly, and deliberately. And he pointed it right at the center man in the first row of the jury box. "I am now," he said, with his cheek against the stock of the gun, "at the greatest distance Mrs. Cobb could have been from that window when she fired the first shot."

And how far did the greatest possible distance seem? Right now, as close as cold-blooded murder. Nothing. No space. That's what Tyrus thought, as his heart began to break in shame. He hated that this was happening. That the Cobbs were losing. That they'd lost. Shamed for-*damned*-ever, thanks to his best friend.

And now, "*One*-one thousand . . . *two*-one thousand . . . *three*-one thousand . . . *four*-one thousand . . . *five*-one thousand . . ."—and as he counted five, Whiteacre, his skull gleaming, took a three-foot pace forward, right toward the center man in the first row of the jury box, at whom he kept the shotgun directly pointed—then—still against the stock of the gun—"*Six*-one thousand . . . *seven*-one thousand . . . *eight*-one thousand . . . *nine*-one thousand . . ."—and now the prosecutor took another full three-foot pace forward, so that he stood only six feet from the center man in the first row, who Tyrus knew would find his mother guilty, no doubt in this rotten world that he would—and "*Ten*-one thousand." Then, as the gun barrel, pointed right at the man's face, seemed almost to touch him, the trigger sounded, loud as a shotgun blast, *louder*, its *click*—though out through that sound still came Whiteacre's words: "*Eleven*-one thousand."

It must have been a minute—the longest ever—that the man took to replace the gun on the evidence table, to take his breaths and recompose his thoughts, and to turn and reapproach the witness.

And now, Joe, just a few more questions. You ran, Joe, that night, to the Cobbs'. You found the backdoor unlocked. You ran to that upstairs bedroom. And the blasted window, was it easy to pass through? It was nothing, to pass through. I see. All shot out. And when you passed through that window and went to the Senator's body on the roof, did you see anything in, or protruding from, the Senator's coat pocket? You saw what appeared to be a pistol. Thank *you*, Joe. Thank you *very* much. And you told your father. And then your father, after he'd come back from the scene and looked for himself—he told you? There was no pistol. In the coat, nothing. Thank you. And now two last questions, Joe. When you came back toward the room to pass in again through the window, Mrs. Cobb was standing where? Right by the window, looking out. And my last question, Joe—Mrs. Cobb, was she crying?

"I can't say she was. No. Not that I saw."

The boy thought now of actual prison. A real twenty years—for his mother. It had been only a nightmare dream. But now it was real. He'd been taken up and moved back and forth by one voice after another in this godforsaken *trial*, but he was sure there was nothing Fenton could do anymore. And—strange—he had a desire not to separate himself anymore from Joe Cunningham, but to begin their friendship all over again, knowing it would take no more than a quiet word of thanks for the milled ashes.

Fenton. Thomas Fenton. Tom. What could the boy think? Not much anymore. His damned brain-furies were ready for any move he made. But the lawyer was at least nothing slick. Not any pretty man. Face a bit pocked. Hair a rumpled salt-and-pepper. A two-suit man, weekday and Sunday. No more. And he was coming at Joe friendly, which the boy thought was maybe best; he couldn't say anymore. And it was real sort of soft and friendly the way Fenton was asking Joe now if he ever really *measured* that angle between windows. No? Well, would Joe forgive him if he did? And would Joe agree now, that his estimate could have been off? Well, no need to be embarrassed, you were just guessing anyhow, weren't ya, Joe? And did you *see* anyone, Joe, pass *across* that side window, you know, stepping from the back of the room across the side window over closer to the front window—which you'd be able to see, wouldn't ya? No, ya didn't? And about light, you know how it *spreads*, don't ya, Joe? Do you think you could have seen the spread light, not the real fire of the blast? Sure, it could easily have been the spread light. Sure it could.

"And the Senator's body, Joe, did you linger over it? Take a long look? Study what you saw, I mean when you thought there might have been something in the Senator's pocket?"

"No, sir. I took one look and backed off. I almost fell. I was scared to death and heartbroken."

"You've called the Senator's lying there mortally wounded the worst thing you ever saw. Did you have tears in your eyes, Joe?"

"Yes, sir. I was cryin' like a child."

"I understand, Joe. I understand. When you looked at that body, just for that second there, before you backed off, nearly falling over, your eyes were filled with tears and you were scared to death. I understand that, Joe. We all do. And now, if you would, take it back a bit for us, all right? When you were still up in your own bedroom, at your own window, did you hear any *words*, Joe. I mean at any time, before the first blast or between the first and second?"

"No, sir. I did not. Not a single word. And my window was open."

And did Joe in the ten years he'd known the Cobbs at any time other than that one, see or hear the Cobbs argue? No? And did his own mama and daddy ever argue and use harsh words, the kind they wished they hadn't said? Once or twice—but you hope they forgive you, Joe, for saying that? I'm quite sure they think it's no thing that needs forgiving, telling the truth, about something that's just natural. I'm quite sure they think it's no thing that needs forgiving. But tell me now, Joe, is it the truth that your mama and daddy love each other?

"As much, sir, as I've ever seen two people."

"I'm sure that's true, Joe. I'm sure that's true. And they are happy."

"Yes, sir, they are."

"Yes. And thank you very much, Joe. No further questions, son."

There was no convincing himself that Fenton's words did anything to cancel Whiteacre's. His furies were on the every-minute watch. But for a second the boy allowed his mind the thought that *if* one word canceled out another, it would at least turn things in the end into a pure gamble, anybody, the Cobbs just as much as anybody else, having a chance. And he let himself think that maybe Fenton had restored Joe Cunningham sufficiently to grace so that Tyrus Cobb could once again cut him loose.

"The State calls the Reverend John Minifield."

The ghost-gray preacher man. The boy wondered now what would come from the Cobbs' other neighbor, who as he walked up behind, out from the courthouse vestibule into the tight-packed courtroom, made even his mother's head turn, for the first time, around past her lawyer. But she sent no look her son's way. Those blue eyes (and if beauty could win the minds of men in a jury, those eyes were the best Cobb case) followed only the thin, pale minister: that voice who'd told the boy there was a hard part of us called shame that, without help, could never in this world find a way to forgive the part of us it was ashamed of. And did the preacher swear to tell the truth? Even with those eyes right on him, he swore.

And what the minister heard that night, through a window open like Joe's, was a clambering, which aroused his attention. He could say now, of course, that it was the Senator he heard, climbing the rose trellis to the porch roof. And then what he heard was a stepping over the roof, and then a tapping—on the window. And *yes* it was the kind of tapping that one could think of as a call from someone identifying himself to another who knew him. Yes, he could say that. And then what he heard was a second set of tappings; then a third, the last loud enough so that it could be thought of as having possibly threatened the glass. And then he heard a gun blast. And he thought, my God, he has shot her.

"He has shot her?"

"Yes, because, that day I heard, as I was trimming hedge, a rather fierce argument, between Senator and Mrs. Cobb."

"Go on."

"Well, the argument I heard, too, was about the Cobbs' son Tyrus. About his achievements, which gave Mrs. Cobb happiness but about which the Senator didn't then want to hear. And then it was about Mrs. Cobb's happiness, which she claimed as a right. . . . She said she would not stand Mr. Cobb's taking it from her. . . . His criticisms. His not loving her."

"Yes. Go on."

"And then I heard what I'm sure was a slap. And then what sounded like someone falling to the floor, at which point I retired."

A slap? He was sure? Yes. And someone falling. Yes. And then he retired. Understandable, indeed, yes. But now if he could return to the night in question, and what he heard next, after the first blast. Yes. What he heard next was a man groaning. And he thought, *she* has shot *him*. Or someone has shot him.

"*Someone?*"

"Yes. I . . . I had thought, for some time, that the Senator . . . that he needed to watch his house. I say this, because . . . perhaps a half-dozen times, I had seen, well . . . Forgive me, but I had seen a *man* either entering or leaving the house, and these were times when the Senator, and the children as well, were away from home."

And the boy said in his mind—let it fall on the hardest rock that ever was. This was his thought about the minister's sermon to him. Shame! Christ! Who, beyond all coincidence, *must* it have been who put those words of warning in his father's mind, *twice*. Watch your house. With all that other lurid suggestion. And those words got to the *Record*, too, so the minister spread his damned gospel. And what did his words do but cause his father's death, the way they made his mind so crazy with anger. There was your manslaughter, and your damned cause. And that filth preached sermons to Tyrus Cobb. Well Tyrus Cobb has got a fire and brimstone sermon for you, preacher man. And it is resting right now under his coat.

"And next, Reverend Minifield, you?"

"Then, after some moments . . . and I would say, yes, about ten seconds, I heard a second blast. I then called Constable Crichter, who told me to stay put, which for some time I did. But then perhaps a minute passed. And now I went from my study to my east window, my bedroom window, to see."

And what he saw was a figure stretched out. A dead man, he was sure. No motion. No sound. But then a figure coming out from the Cobbs' bedroom window, and kneeling at the body's side. And what he thought was, *this* was the killer. But then he heard this someone cry out something like *O my God!* and he recognized the voice of Joe Cunningham and saw him step back away, nearly stumbling, just as Joe had described himself as doing.

"Thank you, Reverend Minifield. Your witness, Mr. Fenton."

Fenton's witness. The boy wanted to climb out of the row where he sat crammed in by Royston, right and left, and step up and say to Fenton, let me have a word or two with this murdering, pathetic filth. That Fenton, however, had no intention of being friendly one bit to the man of God, but rather of making him sweat his Christian blood, quickly was clear to the boy, and satisfied him. And what Fenton did first was set between the preacher's study windows and the Cobb bedroom not just the lot space but also the bedroom of Tyrus Cobb and showed that it came to quite a *separation* across which the Reverend was reading mere sounds. And did not the Reverend, when he heard that clambering, think for even a *second* that there might be someone other than the Senator attempting to get into the Cobb house? No? Interesting, that kind of certainty! But before he heard the tapping, the Reverend had said, he'd begun to listen carefully. Would it have been because he'd become *apprehensive*? No? The Reverend had said that he could interpret the tapping as friendly. Was there a kind of friendly clambering sound, one that let one know even in the middle of the night that whoever it is that is climbing his or *her* porch toward his or her window is friendly? The Reverend couldn't say? And did the Reverend hear any voice? Any calling? Any name? Any *identifying word of any kind*? No? None? The Reverend was not a married man. But if he were a married man and was coming home to his wife and found himself locked out and decided to try his window but found that locked, too, would he just tap? Would he not also, in the middle of the night, call a name, especially if he were *not expected*? All the Reverend knew is that *the Senator did not*. And for that, let the Reverend be thanked indeed, very much. But the Reverend had thought after the first blast that the Senator had shot Mrs. Cobb. And that after the groans, *she* had shot *him*. Or that someone had shot him. And then, some moments later, when he saw someone on the Cobbs' porch roof that it was that *someone* who might have done the shooting. Would he allow, then, that there were confusions in his mind? Ummhmm. And does he recall what his words were to the constable? Does he recall that those words were *Someone has been shot!* Because if he does not recall them, there is here the transcript of the constable's deposition. And would the Reverend agree that had he gotten it right that night and said *The Senator has been shot!* that the constable would certainly have remembered that!

"You say, Reverend Minifield, that after you'd gone to your bedroom window, you saw a man come out on the Cobb porch roof and look over the body. You *did not* at first think it was Joe Cunningham, *did you?*"

Minifield took out his handkerchief from his inside breast pocket and patted his brow. "No," he said, and lowered his head to watch himself replace the handkerchief.

"No, Reverend Minifield, no you did not. You may not have been apprehensive before, but you were by this time, as we know, more than apprehensive—let's say again you were deeply frightened—and you *did not* think it was Joe. You thought you were looking at a *murderer, did you not!*"

"I . . . Yes. Yes, I did."

"And you thought this person too was a person you'd *assumed* had given the Senator reason, as you say *so* . . . very . . . interestingly, 'to watch his house.' Am I correct?"

"Well . . ."

"*Yes* or *no!*"

"Yes."

"But it was no one but Joe Cunningham, who'd come to the Cobbs' over the years countless times, and for no intention other than a good one, whom you were not able to recognize until you heard his *words*, even as you peered out at him, and though you'd known Joe all the years of his life!"

"True."

"Yes it is true, Reverend Minifield. Yes it *is true*. And about this man you say you saw at times at the Cobb house. . . . Did you ever exchange a word with him?"

"No."

"Did you ever come close to the man, close enough, that is, to see exactly who he was?"

"No."

"In other words, Reverend Minifield, you never once made sure about this man, about his identity, his purposes, his intentions—and *that*, Reverend Minifield, is because you prefer theory to fact, or imagination, to fact, is it not!"

"Objection! Counsel is badgering the witness!"

"Sustained. Counsel will refrain."

"Let me ask, then, Reverend Minifield, are you lonely?"

"Objection! Your Honor, what *possible* relevance!"

"Sustained! You will confine your line of questioning to the case at hand, Mr. Fenton. This is eccentric."

But the boy thought *not*. He thought that *there* was their story, if they had to have one. There was their motive. Right there! But Fenton let it drop. And he had no further questions.

And now, with a calm that was to be taken as final, the skull rose to say, "Your Honor, the State rests." The boy knew these words at some point had to come. And at last now they did. He was thankful, but he was afraid. He had no idea if enough had been done—for the Cobbs, or to them, by Fenton, or Whiteacre. He couldn't think. Didn't know how to think in this place.

Then another hiatus. And a mere shuffling of papers at the desks, but which came loud because not a soul in the fifteen rows stirred. The boy had no thought. He wouldn't have known what to tell Fenton, except that he took pleasure in every knife-word he stuck in that gray saint, who seemed to have disappeared out the same back door he came in by. And were he not so relieved *knowing* now he could ignore that preacher's sermon all the rest of his born days, he might have wished out a magic word to wherever the man had gone, to say to him *You're dead, Reverend, sir.* But he had no thought, or plan, for saving the Cobb name.

"The Defense, your Honor, calls Mrs. William Herschel Cobb."

He took in the words. And, strengthless, he thought, this comes, too. He knew it had not been Fenton's plan, to call her. But she would have her say. Would it make the difference? Could it?

The boy thought, then . . . for the first time in these *how many* hours or minutes, of Charlie. Of her asking will there be a strangeness now. . . . And of his lie to his girl, which more than ever now was a lie, for what possibly could be more strange than the feeling he had right at this moment. And yet, though he had a hard desire, as his mother received some last whisperings from her lawyer, to walk up and show her the gun—to turn her damned head with the words *Look at this!*—he wanted her to win.

How many times these past days had he thought how *not guilty* does not mean *innocent*? But he didn't want innocence. He wanted greatness—that hardest damned thing of all, if you want the real truth. And he felt a sudden, perhaps insane assurance, strong maybe because it shot right out of his sick weakness, that sufficient energy for a dream like a Julius Caesar's *did* come best from never surrendering a first concession, or weak admission, as he knew his mother would not. From denying everything, every contrary sign, every soft inclination to relent, even if that meant he'd never tell Charlie the whole truth . . . and nothing but the truth. God bless her. But let it fall on *rock*, that preacher's sermon. He didn't want grace, if it meant going soft, and losing his best possible chance—on the *diamond*. He liked the word. Yes. And did he not know all along that Amanda Cobb would take the stand.

As she swore she'd tell the truth, she made it clear, too, why there were many who would say that hers was the most beautiful time of a woman's life.

"Do you think, Mrs. Cobb," her lawyer now began, "that there must be something about the word *accident* that those who accuse you just do not want to hear?"

The boy thought perhaps Fenton should just wait now and that she should remain silent, looking as beautiful as she looked—and then that Fenton should say, "No further questions."

But, forgive her, about her accusers—she thought, sometimes, perhaps . . . And, please, she wanted them all to understand that she didn't expect her husband that night, that she didn't know who it was, that never at any time in their marriage of twenty years had he come home and not either used his key or rung the bell, never. Never. So she prayed they all . . .

Fenton understood. And in a tone that suggested there was perhaps no other question that needed answering, he asked her, "Mrs. Cobb, did you love the man you married?"

"Oh, my God," she said, touching her cheek, keeping, the boy knew, her crippled hand on her lap. "Oh, sweet Lord . . . I was so young when I married Herschel. . . . I didn't know what I had. I had no idea. And when after a few months I could really see . . . And then after years, when I so deeply knew. . . . That what I had was the most perfect of men. I loved him as much as I possibly could love him."

The boy could read her equivocations. And her words tore him. He could feel the tension and anger that would be his life's energy as—just as much as he wanted to kill anyone who would try to touch her—he wanted the truth to come up and strip her soul naked. He felt the weight of the gun strapped hard against his pounding heart.

"And did you quarrel with your husband, Mrs. Cobb?"

"Honestly. In truth. We would sometimes, in the way of wives and husbands. And I suppose Joe Cunningham may indeed have heard us quarrel over Tyrus. We did have our differences there, his father believing for a long time most passionately that Tyrus should pursue a medical or a military career; and I believing that a calling, you know, can come only from within. But not long after Tyrus left to become a ballplayer, I overheard his father saying to him on the phone that he wished him not, as a ballplayer, to come home a failure. I remember those words, as I am sure Tyrus does and always will. And that would be Herschel's way, to come round in time."

She stopped, bowed her head . . . as if her last thought had suddenly started a new one—one that was a trouble to her heart. She said, "One morning . . . after Herschel's death, I . . . I was going through his papers . . . some reminiscences. And I saw a newspaper clipping from the *Atlanta Journal*. It spoke most favorably of Tyrus's abilities—and Herschel . . . clearly had in secret treasured it. That was his way. His truth was a secret that one needed only to wait some time for. And it all would have come round so beautifully—with Tyrus, I mean. So beautifully. I know this."

The boy felt again every eye on him. The *casus belli*. And his anger now was the anger of resentment. As much as he hated everyone in this room for bloodhounding his mother and father, he hated his mother and father for dragging him into their disgrace. But having nowhere to go, all options equally bad, put you everywhere *at bay*, which he loved, as he loved his mother's taking the stand. But if she failed?

"And at any time in your twenty years of marriage, did your husband ever strike you, Mrs. Cobb?"

"Never. Never once in twenty years. Not one single time."

"Thank you. But was there an argument that day before the shooting, between you and your husband."

"Herschel and I did have words. I confess we did. And I will regret this till the day I die."

"They were over your son Tyrus, and his career choice?"

"Well, yes, as I recall. But really over nothing. It was as much over our little Florence, our twelve-year old, about the coming year in school. And was she reading and preparing.

You know how schoolmasters care—care so very, very much—but how mothers want to see their children free to enjoy life, too. And in the summertime. But this was all that it was over. Something. But nothing. Nothing that wouldn't have resolved itself peacefully, too, as all these things with us did. There were just moments. For us, as for everyone. And what Reverend Minifield heard—was nothing. I had heard before what he had said to Mr. Crichter. And I kept thinking what—what would he have heard—because he is a good person—he wouldn't . . . But what would make him say he heard the sound of a slap? I kept thinking and thinking of the day, and nothing came to me. Nothing but maybe a fly, which had lit on Herschel's own bare arm, and stung him, and made him say some words of anger. I recalled this. And that he had struck at it. I don't know."

But the boy knew. He knew all now. Knew she'd seen his father clear as day in that window. That she'd murdered him. That there was a hardness inside her beauty harder than anything in his father—a hardness going back to her and Nehemiah Pylades Chitwood, that sorry, damned slave of his own damned war disease, which a pathetic honor made everyone keep his or her mouth shut about. He wanted to shout out, "Can't you see she's a cold-blooded, murdering *liar!*"

"Thank you, Mrs. Cobb. Thank you, ma'am. And now . . . I understand that this is difficult for you. But can you tell me now . . . again . . . on the night in question, when you first heard the sounds of someone climbing toward the roof of your front porch, about your state of mind."

"I was all alone," she said. "Paul was gone to Atlanta, and Florence was with friends. I was almost asleep. I'd been trying to sleep since eleven, but the night was hot, and I hadn't yet managed. But when I heard sounds, still, I wasn't sure at first if I wasn't dreaming. I recall thinking that I must be. . . . But, all alone, I became afraid, as the sounds contin-ued, and I woke, fully. I sat up. The sounds were louder, and getting still louder. I thought—an animal. But the sounds were too heavy. And they had no accidental direction. They were coming. And as they grew louder still, I began to panic. I thought now it must be a housebreaker, or worse. I couldn't imagine anything but this. And the sounds kept coming. I was terrified. But then the gun . . . came to me. God forgive me. Herschel and I didn't agree about that gun. God forgive me for thinking now I was right. . . . Oh God forgive. . . . Please forgive me." She bowed her head. She took her kerchief to her eyes, then squeezed the handkerchief hard in her hand beside her face. "But I was all alone. I was all alone. And the sounds were those of a man—I knew it—now on my roof. Coming across to my window. I rose from the bed thinking this wouldn't end till I was dead. It was going to keep on happening till I was dead, and worse than dead.

"I reached for the gun. And as I did, I heard the sounds right at the window. . . . It couldn't have been Herschel. I never thought Herschel. It could not have been. The thought never came to me. And I was all alone. And when I turned I saw a man at my window, trying to open it. I never heard taps. I don't say Reverend Minifield lies; I say only that I never heard taps. I was too terrified. All I heard was the approach of what I was sure would be some horrible thing and then the end of my life if I didn't act. I hated holding the gun. But then I became something else—as I held it. I was thanking God now that I had it. I was thanking Herschel. Oh my God, my sweet Lord God, I was thanking Herschel . . . when I fired. I never heard any taps. Never any words. Never my name. And why—why ever would that have been, if it had been Herschel! Never heard anything but the man trying to open my window. And it could not have been Herschel. Oh God forgive me. Not Herschel. God forgive me. Please! I fired. And he did nothing. He just stood there. He seemed to me to come even closer. And still to be trying to get in. And I promise you, I heard no words. No cries of my name. I heard nothing, except his hands on the window frame. And

I saw him now seeming to push up the window to enter. I was certain I had missed him. He still stood there. I know nothing of guns. I never heard the window glass breaking. I couldn't see that it was broken. I was thanking God I had it locked. Oh my God. My God. Why did this happen? Why! But I couldn't think. I saw only the man, seeming to be opening my window, so I did . . . I did step closer. But I still could not see him, in the dark. I may have waited. Yes. I may have waited. I promise you in all honesty that I am not certain why, but it must have been to see if he would fall. I waited only to see if he would fall. It must have been. And I did come closer. Yes. I did. But I could never say how far. I came closer because I feared I had missed him. Please believe this. Please. And there he still stood as if still trying to get in. It could not have been Herschel. Why? Why ever in this world *would* Herschel have come to our window like this! I could never have thought. And I was all alone. And there he stood, still. So I fired again. I think by this time I had my eyes closed. In all honesty, I believe now that I just guessed where to fire, thinking much more that these were the last moments of my life than that I was about to do what in this horrible horrible accident I did do. I swear to you in all honesty it was not on purpose. I had no *purpose* but to save my life! It had to be the kind of horrible man that gentlemen defend us against. And I was all alone. And I fired. I think I must have had my eyes closed. Because I remember a time of waiting. I was waiting to see if I would die. I remember this now. Yes. I was waiting to see if I would die. And when I didn't—or thought I hadn't—I opened my eyes. And he was gone."

She bowed her head and covered her eyes with her hand, squeezing her handkerchief with a grip that made her tremble. Fenton said nothing. The courtroom was silent. Tyrus wanted not to look at the men in the jury box, for he was certain now that they would never convict her, but that if he looked he might magically change the world and they would find her guilty. He couldn't look. But nothing was happening. The silence continued. No sound.

But now Fenton, softly, "Your witness."

Then silence again. A silence that now continued, a long time. So long, Tyrus thought, that the prosecutor was waiting for the coming, in that room, of some spreading eagerness to hear sound. The boy began even to feel an anger, as more time passed, thinking Whiteacre was stealing the thunder of Fenton's silence; for he was beginning himself to feel an eagerness to hear the sound of some word.

Then, at last, a clearing of the throat, and, quiet, polite: "You were young, Mrs. Cobb, when you married?"

"I was just short of thirteen."

"You were twelve."

"Yes."

And Whiteacre wanted to know this because he found it interesting that she would just now have spoken of her defense of her daughter, who was twelve, from a perhaps overbearing father. And there was her defense of her son from a father who seemed to her too imposing with his definite and strong notions of what life that son should choose. And what he wondered was did her husband force *her* into any choices, or into being an adult . . . before her time?

"*Objection!* Relevance! To say nothing of the *insinuating* nature of certain of the State's remarks."

"Your Honor, I'm trying to establish *motive*. I can see no relevance issue here, whatsoever. And as for insinuations, are we to be so *polite* that we let truth escape, when a man has been torn to pieces by a shotgun?"

Whiteacre was allowed to continue, but he must confine his questioning to events *recent* in the Cobbs' marriage, which came as a relief to the boy, who wondered, over the crazy space of a sinking of his heart, if he burned the wrong book and if his father's had been found and read by Whiteacre, the man seeking an echo for the everything he already knew. But the skull had to begin his story at a point decided by the judge, and within those confines there might not be enough motive *for* a story.

Whiteacre scowled and breathed loud through his nostrils in frustration and seeming disgust. "The truth. The truth, Mrs. Cobb. A witness has testified that the sound of a slap or blow came from your bedroom, as you and your husband argued—and you have admitted that you and your husband were arguing—only hours before he was shot. That the sound of a slap or blow came, and after that the sound of someone falling to the floor. That's what Reverend Minifield heard, as he heard you and your husband in what he described as deeply angered argument. And as recently as three weeks ago, in deposition, you said you had no explanation for this witness's hearing what he heard. Is that not true?"

"It is true. But as I have said, I was still going back over that time to find an explanation. I said this at the deposition as well. And I was simply confessing *honestly,* Mr. Whiteacre, that I could not at the time of the deposition conceive of an explanation. Had I been inclined to concoct something, I would by that time have concocted it."

"No doubt. No doubt. But then, from somewhere, came the fly."

"Through the window, I would guess."

Tyrus ventured a quick look at the jury box to see if there were any smiles. On some faces, yes, but not on all. Then all grew serious with Whiteacre's next question.

"Do you mean the window that was at the time of the shooting *locked*? Because all the windows, upstairs and down, as well as the doors, all were *locked* at the time of the shooting, were they not, Mrs. Cobb? Can you explain that?"

"The back door was not locked."

"And can you explain *that*, Mrs. Cobb! Could it have been, Mrs. Cobb, that someone in the house, before Joe Cunningham's arrival, exited *from* that back door?"

"I simply forgot to lock it, sir."

Yes. He was sure she had. And he was sure that her

husband's not entering through it could not have been because it *was* locked at the time he might have tried it. And on a night so *hot*, so *hot* that she was tossing and turning on her bed in the *heat*, why, one wonders, would she keep the house sealed up so tight. Of course she was . . . *alone*. All alone—as she testified no fewer than *seven* times. And so yes, she perhaps had sealed down the house to keep herself safe—but from *what!* It wouldn't have been, would it, from some sudden return of her husband?

"It was from burglars."

Yes. From burglars. And how many burglars had broken in at the Cobbs' over *twenty years*?

"I will quote my husband, Mr. Whiteacre. 'There is always a first time.' And that of course is why he wanted us always—and this indeed goes back to the first days of our marriage—to keep a gun where we slept, just in case we might need it."

"Any guns kept anywhere else?"

"I'm not sure what you mean."

"Indeed! Let me be specific! Your husband's pistol, *where is that?*"

"*Ob-jection!* There has been *no* sufficient establishment of the *presence or existence of any pistol!*"

"Sustained!"

"Yes. Yes. Yes. Indeed. We have only that puzzling image of something pistol-like that seemed to protrude from your husband's jacket pocket. And just as sure as I am, Mrs. Cobb, that you really did forget to lock that back door, I am sure you have no idea of what Joe Cunningham *means* when he says he saw something like a pistol on your dead husband's person! And in this same way, I am ever so certain, Mrs. Cobb, that you did not, when Joe ran for his father, go out that window to retrieve something that might tell a story."

"No. No I did not!"

"No. No, I am sure you didn't. That would have been a

business too bloody altogether, Mrs. Cobb, retrieving evidence from the body of your slaughtered husband, as he lay there in gore and pools of blood, and hiding that evidence, locking it away in some safe place. Too bloody altogether!"

"Stop, Mr. Whiteacre. *You're* making up a story! *You are!*"

"Am I, Mrs. Cobb! You wouldn't know about guns, not you, the daughter of Captain Nehemiah Chitwood, oh no! A plantation girl like you wouldn't know that when you fire a shotgun straight at someone from twelve feet, you *don't miss!* But indeed you might have feared not that you missed him but that you didn't finish him! You might have feared *that!* So what you did is step closer, and closer, with your eyes wide open!"

"No! No! I was in terror! I shut my eyes and prayed before I fired! For which God forgive me! God forgive me!"

"Indeed may He! Mrs. Cobb. Indeed may the Lord God hear your prayer, for you will need it heard! Because you did finish your husband! Cold-bloodedly ended his life! Confess it, Mrs. Cobb! Confess that you saw him clearly—*From the first!* That, having shot him deliberately once, you waited deliberately to see if he was still alive and that when you saw, from no more than the length of a man's body away, that he was still alive, you took careful aim again and *ended him! Ended his life so that he would never be able to speak a single word against you! Confess it! Confess it for your soul's life! You will never have a day of peace unless you do! Cleanse your soul, Mrs. Cobb! Save your life before God! Confess!*"

"No! No! You're making up a story, sir! This is all a story! You can't trap me in this lie! I'll never confess to something I did not do! You have no evidence of any of the things of which you speak! Just words and words! That's all you have!"

"Eleven seconds, Mrs. Cobb. We have that! And you had that, to take dead aim at your husband's head. At the face of the man you hated. Confess that you hated that face, Mrs.

Cobb; and that you hated that man, who said you were no good even from girlhood, and who struck you hard with his hand, and whom you threatened—because he was *no gentleman* to you—and because you hated what he did to you, with his tyrannies, and with his words, and with his hand. And that for years you hated him. And that you saw the face you hated, clearly, *clearly* that night. The face that kept you from your *happiness!* And that slowly you came right up to that face, nearly eye to eye with it, before with the coldest-blooded deliberation, with dead homicidal purpose, you raised that shotgun and pulled that trigger a second time. And you didn't cry, Mrs. Cobb—you did not shed a single tear—because with that second blast you ended something hateful to you that went back a long, long time. Isn't that true, Mrs. Cobb? Isn't it true that the real cause of this went back a long, long time: that it had been coming, a long time. Isn't it true! Isn't it true that your whole life since girlhood had been frustrated, that you sought release! Confess it!"

She paused. She waited to gather herself. And then said, "Mr. Whiteacre, you are making up a tale. That is all you are doing, making up a tale."

Whiteacre sniffed with contempt. He took a long breath. He looked only at her, not at the judge, to whom he now said, "I have no further questions, your Honor."

As she stepped down, less graceful than when she rose, clearly shaken, her son believed he had enough power of anger to stand down the entire room—enough strength coming into him, he was sure, from his keeping the gun tight against him, hidden beneath his high-buttoned jacket. But his heart sank again, in weakness, when he heard Fenton say, "The Defense rests."

Chapter Sixteen

THE FINAL WORD

No one moved. The boy read the silence as a sign that word *had* canceled word, Whiteacre's wiping Fenton's clear, and that all that was left now was some chance he couldn't cause. Anybody's guess.

"Mr. Whiteacre?"

The prosecutor rose once again, and nodded to the judge. He walked to his stage again before the jury, and faced them. He folded his hands together and looked thoughtful, then spread out the fingers of his hands still folded.

"The Cobb home, gentlemen of the jury," he said, "was not a happy one." He released his folded fingers and set his hands behind his back. "Unless, of course," he said, "that you really do believe that it was a fly that stung Herschel Cobb in those hours before he died."

The boy instantly, at this, burned with rage and contempt, even as he knew, and feared, that the jury might be as satisfied with Whiteacre's scorn as he was ready to fight against it to his last hour. For the prosecutor's scorn appealed to something in himself as well.

"It was no *accident*, gentlemen, this killing. What it was, was the fatal conclusion to an unhappy union."

Yes, it was, gentlemen. And the skull *would* now draw a hard line of connection between a stolen childhood and a last desperate attempt to recover happiness—her *right*, gentlemen, as she called it. And he would ask the jury to ask itself, "if Reverend Minifield had maybe *good cause* to think the Senator might want to watch his house? If the Senator had perhaps heard things about his wife? If he had come to discover things about her? Had come to have suspicions? Had himself intentions that night—dark purposes, which made him—that fatal night—*not* ring his own doorbell, but take instead to his roof—so he could come to his own bedroom window—and tap there, taps of an announcement, taps, as the Reverend has said, saying Your Husband Is At Your Window?

"But of course Mrs. Cobb didn't hear those taps. Didn't hear them though the Reverend said they were to his ears about as hard as the glass could bear. She was all alone. So, she says, she was too afraid to hear the taps, though she had heard everything else; the sounds, the *sounds* she said were what in fact so terrified her. Terrified her as she waited . . . all alone.

"And yes—all alone. No less than countlessly did she remind us of this. What cause for that? Would the cause be sick, nervous, *guilty* worry that we would believe she was *not* alone? Just as we might believe she *lied* when she said she forgot to lock the back door.

"Oh, she was afraid, gentlemen. She was afraid, all right. But the cause of her locking down the *entire* house, upstairs windows included, on a sweltering, *Georgia* August night, was not a fear of burglars but of her *husband*, who might catch her in the act of something. She had this, and one other fear. And that fear, gentlemen, was the fear of disgrace. A fear of disgrace so great that she would do whatever it took to remove all signs of it. For what would a pistol, gentlemen, become, if, as Joe Cunningham saw it, a pistol was there in the Senator's pocket? If it had been out, and in the Senator's hand, well, she could have claimed self-defense, although that would have involved scandal and *disgrace*, a shame which, as I say, she at all costs seeks to avoid. At the cost of a man's life! For she killed him, gentlemen, *she killed him* not to be exposed and shamed.

"But Joe Cunningham came too quick for her to go out and put the pistol in her husband's hand. And Joe saw when he got there that what the Senator had was still in his pocket: that it had not been taken out. So after Joe left, she couldn't put it in his hand. But maybe she could take it and hide it. Get rid of it. Make it *not exist*. Because what a pistol becomes in this case is evidence. Evidence of animosity. Evidence of trouble in the Cobb home. Evidence of *long-lasting unhappiness, hatred, and war*. And so when she could, she made a move to retrieve it. And when she'd retrieved it, she took it and she hid it in some place where it would never be found. Some dark place where it will forever tell the Cobb story, terrifying even the silence and darkness that covers it up. And what, gentlemen, Amanda Chitwood Cobb could *say*, when the evidence of shame was deeply enough hidden, was the word 'accident.'

"But this killing, this ending of a life, this *slaughter* of a man—the most horrible thing that young Joe Cunningham ever saw—was *no accident*. She would have you believe that she closed her eyes as she approached the window, closer and closer, as she brought herself face to face with the man in that window. But, gentlemen, don't *you* close *your* eyes. Look at that window. Look at the man. Look for a good, long time. And come closer. And closer. See the man still more clearly, as she did. And listen—listen closely, with your hearts and souls. Did he whisper her name? Did he beg for *mercy* as she raised the gun the second time? Or did he say a last angry word? Did he die in anger? What was the look on his face before she took aim again and turned that face into a river of blood. Was it a word of anger? A plea for mercy?"

The prosecutor shut his eyes. Let his breath be heard. Then let silence fall. He waited his time, then raised his head and looked upward, in thought.

"But let us now," he said, "with the pulling of that *second* trigger, turn our thoughts to justice. To justice before God. Let truth and *justice* guide you, gentlemen, for all our sakes. For the sake of Mrs. Cobb herself. For living a lie, living unconfessed, great and deep sins unexpiated: this is not life. It is not the soul's life, the life that is real. Let the truth set her free of a hideous *role*, of a continuing false lifetime of lying, which is an endless repetition of her sin. Before God, bring her back, gentlemen, to the power of truth, to a beginning of repentance. Think in your hearts and souls what a *hardened* life you condemn her to, if you do not find Amanda Chitwood Cobb guilty. For only the truth can set her free."

He bowed his head now slightly, waited another moment, and said quietly, "Thank you," and returned to his desk. He set his hands on the surface, then refolded and stared into them.

Tyrus, the evidence a crushing weight against him, again could not clearly form a thought. Some other time his mind might free him from the net of Whiteacre's words, but it couldn't now. A life in the truth. Who in the entire damned world felt more than Tyrus Cobb, the *need*. Christ, he hoped the word that came from that jury *would* be *guilty*. But no! *No!* He would never confess to any goddamned shame, not while he still breathed. And he would by God be the greatest ballplayer who ever lived.

"Mr. Fenton?"

"Thank you, your Honor."

Fenton now rose again, and approached the jury box, then began slowly to walk back and forth before it, halting at last before the man in the front row, center. "Mr. Whiteacre, gentlemen, has created enough of an atmosphere so that I cannot ask you simply to whisk it away. I understand that.

But the State, gentlemen, has *not* met its burden. It has *not*, with the kind of credibility we must demand, presented a case at all, let alone proved one. Don't be fooled by the words of an able prosecutor. There is only one living witness, gentlemen, to this shooting—and that *only* witness is not the good Joe Cunningham, nor is it the good Reverend Minifield. It is Amanda Cobb, and she has told you what happened. She has told you that what happened was an accident. And she has told you that, because it is true.

"We could, gentlemen, I know this, grant everything the State suggests and insinuates regarding conditions previous to the death of Senator Cobb, the great buildup, if you will, the great dramatic story. Mind you, we grant *not one* of those things the State has insinuated. Not the first. But did we, it would make no difference. Did we grant all of them, it would make not one whit of difference. For in truth *all* we are here to assess are these questions: Can we have some *reasonable doubt*, any at all, about the State's claim that Mrs. Cobb would *know*, in the dark of night, at a late, late hour that the sounds made by an unseen man approaching her window were those of her husband? Can we doubt, reasonably—can we not have *some* honest doubt—about the State's claim that she would know they *were* the sounds of her husband when he specifically told her he would *not* be coming home that night? When he had never entered the house in the manner he was entering it that night? When he did not ring the doorbell, as he always would have, if he did not use his key? And when he did not call her name as he approached? And is there not somewhere some reason for doubting the State's contention that Mrs. Cobb would *not* have been terrified as those sounds approached, but been purely cool and calculating? Calm and intentional as she heard them all alone in her room? That she would *never* feel a frantic, blinding terror? That the clear, simple explanation she gave for the much-discussed lapse of time between blasts could not *possibly* be an honest one? The State *must* establish, gentlemen, that there is *no* room left for a reasonable doubt on these questions. *No* room. But your job is simply to determine whether there *is* some room somewhere for a reasonable doubt—and then, if you do so find, to let Amanda Cobb go free.

"I ask you not, gentlemen, to see the face of the Senator, but, rather, to consider again the darkness, the aloneness, the terror; to consider the danger, or what to a terrified mind appeared to be one, of a kind that the Senator himself had wanted always to be prepared for, and made sure his family was prepared for. It was, gentlemen, as you know, *not* Mrs. Cobb who secured and placed and loaded with shot the weapon that killed her husband, but the Senator himself, who thought forever that a gun should be placed in readiness for a night when deadly danger might come upon his family, who wanted the gun ready especially for nights when he and Mrs. Cobb were not together. But a gun itself is a dangerous thing. And accidents will and *do* happen—do happen even if that fact disappoints the desire and hunger among some for a *meaning* to all that took place that night—a dark *meaning*—which there is not.

"We will never know, gentlemen, why the Senator came back that night. Not a first one of us will ever know that. We know only that he did, though he had said he would not.

"Nor will the first one of us ever know why the Senator chose not to ring the doorbell that night but rather to climb the flower trellis at the side of his porch and thus up to his own bedroom window. We cannot know. We know only that the things he did and didn't do that night, and his never calling out his wife's name, and his never in any way identifying himself . . . cost him . . . his life. But, forgive me, I say not 'tragically'—because that suggests again some dark story—rather I say 'horribly, accidentally,' the words the truth asks us to say."

Fenton had begun a quiet pacing. He now halted, and faced the jury again square and middle, his hands free and emphatic.

"Gentlemen, the *soul*. Mr. Whiteacre has spoken of freeing the soul with the truth. Let me implore you from the deep heart of my own soul, again, to free yourselves of all hunger to find meaning where there is none, to find intention when there was none, to find the cause of things to be some longstanding animosity between a good husband and a good wife when there was *none*. Mr. Whiteacre has said to you that the Cobb home was not a happy one. I have said that this assertion would make no difference even were it true. But it is *not true*! And I ask you to save the reputation of a good and beautifully souled woman, and of her good and great family, and of her husband and her union with him, and of her children—to act as saviors indeed—for the desire in us to find a meaning that interests us is so great at times that we will sacrifice to it not only the truth but human lives. Good lives. Good people."

He folded his hands again, bowed his head, then raised it. "Forgive me now, gentlemen, the last reminder, which always comes now. I know you don't need it. Don't need to be told that in the end, in this country, you are not asked to play God and to know things you cannot know. And in this case, *all* you are asked to determine is if there is any reason *at all* here to believe that this sad death might have been nothing more than an accident. An accident. And, gentlemen, how could it not have been—for I will tell your own good hearts and souls that this is a lady"—and he now pointed to her where, in her powerful beauty, she sat faced forward, her head slightly bowed—"a lady who has now already suffered an unbearable agony of loss and loneliness and feelings of desertion, a lady who although she is fully blameless blames herself hour after hour for a death she was not responsible for, but which—and don't we know the heart and soul of grieving love?—she has placed herself in hell for, day after day. It is your blessed opportunity now, gentlemen, to save her with the truth, to acquit her resoundingly, and so to resurrect her from the hell of her own grief and sorrow. Or at least to help her with a beginning."

He now turned square to the jury again and, folding his hands, bowed his thanks to them. He bowed again slightly, then took two slow backward steps, and turned away. He went back then to his seat at the table, where he once more folded his hands and looked at them in silence.

The jury then by Judge Sudduth was quietly ordered to retire. The boy watched the twelve rise and begin to file out and pass on into the private chamber, and then the door close behind them. Then again there was silence. Not a soul in the room moved. For how long a time—before finally a stirring, and then rising of individuals, and then of groups? The boy didn't know. And he remained motionless.

He knew where Paul had sat, and Joe. He moved his eyes. They were gone now, his brother, and the friend he'd never speak to again. And Minifield was gone, the preacher man, and true killer. And the black-haired man, who was no one the boy had ever seen. And Sudduth. Whiteacre. The defense and defendant still sat—though there was a rustling now at their table. The boy looked up, and he saw his mother—looking back. For someone else? Someone, some lover, who would stand up for her and *himself* confess if she was found guilty? The boy thought, felt, that this could be true. Was she looking for some other? He looked at her— and saw she was looking at no one but him.

And he found himself now staring back. She knew he knew. Everything. Would they acknowledge it all now? He could take out the pistol now. He could have for her a private and very real trial. All in an instant of truth. He could be the truth, with the gun. Or he could keep it concealed and be a lie. How were they looking at each other? With just enough truth, the boy found himself right now hoping, just enough so that nothing would in their lifetimes ever be admitted, but everything always known.

She rose in her beauty, surrounded by her defense. And

she turned away and left through a side door under the shield of Fenton and her other lawyers.

Her son sat now alone. The empty courtroom seemed like a church, and he a sinner. He felt a pang of bitterest resentment that he would be here, feeling this way. He felt no desire to forgive, although always there was the exhaustion in his heart of a person who knew his life was wrong. He would marry Charlie in a church. Someday he would, before God. Someday he would get himself right. But first he would have revenge. And he felt the power of his anger now as deeply as he felt his powerlessness even to think of his beautiful girl, the girl he was born for as much as he was born to be a ballplayer. He felt the weight of the gun. What a sound it would make in this hollow place.

He wanted to strike out. To damn kill. If they found her guilty—to kill *her*—*her*, for the way she'd shamed the name Cobb forever. Her for killing his father. Or *him*, if he could dig the man up alive and then send him back with a bullet to his heart, which he deserved, for making his son sit here alone like this, feeling like this. Or himself, to be finished with it all. And to show them all, especially those two he would set beside him in his tomb.

But if they found her *not* guilty? And though Whiteacre's words made him think everything was over—completely—Fenton's had brought him back to life. Had his mother's lawyer's words done enough? He felt still that heavy weight of the gun against his heart. But he thought maybe Fenton had won a victory. And if he did? Sure as hell Tyrus Cobb, around those two sweet words, *not guilty*, would take the hardest stand anyone ever took. And for the mother who wanted it, and for the father who secretly wanted it, be the greatest ballplayer who ever lived.

How long had he sat there, thinking this? He couldn't say. No one was here, not even the bailiff, who for a long time had stood by the closed jury-room door. Only Tyrus, who, as in the deep silence he had begun to hear it tick, thought now that he would take out his gold championship watch—to see if by the amount of time passed he would be able to know—guilty, or not guilty.

But then time struck from the bells, like a church's bells, from the top of the courthouse. The jury had reached a verdict. The bells now rang it so loud that no matter what it was, guilty or not guilty, the word of the verdict would spread everywhere, no stopping it—guilty or not guilty.

In no time they returned, and packed the room again tight, his mother and her defense, the prosecution, the judge, the witnesses, the crowd, that black-haired man. It seemed to the boy they'd all been hovering close and watching him through spy holes, waiting for the moment. And the bells kept announcing it, for this was a trial of interest to everyone around. And hearing them clang, the boy thought—would he become the greatest ballplayer, or use the gun? Use the gun, or become the greatest ballplayer? The bells kept clanging. And the crowd was back in so quickly they were all seated and silent before the bells stopped sounding.

In the silence that now fell complete as the bells' echoes faded, Tyrus could not have said how long the twelve had been out. Twenty minutes? Two hours? Not guilty? Guilty? He felt that weight of the gun.

The bailiff stood again at the jury-room door. And now he opened it. The boy felt every savage resentment, every repentant cry in his heart, every desire to live and every desire to die that he had ever felt. He felt, as the jurymen came back in, in file, every rage, every desire to end his life, or to kill. He felt the weight of the gun lightening. Or would his weapon be the breaking of *records*? Guilty or not guilty?

"Has the jury reached a verdict?" The words of the judge now happened, in this court of truth.

The foreman, the man in the middle, the one at whom the prosecution had pointed the Cobb gun, now rose. He held a piece of paper in his hand. He said, "We have, your Honor."

Then the words came: "The defendant will rise." And Tyrus hated and loved her with all his heart. He felt the gun against his heart. And his true life's calling: never to admit a thing, never, and to be—not guilty, unrepentant—the greatest ballplayer who ever lived. He had begun himself to rise now from where he sat, as he saw his mother rising.

And the question: "As to the charge of voluntary manslaughter, how say you?"

And the words, which Tyrus rose to hear: "We find the defendant . . . *not guilty.*"

Afterword

"I never saw anyone like Ty Cobb. No one even close to him as the greatest all-time ballplayer. That guy was superhuman, amazing."
—Casey Stengel, 1975

It wasn't until 1912 that the Hall of Fame catcher Ray Schalk began his career. But when I was a kid on the South Side of Chicago, I met the man in his tough, gnarled old age; and that was enough for me. I knew for a fact that Schalk's career-long battle with the great Cobb was one of the fiercest of their era. But I'd also seen Schalk the man, and had the truth of history confirmed for my imagination in a boyhood memory of an old catcher's knotted hand. It was a truth that mattered to me, so I put Ray Schalk in my book—but with a slightly altered name, since, having him catch for the Sox in '05, I was moving him back seven years before his time. And I often made here alterations in time and place, taking things from Cobb's later battles and compressing them into the quarter season I had to work with, so that my imagination would have what it wanted for its story of a mind and soul. I call Cobb always Tyrus, because it was his real name and the name he was known by until he'd been up some time in the majors, but also because it is *no longer* the name he is known by and the differentness suggests the distance (or can we say sometimes the deeper, more intimate imaginative truth?) of fiction.

I altered the name of Amanda Cobb's father, too, from Caleb to Nehemiah Pylades Chitwood. Why Nehemiah, why Pylades I'll leave to those who like to guess at these things. Why *not* Caleb—because I knew nothing of the real Captain Caleb Chitwood and I thought it truly unfair to attach the man's name to the father in this book, who came to me from stories my kids have told me about several fathers of friends of theirs, Viet Nam vets: stories of heartbreaking lostness, deep substance addiction, family terror, and (in one case) a self-inflicted fatal gunshot.

That there was trouble in the Chitwood home in the years after the Civil War I simply, and perhaps very unfairly, *assumed*—because of a conversation I had one day, now maybe a dozen years ago. I had gone to the courthouse in Lavonia, Georgia, to see if I could get my hands on records of the 1906 trial of Amanda Chitwood Cobb; and from the old "historian of Franklin County," I got only a smile, a wink—and the word that those records were gone. I operated then like a novelist, not a historian. I asked no further questions, treasuring too much the notion that Cobb himself had gotten hold of the records of his mother's trial and buried them where they would never be found again. The old man and I sat then in a side room of the courthouse that for a good many of the years of his retirement had been his second home. He told me things he'd heard about Amanda Cobb that I'll leave unmentioned, except to say they did very much suggest some kind of dark, troubled background to her life. But I will, from the old man, pass along an image that stayed with me all through the writing of *Tyrus*. He told me that from the son of one of Cobb's very few real friends, he'd heard that in a visit to the Royston tomb where he buried his mother and father (and where he himself now lies across from them, the lily of peace in the stained-glass window between), Cobb, then sick and aging, standing in the tomb, voice choking, told his friend that the night his mother killed his father, she was not alone.

Later that day, I went to Cunningham's Furniture store in Royston (a town I knew in the way I know a hundred small, far-off-the-main-road, forgotten towns in Mississippi; and a store I knew from having seen in every one of those places the very same store, still offering, under a twenty-years' neglected sign, goods so long unsold you can't believe there's a soul in there, still trying). I talked, at Cunningham's, with a lady whose maiden name was Chitwood, old as my historian, and just as lively, who told me about footprints said to have been found out back of the Cobb house the morning after that shooting more than eighty-five years before and that "Aunt Mandy" saw Hershel Cobb clear as she was born. But that Herschel Cobb was a hard man. And hard especially on his elder son.

I didn't stay in Royston more than a few hours. I visited the graveyard and saw the tomb. I went to the library to find out that, no, they didn't keep old *Royston Records*, or have microfilm (In some way he doesn't tell us, Cobb's biographer John McCallum did get hold of the issue of the *Record* that gives the account of the killing; and what I have here in the novel is taken from McCallum's quotations). And the thing I came really to see, the Cobb house, with its porch and porch roof and upstairs bedrooms and windows, I found out, had long years before succumbed to fire. I went to the town hall/police station, where they had a small Cobb display, which attracted no one else while I was there, but which included a recording of an older Cobb's voice. I'd never heard his voice. It was strange, putting on the head phones in that frmtquiet, nearly vacant room, which seemed to be merely some waiting room of the sleepy Royston police station. I had a sudden imagination that I might receive, from the man whose story had so taken me, some barked, infuriated warning to leave his life the hell alone. But what I got was a public Cobb, addressing in platitudes a town he never in any real way returned to, except to be buried in the tomb he built. I liked it, though (and yet why any surprise?), that after all his years up north and later in California and Nevada, there was still the sure sound of Georgia in his voice.

By the police dispatcher, I was given a Xerox copy of a letter from William Herschel Cobb to his son Tyrus, dated Royston, Ga., January 5, 1902. In this letter, which Cobb kept all his life (and which the niece of Aunt Mandy said I should look at if I wanted to get clear the idea of the father's sternness, "for the boy was hardly fifteen"), there is affection, if seriously formally expressed. There is poetry. And there is its concluding thought: "Be good and dutiful, conquer your anger and wild passions that would degrade your dignity and belittle your manhood. Cherish all the good that springs up in you. Be under the perpetual guidance of the better angel of your nature. Starve out and drive out the demon that lurks in all human blood and is ready and anxious and restless to arise and reign."

I ended those few hours in Royston at the Cobb Medical Center, a hospital Cobb built for the town, one could guess, finally to placate the father who'd been so bitterly disappointed that his son had not chosen a career like medicine, but had become a ballplayer. There's a portrait on the wall, in the lobby of the center, of Ty Cobb's mother in her sixties, looking as if, for anyone with a close question, she would have only a Southern matron's distant answer. My Franklin County historian suggested I go and "take a look at her."

As far as I know, there is no Church Street in Royston. The Detroit in *Tyrus* is, though based on a fair amount of research, far more a place of my imagination than it is any real city. I didn't study trains. I've just ridden the City of New Orleans, more times than I can count, between my home in Chicago and my other home in Mississippi. And my going back and forth, north-south, south-north, as often as I have over twenty-five years is surely one reason I wrote this book, which I like to think is about America. I'm certain the great documentarist Ken Burns has it right when in his attempt to get at the heart of the American character, he gives as much attention as he does to the Civil War. And to baseball. The foci here, and the intent, are the same.

But I wrote this book, too, because in Ty Cobb's story I saw the story of Orestes and the story of Hamlet: of a son whose mother killed, or was involved in the killing of, his father, to whom also she was unfaithful. And a son who represented something central to a nation's aspirations, and its troubles. Following Ken Burns makes me seriously nervous. Following Aeschylus and Shakespeare makes me laugh hard at myself. But if I leave to American writers better than myself the idea that we have in Ty Cobb some kind of an American Orestes or of an American Hamlet, which I think we do, then I am more than satisfied.

When reading the outstanding biography of Cobb by Charles Alexander, my *vade mecum* sure and steady, I found myself respectfully admiring, again and again, Professor Alexander's historian's restraint. He very judiciously, responsibly, stops at the facts. In light of those facts, though, Professor Alexander does allow himself the speculation that exactly at the time in which *Tyrus* is set, Ty Cobb may well have been nearing psychosis. Alexander is the first to report that in his second season, just some few months after the time at which *Tyrus* closes, the still deeply traumatized Cobb had to leave the Tigers and enter a sanatorium for some weeks. If Cobb is a Satan figure, he's by no means the simplicity that demonizing sports lore has made him out to be. His grief, I think it's fair to say, was of Shakespearean proportions. His response to his grief may have been every bit as belligerent and ferocious as the demonic lore has it (and as my book has it). It seems he chose with furious anger to *be*, and not *not to be*. But his mind was very heavily burdened.

And I must admit, too, that I've always smiled at the notion that flying spikes, however directed or sharpened, even *begin* to match the true deadly violence of the quite common 90 mph brushback pitch (especially in the days before helmets, the days in which Carl Mays killed a man with his fastball). I'm a bit amused as well by any singling out of Cobb as a racist when the game in which he played banned African Americans from a time well before he got there and for twenty more years beyond his retirement (and when one thinks of the filth that, even longer after Cobb was gone, Jackie Robinson had still to endure—up north).

But I'm not interested in playing apologist for Ty Cobb. He *was* a violent man. One night when he and his wife, Charlie, were accosted by two thieves, he chased off both men, following one whom he'd disarmed to the end of a blind alley, where with his own gun he may have pistol-whipped the man to death. And he was every bit the child of the supremacist defeated South. I wrote about him, in fact, because he did suggest to me, not just Orestes and Hamlet, but Milton's great fallen angel. And I gave to Herschel Cobb a few extra years in the Georgia state senate just so he'd be there at exactly the time when Georgia was constructing its version of the Deep or *Solid* South's Jim Crow apartheid. I wanted Senator Cobb implicated, as one suspects the father of Ty Cobb would have been, had he still been in Atlanta in '05.

I promised myself, though, that I would never neglect to mention, in some foreword or afterword, a conversation I had maybe eight years ago now, down in Naples, Florida, in one of the quiet, older sections on one of the bays in Port Royal. A friend of my mother had a friend whose father had been for many, many years one of the closest friends of Ty Cobb; and when Mrs. S. was a girl, back in the 1920s, Cobb was a frequent visitor at her family's Cleveland home. I don't know. Is it just natural, when there's no lost brightness, or happiness, or aliveness, that old age, especially in a beautiful woman, will bring with it a remarkable graciousness? Or did Mrs. S. speak to me from a time now gone by? There are details I recall. She spoke of tricks her father had, to get Cobb in a sure good mood. How he'd ask Cobb to tell that old story about the black snake he saw whoop the rattler. Or about how Cobb would break from the crowd and play ball with her and the other children, not just once, but lots of times. How she would never forget, "Thata *girl*, Colleen! Way to *hit behind the runner*!" The day was as beautiful as any I can remember. The light on the bay and the air coming in off the wide blue water brought the kind of comfort and peace that do make you think, this is a dream. And what I had in my mind always when I tried to bring my Charlie to life, was the way the beautiful Colleen S. said to me of the Cobb she knew long ago—that above all else, above *everything*, "He was a gentleman."

I lied about the pistol. Not in saying there was one. There was. Rather in saying that it was ever missing, that Amanda Cobb had gone out and gotten it, and that Tyrus Cobb had then gotten it from the place where she'd hidden it. The fact is that it *was* found in the dead Herschel Cobb's pocket (so add to the Hamlet story that the father did want to murder the mother). Nor was there ever any book titled *William Herschel Cobb: Turning Points of His Life, Commencing with His Coming into His Profession.* I'll talk below, very briefly, about some purposes behind these fabrications. Here I'll just say they all *were* purposeful devices. As was my back-dating a bit Cobb's first acquaintance and early romance with Charlie, who, as I've said, did later in fact become his wife.

As the millennium ended and ESPN was polling its pundits and making its rankings of the One Hundred Greatest Athletes of the Twentieth Century, I wondered where Cobb would come in. As it turned out, they ranked him twentieth, all sports considered; fifth among baseball players, following Ruth, Mays, Aaron, and Williams. There's something exhausting about special pleading. You feel tired even before you start. After all, you're not gonna convince anybody—although I have gotten firm nods of assent here and there when I've said that the best player I ever saw (and I saw Williams a little bit and Mays and Aaron a lot) was Roberto

Clemente. About this I'm really passionate, actually—because (and I think that asking opposing fans which player makes your gut tense hardest is about as good a measuring of greatness as there is) as a Cub fan what did I come to *know* but that Clemente, preternatural jump, runner-halting tomahawk missile of an arm, was the best damned outfielder, Mays not excepted, that I ever saw or ever will see and that when we got out Willie Mays or got out Henry Aaron, we breathed a sigh of relief, but that when we got out Roberto Clemente, we thanked God for the miracle. And I am, by all accounts assured, *positive* that that was exactly the feeling opposing fans had if their team was lucky enough to be able to retire Ty Cobb.

That at the first inductions to the Hall of Fame, in 1936, sportswriters who hated him gave more votes to Cobb than they did to anyone else, Ruth included, is fairly well known. Not until Tom Seaver's nearly unanimous vote was a vote percentage as high as Cobb's ever matched. But less well known is a poll that Cobb biographer Gene Schoor reports on, taken in 1942, of over one hundred former great players and managers—including obviously a high number who would have been on the field when Cobb and Ruth were on it (which would be a far cry from the location of *all* ESPN pundits). To be exact, there were 102 who voted; and of those 102 votes, 60 went to Cobb, 17 to Honus Wagner, 11 to Ruth, 4 to Rogers Hornsby, with other nominees dividing the remainder.

But Ruth, Mays, Aaron, Williams—they're all home-run sluggers—and there it ends, for Clemente, too, with his measly 240 career four-baggers. And yet there's a clock in center at Wrigley about a million feet from the plate and the only player ever to threaten it, with one mythic, breathtaking shot, was Clemente. And there's a story about Cobb, perfectly true, that I include among my very favorites. He was stubborn about the home-run thing. And when the game changed from the "inside" ball of which he was the undisputed master to the Babe's big-bash parade, he simply refused to change. He *wouldn't* swing for the fences. But one day, near the very end of his long, long career, he said to the sportswriters in St. Louis, who wouldn't let up with their questions about his ornery preference for old ways, *All right*, if you wanna see home runs, you come out and watch for the next three games. The result?—and don't ya love stuff like this—*five* homers in the first two games and a very near miss in the third. That Cobb had Olympic speed may not come as a surprise to those who know his story on the paths. But that he was a big man, 6' 1" and playing for most of his career at just under 200 pounds (which means what in today's terms, 6' 3", 220?), *might* come as a surprise. ESPN take note: he could have hit home runs if he'd wanted to, and a lot of 'em.

And it wasn't runs batted in that mattered so much in Cobb's day—it was runs scored. Cobb, then, would have watched very closely this summer of '01, when Rickey Henderson, seventy-three years after the Tiger star's last game, finally broke the record that, of the ninety he retired with, could have mattered to him most. After, that is, the record for lifetime batting average. But that .366 is in no danger whatsoever. It looks good to last easily a hundred years; and if they ever raise the mound again, or allow spit on the ball— it could last a thousand. He was a ballplayer, all right, the son of Herschel and Amanda Cobb; and nearly a century after his debut, one might still nod at the judgment of Ring Lardner's everyman, that he was "the greatest of 'em all."

I see him in his last months, broken by physical illness, friendless, armed with a gun and half mad, or drunk; and I know why a film was made, and a play was written, about the man in those terrifying days. The spellbinding account by Cobb biographer Al Stump, who also was the "ghost" for Cobb's autobiography (one of the best ever about/by an athlete), is an unforgettable story of demons never exorcized. And sure as I had anything in my mind as I wrote *Tyrus*, it was the man's end as Al Stump and others give it to us. Over the years, Cobb had made money, multi-millions, getting good tips from car makers, having good friends, but mostly having a mind spectacularly like a razor; but he sank in a final complete isolation and paranoia into a sick, pathetic miserdom. So many stories. So many. All sad. And all, it seems clear, about unresolved, unrelieved rage. Hate lists, that he carried in his pocket. Houses booby-trapped in case any intruders, like a former wife, might try anything while he wasn't looking. Family—five children, all of whom he'd loved—but finally separation from them all, though there had been one deathbed reconciliation with a dying son who'd disappointed him. I wanted the gun this tortured man carried so many of his days, and slept with so many of his nights, to be always the gun his father had carried; and so I had his mother, whom I made terrified and compelled by shame, hide it away in a place to which her son would inevitably be brought by a fatal curiosity. A son who, whatever he may have revealed to a friend in the Cobb tomb, only spoke once to John McCallum and only once to Al Stump about an event he called "an accident." But about the "accident," he said to both men the same thing: "I never got over that."

It was in the great summer of '61—Billy Crystal's summer—with Mantle and Maris electrifying the country with their unforgettable race to catch the Babe—that Ty Cobb died. I see the great star of the past lying on his deathbed, and I imagine sounds coming from somewhere of a radio broadcast of a Yankee game, cheers for those home-run boys, whose type of baseball had long won the day. And of all the many images of Cobb that moved me, perhaps the one that moved me most was indeed that of him lying alone, dying that summer in Emory University Hospital. There was a tape-recorder microphone, which he could no longer hold, strung over his bed; for he was still dictating things for his autobiography, a book he wouldn't live to see. And still there was the terror and the haunted miserdom—for, on his hospital bed table, Cobb kept a satchel holding a million dollars in negotiable securities, and, next to that, a loaded gun. But there was also his mind in that solitude, going back to the days of Ed Killian, Billy Armour, Wild Bill Donovan, and Matty McIntyre; and his voice, with no one there listening, telling his story.

She did come. It is said that he was already gone from the conscious world and so he never knew. But Charlie came. He'd failed over so many years to conquer those raging passions that his father had told him he must conquer—failed so many times to defeat the demon that lurks in human blood—that she had had, years back, to leave him—though with nearly everything in him he had fought the divorce— fought hard against a failure in his marriage, which, however, could not hold together against the relentless dark energy of his unforgiving anger. But she came; and because, for myself, I wanted the image of the two of them in that room to be not cold but heartbreaking, I made her come to New York, over a half-century before, and before in real time she would have, to tell him love is true and fear is a lie, and assure him she was his confidante.